100

"There's so much more to

P9-EDY-997

"[Nichols] has secured her place in the continuum of history."
—*Chicago Sun-Times*

From Nichelle Nichols, bestselling author of *Beyond Uhura*, and acclaimed *Star Trek* author Margaret Wander Bonanno, comes an extraordinary debut novel that will take science fiction fans into a captivating new world.

It is the story of Saturna, born in the late twenty-first century with unearthly beauty and stunning powers. Half human, half Fazisian, her very existence violates both Earth and Fazis laws...and could initiate all-out interplanetary war.

# SATURN'S CHILD

"An involving plot, sophisticated dialogue, and a cliff-hanger ending make this a surefooted start to what promises to be a fine series."
—*Publishers Weekly*

"Definitely keeps you turning pages...Full of good scenes and entertaining bits of world building."
—*Booklist*

*Also by Nichelle Nichols*

BEYOND UHURA

# SATURN'S CHILD

## NICHELLE NICHOLS

### MARGARET WANDER BONANNO

ACE BOOKS, NEW YORK

This Ace Book contains the complete text of the original
hardcover edition. It has been completely reset in a typeface
designed for easy reading, and was printed from new film.

SATURN'S CHILD

An Ace Book / published by arrangement with
the author

PRINTING HISTORY
Ace/Putnam hardcover edition / 1995
Ace mass-market edition / November 1996

The Putnam Berkley World Wide Web site address is
http://www.berkley.com

ISBN: 0-441-00384-2

ACE®
Ace Books are published by The Berkley Publishing Group,
200 Madison Avenue, New York, New York 10016.
ACE and the "A" design are trademarks
belonging to Charter Communications, Inc.

PRINTED IN THE UNITED STATES OF AMERICA

10  9  8  7  6  5  4  3  2  1

To George Coleman...
who proposed to me
when he was eleven.

# Acknowledgments

One evening, over dinner and champagne with my editors, George Coleman and Susan Allison, celebrating the signing of my new contract with Putnam for my autobiography, *Beyond Uhura,* I was compelled to tell them about Saturna, who has been living in my mind since I was a little girl. They both fell silent, looked at each other, then at me. "I'll buy it," Susan calmly announced, and *Saturn's Child* was born.

I am ever grateful to Susan and to George, whom I sorely miss; to Phyllis Grann, who said yes!; to all the wonderful people who worked so hard to make *Beyond Uhura* successful, including Marilyn Ducksworth, Rena Wolner, Mih-Ho Cha, David Groff, Liz Perl, Jennifer Lata, Judy Murello, and Frank Kozelek, all of whom have made me feel at home at Putnam-Berkley, and who never once mentioned the omission of their acknowledgment in *Beyond Uhura*—honest, I thought I had, gang.

Many thanks to Margaret Bonanno, who "connects the dots" so beautifully with and for me, and who delights me with her uncanny grasp of who my characters are and where I wish them to go.

A special thanks to my new agents at William Morris, especially Matt Bialer, Marcie Posner, and Betsy Berg in New York; and Amy Schiffman, Steve Weiss, Lewis Henderson, and Mike Sheresky in Los Angeles; we've only just begun. To Doug Conway, with his foresight before and behind the scenes, who keeps this literary ball rolling; I am truly grateful and delighted to call you friend. To my wonderful son and friend, Kyle Johnson, who loves me and doesn't think his mother is *really* crazy after all these years; and to my friend Carmen "Bunny" Meechan, who puts up with us all.

# SPECIAL ACHNOWLEDGMENT

Before starting the formal writing of *Saturn's Child,* I sat down with Jim Meechan (as I usually do on any new project) to discuss the book. Since this book is the first of a series of books on the adventures of Saturna, I wanted a "bible" that would define the characters, the major story lines, the science and technology I would employ, and the planetary settings, among other things. This bible would then be the writer's guide for developing the actual books.

Jim is an extremely creative thinker and writer, with a vivid imagination, and we think alike in visualizing the future. He has practiced as a research physicist for some fifteen years, written and published more than fifty technical papers for major scientific journals, and lectured throughout North America and Europe, including an invited lecture before the legendary Royal Society in London. This combination of talents has been absolutely invaluable to me in the writing of *Saturn's Child.*

As I labored in finding just the right mix for naming, describing, developing, and defining my characters and the conceptual treatments of story lines and plots in the creation of alien planets, Earth, and our solar system in the late twenty-first century, and certainly for scientific and technological insights so vital to this book, I blatantly drew from Jim's wellspring of imagination (not to mention his word-processing skills in putting it together).

Now I was ready for my co-writer. Jim interacted with Margaret Bonanno and me on a regular basis by phone and in my home (Margaret's first airplane flights) throughout the growth of *Saturn's Child.* I thank Jim Meechan from the bottom of my heart. I do not want to consider what this book would be like without his most valuable input.

# PROLOGUE

The two creatures had arranged themselves on each of Saturna's shoulders. Catlyke sat on the chair back, using two of her four hands to cling to the fabric of the girl's tunic, balancing perfectly, while Mushii had draped his entire mop-like self over her other shoulder, his head tucked under her chin. They sat on either side of her elegant head, watching her work and communing on a wavelength even she hadn't learned to access yet.

*She needs to be told!* Mushii thought to Catlyke, his antennae sparking blue, which meant he was particularly disturbed. *Before she finds out accidentally!*

*I'm not so sure!* Catlyke purred in response, preoccupied with grooming her lustrous fur, combing the tangles out with her nimble fingers. Mushii, Catlyke had observed, was always disturbed about something. Catlyke, who was inclined to be a lot more philosophical, had always thought it was because she had been designed with hands and Mushii hadn't.

*Life is about learning, after all,* Catlyke offered grandly from the vast perspective of her brief years. *Saturna will learn what she needs to know when she needs to know it.*

Unaware of all this mental chatter transpiring in the atmosphere around her, Saturna only noticed that her shoulders were beginning to ache. She shrugged impatiently.

"Do you mind?" she said aloud, though she could have communed with either of the creatures mentally. "You two are gravitationally massive. I'm trying to get some work done here!"

She plucked Catlyke's tiny prehensile fingers loose from the soft fabric of her tunic and set the feline down on a nearby chair cushion; last time she'd removed Mushii first, and it was important not to give either creature a chance to accuse her of

1

favoritism. Then she scooped Mushii onto a cushion at exactly the same height from the floor, ruffling his thick fur affectionately. Did she only imagine she saw him stick his tongue out at Catlyke? Despite his mixed heritage, Mushii was far more Earthian, Saturna thought, than most Earthians she knew.

Then again, in this small colony, how many Earthians did she truly know?

Both creatures were pouting at her now; she could feel it in her mind.

"Seriously, if I don't finish these equations, Krecis will scold me for my negligence again, and he'll be well within his rights. Why don't you two go play in another room for a while, or take a nap or something? I have to concentrate!"

*Concentrate!* Mushii mentally focused so Saturna could fully understand him in her mind. *Daydream is what you mean!*

"Well, so what?" Saturna demanded, still speaking aloud, frowning at the little creature whose large liquid eyes peered up at her impertinently. "I thought girls my age were allowed to daydream. In fact, from all the Earth literature Krecis has been giving me, it seems almost required."

Catlyke said nothing, paying inordinate attention to smoothing the fur at the tip of her long, twitchy tail. Did she look smugger than usual? Mushii wondered. Was she laughing at him?

*What do you daydream about?* he asked Saturna with honest curiosity, cocking his head to one side, his antennae twinkling a soothing pale green now, which meant he was feeling much calmer.

"Never you mind!" Saturna scolded him, her skin tones iridescing from their everyday warm matte brown into something a bit more russet tinged with coppery highlights; in simple Fazisian terms, she was blushing. "I mean it, now! Stop pestering me and let me get back to work."

She did try, focusing all her attention on the advanced calculus on her screen, which she could usually solve faster than some of the colony's computers. But it wasn't long before her luminescent eyes strayed dreamily toward the windowport and its too predictable view of Titan's somewhat gloomy local landscape. Saturna watched the huge amorphous methane "flakes" solidify in midair and tumble slowly to the ground, as they had been doing since Titan was captured by Saturn eons ago, but she wasn't really seeing them.

As always in times of crisis, she was seeing him, even though he was light-years away in the Milky Way Galaxy.

✍

"Watching" her in his mind, standing but a half-klick distant, the WiseOne Krecis marveled as he always did at the young woman's clarity of soul. On the cusp of adulthood, she was becoming more than even he had dared to dream.

This, he thought, is our legacy. This unique being is the culmination of all we have striven for, all we have achieved in this place so far from home! She is so very young, and does not begin to know who—or what—she truly is. Were we wise, were we right, to do what we have done to bring her here? Most important, for mine is the greatest responsibility, was I right?

# CHAPTER 1

Once in a blue moon, as Earthians would say, the methane-laden atmosphere of Titan actually thinned enough so that one could see the distant rings of Saturn. Krecis remembered the very first time he had seen them.

&

"Propulsion interrupt in primary engine..." The voice had blared throughout the ship. Lights flashed on every panel amid an eerie chorus of alarms. Krecis was only too aware of the seriousness of a propulsion malfunction.

"Bearing?" he'd asked his helm once the shuddering stopped.

"Seventeen-oh-one point three ... mark," Zandra had reported calmly, though Krecis knew she was feeling anything but calm. They were only a few billion klicks off course, but rapidly increasing the discrepancy.

Reports were flooding in from every deck of the vast ship. Biotech had stabilized, but with possibly as many as half the root-stocks either outright destroyed or questionable; Enviro-Control was still borderline and grav had only just returned to normal levels. How ironic, Krecis thought, to have come this far only to experience propulsion problems at the last moment!

And if they were severe enough, to have forfeited the lives of everyone on board.

They were supposed to have entered into a tight orbit around the asteroid belt between the fourth and fifth planets. Here, a plethora of mineral wealth was waiting for the taking. Having navigated with breathtaking accuracy between their two star systems, Krecis considered this eventuality particularly frustrating.

They had come from a system Earthians called Vega, from a planet they themselves called Fazis. Over the past several centuries they had sent multigenerational ships out into the void between, often linking several of them together to form permanent colonies. The most distant of these from the home-world, Outlyer-21, hung like a jeweled pendant a mere fifty million miles beyond the orbit of this system's farthest planet. Some Fazisians had lived their entire lives on these space stations, though Krecis was not one of them.

He and his crew had come the long way around, from the homeworld. Had they journeyed this far only to succumb to a split second of failure?

"Situation analysis?" Krecis asked his helm with quiet control.

"The power loss severely decreased our velocity," Zandra said with a calm to equal her spouse's, deciphering readouts with lightning speed, "and the fifth planet's gravitational force has whipped us off on a new vector."

There was no accusation in her voice, no faultfinding; the damage was done, and the result of any one of a dozen variables, not least of which might have been Fazisian error.

"Accepted," Krecis said. It was all that could be said until their true bearing was understood. "Query: Where are we?"

Zandra did not try to hide her astonishment at the readings as they came up on her screen. "We are actually heading into close orbit about the fourth planet!"

The screens had gone down the instant the crisis klaxon blared; they'd been flying on emergency system instruments for nearly seventeen minutes. Static swirled and images flickered as Vaax muttered to himself at NavComm, trying to set things right.

"Better to be in orbit about the wrong planet than strewn across its surface," Krecis offered in an attempt at bitter humor. A ship's commander on longrange had to be philosopher, priest, and crisis counselor as well as chief scientist, plumber, paramedic, and occasional washer of soup pots. It had taken Krecis a third-age of preparation and experience to even qualify for this assignment; at the very least he could keep his people focused on the job at hand.

"We can retro back on course," Zandra said.

"No!" Krecis commanded. He knew the dangers of a major retro move following ion engine failure. "Too risky. Maintain course."

"Acknowledged," the helmsman responded.

Krecis quickly realized that the forces of the universe now dominated his ship's trajectory and he must use them, not fight them. There was no other choice at this point than to enter the domain of the fourth planet, find a suitable landing site, and correct the engine problem. His decision made, he calmed the crew as only he could, as the Fazisian craft hurtled toward the fourth planet.

"Image!" Vaax offered finally; he sounded grumpy, meaning the screen was not as clear as he'd expected it to be. Vaax expected perfection from his instruments, even after all that shaking around.

"It's really ringed!" Zandra said, as the extraordinarily beautiful gas giant loomed on the forward screen. Her fingers began to pepper instructions into the analysis program even as her jaw went slack with awe at the sheer beauty of the thing. "An impacted satellite? Interstellar dust? Ice crystals, perhaps? What causes something like that? There's no analogue in any of our systems." She studied her readouts, answering at least one of her own questions. "They're barely seven *korros* thick! How is that possible?"

"Analyze later," Krecis advised, not wanting to curb her enthusiasm—but unless EnviroControl got back within normal parameters soon, the entire issue would be moot. "Meanwhile, you and Vaax must plot us a course that guarantees we don't hit anything."

"Easy for you to say!" Zandra remarked, but as usual, set about doing the impossible.

It was why Krecis had married her. It was why, when she died, he had never married another.

❧

They had not been aiming for Saturn at all, but in fact for the asteroid belt between the last of the gas giants, Jupiter, and Mars, the first of the four solid inner worlds—the fifth and sixth by Fazisian notation, which counted planets from the outer edge of a solar system inward. Mercifully, Jupiter's gravitational field had grabbed them and spat them out toward Saturn, rather than driving them directly into the system's primary. Considering this alternative, things could be worse . . . much worse.

Krecis wished now that he had not ordered the crew to jettison a lot of the heavy mining equipment when it was clear that the slingshot effect was not directing them onto the desired course. It was one of those split-second decisions every commander dreaded but was fully prepared to make: Hold on to the expedition's essential tools a moment too long and risk losing the entire ship? Or jettison the hardware and then face the dreaded message on holocom as soon as one reported back to the homeworld? He was sure that message would read out like this:

"You've essentially defeated the entire purpose of your mission. Return to Fazis. Repeat: Return to Fazis at once."

He decided not to report his action for now. Fazis was many light-years away. By the time he reached Fazis Prime, he might be deemed too old or too unlucky for another offworld command. Such mischance might mean the end of a career, or worse.

His thoughts rolled back to what had happened to Gremar's ship in the Pictor System, though Gremar hadn't been so fortunate as to lose only the machinery. There had been casualties and a bulkhead breach, and by the time the ship limped home nearly a decade late (leaking radiation so badly it had been unable to dock at any of the stations, which were strung out on an indirect route anyway), half the crew was dead.

The battered vessel was located in-system and brought in tow after eight years comm silence on the very day Xeniok acceded to the throne following the Fazrul's vote of confidence. His father, the Old Ruler, who had been nearly three-quarters' age when he sired him, was dead and could not advise him. The thought of what Gremar and her crew had endured to return this far filled the Young Ruler with horror. His very first major decision was to announce suspension of the offworld program, indefinitely. It was Krecis who had gone to the capital to try to talk him out of it.

He and Xeniok had been lifelong friends and cohorts since they had roomed together at school. Krecis was counting on this now, to persuade Xeniok where no one else could.

"We will not, of course, recall the colonies already established," Xeniok announced, barely mollified once Krecis had stated his case. The royal "we" sounded strange to his own ears, and he was genuinely torn by the dilemma. "But to continue to extend ourselves into other star systems seems dangerously foolish, my friend!"

"Then you condemn the outlying colonies to eventual atrophy, my lord," Krecis reasoned. At ease with himself and his status even at so young an age, he had no problem addressing his former academy roommate by the honorific, and would continue to do so for the rest of their lives. "And you give our youth nothing to strive for. That which does not grow must die."

He had continued to argue in this vein throughout the dinner hour and well into the night; it was in fact dawn before he left the palace, his mission accomplished. Whenever a retainer stepped into the Ruler's private rooms, an inquiring eyebrow raised as if to suggest that, old friendships notwithstanding, Krecis was overstaying his welcome, he or she was waved away. In truth, Xeniok needed to be persuaded, and who better to persuade him?

"Have I ever won an argument with you, Krecis?"

"Not to my knowledge, my lord," Fazis' most gifted scientist had answered, and returned home confident that the Fazrul, after a show of a few days' haggling, would affirm what the Ruler had decided.

❧

That was a quarter-age ago! Krecis thought, contemplating the still-uncanny beauty of Saturn through the methane mists of her largest moon; Titan was his own private realm, assigned him by Xeniok in exchange for his loyalty and his insistence that the exploration of space not be abandoned. Now it is Xeniok's son who will rule, once he has proven himself by leading the second expedition to this alien system. And all because I spoke my mind. How different would the universe be if I had kept my peace?

If he had any regrets, Fazis' most gifted scientist kept them to himself.

☞

"How can you be so eager to leave this beautiful world?"
Zandra had mused as they stood on the balcony overlooking
the Allellul Valley and its tributaries the night before the Fazrul was to vote on the cause Krecis had so eloquently
pleaded. The rivers sang purple and magenta beneath the gathering methane mist rising off their banks, and small crimson
lizards beat their wings together in plaintive trilling in the
terraced gardens. The planet Fazis, centuries after they'd
nearly drowned it in debris, was once more as beautiful as its
inhabitants.

They called themselves Fazisians. In a language of gutturals
and fricatives suitable to their flexible vocal cords and a res-
piratory system which had evolved in a methane-dense atmosphere, they had created a highly artistic as well as
scientifically advanced culture. But two generations before
Krecis and Zandra were born, there were some who grew lazy
and others who grew greedy, and an entire world suffered.

Offworld travel had saved them. Now Fazis Prime was a
world of gardens and forests once again, its heavy industry
removed to orbiting factories and airless moons, and strin-
gently monitored for violations, and the three other habitable
worlds in the system had been colonized so that even the lazy
ones would have somewhere to live. And they were still
among the most attractive beings in the galaxy.

Bipedal and erect, they had clear bright eyes beneath upslanting browridges almost like a second set of eyebrows, and
their eyes were almost universally a brilliant green. Their
bronze-toned skin ran the spectrum of every known shade of
brown and russet and gold with each emotional change. Their
crowns of silky-to-feathery purplish-blue hair and iridescent
orchid nails would someday be envied and emulated by Earthians of both sexes.

It was the methane, Earth's scientists would ascertain once
the atmospheric composition of Fazisian worlds was made
known to them. The inhabitants of Fazis, surprised to learn
that Earth's atmosphere did not also contain ten percent methane, agreed.

They could see in the dark. They could hear in registers

Earthians could not. And they were telepaths. What more could any intelligent being desire?

Except the stars.

Zandra was teasing. Her question to her spouse was purely rhetorical. How could either of them leave their homeworld? What Fazisian of exceptional talents and intelligence could not? It was what both had been groomed for since they'd achieved perfect scores on their first-form tests when they were barely old enough to clamber onto a chair and tap into a compscreen. It was what they had lived their whole lives for—aside from each other, of course—separately, on training missions to the near moons and the in-system worlds, and now together on this culminating mission.

Ordinarily only those a half-age or older were permitted to lead an exploratory mission; two as young as Krecis and Zandra would usually be offered assignments on any of the colony worlds, a place to conduct their advanced research as well as a paradise in which to rear their children. But if Krecis was the most gifted scientist of his generation, Zandra was second best, and there would never be any children.

Was it Zandra's brief exposure to radiation during the solar storms the year she commanded the ferry fleet between Fazis Prime and Fazis Second, as some healers had suggested, which determined that as lifemates they would never bear children, or was it the illusive infertility gene that had plagued Krecis' lineage for centuries? The most exhaustive research had failed to find a cure for the sterility gene that skipped generations, only to show up unexpectedly down the line. Neither of them ever spoke of it, though both would have been well within their rights to seek another mate. That neither had done so endeared them to each other all the more.

Krecis did not answer Zandra's question for some moments, and his silence spoke volumes. Both knew their ship would go farther than any Fazisian ship before, and the nature of their assignment meant it would be decades before they returned, if they returned at all. And the selflessness of Zandra's question—she did not mention how she might feel about leaving her homeworld—moved him to tears. He had merely put his arms about her and cradled her head against his shoulder;

the mist-shrouded stars, the soughing trees, the trill of lizards, answered for him.

"If the Fazrul votes against Xeniok—and rare though it is, it has been known to happen to a Young Ruler—then the decision will be made for me and I will not leave this beautiful world. Nevertheless, I intend to sleep the sleep of the unconcerned this night. Let tomorrow bring me its answer. Besides . . ." And here he kissed her brow just at the hairline, warming her skin against the evening's chill. "I have my world, my universe, right here. From now on, I shall take her with me wherever I go."

They had both slept the sleep of the unconcerned that night, though not before such activities as altered all their emotional colors through the entire spectrum several times over, and in the morning the Fazrul affirmed their support of the Young Ruler and his decision. The tragedy to Gremar's ship notwithstanding, Krecis and his crew could go.

"Stay in touch, my dear friend!" Xeniok urged him the night before departure. "I will need to know everything that transpires with you and Zandra, even beyond the official reports."

Krecis nodded. As usual, his closest friend shared his own thoughts. A Ruler's life was never private, and official communications could be descrambled no matter how carefully they were coded. However, Xeniok and Krecis had learned over the years to communicate without using words, without finishing sentences. It seemed as if the two minds were one, allowing them to trade thoughts and ideas without the possibility of interception by anyone.

"I will do what I can, my lord," Krecis promised. It was all he needed to say.

"All my love to Zandra," Xeniok said with especial warmth.

"And hers to you," Krecis replied formally, though the emotions behind his sentiment were anything but formal. He and Zandra and Xeniok shared a complex past. But today was for the future. The two friends embraced, and Krecis took his leave.

☙

Fazisian ships finally had the technology to go from one star system to the next, and their use of ionized heavy elements such as uranium for ion propulsion provided unprecedented speeds. Krecis and Zandra's journey was made in increments, leapfrogging from one outlying colony to the next, gathering data, charting every comet, every asteroid, every cloud of interstellar dust they encountered along their way. They would berth at some colonies for a month or more, loading and offloading cargo, taking on new crew members and dropping others off; in some places they stayed only long enough for the next departure window before they were off again. The journey was an end in itself, invaluable in terms of research, and yet Krecis never lost sight of his goal: the Earthian system (though he did not know enough to call it that yet) and the search for intelligent life there.

"Nonsense!" was the opinion of the commander of Outlyer-21, the last colony on the frontier some fifty million miles from the outer fringes of the unexplored system. "This is about economics, not fantasy. You've been sent this far because that system is replete with the mineral wealth we need. Xeniok and the Fazrul have promised every Fazisian his own personal asteroid to tether in his back garden. Let's not pretend it's about anything else."

Krecis had smiled and spread his expressive hands in a generous gesture. The Fazrul was noted for its promises.

"One has to keep a pragmatic view, Commander," he said. "As long as it grants me and my scientists permission to go forward, I have no quarrel with the Fazrul's true motivation."

The commander leaned forward across his expensive *col*-stone desk, carved from a single slab harvested from an in-system asteroid by one of the earliest expeditions, transported across parsecs of space, and appraised at twice its weight in argen for its rarity.

"There are no other intelligent life-forms out here," he insisted. "I personally have monitored every sound emanating from that system for over an eighth-age, and it is nothing but random noise."

"As you say, Commander," Krecis replied magnanimously, thinking, *Perhaps what seems random noise to us has simply not been recognized for what it truly is.* He deliberately left his thoughts open for the commander to read.

"Nonsense!" the commander repeated. "Over one hundred expeditions to the four systems nearest our own..." He tapped the golden surface of the desk imperiously with one long-nailed finger. "And not one found anything more intelligent than a *keri*fruit on any of a dozen likely planetfalls. Every longrange commander likes to flatter himself his mission will be the exception, Krecis. Don't lose sight of your goal!"

"I, Commander?" Krecis did not need to say anything further. He was a scientist, and not noted for delusions. "If my ship provides the Fazrul with sufficient profit, it will fund further scientific missions in the name of . . . further profit. That, and only that, is my goal."

&

And yet circumstance, which Krecis had always trusted once every logical step had been taken, had seen fit to thwart him in pursuit of his goal. He'd had to jettison much of the mining equipment to save his crew. For what possible reason was he loitering about this alien star system now?

Vaax had laid in a path just beyond the outer ring, and Zandra was successfully negotiating the trajectory and literally threading the ship through. She had brought up the aft-screen view of the retreating planet as if unable to take her eyes off it. Krecis leaned forward from the command chair and tapped one orchid nail against the helm console.

"Study your pretty rings later!" he advised softly, in what to anyone who did not know him might have sounded as if he were scolding. "Find me a reason for staying here."

*Find me a reason, O my beloved, to give to the somber faces on holocom once they learn I cannot bring in tow the train of countless ore modules they have commissioned us to bring. Find me a reason which speaks of the future and not of profit margins!*

*Of course!* Zandra thought back to him on their most intimate private wavelength, and this time set about finding the impossible.

Earthians called it Titan.

∅

It had a solid surface and a nitrogen atmosphere with a substantial methane content. Its frozen lakes and seas could support methoponic farms to grow sufficient food for a hundred times their number. Scans had shown veins of what appeared to be incredible mineral wealth, which possibly could be mined from the surface. There was the almost incredible possibility that its seas contained trace of life, and most astonishing of all, it lay in the path of a constant flow of active radio transmissions from *something,* in fact several somethings, inhabiting the inner worlds. Having listened to those transmissions for the greater part of fifty Fazisian years now, Krecis knew enough of their languages to call Saturn's largest moon Titan too.

As was often the case, Krecis found himself laughing at himself. After fifty years of monitoring the radio transmissions of the *four* intelligent species inhabiting the inner planets of this system (ah, the look on the face of the commander of Outlyer-21 when he had reported that!), he had learned the names by which they called themselves, their sun, its planets, their satellites, and even some of the larger asteroids which separated the gas giants from the smaller planets closer in. Further, he even knew some of their slang, though he had forgotten which species had coined the phrase "once in a blue moon."

Thus, once in a blue moon—which Krecis assumed meant rarely, since not once in his fifty-year tenure on Titan had he or the colony's computers noted any alteration in the color of any of the system's satellites—the methane-laden atmosphere of Titan cleared enough so that one could see the rings of Saturn with the naked eye. Computer-enhanced imagery could of course provide sharper images accompanied by more data readouts than one could digest in an afternoon, but sometimes, as Zandra had taught her spouse, it was much more pleasant to appreciate a thing for its sheer beauty alone.

In his late love's name, Krecis beheld the rings of Saturn through the rusty "snow" of Titan's atmosphere, and thought of what was to come.

A second ship had been sent from Fazis, this time bound

directly for the colony on Titan. Aboard was Tetrok, Xeniok's son and heir apparent to the Fazisian throne and, not incidentally, one of the most gifted scientists of his generation. It was he, with Krecis at his side, who would greet the Earthians, of whatever species, when they arrived. For, in time, they would arrive.

Four intelligent species in the same system! Krecis thought with quiet pleasure; the Fazrul had deemed the discovery significant enough to grant him and his crew permanent settlement rights on their frozen moon. What did they look like? Did their planets of origin hold the key?

He and his scientists had taken to referring to them collectively as Earthians, since they referred to the seventh planet as Earth and it was the seat of their government. Even this, Krecis thought, might be significant. Had it been a series of peaceful or of violent contacts, or perhaps both, which had persuaded the inhabitants of three of the other inner planets to allow the Earth species to govern them? Would this make them more, or less, receptive to the discovery that there was a Fazisian colony in their system? And, most puzzling of all, which of the four planets had they come from?

&

"Obviously the four closest to the primary!" Vaax had concluded with a young man's impatience when, in the second year of discovery, the radio signals had been detected, run through the computers, and determined to be genuine, recent, and generated by something at least as intelligent as they. "Four totally diverse sets of environmental parameters would explain four different species."

"The ninth planet's entirely too hostile!" Zandra had countered to temper his enthusiasm.

It was night-cycle, and nearly everyone was in a sociable mood. The few solitary souls who preferred to be by themselves after the evening meal had already gone off to their quarters to read or view entertainment cubes from the colony's exhaustive library; everyone else had simply hung about the commissary. There was music from one corner, in another some sort of silly improvisational game which alternated exaggerated mime with a great deal of shouting, and, here among the command crew, a heated debate.

"Too hostile for us, maybe!" Vaax argued. "But maybe not for them. The odds of finding any intelligence this far out were astronomical. Who's to say they aren't so different from us that—"

"Let us at least pray they have the same number of arms and legs!" Fariya chimed in. It was she who had first detected the radio waves. "I should hate to have to defend myself against one otherwise."

"We'll assume Xermik's Law holds sway in this system as well as our own," Krecis suggested. "The concept that all intelligent life within the same galaxy has a certain evolutionary symmetry of form is . . . comforting."

"Four species, four worlds!" Vaax insisted, as if his entire reputation as a scientist depended upon it. "A highly heat-tolerant species for the ninth world—"

"Which is also anaerobic, since this last world has no atmosphere at all," Zandra pointed out, though she let the young man have his say, however erroneous it might prove to be. Who knew? He might even be right.

"Even greater tolerance for your species from the eighth world," Krecis reminded them both. "Beneath all that sulfur and carbon dioxide, it's even hotter. And this extraordinary species can also breathe in all that soup. That's news to me."

"What of the seventh world?" Vaax demanded aggressively; he knew he was being humored and didn't care for it at all. "It's mostly nitrogen, not a trace of methane at all, and also mostly water. What could possibly live there?"

"A species dominant enough to bring the other three into governance," Fariya suggested. "I'd like to imagine a waterborne species, all sparkling scales and flippery fingers."

"At least the sixth world's habitable," Vaax offered defensively.

"Again, if you like breathing $CO_2$," Zandra said. "It is the dominant atmospheric component."

She saw the young man's crestfallen look and decided it was time to stop the teasing. *That's enough now!* she scolded Krecis and Fariya on a wavelength Vaax had not yet mastered. "Vaax, we're not making fun of you, honestly. We know no more than you. But it's my belief that, excluding that inner-most planet—"

"Mercury," Fariya supplied.

Zandra glanced sideways at her. "I beg your pardon?"

"Mercury. That's what they call it. We've intercepted several recent transmissions about some unmanned probes they've put in orbit."

"Ah. Mercury, then," Zandra corrected herself. "Mercury is far too hostile to support any form of life which exists outside a children's holovid, but the seventh planet seems most hospitable in spite of all that water—"

"And the virtual absence of methane, except for traces above what seem to be their major metropolises." The game in the far corner had stopped between rounds, and one of the gamesters was passing their table with a tray of fruit juice from the dispensers; his team had been studying this very phenomenon. "We think they manufacture their own methane. Possibly to compensate for the lack in the atmosphere, which suggests Earth may not be their point of origin at all."

"Interesting!" Fariya said thoughtfully, though whether she meant the gamester's theory or his person it was hard to say; she'd been flirting with him since they'd spent thirty hours together in a very small access conduit rebooting the EnviroControl computers following a recent power outage. Zandra made a humming noise in her throat to get everyone's attention.

"Nuclear winter," she said.

"Ah!" Krecis said. It was the very thing he'd been thinking.

"Again, let's eliminate Mercury from our consideration, which means at least two of the four species would have had to evolve on a single world . . ."

"Or perhaps that puzzling asteroid belt between what we now know as the fifth and sixth was yet another world which met with some catastrophe, such as a comet . . ." the gamester offered.

"And the survivors emigrated to the sixth world," Zandra finished for him. "There they discovered a species already established. We know there is water on the red world; our spectroanalysis of the polar caps proves that. Perhaps this species destroyed their own atmosphere, as we almost did on Fazis, or perhaps some natural phenomenon. Those volcanoes were not always so quiescent—''

''Nuclear winter,'' Krecis finished for her. ''Perhaps species-induced. Not the case with the eighth planet, however. I doubt any species could be so destructive as to create that hellish atmosphere.''

''A natural phenomenon, then,'' Zandra concluded. ''All in all, it became necessary for all four species to end up on the seventh planet, from which they are in the process of repopulating their system. We know they have colonized Earth's satellite, and the sixth planet—''

''Or perhaps that species never left its world, but adapted somehow,'' Fariya interrupted, more to impress her gamester, whose fellows were calling him back for another round.

Zandra shrugged. ''Whatever. It is all theoretical until we can find a way to interface our communications with theirs, or until we meet any or all of the four species face-to-face.''

''What if all four species evolved on the same world?'' Fariya wondered, loud enough for the departing gamester to hear.

Vaax had to have the last word. ''Ridiculous!''

∞

Fifty years later, Krecis thought, and still we do not know! We are forbidden by the Fazrul to contact them directly. Therefore we must wait and see.

Though apparently not for long. For not only was Fazis sending an expedition to Titan, so was Earth.

# CHAPTER 2

"Economics," Bydun Wong, chief counsel for the Earth Space Council, told Dr. Nyota Domonique as they sat in his posh office in the executive tower overlooking the meticulously landscaped grounds of ESC headquarters. His round, ageless face wore its official smile, which meant he was particularly pleased with himself. "You're a biologist. You know what's out there, and what it can mean in terms of resources. Let's dispel any romantic notions about Planets for People before we begin, shall we?"

"Whatever you say, By," Nyota replied. Darwin's First Rule of Survival, she thought: Never argue with a lawyer! She flashed him one of her own dazzling smiles.

Strictly speaking, Bydun Wong was not even nominally Nyota Domonique's superior. Had she gone to law school instead of concentrating on microbiology and linguistics, she might easily have had his job. Dr. Nyota Domonique was a distinguished scientist and space explorer; her quiet dignity was always disturbing to Bydun Wong, who was more comfortable intimidating than deferring.

Dr. Domonique had been an administrator on Mars, running the biospheres as well as supervising most of the active experimentation. Bydun Wong was a brilliant legal mind, and a pompous ass. The media had dubbed him "Dr. Inside" and her "Dr. Outside." As their jobs were interdependent, they were, as Wong himself liked to say, "equal partners in space exploration." Dr. Domonique was no ordinary space jock. Still, the Earth Space Council cut her orders, and it was Counselor Wong's job to clarify the parameters.

After x number of years of working with him, Nyota had learned that the best way to manage Bydun Wong was to tolerate his long-winded verbiage rather than argue every point

along the way, especially since experience had taught her that
these spiels frequently turned his logic back on his own argument.

Wong had folded his soft hands on the desktop and settled
himself contentedly in his ergonomically designed chair. As
he droned on, Nyota's mind wandered. Had he ever been in
space? she wondered. Oh, maybe the occasional hop to Selenopolis and back on official business, but that was all. The man
looked far too comfortable here on Earth. She, on the other
hand, hadn't felt entirely at home on her homeworld since her
first "joyride" back in undergrad.

Nyota lived for space, found it almost unbearable to cool
her heels for any extended time on Earth. And she'd just been
handed a long-term assignment that could keep her offworld
for the next several years! She ought to be ecstatic. First, however, she had to endure Dr. Inside for a few eons longer.

"To reduce this mission to its simplest terms," Wong was
saying, as if she didn't know, "we're sending you and your
crew to Titan to study Saturn at close range and to map and
catalog every square millimeter of Titan's surface. If you happen to find preanimate hydrocarbons under the ice, so much
the better."

"Of course, sir," Nyota replied, forcing her attention back
to Wong. "Although that isn't what you've told the media
people."

Counselor Wong started to say something, then changed his
mind. Coddling the media people was the second hardest part
of his job; obtaining funding from the Earth Space Council's
contributing territories was the first. And the official public
relations speech that habitually snowed the media and the man
in the street wasn't going to work on a veteran spacer like
Nyota Domonique.

"The media need to have their hands held," he reminded
her. "They flatter themselves that they speak for the common
man, and the common man needs to know where his money's
going. That hasn't changed since the space program was in its
infancy . . ."

Nyota sighed. She'd heard it all before. In the early days of
NASA and other individual national space programs, the
scramble for funding had been constant. The average person

simply hadn't understood that the progress and evolution of
his species on Earth relied to a great extent upon what was
learned in space.

Nyota knew. It was Skylab's discovery of underground
stream beds in the sub-Sahara over a century ago that had
saved her grandmother's village in the droughts of the 1980s.
Without that eye-in-the-sky capability, her entire family might
have died, and Nyota herself would never have been born. In
the past century the many medicines and metallic solids that
could be manufactured only under zero-g conditions had improved the quality of life planetwide. It was no mystery to her
why she had been drawn toward space.

"... and, to be honest, the Jupiter colony went over budget,
but the budget wasn't realistic to begin with . . ." Counselor
Wong was still talking. Nyota stifled a yawn. "The usual malcontents in the regional councils are making noises again. The
money's there; it's just a question of how it's allocated. You
may even find some of your crew rosters altered because
someone owes someone else a favor. This Titan mission is
going to be scrutinized very carefully, and you'd better bring
something worthwhile back with you."

"How about the specs for country estates for people who
hate hot weather?" Nyota quipped; her sardonic wit had gotten
her into trouble more than once, and joking about the ultralow
temperature on Titan was probably not the politically correct
thing to do with "Emperor" Wong.

"You've got the general idea!" Counselor Wong said dryly,
not allowing the slightest trace of a smile at her bon mot.

When Nyota Domonique's mother was still cutting her baby
teeth, the people of Earth had finally grown up. Tired of sup-
porting armies and arsenals to defend themselves against themselves, they had at last laid down their arms. National
governments had given way to regional federations—there
was a North American Federation, a Pan-African Federation,
a Pacific Rim Federation, and so on—all of which sent representatives to an interconnected group of governing councils.
There was an Economic Council, an Environmental Council,
a Council on Law Enforcement, and of course, an Earth Space
Council—in short, a council for all occasions, all of them under the aegis of the United Earth Council, the UEC.

Growing out of the old United Nations, the UEC modeled itself on the U.S. Supreme Court, streamlining judicial functions, evolving into a strong, unimpeachable power. In time it completed the work begun with the fall of the old Soviet empire and the tentative handshake that ended a Middle East conflict six millennia old. Even the Irish Republican Army had finally given up and gone home for a cold one and to watch the good news on the telly when Britain ultimately relinquished sovereignty over Ireland. By the time Nyota Domonique was a twinkle in her father's eye, Earth was slowly but surely approaching the ideal of a global village, despite the fact that the various economic territories still retained a great deal of autonomy, particularly where the allocation of funds was involved.

In a fever of enthusiasm coinciding with the new century, space exploration had flourished, though in deliberate, economically sound steps. Following the construction of the first Friendship Space Colony at the LaGrange point between Earth and the Moon—at the time, a giant step from Space Station Freedom—colonizing the Moon itself had been the next logical step.

Selenopolis was populated originally by research scientists and mining engineers. Soon thereafter followed all the professions, from lawyers to energy station attendants to fast-food chains. The inhabitants prided themselves on being "Selenopolists," all but independent from Earth, though they still sent representatives to the Earth Councils. Sergei Saranov, a Ukrainian by birth, was now the Governor, and he and his followers actively promulgated independence from Earth, since they felt with some reason the Moon colonists were giving more to Earth than they were receiving.

From the Moon the next step had been a freewheeling station midway to Mars. Finally, a foothold was made on the Red Planet itself, which within a mere twenty years had flourished beyond anyone's belief. In another decade or so, it too would be flexing its independent muscle.

By the time Nyota Domonique was old enough to be kissed, the exploration of space was rapidly moving toward the outer planets. Nyota had been sweating out the orals for her doctorate in genetics when the announcement came that the ESC would indeed be launching an expedition to construct a permanent station in high orbit above Jupiter.

⌘

Twenty years later, Nyota Domonique stood at one of the observation ports on the outer rim of Jupiter-1, watching the tech crew ready her ship, the *Dragon's Egg,* for the final leg of its voyage. Wong's parting words to her still rang in her ears:

"I've given the media my best philosophical shot on humankind's Place in Space," he said. "But it's no secret that what we really need is a space discovery home run.

"Officially, your mission is to determine whether Titan would make a good extension colony someday. You're to confirm in person what flyby probes can't really measure through the methane atmosphere. Query: In spite of the extreme cold, is the body habitable? Unofficially, your assignment is to find some evidence of biological life on that frozen orb. That's the kind of discovery we need to really solidify support for future space exploration. We're counting on you, Nyota. If anyone can pull it off, it's you."

Embarrassed by his own uncharacteristic display of warmth, Wong collected himself and continued.

"Every ten days from the time you make planetfall on Titan, you'll send us *two* separate reports," he concluded, shaking her hand in farewell. "Both will contain essential topographical and geological data, astrophysics, local 'weather.' The 'official' report will detail the colony-extension theme, the 'unofficial' report will ideally confirm evidence of biological life. This office will decide how much of which report to issue to the Councils and the media."

Still, something about it just didn't add up. The words were out of Nyota's mouth before she could stop them.

"I'm just curious, By. The ESC's sudden eagerness to send a ship to Titan wouldn't have anything to do with those radio signals we intercepted all those years ago, would it?"

"Nothing whatsoever!" Bydun Wong had assured her, his smile wider than ever, which convinced her more than ever that he was not telling her the truth.

Officially, the "messages" had been dismissed as either static, solar noise, or badly decayed Earth signals; the most popular theory was that they were time-delayed feedback from old twentieth-century signals that had somehow looped back into the Solar System instead of dissipating out into space. An echo, in other words, of the radio chatter of people long dead, maybe even reruns of *Star Trek* rattling around loose in space, meaningless. In no way, official sources had stated repeatedly, could these radio signals be construed as originating with any extraterrestrial intelligence.

Nyota thought differently. She'd been there when the signals were first intercepted.

∞

She'd been on her first deepspace assignment, aboard Beth Listrom's interplanetary, the *Venture VI*. At least she'd always thought of *Venture* as Beth's ship, since Beth would eventually command her, before being promoted to commander of Jupiter-1. But in those days Beth was a lowly ensign, and Nyota was low man in the bio lab, sterilizing beakers and starting countless culture bases to record how they behaved under different g-forces, exposure to various radiation "soups," and other deepspace factors. She sometimes thought such scut work was designed simply to keep Level 4 techs from having too much fun in space.

It was night shift and she'd been floating back from the commissary with a container of tea, hand-over-handing it down the corridors, since the artificial-g was shut down for emergency repairs, when Listrom called her into CommOps.

"Hey, Nyota? Got a minute? I want you to listen to something. Tell me I'm not going bonkers."

She boosted the gain and handed Nyota a headset. The two young women listened intently, their heads together, for several minutes.

They were a study in contrasts. Beth was big and blond and blustery, her northern European ancestry obvious in her pale blue eyes and the milk-white skin she spent hours under UV lamps trying to tan. Nyota was petite and dark, with liquid brown eyes, small graceful hands, a mane of thick, silky blue-black hair, a dazzling smile, and a singing voice with a three-octave range. They had been close friends since they'd trained together for the space program. By now they were close enough to tease each other constantly.

"What am I listening to?" Nyota asked, putting the headset down after several minutes, pretending she hadn't heard a thing. If she had heard what she thought she'd heard, they could both be in a lot of trouble.

"Oh, give me a break!" Beth said. "Don't tell me you can't hear it!"

"Hear what?" Nyota asked, all innocence.

"Tell me you don't hear voices."

"Beth, honey . . ." Nyota floated out of the restraint harness and looked as if she was about to leave. "If you're hearing voices, it's Psych you want to talk to, not me!"

Beth grabbed her arm. "Dammit, get back here and quit fooling around! You're a linguist and you've got perfect pitch. If you can't hear it, no one can."

"Well . . ." Nyota looked at her out of the corner of her eye. "I might have heard something . . ."

"The hell you say!" Beth snorted, hitting the replay. "Listen to it again."

They did. It did sound like voices, voices talking underwater, or voices on an old vinyl record playing at the wrong speed.

"Can you speed it up a little?" Nyota asked.

"Sure," Beth said, frowning but doing it. Nyota listened intently, and then began to laugh.

"Want to let me in on it?" Beth demanded grumpily.

"Satchmo!" Nyota said.

"Say again?"

"Louis 'Satchmo' Armstrong," Nyota explained patiently, as if anyone but Beth would know such things. " 'Satchmo' was short for 'Satchel-mouth.' One of the jazz greats of the last century. He played a down trumpet, and he sang with a lot of gravel, just like that."

Beth was goggling at her.

"My grandfather had some antique vinyls that *his* grandfather left him," Nyota explained. "We used to play them when we were kids; we thought they were a riot. Honestly, Beth, you ought to try expanding your cultural horizons a little."

"Hmmph!" was Beth's answer. It was a sore point between them. Beth was pure military. She worked hard and she played hard and she didn't have time for what she called "cultural fluff."

"Anyway, that's who they sound like." Nyota shrugged. "Satchmo."

"They," Beth repeated. "So you don't think I'm going bonkers?"

"Oh, too late for that!" Nyota said, ducking as Beth took a less than playful swing at her, a silly thing to do in zero g; her chair swiveled a full 360 degrees before she got it back under control. "But it's got nothing to do with this. There's someone talking out there. I'd stake my career on it."

My career! she thought. One hundred and forty-four petri dishes sitting on their trays waiting for me to check and see if anything's growing in the medium, and you know what? All of a sudden, I don't care! Whatever Beth's just reeled in out of the static and the solar noise is far more important than any of that!

Ask any Earthbound expert about the possibilities of contacting extraterrestrial life and the response was always: "Perhaps someday, but not within our lifetime." For all the SETI-arrays and high-orbit receivers gathering data from above three planets now, the official position was still one of hopeful skepticism. Positive reports had been made sporadically since early in the twenty-first century, but the "official" analysis always rejected the possibility of intelligent communication. Only the young, on their first deepspace mission, could dare to feel differently.

Nyota's tea grew cold, her culture media languished unwatched in the lab as she and Beth continued to listen. She knew she'd catch hell from her supervisor for not recording her 0100 findings—which would be no different from the 2400 ones—but she'd take that risk. She simply had to find out where those voices were coming from.

"They are definitely voices," she decided finally. "At least two, maybe three distinct individuals. Do you hear the variations in range? And one of them slurs his—her?—s's just a little. Hear it?"

"Uh-huh," Beth said, though she didn't really.

"And there's a decided linguistic pattern. You hear that 'gth' sound that's repeated at the start of some words and the end of others?"

"Hey, you're the language expert!" Beth said, more concerned with recording all of this for her end-of-watch report. "How many languages do you speak anyway?"

"You mean fluently?" Nyota asked vaguely, paying more attention to her headset than to Beth; she failed to notice that Beth looked like she wanted to hit her again. "Four. Well, four and a half. My Chinese is a little rusty . . ."

"Your Chinese is a little rusty!" Beth snorted. "You're a kick in the head, you know that?"

Now Nyota gave her her full attention. "Hey, come on! You're at least bilingual yourself. You'd have to be or you wouldn't have qualified for CommOps. And that's not counting all the decode lingo."

"I'm just a tech," Beth demurred, holding the headset against her ear again. Now that Nyota had pointed out the nuances, she could hear three distinct voices as well. She listened, wide-eyed; this was scaring her. "You know what? I think I'm going to have to report this all the way home to HQ."

"Shouldn't we try to figure out where it's coming from first?"

They tried, staying on it until the artificial-grav kicked in at 0700, when Beth shooed Nyota out before the day shift, and her exec, arrived to give her the lecture about "unauthorized personnel" loitering in CommOps. But the signals' exact vector eluded them. Between their own transmissions kicking out of the Mars bases, local ship-to-ship chatter, and garden-variety static, they never did get an accurate fix on it. Beth Listrom logged it as "apparently emanating vicinity Saturn" and, without bothering to wait for her exec's approval, called it in to ESC HQ on Earth on a secure frequency.

From *Venture*'s position roughly halfway between Earth and Mars there was a twenty-minute turnaround on transmissions to Earth. Listrom's exec hadn't finished chewing her out for insubordination when they got the answerback:

" 'Message received . . .' " Beth decoded aloud so the boss could hear and make sure she wasn't concealing anything; she

clung to the headset for dear life and refused to relinquish it.
" ' . . . and taken under consideration. Maintain Level-one security . . . ESC-one out.' "

With that she'd handed over the headset and confined herself to quarters for ten days. It was worth it. If those transmissions were what Nyota said they were, she wanted to make damn sure they got the credit.

✍

They never heard another word. Back home, Decrypt had crawled all over the mystery transmissions, turning them inside out and upside down while simultaneously denying to the media that anything like an alien transmission had been picked up inside the solar system. The story leaked anyway, and speculation about little green men ran rampant for a couple of weeks and then, in the wake of some holovid star's scandalous affair with an Olympic skater *and* her two husbands, gradually became less and less important in the public's mind. Most people on Earth knew it took months just to reach Jupiter-1 with an optimal launch window; the notion of extraterrestrial visitors traveling light-years just to play tourist didn't have much popular appeal anymore. The man in the street had taken to echoing the experts:

"Maybe someday, but not within our lifetime."

Having heard those Louis Armstrong voices, Nyota Domonique had to wonder. She'd kept the memory of those sounds running through her mind all these years—being a qualified esper with a high eidetic rating helped—and it was the only record she had. A good soldier, Beth had refused to dub the tape, and Decrypt had declared the report "inconclusive," with a strong suggestion that Ms. Domonique stick to her areas of expertise and let the brass worry about little green men.

If anything further was ever intercepted, no one was talking about it. And the vehemence with which it was suggested that she mind her own business had had Nyota wondering ever since.

✍

"So now you get to find out for yourself," Mark McCord observed, treading catlike and quiet on the carpeted deck to stand behind her at the windowport in the outer torus of the station. He studied the view with her, even though as civilian commander of Jupiter-1, he could look at it anytime he wanted.

Nyota willed herself not to jump out of her skin. Mark's esper rating was as high as hers, but she should have felt him sneaking up behind her. It was her own fault he had read her thoughts, since she'd done nothing to shield them. Not that she'd ever succeeded in shielding from Mark, nor he from her, which was what had added such spice to their early relationship.

"My favorite part of the sky," he added, when she said nothing.

How long had it been since they'd decided it was better to be friends than ex-lovers? Mark had been with Jupiter-1 since it was nothing more than a skeleton, fragile-looking titanium struts gleaming defiant against the darker than dark of space like a child's toy, with a longrange shuttlecraft clinging to its underside like a gigantic cocoon. The station itself had evolved into a kind of hive, buzzing with structural engineers and environmental-control experts modifying the old Mars-1 design to adapt to the particular problems of Jupiter orbit. For the next two years interplanetaries had lumbered into the airlocks carrying maximum payloads of structural metals, prefab plastic modules for everything from computer consoles to toilet seats, plus the hardware for both, along with the best rations, the latest entertainment vids, and of course, the wall-to-wall carpet. They left with their cargo bays empty except for personal mail, and gradually the station had taken shape, becoming a viable colony which required only the occasional supply run from Mars to keep its denizens fed and happy. Toward the end the designers had scavenged the shuttle itself to construct a holovid arena; it was symbolic of their intention to be permanent, and never go back.

Beth Listrom and her military complement had arrived piecemeal, part of the interplanetary turnover bringing the short-term consultants out and defense forces in, once the main structure was in place. But Mark McCord had been there from the outset, a CEO who wasn't at all shy about occasionally sliding that long-muscled torso into the close confines of an airshaft and getting his hands dirty. He could point out the structural plates in the main torus that he had sealed in with his own hands.

"How the hell am I supposed to run the place if I don't know how the pieces fit?" was how he'd explained it to Nyota in the first personal transmission he'd sent her when Jupiter-1 first became operational. She'd put in for assignment to the station herself, but HQ had needed her expertise in running the Martian biospheres instead. Considering the up-in-the-air quality of her relationship with Mark at the time, it was probably just as well.

That was a long time ago, Nyota thought now, not even bothering to turn and look at him. She could see his rugged face with its broken-looking nose—souvenir of a bar fight on Selenopolis, he'd told her—reflected in the windowport, just behind her left shoulder. When he put his warm, calloused hands on her shoulders she didn't shrug him off; in fact, she leaned into him a little, just for old times' sake.

"Reading my thoughts again!" she scolded him, smiling. "As I recall, that was only one of your annoying habits."

"Set in my ways, I guess," he murmured, closing his eyes and breathing in the scent of her, remembering how well they'd fit together once upon a time. "Seriously, if they are out there, it should be you who finds them."

"Oh, but Mark, we know there's nobody out here but us chickens!" Nyota said ironically. She'd had that very same conversation with Beth only last night. The intervening years had somehow persuaded Beth she hadn't heard what they'd both heard, and she'd changed her tune to the official one.

"We were both young and dumb and starstruck," Beth insisted over her third Red Martian. "If I heard it today, it would sound just like *Star Trek*."

"I can't believe you're serious," Nyota remarked, but Beth had changed the subject.

"Whatever you say," Mark said now, giving Nyota's shoulders a final squeeze. Uncertain if she could block her thoughts from him even after all this time, Nyota tried not to remember how it felt to run her fingers through his hair and along the muscles of his chest and arms, or how his mustache tickled. "Still, let them know that if they're in the neighborhood they can always stop by for a drink. I'll even dip into my private stock of Guinness."

"I'll certainly be able to give you plenty of advance warning!" Nyota turned then and stroked his face—once, briefly, for old times' sake. It would be a long time before she would see Mark or Beth or anyone from the station, unless she counted visual transmissions. It was the damnable thing about space travel, the time involved. It almost guaranteed against close personal relationships.

Mark McCord didn't have to read her thoughts this time to see them in her liquid brown eyes. His own gray eyes crinkled at the corners with what might have been a sad smile; he nodded without another word and began to walk away, back to work. They would see each other again at the formal send-off at the airlock just before the *Egg*'s departure, but this was the only private goodbye they could allow themselves. Nyota turned toward the windowport, too quickly, so she wouldn't have to watch him go. If she brushed a tear or two from her thick eyelashes, no one noticed.

*∞*

Depending on the conditions they found on and around Titan, the crew of the *Dragon's Egg* could stay for a minimum of six months or, with the ESC's go-ahead, hunker down on closed-system technology for years until the next window. The decision was the commander's to make, though every crew member had a right to be heard. Decades in space had convinced ESC administrators of the wisdom of relying on *in situ* judgment. The longer a crew stayed out in space, the more important it was to them to know that their needs mattered. No one wanted to risk so much as a single member of a team going space-happy so far from home.

Closed-system technology! Nyota thought, making her final inspection tour of the *Dragon's Egg*. In full hardsuit—including Velcro toeholds, even though the constant rotation of the station torus created its own artificial-g—she was down in the hold taking inventory of literally tons of freeze-dried rations, hi-pro and vitamin supplements, and Meals Ready to Eat that would sustain them while they waited for their onboard hy-droponics lab to kick in and provide the fresh veggies. What they ate after the prefab meals ran out, no one wanted to talk about.

Was it any more repulsive to think of recycling solid waste into nutritionally balanced meals than it was to think of drink-ing and bathing in your own filtered sweat and urine? Every spacer had bouts of squeamishness about the entire subject at least occasionally, and there was always at least one joker in every crew whose lunch table humor could make it stick in your throat and threaten to come back up again, but you coped. Very simply, in this latter half of the twenty-first century, it was the only way to fly.

# CHAPTER 3

Heads turned whenever he strode across the courtyard to his father's chambers. Heads had turned to watch Tetrok ever since he was a child.

It wasn't just that he was handsome. Most Fazisians were handsome. It wasn't just that he was heir apparent to Xeniok's throne. His father, at one hundred years, had not even reached half-age, was still in excellent health, and might rule for decades yet. Further, there was no guarantee the Fazrul would support Xeniok's heir as next Ruler when the time came. It was well within the realm of possibility that he would live the rest of his life as an ordinary citizen. It was not heritage that made men as well as women turn and watch Tetrok as he passed, but something more subtle. He had what Earthians would call *charisma*.

It haunted him. While his father had wisely enrolled the boy in general schools rather than appointing him private tutors, even giving him an obscure family name and sending him offworld to a provincial capital so that neither his teachers nor his fellow students knew who he really was, something about him inevitably attracted their attention. True, he was one of the brightest students, but it was more than that. As he grew into young manhood, it became more complex.

Tetrok was gregarious, popular, and fun to be around—a natural-born leader possessing such a unique blend of wisdom and charisma that his many male friends easily accepted their role as his followers. But in fact, Tetrok was a loner. Young women found him irresistible, but soon grew frustrated at their inability to reach the inner core of him.

Like all Fazisians, Tetrok was a telesper. Like all Fazisians, he had been trained in mindshare, and when he was fully shielded, no one could reach him. There was a watchfulness about him which made others, his peers and his elders alike, equally watchful of him. Tetrok was an enigma.

"Why do you always hold back?" his distant cousin Nebulaesa would ask when they had barely entered adolescence, and were learning the fine points of telepathy. "Krecis says it's selfish not to give equally when minds touch."

"It's the way I am," Tetrok had answered, fully realizing that the answer was insufficient.

Tetrok had no siblings, an advantage to a Ruler's son who would thereby automatically be first in the succession should Xeniok choose to step down. But while the succession was hereditary, it must be submitted to vote by the Fazrul, and if the Fazrul refused the Ruler's first choice, there must be other choices.

Second after Tetrok was his first cousin Valton, offspring of one of Xeniok's several sisters. Born in the same year, he bore enough resemblance to Tetrok so that at first glance they might almost be mistaken for twins, though two more divergent personalities would be hard to find on all of Fazis. Next were the two sisters Nebulaesa, who was Tetrok's age, and Zeenyl, several years younger, enough removed in consanguinity to marry either of the males if they so chose, which was how the succession had been preserved in ancient times. Third and fourth respectively in line, either girl could aspire to ascend to the throne on her own, or become co-Ruler by marriage if she preferred.

All grew up beneath the scrutiny of the Fazrul and, through the Fazrul, beneath the eyes of all of Fazis. If Tetrok chose to keep himself to himself, this might be why.

"It's because he is selfish!" his cousin Valton offered instead, vying with Tetrok for Nebulaesa's attention when they were in their teens, their hormones surging. "He wants to read our thoughts without sharing his own!"

"He doesn't need to read your mind to read your thoughts, cousin!" little Zeenyl had said gravely on that particular occasion, startling the others. She was so quiet usually that they often forgot she was around. "You always make such awful faces, even I know what you're thinking."

Zeenyl's telesper abilities were not as strong as her three elders', were less developed in fact than in most children her age. Her parents had expressed concern; Krecis, her tutor, had suggested her talents lay elsewhere. But for her to admit to such weakness before Valton was a serious matter.

"Do you, little one?" Valton had pounced on her then, tickling until she squealed. "Then how did you not know I was about to tickle you?"

He didn't give her time to answer, but continued tickling until she was out of breath. Stubborn, she would not beg for mercy and her sister, Nebulaesa, tried to intervene.

"Valton, stop it!" she cried, tugging at his shoulders. "She's much smaller than you; it's hardly fair!"

But it was Tetrok who forcibly made him stop.

"Enough, cousin," he said without raising his voice, though his hands held Valton's wrists with as much strength as Valton possessed, and a slightly stronger will. "Has it ever been told to you that you don't know when to stop?"

"Constantly!" Valton nearly shouted, yanking himself free, his moment spoiled. "Most frequently by you!"

Tetrok had shrugged then, not wanting to quarrel. *The whole world is watching, cousin. You would do well to govern your behavior by that. I only meant to warn you!*

Valton heard the warning in his mind and disregarded it. And Krecis, mentor to them all, saw the future of Fazis unfold before him, and took note. If there was an intrinsic flaw in hereditary rule, he was observing it.

☙

"How do you hope to rule if you do not trust?" Xeniok would ask his son, from the time his first games tutor complained that it was impossible to best the boy at any of the interactive games; the tutor had implied some level, not of cheating exactly—one did not lightly accuse even a child of the ruling family of such a transgression—but of privileged information the boy ought not to possess.

Tetrok had shrugged his stringy shoulders; he was growing tall rather than broad this season, and his wrists dangled out of his sleeves. "It was only a game, Father. Xerec takes these things too seriously."

"Is that an apology or an explanation?" his father asked mildly; it was impossible to be stern with the boy.

"Neither," Tetrok answered with a trace of stubbornness. "Merely an observation."

"An observation!" Xeniok had repeated for Krecis later that day. "What am I to do with one so young who is so full of 'observations'?"

"Give him his head," Krecis suggested. "He may surprise you."

It had been Xeniok's idea to appoint Krecis the children's unofficial tutor whenever he was planetside. Krecis was of a noble line but not of the ruling family proper, and as master scientist and member of the Order of Telespers, could enrich the youngsters' education in any number of areas.

He took them on field trips to catalog the flora and fauna of their world, taught them logic and dialectic beneath the pristine amber skies, took them soaring through the labyrinthine mysteries of the inner mind as easily as piloting a skimmer above the surface of a sea. For Xeniok's part, it was gratifying to the Ruler to see his dearest friend, who had no son, providing wisdom to his own.

✍

Down the years to Tetrok's adulthood, Xeniok would take Krecis' advice and come to call often upon his son's observations. Yet it was with some relief that he received the news that Tetrok had been chosen, as top of his class in the Offworld Academy, to lead the next expedition to the Earthian system. Perhaps in space exploration the young man's true abilities would emerge, honed into leadership in the decades he was gone.

"There will be a celebration for your send-off," Xeniok informed his son, letting his pride at the sight of him in his offworld uniform slip through his mental shields. "Your mother and aunts and cousins have something elaborate planned, though you must of course pretend it is a surprise."

"Of course, Father," Tetrok answered, an amused smile tugging at his expressive mouth.

"While I will also take part in the festivities, I don't know if time will permit me a true farewell," Xeniok said with some emotion; he took his son by the shoulders. "That I wished to do in private. You will be gone a long time."

"That goes without saying," Tetrok said, uneasy with the emotional turn the conversation was taking. "I will miss you, too, Father."

"You don't need to be told that the Fazrul will be observing you far more keenly than it would any ordinary offworld commander."

*To see if I am worthy to lead when you grow weary of the task, Father. Yes, I know!*

"I will conduct myself as I would were I an 'ordinary' offworld commander—whatever that might be," Tetrok said aloud. "My crew has entrusted me with their lives. That is no less important to me than governing a world."

The answer satisfied Xeniok, who kissed his son farewell and said no more.

✍

Tetrok's ship had almost reached Outlyer-21 at the outer edges of the Earthian system in a matter of months, a fraction of the time it had taken Krecis and his crew to come the long way around. Krecis wondered if such breakneck speed would affect the mind-set of these newcomers sent to expand upon his work here.

The Fazrul had granted Krecis complete autonomy on Titan; he answered to no one but the Ruler, and he had ruled wisely. Under his tenure the entire satellite had been explored and charted. Ecologically sound mining operations harvested the mineral wealth that Fazis needed. Research laboratories as sophisticated as any on Fazis Prime had produced a number of genetic breakthroughs, especially in improving plant and animal species by judicious exposure to the increased methane levels of Titan's surface. Despite its precarious beginnings, Krecis had made his colony work. He was pleased with his small realm, and the Fazrul was pleased with him.

But now the Fazrul deemed it necessary to explore and chart the entire star system; it was why the new Wingcrafts had been designed, and why Tetrok was the first to command one. Krecis wondered if this was wise.

It is not ours! he thought. What right have we, who are interlopers here? The Fazrul had taken his objections under consideration, and sent Tetrok's ship anyway.

Tetrok had all the necessary credentials to explore a newly charted star system, if that system was uninhabited. Degrees in physics and astrogation, high esper and leadership ratings in all scan levels, indicated that he possessed the technical skills to do the job. But was the man behind the training much changed from the boy Krecis once knew? And who among them, even Krecis himself, had the qualifications to negotiate with not one but four new species, as likely different from each other as they were from Fazisians?

It is Tetrok who will first encounter the Earthians regardless, Krecis thought, for they are coming here. Was this justification for whatever happened when they did?

The relative positions of the two approaching ships were marked on a holochart which dominated one wall of the command center, altering daily as each neared Titan. Tetrok's ship would arrive at Outlyer-21 within days and then proceed into the system; the more ponderous Earthian vessel had left the orbital station beyond Jupiter and would not arrive over Titan for nearly four months. But it would be Tetrok who would decide whether they would actively intercept the Earthian vessel, or lie in wait on Titan and allow themselves to be discovered. Krecis might be the final authority on Titan, but he had no jurisdiction beyond its orbit. Would the heir apparent seek his advice or not?

Even as he studied the holochart, Krecis studied the file on Tetrok, as well as the handsome young face whose holo graced the file. Had the younger man changed overmuch since he had been his pupil nearly a quarter-age ago? Even a Fazisian could not get an esper reading from a holographic image. Even Krecis, his telesper skills honed to the high-priest level, could not get a read on the Earthians.

He had tried. For decades he had studied the intercepted radio messages, until he prided himself that with the aid of the central computer's linguistics program he could make himself understood in all four of their languages. But if they had holocom, it was incompatible with Fazisian technology. So too their mental powers, if they possessed any.

How many nights on his offshift had Krecis honed his mind against the four languages—the musical one, *Chinese,* which was closest in spirit to Fazis' tongue, the quixotic *English* with its plethora of synonyms for a single thing, the hard-to-pronounce *Russian* and *French,* the first of which seemed to be spoken from the back of the throat, the second from somewhere above the bridge of one's nose—sending his mind out in the hope of reaching some unknown mind? His fellow Fazisians had complained.

"Your mind is too powerful, OldOne," Vaax, sent as spokesman by the others, chided him, meaning the title as a compliment. "No matter how carefully you shield, some of us can hear you in our dreams."

"Forgive me. I shall have to stop, then," Krecis answered solemnly.

"You ought not to be alone so much at night," Fariya suggested gently, thinking, *Zandra is dead. How long will you mourn?*

"It was so as not to mourn that I engaged myself in this communication!" Krecis had said aloud and none too gently. After that no one criticized, but he abandoned the search.

If Earthians had mental powers, they too were on a different, and possibly incompatible, frequency. There was nothing to do but wait. One thing longrange space travel taught one to do well was to wait.

*⁂*

Nebulaesa watched the sleek vessel fold its solar sails like oversize iridescent wings as it slowed to synchronicity with the rotational speed of Outlyer-21's outer torus. Recent Fazisian design criteria were based upon environmental themes, and spacecraft deliberately mimicked forms which had served the natural world since the beginning. These latest additions to the offworld fleet were like gigantic insects, right down to a carapace-fuselage where the now folded sails concealed themselves as part of the overall design—streamlined, efficient, but also beautiful. As Nebulaesa watched from the main airlock's security post, the ship bearing the heir apparent heeled over in the most graceful docking maneuver she had ever witnessed.

Everyone on Outlyer-21 had been briefed on the design of the new ships, but this was the first one to actually loom out of hyperspace and approach the outpost's docking ring. The usual traffic consisted of freighters and ore drones and the occasional government courier, ordinary ships on ordinary missions. The Wingcrafts were something special. Every tech on the station was itching to have a closer look at this one.

Nebulaesa watched for a different reason. Yes, it was her duty as the newly assigned commander to greet each incomer, but she also had a personal reason. The Wing's helmsman was her younger sister, Zeenyl, and it was she who had executed the pure choreography of the docking maneuver. Nebulaesa had not seen her sister since before Zeenyl's marriage to Phaestus, had not even met her new brother-in-law at all. She was eager to remedy that.

How eager she might be to see Tetrok again was something Nebulaesa kept to herself.

The year before both boys left for the Offworld Academy, where she would follow them a year later, Nebulaesa confessed to Tetrok that she loved him. Tetrok's response troubled her to this day.

"Good, I'm glad!" he'd said, never once saying "I love you" in return. Their affair had been brief and incendiary—they were both very young—ending as abruptly as it began, but not before Nebulaesa found out, too late, that it was Valton who loved her more.

*

How long she stood at the airlock in her official capacity, greeting each crew member as she or he stepped through, the chronos could easily tell her but, lost in her thoughts, Nebulaesa paid no heed. She knew that as a member of the bridge crew Zeenyl would be among the last to leave the ship, second only to her commander.

As to how she was to greet Zeenyl without revealing too much of her lingering feeling for Tetrok . . . Nebulaesa was still pondering that when someone spoke her name.

"Commander Nebulaesa?"

"Phaestus!" she said graciously, instantly recognizing the slightly distracted look of the dedicated scientist from the countless holos Zeenyl had sent on her personal channel. She took both of his hands in hers as was customary and kissed his cheek. "Kinsman—welcome!"

"My gratitude," he answered, holding her hands in his own a moment longer than strict protocol required. A sensitive man as well as a brilliant one, Nebulaesa noted; would her sister have chosen less? "As a mere scientist and not a member of the crew, I've managed to escape a few moments ahead of the others. They're still battening down."

"Understood," Nebulaesa said, and the two simultaneously opened their minds to each other.

There were countless levels to a Fazisian's mind, and the high priests spent lifetimes accessing new ones. For the average person, the earliest level mastered was a kind of warmth, a welcoming wavelength which spoke wordlessly of trust and friendship, particularly when greeting a new member of the family. It was thus that Nebulaesa and her new kinsman were communing when Zeenyl and Tetrok emerged at last from the sleek ship.

Stoic though Fazisians tended to be, they were also deeply affectionate. Siblings as close as these two needed no words to greet each other; Zeenyl and Nebulaesa embraced in breathless silence.

"Sister!" each said simultaneously, as they held each other at arm's length, their musical laughter harmonizing.

"You're flourishing!" Nebulaesa pronounced of Zeenyl. She nodded toward Phaestus conspiratorially. "He must be good for you!"

"I could not be happier!" Zeenyl announced, though a small frown creased her brow. "But you look tired!"

"It's nothing!" Nebulaesa dismissed it. "I am ... still learning my new responsibilities. As replacement crew, we arrived barely a hundred days ago ourselves."

"Just so." Zeenyl nodded her understanding. Nebulaesa had turned her attention to the last to arrive.

"Tetrok," was all she said.

"Commander," he replied, deliberately choosing the formal mode. Tetrok was shielded, as always. Nebulaesa had expected no less.

Zeenyl watched the two of them. It took no telepathy to sense the negative energy crackling between them.

"Now we are all together except one!" she said, trying to

break the tension, though her words had the opposite effect. To mention Valton in Tetrok's presence was to risk much; the two had been at odds since early boyhood. As for the strange, lopsided love triangle that had been Valton, Nebulaesa, and Tetrok . . . Zeenyl regretted her words, sought some way to take them back. "And Krecis, of course."

"And Krecis, of course!" Nebulaesa repeated gratefully, taking the cue. "Dear Krecis! How I envy you both the privilege of working with the OldOne. You must tell me everything that transpires on Titan, everything! But for now, let me personally escort you to your quarters."

She walked slightly ahead of all three of them down the curve of the docking ring; she could not meet Tetrok's gaze overlong. The gravity here was slightly denser than aboardship, and new arrivals always walked as if they were sinking slightly in mud.

"After you've refreshed yourselves, I hope you'll join me for dinner," Nebulaesa went on, when she could trust her emotions to stay inside her where they belonged.

Her official voice masked a welter of feelings. Old feelings for Tetrok, which had not altered since the night he'd kissed her fingertips on the seawall of the academy and told her that while he would always think of her as a friend, their destinies would inevitably draw them apart, so it was best to go their separate ways from that moment on. Nebulaesa had cried, pleaded with him, forgetting her pride.

"Tetrok, I understand what you're saying—the time, the distances that will keep us apart. But if we love each other—"

"Nebulaesa . . ." He had made a negative gesture, telling her he was not listening, either with his mind or with his heart, to whatever she was about to say next, yet she persisted.

"I don't even have to be the only one! I don't mind if you have others, as long as you and I . . . Just don't take yourself away from me entirely!"

Again he indicated he would not listen. "In time you will find another, someone who can give himself entirely, someone less selfish than I. Valton is right about that, you know."

Nebulaesa only wept; it was she who refused to listen to him now. Tetrok had had his way—Tetrok always had his way—and they had separated, leaving Nebulaesa hurt and angry but loving him all the more.

Had they been wise to initiate a love affair after they'd been so close as children? Was there any way it could have ended except in sorrow?

Added to Nebulaesa's old sorrow was the new sorrow that Zeenyl and her spouse would be here scarcely overnight before the graceful technological butterfly that had brought them this far took wing for Titan.

☙

"Why is it," Major Copeland asked from the commstation, yawning and stretching her arms high above her head, "that the final leg of any mission always seems the longest? Have you noticed that, Commander?"

"What's that, D'Borah?" Nyota asked informally. The flying bridge was on autopilot and these two were alone at stations; Nyota had been scanning a report from Hydroponics and wasn't really listening.

"I said, we've been out here for months, with only a few weeks left to go, the work load's only going to increase as we get closer, but I feel like time is dragging on my hands. Cabin fever? I don't know. I just can't wait to get some dirt under my feet again, even if it's cryogenic Titan dirt."

Nyota shook her head; she couldn't disagree more. "Hmmm . . . Seems like every place I've touched on is just a stepping stone to the next. I can't stay anywhere for long. Can't wait to see what's over that next horizon, I guess."

D'Borah Copeland smiled. She could have been Nyota Domonique's older sister and, off duty, she often assumed that role. Even though she'd graduated two years ahead of Nyota, she was one of those career fliers who let the promotions find them rather than seeking them out; it wasn't that she was unambitious, just that getting ahead wasn't that important to her. Playing mother hen to her commander was.

"That's just because you've never found a reason to stay," she said knowingly.

Nyota knew exactly what she was talking about; they'd had this conversation more than once.

"Any man who couldn't follow me into space wouldn't be

worth my time!'' she said sternly. ''And that's all I want to say on that subject!''

Now it was D'Borah Copeland's turn to shake her head. ''Pity! You'd make such beautiful children.''

Nyota looked at her under her eyelashes. ''Major, it seems to me that at the start of this shift you promised me a long-range scan on large debris on a thousand-kilometer course ahead. Have you done that yet?''

''Large debris'' meant anything pebble-size or bigger; a thousand-kilometer scan could take days, depending on the density of debris in the area. ''Dustbusting'' was the most polite word the crew had for it; it was like sifting an entire beach through a sieve, and the commander knew it.

''I was just about to complete—'' D'Borah began.

''Well, good. I'm glad you haven't completed it, because I think you should expand your scan to micron-size or smaller. We don't want anything gumming up the intakes as we get close to Saturn's gravity-well, do we, Copeland?''

D'Borah realized Nyota had just done something she was famous for—shifted as smooth as silk directly from formal to casual to command mode at the flick of an eyelash—and she, D'Borah, had been told in no uncertain terms to mind her own business.

''No, Commander, we don't!'' she said crisply, and went back to her dustbusting.

&

Tetrok studied Krecis' holochart, where his own Wingcraft had come to rest on the surface of Titan, while the Earthian ship continued to move inexorably toward them. In one corner of the command center, a wide-band receiver picked up a continuous stream of intraship chatter in the musical language, Chinese.

''This is exciting, Krecis!'' the heir apparent announced with as much enthusiasm as he could permit himself.

''Exciting? Perhaps. But also, you'll forgive my saying so, somewhat worrisome.''

''Worrisome? How so?''

''We don't know who they are,'' Krecis said, gesturing toward the moving light that would very shortly alter the course of at least local cosmic history. "We have no precedent for this, neither as to the psychic impact upon either species, nor even as to simple protocol. And there is, primarily, the question of whether they come armed."

"Their ships move so slowly," Tetrok pointed out. "Nearly a year to pass between two in-system worlds. How many centuries would it take them to come as far as we have? Surely their technology cannot surpass ours."

"Can we be sure?" Krecis wondered aloud, even as he invited the younger man into his mind.

*Does the ponderousness of their ships necessarily mean they are not as evolved as we, or rather that they have focused their technology on alternate priorities? Consider . . .*

A landscape bloomed suddenly in the younger man's mind, startling him. Tetrok's journey had taken him directly from Fazis Prime to Outlyer-21; while he had spent his youth amid the exotic flora of Fazis Fourth, that colony world had contained nothing so exotic as this. How much of this was Krecis' imagination, how much based in fact? There were legends of ancient Fazisians who had been able to project their minds to places they had never been, but these were considered largely infant-school tales. Had Krecis discovered some long-lost skill, or was he merely extrapolating?

*I do not know!* Tetrok heard the older man's mindvoice within his own mind. *But these are the ghosts which populate my dreams.*

Figures, ghostly, appeared against this landscape now, unscrolling across Tetrok's mind, moving as if in fog—bipedal, indistinct, somewhere in a middle distance lacking referents. How large were they, of how many genders? Were they individuals, or, like some of the animal life on Fazis, of a communal mind? What was their command structure? Were they espers? Did they only appear to be walking upright, or were they perhaps swimming in some invisible ether? What did they believe in? Were they without a sense of the Supreme Being, or did they worship, as Fazisians did?

As they moved across his inner eye, Tetrok found himself distinguishing four distinct species, but what differentiated one from the other he could not tell. This much detail surely was not known; he was looking at the inner workings of Krecis' agile mind, and what he had concluded from the scant hard data at his command.

Tetrok watched as the four species moved up an entry ramp into a ship.

*Yes,* he heard Krecis' mindvoice once again, tinged with self-deprecating humor. *I fear I lack imagination here. It does look alarmingly like one of ours!*

Screens and instrument panels, consoles and chairs, the very color schemes common in the ships of Krecis' generation, were reproduced in the interior of this supposedly Earthian ship. Indicators were all marked in Fazisian script—a fine point, Tetrok realized. Who was to say what manner of writing these four species might have in common, if they had writing at all? Perhaps they marked their instruments with scent glands hidden in the palms of their hands, or with musical tones, or light, or esper codes. The young man almost found himself transported into this figment of the elder man's mind, more real than any holo image. With a little bit of imagination he might reach out and touch one of these obscure aliens, clap him (her?) on the shoulder.

And forfeit his life for it. Krecis was right, Tetrok thought, raising his mental shields with a snap, shutting the image out. There was no protocol for such an encounter, none at all. Who was to say that what a Fazisian considered a friendly gesture might not be construed as a profound insult by some, if not all, of these four strange species? What were they to do?

Tetrok's shields had not prevented him from seeing Krecis' final construct for this foreign landscape—a ship armed with deadly weaponry, and with full intent to use it. Tetrok gave the older man an inquiring look.

"It seems reasonable," Krecis answered with a shrug. "A slow ship makes an easy target. Would they not come fully armed?"

"What do you think, OldOne?" Tetrok asked thoughtfully. "How do we approach them?"

Krecis slipped his hands into his sleeves. "I have not been informed of the extent of your orders from the Fazrul—"

"Which is your indirect way of asking me what they are." Tetrok smiled, appreciating the older man's subtlety. "While I remain on Titan, I am under your command. My decisions once I take the Wingcraft out into the system are largely discretionary. I am to report in to my father and the Fazrul at regular intervals, of course, but essentially I am on my own as to the day-to-day.

"The Fazrul wants this system charted, with as little risk as possible to life and property. Whether it takes me one year or twenty—and there are some in the Fazrul who would not mind my being absent for twenty—whether it is done covertly or with full knowledge of the inhabitants, is up to me."

"A heavy burden of decision for a commander on his first mission," Krecis said carefully. If Tetrok had tried to reach his mind just now, he would have encountered shields even more powerful than his own.

"Especially a commander whose every breath is recorded by the Fazrul. Krecis . . ." The ever-confident Tetrok hesitated. "I will need your advice."

He has thought about this, and deeply! Krecis realized. Perhaps he has thought of little else since he left Fazis. "Let me ask you, then: How does it seem to you? How does it seem best to treat with the four species when they arrive?"

"I can only treat with them as I would wish to be treated were I to find an unknown race nesting on a satellite in the Fazisian system," Tetrok said thoughtfully. "And that is to let them find us. To go out into orbit to meet them—particularly in a Wingcraft of superior speed—would most likely be viewed as a threat."

"Whereas to remain passive on the surface is to leave ourselves vulnerable to their weaponry."

"Only if they choose to use it, OldOne. And we will know that as we scan them coming into the system."

"Which will not be soon enough to defend ourselves," Krecis finished for him.

Tetrok reached out for Krecis' mind and found it decisively shut to him. He remembered what his father had said about never being able to win an argument with Krecis. Even as a boy, Tetrok had known better than to try. Only Valton, poor stubborn Valton, had dared. And Krecis—in the interests of improving the boy's skills at dialect, as he explained it—had bested Valton, as he did most adults, every time.

Tetrok had found it an interesting lesson. Throughout his

youth he had watched Valton challenge Krecis at family gatherings, watched the OldOne take the challenge with a twinkle
in his eye and give the young man the best of his wisdom and
rhetorical skills; Valton had foundered every time.

"Have mercy, cousin!" Tetrok tried to tell him once. "On
those of us who must watch the slaughter if not upon yourself.
You cannot win. It's no shame to admit the OldOne surpasses
you in age and experience. Stop torturing yourself!"

"I will win!" Valton had answered breathlessly, as if it
were a contest of bodies as much as minds and wills. "Though
it takes a half-age, I will win!"

He had said it with enough fervor to make Tetrok profoundly uneasy.

One entire solar system and nearly a quarter-age distant,
Tetrok wondered now if the OldOne was testing him as he
had tested Valton, or merely helping him to clarify his thought.

"We are the interlopers here," Tetrok said finally. "If the
Earthians are an aggressor race, they will destroy us eventually
anyway. Better to know this earlier than later. And I would
prefer to think them wise enough to interpret our remaining
on the surface as a gesture of goodwill."

Krecis nodded, satisfied with the answer.

"And in all things"—Tetrok clapped the older man on the
shoulder—"I will rely on your judgment, OldOne."

OldOne! Krecis thought. They all honored him in this way
now, and it was an honor. Yet, in truth, he had never felt older.

*

"It doesn't look real!" everyone aboard the *Dragon's Egg*
kept saying to each other.

"It," of course, was Saturn, the only thing visible on their
aft screens for days now. Aft screens rather than forward because Commander Domonique had ordered an old-fashioned
retro approach from the instant the big gasball had reached
out and grabbed them. Let the planet do the work of pulling
them down toward its surface, while they controlled the speed
of descent with retros until they were low enough to pick their
way among Saturn's eighteen known moons and find the one
they wanted.

There'd been some muttering among the crew about doing

things bass-ackwards as the helmsman had swung the big ship around on its axis so that it would back toward the planet; DefCon was particularly disgruntled.

"This isn't the siege of Aqaba!" Nyota, ever the historian, told them sharply. "You can turn your guns around if you need them. What the hell do you think you'll be shooting at on Saturn, anyway?"

Nyota Domonique seldom swore; she didn't need to. But weapons types needed to be spoken to in a language they could understand. The grumbling stopped.

Still, it was so strange to keep seeing the thing in back of them.

"It doesn't look real!"

Crewmen greeted each other with it as they glided past each other in the narrow corridors, in the commissary, the gym, the labs. It was de rigueur on the flying bridge because the planet was so huge it literally lit up the inside of the bridge with an eerie golden light. It became the universal buzzword, replacing "Good Morning," "How are you?" and even "So what are you doing when you go on offshift?"

"It *doesn't* look real," even Nyota Domonique had to admit, though the computers were spitting out reams of hard data on it at an ever more frenetic pace the closer they came. "But oh, you beauty, you certainly are!"

She sat tilted back at the comm gazing at it for hours, losing herself in the intricate beauty of the rings even as her mind balked at the fact that they were less than ten meters thick in places, concentric whorls of dust and of water ice held in this precise configuration for billions of years, so bright with reflected sunlight that they could be seen from Earth. And if one could tear one's gaze away from the rings, there was the planet itself, its surface seeming no more than layer upon layer of undulating gaseous veils of greenish gold—a vision, a magical fantasy of a planet, hardly a real place at all. Far more serene than its tumultuous bigger brother Jupiter, warmer and less remote than its outer cousins Uranus and Neptune, Saturn was, above all other things, mysterious. Yet to Nyota it said home.

Did she only feel that way because this mission was probably the high point of her career? At least that was how the

history books would characterize it. Never mind her early genetic work at Biosphere III which had produced hybrid grains
hardy enough to survive Martian winters; historians wouldn't
consider a breakthrough that could feed an entire planet half
as glamorous as what she was doing now. Never mind that
thanks to altered genetics and improved nutrition, an Earthian
could expect to live 170 years or more and Nyota was still a
young woman. What could she possibly do for an encore?
Cure cancer, she supposed; there were still some resistant
strains that had eluded the best of research efforts. But that
didn't hold the same visceral thrill as being the first Earthian
to watch Saturn looming on her event horizon and call it home.

*Something's going to happen here,* Nyota thought, though
she had no idea where the thought came from. *Something
that's going to affect my entire life.*

Meanwhile, there was work to be done.

*∞*

"Eighteen moons!" Luke Choy, the *Egg's* helmsman griped,
steering a course around one of the smaller ones, Epimetheus.
He'd swung the big ship around frontwards and was running
her on manual, cutting a fine line between steering too close
to each of the odd-size satellites as he approached them and
getting yanked off course by the big planet that from this angle
completely dominated the screens. At home he'd been a Virtual Reality Championships semifinalist with reflexes like an
android, but the stakes here, namely his life, were a little too
steep. "Oh Ma, I'm glad my life insurance is paid up! This is
like tiptoeing through a minefield dragging a loaded dogsled."

"Complaints, complaints!" D'Borah Copeland offered
from NavCon.

Commander Domonique said nothing. She knew Luke
worked best when he complained most. He was the spoiled
brat among her crew, youngest grandson of the consortium
chief whose company had commissioned the *Egg,* a space-law
student with a helmsman's Class 1 license and an itch to go
offworld, who'd been jumped ahead of several equally qualified candidates when his grandfather called in some favors.
The rest of the crew was aware of this, but four years in the
trenches had proven that Luke could cut it, so most of the

resentment had worn off. Still, the bellyaching this close to landfall could get on anyone's nerves.

"Dodging rocks! That's what we're doing—dodging rocks," Luke went on, oblivious of the glances exchanged behind his back. "It's worse than one of those old two-D sci-fi movies. Not one of them's the same size, they've got the most erratic orbits I've ever seen outside a video game, and the trace elements are playing hob with my instruments . . ."

Copeland and the rest of the crew sighed and blocked him out. Only Nyota seemed indifferent to his raving.

"And who named these idiot things anyway? Iapetus, Hyperion, Tethys—"

"Prometheus, Pandora, Calypso, Helene, Titan . . ." Nyota interrupted finally, turning off his faucet. "Count your blessings I don't make you dodge them all. Copeland plotted you the tidiest trajectory she could. What do you want, a cakewalk? If you don't think your skills are up to it, I can have you relieved."

That settled him down. "I'd rather get out and push!" he muttered, by way of having the last word.

"Don't give me any ideas!" Nyota shot back.

"Designated target Titan in Sector L-four," Copeland reported quietly.

Not as large as Ganymede, about the same size as Callisto, swathed in rusty clouds of icy methane, Titan hung well beyond the rings, complementing the golden surface of the mother planet like a bright orange-red jewel, an amber pendant displayed to advantage against pale alien flesh.

Throughout the ship the crew seemed to let out a collective sigh. They were scientists all, and not one would admit aloud to anything as sentimental as being taken by the beauty of a new world, but the chance to be the first Earthians to see something like this was the real reason every one of them was out in space. Even Luke Choy managed a moment of silent awe.

"Let's not get too comfortable, people . . ." Nyota started to caution them, when something on the readout screens caught her eye.

Actually, two things caught her eye. One was a peculiar reading on the surface scanner; the other was what the computer seemed to think it meant. Choy was easing the big ship into a power-sustained orbit just above atmosphere; what the naked eye could see on the screens was a roil of cloud as thick and pink as cotton candy. But the scanners were calibrated to ignore atmosphere and produce clean surface images. What Nyota was supposed to be seeing was a landscape of crater-pocked rock and extinct volcanoes covered with massive lakes of incredibly cold methane ice—and they were there all right, clear as the airless surface of Luna on a winter night. But there was something else.

"Analysis!" she said over her shoulder to Copeland. "What are we looking at down there?"

"Down where?" Copeland demanded crisply. "Give me an exact grid and I'll tell you."

"Sectors J-seven and K-seven through nine," Nyota shot back, standing corrected. "There's a little bit of something sticking out into I-seven as well."

Copeland localized the grid and enlarged it. "Uh-oh," she said.

# CHAPTER 4

Ever since the death of the *Challenger* over a century before, no one, but no one consciously said "Uh-oh" on the flying bridge of an Earth ship. It was a spacer's superstition, like the actor's taboo against whistling in the dressing room or mentioning Macbeth. Copeland realized what she'd done and clapped her hand over her mouth.

"I'm sorry!" she said into a silence made that much louder by the blip and whir of instrumentation everywhere around her. Everyone on the bridge was frozen in place, staring at her in horror. She could almost imagine the entire ship going silent, listening, waiting for disaster to strike. "I'm sorry, I didn't mean—"

"It's all right!" Nyota Domonique said, a little too quickly. "People, it's all right. Let's not get space-happy here. Tell me what you read down there, Copeland."

"Yessir!" Copeland's fingers flew over her board, her shoulders hunched in gratitude for being let off the hook.

"The rest of you, as you were!" Nyota said—again, a little too sharply, but it had the desired result. Her command mode brought everybody out of their self-imposed trance: bodies leaned over instrument panels in exaggerated attention to detail; fingers pulled information out of buttons and toggles at superhuman speed.

When she was sure no one was watching her, Nyota let out a sigh of relief. Someday, she thought, I'm going to bark and they're not going to jump. Then what? She scanned the bridge with narrowed eyes, drumming her fingernails on her chair arm, trying to keep her heart from pounding. She knew what those strange shapes on the surface of Titan looked like to her. If the computers agreed with her, would her reaction be one

54

of joy or dread? She watched the readouts coalescing on her screen and suddenly burst out laughing.

"Sir?" Ensign Choy swung around in his chair, alarmed.

"Check your chronometer, Ensign," Nyota said, suppressing a laugh.

They all did. The date was April 1, 2089.

"I'd almost be relieved if it was a joke!" Copeland said. Nyota glanced back at her and Copeland shook her head.

"Give me what you've got," Nyota said calmly.

Copeland took a deep breath and began. "The good news is Titan lacks a magnetic field, so we don't have to recalibrate for that. The bad news is the atmosphere's an absolute chemical stew and it's constantly moving, so any readings I give you will be accurate only within seven percent, plus or minus."

"I'd consider those acceptable odds," Nyota said, though she would have preferred them a little tighter. "Cut to the chase, Major. Tell us what we're looking at."

"Those are not just odd-shaped rocks, Commander," Copeland said deliberately. "They're artificial constructions of refined metals and thermoplastics laid out in an ordered design."

"Meaning . . . ?" Nyota prompted. She'd opened the intercom so their conversation would be heard throughout the ship. She wanted everyone to hear it and think about it before they did anything further.

"They're buildings, Commander. Someone's been here before us."

Someone—was it Choy?—began humming the theme from *Thus Spake Zarathustra*.

"Belay that!" Nyota snapped, and the humming subsided. "Helm, go to station keeping; hold present position. Navigator, scan all frequencies for radio transmissions. DefCon, go to standby. Repeat: Standby status only. If anything down there wanted to start shooting at us they would have done so already; I don't want anyone getting trigger-happy up here."

"Aye sir," Choy and Copeland said in unison.

One step at a time, Nyota thought. My entire crew has just snapped to attention; even the ones on offshift have stopped whatever they're doing to see what happens next. The procedural manuals are very specific, and if I vary too much from SOP, Choy will be the first one to dust off his law degree and lodge a protest. Slow and steady and don't alarm the crew!

While she waited for Copeland's report, Nyota leaned forward at the con; now that the shapes had been defined, it was easier to see them for what they were. This was obviously a colony compound of some kind, a cluster of living and working quarters interspersed with storage sheds and what, if form suggested function, were most likely a power plant, a fuel dump, an atmosphere converter, and what looked like some sort of greenhouse. None of them could possibly have been designed by anyone from Earth.

Space exploration had wrought a wonderfully creative havoc with traditional Earthian concepts of architecture, as architects and structural engineers grappled with the problems and challenges of different g-forces, extremes of temperature, the availability of materials on the worlds where they were building. An apartment complex on Mars was radically different from one in Selenopolis; the Jupiter-1 station might look almost identical to its prototype, the old LunaMars-1, but it was constructed of entirely different materials. Yet as otherworldly as some of those modern structures might seem at first glance, they were definitely Earthian.

Just as this compound was definitely not. These structures were at once beautifully functional and functionally beautiful. But what made them different? Were the angles more angular, the symmetries more or less symmetrical? What colors were these, at once more subtle and more brilliant than anything an Earthian could accurately describe, if only because no Earthian eye had ever seen them, no Earthian brain ever registered them before?

What they were looking at was a completely self-sufficient colony, constructed by beings from another star system on a satellite of the sixth planet of their own system. Maybe it wasn't the only one. There was a suggestion of roads leading off from the middle of the compound like wheel spokes in all directions; nothing paved or elaborate, merely an expert grading of the existing bedrock or, more accurately, bed *ice*. What if the entire planet was peppered with similar settlements? Was that where the roads led?

There were no vehicles visible, which didn't mean there weren't any. If she were commander of this outpost, Nyota thought, she wouldn't keep sensitive equipment out in the methane rain. Restless, she listened along with Copeland, hoping to hear those Satchmo voices she'd last heard in her youth. She had no doubt they'd found the source. Even as she listened, she wondered: What of Saturn's other seventeen moons? What if this cluster of habitats was the vanguard of some vast incursion, even an invasion?

*Careful, girl,* she cautioned herself, turning her esper-mind up to full power. *Don't panic until you know what you're dealing with. Relax and try to read them, if they're still here!*

"Commander? I'm not reading any radioactivity whatsoever, on any frequency." Copeland sounded profoundly relieved.

"Thank you, Major. Full scan on infrared, please. Obviously someone's been here before us. The next question is: Are they still here?"

Infrared would pick up heat readings—running engines and warm-blooded life-forms. If their ancestors had been lizards, it wouldn't read them. But they had to start somewhere.

"Another thing," Nyota said. "Rumor has it we have a social psychologist on board. Tell him I'd like to see him on the bridge ASAP."

Tetrok found Krecis in the biotech lab. The small outsystem monitor built into the OldOne's console told him as much as anyone in the command center knew about the newly arrived Earthian ship, but as a courtesy Tetrok had come to speak to the high priest in person. He found him holding something small and furry and newborn-looking in his arms.

"A success," he reported, caressing the creature's golden fur with the tips of gentle fingers. "Twenty days old and she already shows signs of precognition. Once we have her weaned, the real teaching can begin."

As if on cue the pretty thing took one of Krecis' fingertips into her toothless bud of a mouth and began to suck. With a small smile Krecis reached for a feeding tube and gently placed the nippled end in the creature's mouth.

"So soft!" Tetrok whispered so as not to startle it, reaching out to take it and stroking its fur. "You will send her back to Valton?"

"Eventually," the OldOne answered. "Though I should like to breed her first."

Ever since the biotech labs had been transferred from his ship to the surface of Titan, Krecis had overseen the breeding of several dozen animal species in an attempt to adapt them to environments other than Fazis. Altered at the genetic level, then nurtured on special nutrients native to the worlds on which they would be "seeded," these creatures were first sent back to Fazis Prime, to the care of Krecis' former pupil, now head of Offworld Services, Valton.

Tetrok's cousin Valton, second in line to be Ruler if for some reason the Fazrul rejected Tetrok. Tetrok was mindful of this fact at every waking moment.

Whatever else may be said of him, at least Valton loves animals! he thought, remembering his last visit to his cousin's villa before his departure for Titan. The open, airy rooms had been all but overrun by things with fur and feathers. Eventually Valton would transfer each animal to the world for which it had been bred, in order to make room for new ones, but there was always something curled in his lap or perched on his shoulder whenever Tetrok saw him. Now if only Valton got along as well with people . . .

The creature in Tetrok's arms began to purr beneath his touch. He'd expected as much, but he was startled to hear the purring not in his ears but in his mind.

"An animal with esper potential?" he asked Krecis, surprised; for some reason the notion made him uneasy.

The creature had opened its limpid, nocturnal eyes now and was gazing straight up at Krecis.

"The potential has always existed in her ancestor species," he said mildly, holding her gaze as if communing with her. "We have given her genes a little . . . encouragement, so to speak. The rest will be a combination of nutrition and training."

Tetrok examined the contents of the feeding tube for the first time.

"Garpozin?" he asked, noting an odd greenish tinge to the

feeding formula; it was an algaelike substance found on an outlying satellite which had remarkable healing abilities.

Krecis nodded. "Among other things. A formula I have developed from the curatives of several worlds—"

"OldOne." Tetrok cut him off, as if only now remembering the reason he had come here. "The Earthian ship continues to study us. How long do we maintain comm silence?"

Krecis waited until the creature finished its meal, and set aside the feeding tube; he then began to stroke its stomach rhythmically. In the silence Tetrok could hear what had become familiar chatter—the sound of the colony's commsystem reading and translating every transmission, internal and external, that the Earthian ship made.

"Chinese seems to be the dominant tongue," Krecis observed, as if there were no hurry for any of this. The tiny creature in his arms emitted a frighteningly loud burp; the high priest smiled with satisfaction and placed it back in its enclosure, stroking it until it rolled itself into a ball and sighed into sleep. "How long do we remain silent? Until they have studied us sufficiently to decide we are worth communicating with. When they address us, we will respond."

✍

"If they *are* still here," Ensign Choy wanted to know, "is it a good idea for us to be hanging around? What if they've got weapons?"

Copeland nodded toward Nyota, who was swinging her chair in a complete arc to study everyone on the bridge, her esper-mind reading crew morale; every possible reaction from pure skepticism to quiet elation to barely suppressed fear emanated from the minds around her.

"On your screen, Major," Nyota instructed her.

Nyota knew what she'd see before she even looked; her esper-mind had already told her. She watched as the scanner framed and enlarged each grid of the area below. White-hot readings indicated high-efficiency machinery up and running, particularly an oxygen converter that simply ingested the endless supply of ice and broke it down into needed elements. Cooler red-into-yellow sectors indicated less volatile or better insulated machinery—climate control, computer center, living quarters set into the cool blue-to-green of the buildings themselves. Empty black areas indicated unheated storage sheds, although one of them glowed white in the center—suggesting a small vehicle, perhaps an overlander only recently arrived on one of the graded roadlets, its engine ticking into idleness. Deep blues within an aura of greenish yellow in a rhomboidal clear-walled structure suggested a greenhouse lush with rustling foliage. Lastly, there were the heat sources that moved.

Their hands, necks, and faces bloomed in shades of yellow, red, and white, the white predominating about the center of the face, where most mammals exhaled $CO_2$ warmed to blood temperature, sufficient to heat the area around eyes, mouths, and nostrils into the white range as they breathed. The tops of their heads showed bluish green to indicate the cooler topography of hair, fur, or feathers. Bipedal, upright, large-brained, they were also fully clothed, for unexposed areas of their bodies registered in bright to dark blues, indicating some insulating materials which kept body heat in while simultaneously making a fashion statement.

"I guess we're the first Earthlings to get a preview of the new spring line on their homeworld," Nyota observed, to break the tension.

"And no weapons of any kind, not even hand weapons, Commander," Copeland reported, indicating a wide-range scan. "Unless, of course, they're so sophisticated they don't give off heat readings."

"Swell!" Choy remarked. "So what do we do now?"

"It's obvious what we do now!" An unfamiliar voice issued from the gangway leading up to the flying bridge. It belonged to a lanky, wild-haired man whose wrinkled clothes suggested he'd been sleeping in them, which he had.

He seemed to have difficulty pulling himself up by the handrails, as if he'd just stepped out of zero g. When he walked he looked like he was wading in hip-deep water, and when he stopped he leaned crookedly against a bulkhead as if the trip from his quarters to the bridge had exhausted him. He scowled at Commander Domonique to indicate his displeasure at being woken up.

"Langler, Psych," the ship's social psychologist introduced himself tersely.

If they'd ever met, Nyota couldn't recall. Had he gotten on at Jupiter-1, or earlier? Where had he been hiding himself all these weeks, and how had he managed to avoid staff meetings?

Having announced himself, he turned toward Choy. "What do we do now, Ensign? What do you always do when you meet someone new? You say hello!"

❧

"What if they don't attempt to communicate with us at all?" Tetrok wondered aloud. "What if they merely dash back the way they've come and report us to their superiors?"

"Would you?" Krecis asked mildly.

"No, of course not! I would be so overwhelmed with curiosity . . ." The younger man collected himself. "Which is not to say that *they* are. They may be so very different from us . . ."

"It seems to me," Krecis said with a faraway look—was he reading something from the Earthian ship that Tetrok could not?—"that any spacefaring race would have more in common with other spacefarers than they would have differences. They are curious, or they would not be here. They will address us, and we will respond."

❧

"Is that your official recommendation?" Nyota asked Langler, motioning him to come all the way onto the bridge and take one of the empty seats at Ops. "We just 'say hello.' "

Langler indicated with a gesture that he preferred to stay where he was. "Yes, that's my recommendation. They know we're up here. They know we know they're down there. Furthermore, that's what the procedural manuals say you're supposed to do, although they recommend the old mathematical-code approach, like the Voyagers. Me, I'd prefer something more direct."

Nyota studied the newcomer thoughtfully. He was trying mightily to project hostility and insubordination, but there was a soft core to him, something wounded, and she wondered what it was. As if he felt her reading him, Langler shut down suddenly, and Nyota wondered what his esper rating was.

"I'm listening," she said.

"Just send them your basic 'Hi, how are you?' message in all four languages and see what you get back. Maybe throw in a little Beethoven in the background just for style. You know they've been reading our transmissions for as long as they've been here."

"*Do* we know that?" Nyota asked ingenuously, trying to see where his mind was going.

"Why do you think they've been silent since we came into the system?" Langler responded with equal innocence. If he'd ever heard rumors, he didn't let on.

"Valid point," Nyota acknowledged, gifting him with one of her dazzling smiles.

Most men would have responded in kind; Langler's face never altered its mildly annoyed expression. *Okay for you, mister!* Nyota thought. This time, Langler did smile: *Message received, loud and clear.* Nyota turned her attention to the commstation.

"Copeland, take the man up on his suggestion. Message: 'Earth vessel *Lòng Dàn'* "—she deliberately used the Chinese-registry name for the *Dragon's Egg*—" 'sends best wishes to you. Who are you? Please identify on this frequency.' Run that in all four codes; then scan all frequencies for a response until I tell you otherwise." She shot a sidelong glance at Langler. "And use a Mozart disc. It's more stimulating than Beethoven."

"Aye sir," Copeland replied, suppressing a smile, and proceeded to read the message in all four of Earth's tongues, though her Russian teacher had once told her her accent was atrocious. Should she run a compusynth program through instead? There wasn't time. She let her own voice carry it, and hoped she'd be understood.

She was. The answerback came almost as soon as she'd run the program once. Everyone on the bridge heard it. Nyota wanted to cheer. Her lifelong belief was vindicated; there was no mistaking those Satchmo voices.

But they were speaking Chinese!

❧

Oh, the slowness of it! In the movies, Earthlings and aliens made contact in a single scene, zooming into each other's atmospheres in cheeky little Hollywood- or Tokyo-designed shuttlecraft, or beaming in on matter-energy waves. In real life, these things took hours, sometimes days.

Everyone aboard the *Lòng Dàn* knew enough Chinese to order a meal and find the way to the rest room, but even Luke Choy had learned it as a second language and didn't consider himself fluent. How the visitors had learned Chinese or why they chose it instead of any of the other three Earth languages was something they'd figure out later when they had time. For now, the single most important dialogue ever to take place within the solar system depended on a language none of the participants was entirely comfortable with.

Ensign Choy found himself shoved to the forefront, with Nyota Domonique just behind him to whisper encouragement in his right ear while, in his left, Langler the psychologist warned him not to make a fool of himself.

Not that they were actually whispering in his ears. All three of them, along with two DefCon security types whom regulations required them to take along, were sealed up in full hardsuits as if prepared for every possible contingency. They could communicate only via their helmet radios, on an open channel which could have them all interrupting each other if they weren't careful. The result would be chaos.

Which would impress the hell out of their hosts all right. But there hadn't been time for more than a brief rehearsal while they'd suited up, and they were all a little nervous.

"I don't want to hear a word out of either of you," was how Nyota instructed the DefCon muscle. "Just keep your noses clean and try not to shoot each other in the foot. As for you . . ." She turned toward Langler, having to tilt her head back to look up at him. "You and I communicate in English only. I want a running commentary on your impressions on closed channel. Don't worry about interrupting anything else that's going on, if you think you've got something important."

"I've never been accused of being overly polite!" Langler remarked with a grimace that could have been a bitter smile.

Nyota tried not to watch him climb painfully into his hardsuit, which seemed to give him inordinate difficulty until the male security guard—in her mind Nyota had already tagged him and his equally large female companion Tweedledum and

Tweedledee; they looked remarkably alike and she wondered if they were siblings, even twins—gave him a hand. Langler grunted his thanks, looking more uncomfortable than ever. Before Nyota could tear her eyes away, he snapped at her: "Look, I broke my back and both legs in a high-impact crash on Mars-seven twelve years ago. They put the pieces back together, but I'll never be fully functional in normal g again. I'm happiest at zero, which is how I have my quarters set— which is why you've never seen me in the common areas since I signed on. I can function in up to point five g; I have to for physical therapy two hours every day, but don't expect me to be happy about it!"

"I'm sorry, Langler. I—"

"And there's an easier way for us to communicate!" he finished testily. *Open your mind, lady! One of the reasons I'm in my line of work is because my esper rating's the highest on the ship. Higher even than yours, so deal with it! You want to communicate with me, don't waste time on technicalities.*

Nyota's eyes brightened in unconcealed fascination. "Thank you, Langler," she said primly, masking the fact that a mind that powerful frankly intrigued her. "That's good to know."

Choy and the two musclemen had looked from one to the other of them blankly, having missed half of the conversation. Swell! Nyota thought. One high-rated esper and three psi-nulls. Will that make this easier or harder?

"Much easier," Langler assured her. "We don't need any background static from amateurs!"

"As you were, mister!" Nyota silenced him, strengthening her mental shields before she turned her attention to Choy. "Luke, I don't have to stress how important your part of this is. I don't know how or why these people speak Chinese, but you're to be our interpreter. I can wing it for a while, but if I get stuck or if you think I'm missing some nuance, I'm counting on you to bail me out."

Choy swallowed hard. "Yes ma'am!"

"I'll also require your legal expertise," Nyota went on. "Once we figure out who our unexpected visitors are and what their intentions are, I have a feeling we'll all grow old while we wait for the ESC to strangle the whole event in red tape.

Anything you can suggest to ease the situation will be greatly appreciated.''

This seemed to cheer the kid a little. "I'll do my best!''

Nyota patted his shoulder. "That's all any of us can do. Look at it this way: you've guaranteed yourself a place in history.''

Choy sealed his helmet before he answered on radio. "Yeah, especially if I screw up!''

✍

Now, adjusting his booted feet to the light gravity of Titan and the unfamiliar artificial surface they were standing on (he'd been thinking "man-made," but that wasn't right. Alien-made? That sounded so judgmental. Visitors, strangers, new-comers—what to call them?), Choy took small, uncertain steps toward whatever it was that was about to emerge from the sealed door in the opposite wall.

As nearly as they could interpret the answerback, they'd been instructed to land near the compound and enter a specific structure through a designated airlock. The inhabitants seemed to understand that the *Egg* itself would remain in orbit while a smaller craft (in this case a state-of-the-art PLUM or Planetary Lander Unit Module) made the actual landing. As they crossed the hundred meters or so from the PLUM to the compound—Langler had recommended a hundred meters as a safe, nonthreatening distance—they couldn't help bouncing a little in the light g. Only Langler dragged his feet slightly, even here. Nyota blocked any wisp of pity for him out of her mind, concentrating instead on what a ludicrous little party they made, the best and brightest Earth had to offer hopping like kangaroos across an open courtyard.

Were they being watched? Was there any break or opening in the exotic if monolithic facade of the main structure to suggest they were being monitored, even recorded? Though she knew she couldn't be seen through the photosensitive hel-met visor—or could she?—Nyota consciously raised her chin and straightened her posture, if only to keep from hopping so much. There was something to be said for dignity.

✍

"How many shall we meet them with?" Tetrok had asked Krecis as they watched the PLUM descend into atmosphere like a hovercraft on their monitor, then disgorge its five hard-suited passengers. "If only we two meet their five, do they think we are flaunting our superior strength? Must we meet five with five?"

"You know as much as I, Commander," Krecis replied, giving Tetrok to understand that the decision was his alone. It was the way Krecis had taught his young charges under Xeniok's aegis before he'd left Fazis, and he saw no reason to alter his methodology now.

✍

Had there ever in the universe been four children with more promise than those four? Krecis had watched them tumbling about on the Great Lawn, dirt on their knees and twigs in their hair, and thought: The future of Fazis is here in this place; the fate of Fazis is all in my hands!

He had accepted the role of tutor because his old friend Xeniok had asked him; there were those in the Fazrul and even in the ruling family who whispered none too subtly that it was demeaning for one of the most brilliant minds of his generation to squander his time on children. But Krecis considered it an honor. It was the longest time he and Zandra would remain on Fazis, while their ship was readied for what would ultimately end in landfall on Titan. Not demeaning at all to spend one's days in the presence of eager young minds and possibly future Rulers beneath the russet skies of Fazis.

"You cheated, you cheated! It was well within bounds and you moved it with your foot. It isn't fair!"

Valton's shrill voice echoed across Krecis' thoughts.

"Did you actually see me move it, cousin?" That was Tetrok, his voice much calmer. The two girls had stopped to watch the row, and all their thoughts were open to Krecis, making intervention easy.

"Well, not actually, but—"

"Then how do you know it wasn't an earthquake which moved the marker? It must have happened someplace else at one time. What do the rules say about earthquakes?"

"Tetrok, that's silly," Nebulaesa interjected, and little

Zeenyl, smallest and shyest of them, added: "The builders would never have built the palace here if there were earth- quakes . . ."

This would go on all afternoon, Krecis thought, unless it ended in a fistfight; Valton's temper rarely held against his cousin's teasing. Should he intervene or let them solve it them- selves? He was still debating it when he felt Zeenyl tugging at his sleeve.

"Make them stop, please!" the little one pleaded. "They'll be at it for days if you don't."

Krecis rested a hand on her head. "Little one, it occurs to me as they get older that they will be at it for a lifetime whether I intervene or not. Nevertheless . . ."

He strode over to where the game had been interrupted, hoping his mere presence would temper the situation, but Val- ton was purple-faced with rage, and Tetrok wore that superior look which said he would not give in lest his integrity be compromised.

"Tetrok," Krecis said.

The boy turned toward his mentor. "Krecis, I—" he began, but Krecis held up a hand to silence him.

"Think before you speak," the WiseOne advised him. "For, as you know me, you know I already know your thoughts."

Tetrok looked down, studying the turf at his feet. "It's just that he always has to win! It's not as if he doesn't cheat him- self; I've caught him at it."

"And so by cheating him, you show him that his method is best," Krecis suggested. "Does this make sense to you?"

"No," Tetrok admitted, shamefaced; it was Valton who was gloating now. Seeing this, Tetrok shook himself like a colt and shrugged the incident off, giving Valton his best smile: "Cousin, I apologize. I did move the marker with my foot while you and B'Laesa were still in scrimmage. It was childish; I won't do it again. The round is yours. I know how important that is to you."

"As if it's not important to you!" Valton shot back.

Tetrok had been about to walk off the field, back to the starters' position. He turned. "As a matter of fact, it isn't."

Then Valton laughed heartily. "I caught you, cousin, and I

bested you! That is reward enough ... for now."

"Arrogant!" Zeenyl breathed at their departing backs. "They are both so arrogant!"

She returned to the spot in the shade where she'd been reading, the elder cousins' rough games of no more interest to her than their underlying competition to be Ruler.

Krecis had waited until evening to speak to Tetrok alone.

"The incident was out of character," he began. "What were you trying to prove?"

"Nothing," the boy answered too quickly. "It was childish. As B'Laesa said, silly. I should have known better."

Krecis waited.

"All right!" Tetrok admitted. "I was trying to teach Valton a lesson. Trying to make him ... his better self, as you've taught us."

Krecis found this interesting. "Please explain."

He allowed Tetrok's thoughts to trickle into his mind as the boy struggled to put them into words.

"Krecis, it seems as if since the day I was born, though I have always loved Valton, he's ... resented me. If I am chosen Ruler, it's because it's what the people want. If they choose him instead, I will rejoice for him. But he will never rejoice for me. I wanted—I wanted to show him that winning isn't everything."

"And do you think you succeeded?" Krecis asked gently. When the boy did not answer, he did: "Your intentions were noble, Tetrok; your execution was not. Remember this for the future, and your decisions will always be your own."

☙

Ultimately Tetrok chose Phaestus, Zeenyl, and Vaax to accompany him and the OldOne when they went to meet the newcomers. The choice was random—only Vaax was conversant in all four of the Earthian languages—but all three were off duty and willing to volunteer. As soon as she entered the command center, Zeenyl went to the closest monitor to study the approaching Earthians.

"Are you sure they are four distinct species?" she asked of no one in particular. She did not know Vaax well enough to understand why he bristled at the suggestion and seemed about to launch into an impassioned speech. Sensing this, she dismissed the importance of her own thought. "Perhaps they have only sent representatives of one."

"Or the fact that the one in the lead is smaller than the others, or that the tallest one ambulates with difficulty might indicate a certain differentiation—" Vaax began.

"They are at the airlock," Tetrok announced, handing him a breather. "Will we keep them waiting?"

☙

Nyota touched her gloved palm to what she assumed was a control mechanism for the outer airlock, even though it was set into the wall well above shoulder height rather than at arm's length, where Earthians would have set it. When the airlock whooshed open with a sound more familiar than foreign to any seasoned spacer, she stepped confidently over the threshold. Tweedledum and Tweedledee slipped nervously around to flank her, immediately on alert. Nyota sighed. How primitive do we look? she wondered. Even as Choy and Langler passed the airlock's laser eye and it closed behind them, something that sounded remarkably like climate-control cyclers started up with a hum; a frame of light around the inner airlock on the far wall indicated it was about to cycle open. Nyota motioned Choy to step forward and act as their interlocutor.

The monitors built into each suit read a gradual rise in pressure inside the windowless room and an infusion of atmosphere slightly more oxygen-rich than Earth's. Temperature readings yielded 21 degrees centigrade, balmy by comparison to the three-digit subzero outside. Nyota glanced about at her crew; every one of them, even the cynical Langler, was concentrating fiercely on those readings in order to avoid confronting until the last possible moment whatever it was that was about to emerge from that airlock.

It didn't look so terribly different from an Earth-built airlock; nothing scary about it at all. Nyota dared to close her eyes and open her esper-mind one last time. It sent her reassurance. She and her crew were safe, and something wondrous was about to happen. Nevertheless, as the five stately figures

stepped gracefully through the airlock, Nyota gasped in spite
of herself.

They were so beautiful!

All five were tall and stately and slender, their high-browed
foreheads crowned with luxuriant manes of long silky hair in
shades of bluish indigo. Vast intelligence greeted their visitors
in the depths of emerald-green eyes framed by upslanting
browridges almost like a second pair of eyebrows. Their fingernails, Nyota decided, were not painted but were naturally
that brilliant shade of orchid, and most fascinating of all, their
skin tones ranged from buttery caramel through bronze and
russet to a deep chocolate brown and—Nyota decided this
must be some trick of the light here—seemed to change colors,
almost iridescing, each time they moved or spoke.

They were not wearing suits or any kind of protective clothing; if anything they looked as if they'd just stepped out of a
Renaissance pageant. But again, how could someone from
Earth describe those colors, those textures? It seemed to Nyota
that each individual's garb had been selected and designed
precisely for that individual, to display him or her (yes, she
decided—her eyes, safely hidden behind the photosensitive
visor, scanning each of them in turn—one of them was female,
though she was as tall as the males) to best advantage. Their
only concession to the presence of Earthians in their midst
was what appeared to be a very simple breathing apparatus
about the size of a man's hand, which hung like an ornament
at each one's throat; a thin tube extended from the device up
the side of the neck, looped over the right ear, and ran along
the right cheek to end just beneath the nostrils. Were their
oxygen requirements higher than Earthians'? What were they
breathing?

"Methane." Langler's voice crackled in Nyota's ear. Damn
the man! She wished he'd stop intruding into her thoughts.
"They seem to require ten to thirteen percent methane in the
standard nitrogen/oxygen mix. I'm willing to bet you none of
them smokes!"

"Neither do we anymore!" Nyota reminded him, then cut
him off. This was taking too long. All of their conversation
so far had been closed-frequency; they could not be heard
outside their own headsets. The exotic strangers, inordinately

patient, seemed willing to wait as long as necessary for them to communicate. It was time to start. Nyota put her hand on Choy's shoulder.

"All right, Luke. Give them the regulation speech, but do it with feeling."

"Commander?" Choy's voice came through as a squeak. He had his gloved hands on his helmet seal, ready to pop it if she gave the word. "Wouldn't it be easier to communicate if they could see our faces?"

"Just before one or the other of us succumbs to the other's cold germs? I don't think so, Ensign. As you were!"

As far back as H. G. Wells's *War of the Worlds,* Martian invaders had survived Earth's most powerful weapons, only to succumb to the common cold. The theory that Earthians would have absolutely no immunity to offworld bacteria, and vice versa, had never been proven or disproven outside of science fiction, but Nyota Domonique was not going to make her crew the test case. She squeezed Luke's shoulder as hard as she could through all those layers of protective fabric.

*Let's go, mister! Get on the stick!*

She heard him clear his throat and begin his speech, stammering only slightly as he struggled to remember the exact word, the proper inflection. Halfway through, he realized he'd forgotten to open the outside channel. Their welcoming committee waited politely, something which could have been bemusement on their handsome faces. Choy realized with a sinking heart that they couldn't hear him; he was essentially talking to himself. He stuttered to a halt, opened the broadcast channel, and began again.

✍

How often would Nyota and Tetrok laugh about it later?

"He sounded so pompous, really," Tetrok would say. "Though it is a beautiful language—so melodic! But there he was, plodding along, with his commander the gifted linguist prompting him . . ."

Tetrok struck a pose that made Nyota laugh, somehow transforming his graceful height into Luke Choy's smaller, more diffident I'm-only-doing-my-job posture on that memorable occasion. Somehow his deeply resonant voice became Luke's nervous singsong, too.

" ' . . . and we persons from Earth wish to assure you that our ship—is that right, Commander? *Chuán* is "ship," isn't it?' And then you said . . ." Tetrok's voice became Nyota's then, lyrical and sweet; he was an awfully good mimic. Nyota gave him a dangerous look, but didn't stop laughing. " '*Chuán?* Are you sure, Luke? I thought it was *chuáng.'* And then he said: 'No, I'm pretty sure *chuáng* is "bed." We don't want to tell them we came here in a bed, do we?' Then there was the mixup about 'tree,' 'book,' and 'water,' and at one point he even said *mén* instead of *rén,* and I looked aside at Krecis and thought to him: *Does he realize he's just referred to himself as a door instead of a person?* and—"

"And all along, every one of you understood every word we were saying in English!" Nyota accused him. "Did you ever once try to interrupt us and switch languages? No, you just kept tottering along in Chinese, and because you couldn't get the upward inflection on the third syllable correct, we missed half of what you were saying—"

"We thought it was some sort of ritual!" Tetrok defended himself, and Nyota didn't know him well enough yet to know if he was joking. "We thought it was how your different species communicated—"

"Oh, and that's another thing!" Nyota interjected. "Assuming that four languages meant four different species—"

"For all we knew, English was a religious language and we'd be breaking some sort of taboo by speaking it. And all the while you steadfastly refused to remove your helmets. How were we to know you weren't four different species? If I hadn't thought to show you the sterifield, we might still be standing there . . ."

⨏

After what seemed an eternity, Luke Choy finished speaking, his voice fading to a dry croak. The most dignified of the five dignified beings stepped forward then.

"You may breathe freely here," Krecis said in labored but precise Chinese. "We have studied the air of your Earth, and have balanced our air accordingly. If you wish to remove your helmets . . .''

Actually, he used the word for ''hat'' instead of ''helmet,'' and Choy, grateful he wasn't the only one making blunders, almost choked on a laugh. Again he sought Nyota's advice.

''Tell him it's not the air we're worried about but bacterial contamination,'' she urged Choy, at the same time trying not to think of what the eldest of the beings meant by their having ''studied the air of your Earth.'' Just how technologically sophisticated were these people?

*Probably sophisticated enough to have a device that protects them against our germs—a sterifield or something.*

''Langler!'' Nyota warned him on the open channel, cutting across Choy's plaintive plea: ''But Commander, I don't know how to say 'germs' in Chinese!''

''You told me to give you input!'' Langler hissed on his channel before she could answer Choy.

''Try opening your mouth!'' Nyota shot back.

''What?'' Choy, thinking she was talking to him, was now totally confused.

Nyota gritted her teeth, took a deep breath. At times like this, a commander's lot was not a happy one. ''Choy . . .'' she began patiently—she'd deal with Langler later—but before she could go on, someone touched her shoulder.

*Tetrok.* She heard the name like a caress in her mind, but whether he had placed it there or she had plucked it out of his mind . . . Before she could respond, the two security guards moved to intercept him—intergalactic relations be damned; they had their orders—and she forcefully waved them off. As a gesture of trust, she placed her own gloved hand over his bare one, and watched the color of his skin change.

If she spent the rest of her life with them, she would never cease to marvel at the way a Fazisian's skin tones altered with every stimulus. Was it only the warmth of her hand, or something deeper, that changed Tetrok's colors that first time?

Whatever it was, Nyota somehow trusted him implicitly from that moment, allowing him to lead her to a control panel just inside the airlock, as each of the remaining Fazisians took another of her crew in hand and led them all through. Without words, Tetrok gave her to understand that Langler was right:

one of the panel's functions was to emit a mix of ultrasonics just powerful enough to kill harmful bacteria without giving anyone a headache. To show she understood, Nyota removed her helmet, motioning to the others to do the same.

She had yet to see any of these somber beings smile. The biologist in her knew this instinctive show of teeth might easily be interpreted as hostile. But the one called Tetrok had been able to touch her mind with his thoughts; surely he would understand. Nyota met his brilliant green eyes with the warmth of her brown eyes, and smiled.

And Tetrok smiled too.

# CHAPTER 5

Tetrok lifted the sleek furball out of its environment and placed it in Nyota's arms. At first she'd merely been impressed with its beauty. Now she could feel it resonating in her mind.

"Is it native to your homeworld?" she asked, stroking its golden fur. "Does it have a name?"

"It is and it isn't," Tetrok answered. "One parental genome has been altered to help it adapt to its new environment. In addition, we carefully expose it to higher methane levels, and a series of nutrient supplements Krecis has developed in his tenure here.

"All told, we have genetically altered over thirty different species in this way," he went on. "Our hope is to improve our own species in the process. We have learned much about longevity from the work we do here."

"What happens to these creatures once they mature?" Nyota asked, having seen none but the creature she was holding.

"They are sent back to the homeworld for cataloging and further study. Valton, the head of Offworld Services, has several in his personal menagerie."

There was that name again! Nyota thought, picking up the same uneasy resonance from Tetrok that she had the first time she'd heard Valton's name.

"There are other things about this creature Krecis has not yet told me," Tetrok went on, before she could ask him about Valton. "Nor has he given it a name. We do not name living things as your kind do; we let the creature choose its own name."

"You mean it actually tells you?" The creature had awakened, and was bumping the top of its head beneath Nyota's chin, marking her with its silky whiskers in a gesture she found wonderfully familiar. "Or does its behavior suggest a name?"

*"Yes, to both questions."* Tetrok smiled. Nyota handed the animal back to him, pleased at the sight of such a strong man handling the small creature so gently.

*"It reminds me of an Earth species,"* she said. *"It's very catlike."*

The creature turned its golden eyes toward Tetrok in agreement.

         *✍*

It was like a dream.

It wasn't only the light gravity of Titan that made Nyota feel as if she were floating; in fact the Fazisians, wary as all long-term spacers were about the effects of abnormal g-forces on muscle and bone, had managed to augment the gravity inside their compound to something near Earth-normal. Make a note, Nyota told herself: The gravity on their world is not too different from ours. What other similarities do we have, before we start examining the differences?

Fazisians, she thought. They call themselves Fazisians. Their world is Fazis, in the star system we call Vega, and their technology is just far enough ahead of ours so that they can travel between solar systems in the time it takes us to plod from planet to planet in our own. They also live about sixty years longer on average than we do. They've been here for fifty of their years, which is approximately forty-five of ours, and except for those random broadcasts whose existence the ESC will continue to deny, we never suspected a thing.

With Tetrok on one side of her and the elder statesman Krecis on the other, she had studied a starmap in the colony's command center, marveling at the holographic technology which suspended the stars in midair and made it possible to move among them, measuring vectors, comprehending space in a way she hadn't considered before.

Just as the countless Fazisians who had passed her and her party in the corridors on the way here had seemed unperturbed by the arrival of offworld visitors in their midst, those in the command center stepped casually aside from their work consoles to allow the visitors access to whatever information they needed, studying them keenly if unobtrusively as these newcomers moved unimpeded through their world.

Of course, Nyota thought. We're no particular surprise to them, because they've been tracking us since we left Jupiter-1, maybe since we left Earth. The thought should have frightened her, but it didn't. She'd trusted the Fazisians from the moment Tetrok touched her mind. She'd felt rather than seen the exchange of glances among the others at his action, and knew that it was a great privilege to be allowed such ready access to his thoughts. She knew also that this was a highly gifted telepathic species, whose skills would make Earthian esper talents pale by comparison. This too should have frightened her. It didn't.

The starmap had confused her at first, until she realized all the referents were reversed. Of course. The perspective was from Vega to Sol, a travel guide for Fazisians headed toward the Solar System, not the other way around. Seeing her frown, Tetrok had keyed a toggle on the control panel and the map had flipped around.

"Thank you!" Nyota smiled, hoping he would understand the gesture if not the words. He did.

None of this was lost on Krecis, but he had other concerns.

"Your . . . star?" he asked in English; on the way here he and Langler, with considerable help from Vaax, had initiated a tentative conversation in that language, supplemented with a great deal of gesture and body language, not helped by Langler's difficulty in negotiating the corridors in normal g. Now Krecis keyed in commands that enlarged a portion of the starmap, and using a light-pen, he highlighted the sun. "What is its . . . designation?"

"Its name?" Nyota asked carefully. "We call it the Sun, or sometimes Sol. We refer to the system as the Solar System."

" 'Son'?" The female Fazisian who had met them at the airlock—Zeenyl?—turned her emerald-green eyes on Nyota, her head tilted slightly in what on a human would have been puzzlement. "This is also 'child'? And 'soul' is . . . 'essence.' 'Spirit'? Your star is also designated child, and spirit?"

Uh-oh, Nyota thought. If I'm not very careful, she's going to invest the word with all sorts of socioreligious meanings it doesn't have, or used to have and doesn't anymore. How do I keep this from getting complicated?

"Well, no actually—" she began, only to be interrupted by Vaax.

She'd tried to figure out the pecking order here; obviously the authority lay in Krecis and to some degree in Tetrok, while Vaax seemed to be of some middle rank. However, he was also apparently the linguist of the group, to judge from the way the others deferred to him in this particular area. He began to explain something to his fellows in a long expostulatory monologue of which Nyota understood not a word. Part of the problem, she thought, was that Earthian ears couldn't hear the lower registers of the Fazisian tonal range. Damn the ESC for squelching those radio transmissions all those years ago! The years of linguistic work that could have been done! Just then the radio in the helmet she'd tucked carelessly under one arm began to beep. That would be Copeland, scolding her for missing her thirty-minute check-in.

"*Dragon's Egg* to Domonique . . ."

"Like who else would it be?" Nyota snapped, whispering so she wouldn't interrupt Vaax's monologue. "Copeland, I'm busy right now. We're at a fairly delicate point in relating to our new friends and I don't want to be disturbed. You can read us on red so you know we're still alive and well, and since no one's sent a distress call you can assume everything's copacetic. Stand by until I hail you back!"

"Affirmative!" Copeland replied, and broke the transmission.

Nyota looked up to find every Fazisian in the command center contemplating her quizzically, as if they couldn't understand the behavior she had just displayed. Nyota shrugged at them helplessly: *How can I explain it?* Langler would have it figured out by the time they got back to the *Egg*.

☙

"It's the skin tones," he explained by way of not explaining. "They don't understand why we don't change color when we get angry or display any other emotion. Apparently every life-form on Fazis—animals, plants, everything—changes colors due to environmental or emotional factors. It's the methane."

It would become the expedition's new buzzword. For the next thousand years, Nyota thought, every time we or the Fazisians want to explain away a difference between us, we'll shrug and say, "It's the methane." I hope!

"They could read your annoyance at the interruption in your voice and your facial expression," Langler was saying, "but you perversely insisted on staying the same color. It puzzles them. Just as the fact that you and Choy and I come in three distinct 'flavors' made them think we were from three of the four different species represented by our four different languages."

"Not that Earth people haven't made that particular mistake often enough!" Nyota remarked wryly. "I sincerely hope we've set them straight on that much!"

It was Langler, too, who had figured out from his conversation with Krecis why the Fazisians had insisted on speaking Chinese.

"They were monitoring the ship's computer chatter. Ever since they set up this colony they've been culling all four languages out of radio spillage from Earth and the stations, but when they picked up the *Egg*'s transmissions as we entered Saturn orbit, it was talking to itself in Chinese."

"Of course," Nyota said. "*Lòng Dàn* is Chinese registry; she was programmed in Shanghai. I suppose we should be grateful they didn't access deep memory cores and try addressing us in binary!"

"Well, there you have it!" Langler announced, pleased with himself. "They assumed everyone on a Chinese ship would be Chinese. One of four distinct species which, for all they knew, required a different environment from the other three. They're still puzzling over that one."

✍

The dreamlike quality had crept in somewhere during Vaax's monologue, and Nyota had felt her mind drifting. It wasn't just the mesmerizing quality of that low, guttural voice—there was that—it was the feel of the several Fazisian minds communing silently over and under and around the spoken words that was making her dreamy. She felt it as a light breeze against her skin; even inside the bulky hardsuit she was getting goose bumps. A glance at Langler told her he was fighting it too, whereas Choy and the DefCon twins seemed to be oblivious. Nyota made a note of that, too; it might prove useful. Shaking the static out of her brain, she saw Tetrok half turn away from the rest of the group, watching her.

Would she trust him so much if he weren't so unspeakably breathtaking? No, that wasn't it at all. She trusted her own instincts and her esper abilities. She stepped through the holo starfield and went to him. Vaax finally stopped talking, and the others watched.

"I'll tell you what . . . Tetrok," she said in careful English, though she didn't know how much he understood. "I need to get back to my ship soon. Let's you and me cut to the chase, or we're going to be here until the ice melts."

She touched his arm and he understood at once, holding out both of his orchid-nailed hands, palms upward. To Nyota's surprise, his palms were the same creamy brown as the rest of his visible skin. She placed her hands, palms down, on his. Immediately his hands and forearms began to ripple with iridescent bronze and copper highlights, and Nyota heard boyish laughter in her mind.

*Much better!*

Inside their minds the tale seemed to take hours, though only seconds passed in the world beyond. Tetrok showed her his world, his people, their history in brief, the reasons for their venture into space and why they'd come to ground on Titan. He allowed her to see where the roads on the surface of Titan led, and what work his people had accomplished. By the time she reluctantly drew her hands away, still tingling from his touch, Nyota felt she knew these people, and this man, quite well.

"I marvel at what you've done here," she said aloud. "My report to Earth will emphasize that you are not an invading force."

She had her back to them and didn't notice her own crew goggling at her, but she couldn't miss the glance exchanged between Krecis and Zeenyl. She wouldn't realize until she was back in the PLUM wondering why her throat was sore that she'd just spoken in Fazisian.

"Your assessment pleases me," Tetrok answered in remarkably facile English, the corners of his glass-green eyes crinkling in what could have been a smile. "It is most important to all of us."

"Who is Valton?" Nyota asked. She did not notice the other Earthians looking at her oddly. Tetrok made a negative gesture.

Who is Valton? Tetrok thought ironically. Merely my kinsman, my nemesis, a shadow fallen over my life since the day I was born? A man who would be Ruler, to the point of obsession, and who watches my every misstep in the hope that I will fall? My closest peer, whom I might yet have made an ally, until I stole the woman he loved away from him, merely because I could? Ah, Nebulaesa! If Valton had not betrayed me when we were boys, would I have hurt you both?

"Valton is . . . the head of our Offworld Services," he answered carefully. "We all report to him, save that Krecis is a law unto himself on Titan."

This seemed some private joke; Nyota smiled politely.

"Your . . . superior, then?"

"When offworld, yes," Tetrok answered, thinking: Though only until I am Ruler!

They'd dropped hands then, and Nyota collected herself. They'd broken the language barrier, quite an accomplishment for one afternoon; no point in being greedy. Past time to get back to the ship.

❧

The crew had returned to the *Dragon's Egg* and filed a full report; Nyota ordered it sent the long way around to Earth via Jupiter-1. The answerback would take several hours, she hoped. Time enough to have Choy scan the entire ship's library for legal parameters and anything on the books which might set a precedent for first contact. Nyota wanted to have a game plan before the Bydun Wongs of this universe got their fingers into things.

"It's a legal nightmare!" Choy announced gloomily, condensing his findings into a single-screen précis that would be accessible to the entire crew. "Our grandchildren will have grandchildren before this is sorted out."

"Meaning what?" Nyota asked.

Choy swung his chair away from the console and blinked nearsightedly. "It comes down to a question of whose planet is it, anyway?"

≈

"You don't consider that the contact might have been too . . . intimate?" Krecis asked Tetrok when they were alone.

"Is that an accusation or merely a criticism, OldOne? It was an expediency, which solved a linguistic problem that might have hindered us for days. And she . . . Nyota . . . invited it."

"Perhaps she did not fully understand what it was she was inviting," Krecis observed.

Before Tetrok could reply, the holocom sounded, and a figure began to materialize in the center of the room. Unhindered by the limits of Earth technology, the Fazisians on Titan could have their answers from the homeworld almost immediately.

Tetrok expected to see his father appear, fully dimensional, on the platform before them. But instead of Xeniok a younger man, dressed in the robes of the judiciary, took shape.

"Gulibol." Tetrok acknowledged the Crown Litigator in a neutral tone. His presence, rather than the Ruler's, was disquieting. "Is my father not available? Our message was relayed to him."

"He is here with me, having summoned me," Gulibol replied dryly. While holocom could be used to project more than one person at a time, it could also be manipulated so that those receiving the transmission were not always aware of the presence of others in the background. Gulibol was being exceptionally courteous in telling Tetrok his father was in attendance. "It was his thought that, due to the nature of the situation, I should speak for him in his official capacity."

As opposed to his capacity as father to his son! Tetrok thought, not liking the tenor of this conversation in the slightest.

"Very well," he said, no trace of his thoughts in his words. "My father has been apprised of our encounter with the . . . Earthians . . . whose solar system we presently inhabit. What is his—official—assessment?"

≈

"Technically," Luke Choy reported, "the Fazisians are trespassing. They're squatters—for want of a better word—in our system. Duration doesn't count. We're within our rights to ask them to leave.''

''Oh, great!'' Nyota said. ''Dollars to doughnuts, that's exactly what the Councils will decide, unless we present our case to the ESC very carefully. Ideas, people?''

''Dazzle 'em with technology,'' Langler said with an evil grin. ''That hologram starfield was very impressive. If Wong and the Councils can be made to understand that beings with that kind of technical knowledge have been sitting on our doorstep all these years without invading us, I think you can sell them on a good-neighbor policy.''

*But whatever you do,* he added in Nyota's mind, *don't let them know their minds are stronger than ours!*

≈

''Your instructions were to conduct a thorough exploration and evaluation of the star system,'' Gulibol reminded Tetrok unnecessarily. Even in conversation, the man always sounded as if he were reading from some legal tract. ''You have delayed initiating that exploration while you awaited the arrival of the Earth ship, a decision which the Fazrul—''

''May choose to interpret any way it wishes!'' Tetrok said impatiently. ''The Fazrul is not here; I am. It was my judgment that such an expedition would be ill-advised in an inhabited system wherein some of the inhabitants were in fact heading directly toward us. We did not wish them to interpret our intentions as hostile, to see us as an invasionary force. It was our judgment''—his gesture included Krecis, who stepped forward into range of the holocom, though he did not speak— ''that face-to-face contact with the beings who call this system home was of far greater import than itemizing ore deposits or calculating the star's mass to the fourteenth decimal point. Further—''

Tetrok was interrupted by the sound of dry laughter as his father stepped into the holocom's range and made his presence visible. *How he has aged!* Tetrok realized with a pang. *And not just by the time I have been away. Is this the price of leadership?*

''Further,'' Xeniok finished for his son, ''if these newfound beings object to our presence on the threshold of their worlds, we have no right to be digging up rocks in their back gardens." The Ruler turned to his Litigator. "Gulibol, you have done your job. I thank you."

The Litigator pressed his thin lips together and stepped out of range of the holocom, though Tetrok and Krecis could not tell if he had also left the Ruler's chambers.

Thus far Krecis had kept his counsel. Were he addressing Xeniok and the Crown Litigator, he might have taken a different tack. But this was Tetrok's conversation.

"My watchdog," Xeniok characterized Gulibol, indicating that indeed he had left the room, for Xeniok would not mock him to his face. "It is his job, however unpleasant, to argue against every decision I make, in order to provide balance." He leaned forward, as if to touch his son across parsecs of space. There was a quiet eagerness in his voice. "What are they like, these . . . Earthians?"

"Most unusual, Father," Tetrok reported, traces of a young boy's enthusiasm in his voice. "Everything about them is extraordinary, from the variations in their appearance to the sheer courage with which they venture into their own space with such limited technology. I will prepare a full report. To that end, I have invited their leader and some of her officers to be our guests here, if their government will permit it. After that—"

"Just so!" Xeniok responded. "You will do what your training and your instincts dictate. The litigators will have their turn later."

It was some minutes after they had terminated the holocom transmission before Tetrok dared speak his thoughts aloud to Krecis.

"That was far too easy!"

"Of course." Somewhere during the conversation, Krecis had retrieved the small feline creature from its enclosure and was communing with it as he held it in his arms. "But we make what headway we can before it becomes complicated." Almost as an afterthought, he added: "Your father was not alone."

"I'm well aware of that," Tetrok answered. "Gulibol—"

"I do not mean Gulibol."

⚹

"He's not telling you everything, Uncle," Valton said, stepping out of the background the instant Xeniok shut down the holocom. "Has he truly done nothing while he waited for these Earthians to arrive? We both know Tetrok better than that."

Xeniok suppressed a sigh. He did not like his sister's son; he never had. Ever since he was a boy there had been something, not quite devious but rather, discordant about Valton. It was as if he could never permit a good thing to be accepted for what it was; it always had to be turned inside out, examined on its underside, searched for some imperfection, and if none could be found, Valton managed to attribute this to oversight. Nothing in the universe was perfect, and if the imperfection could be found, Valton would find it.

He and Tetrok were of an age. Valton was in fact several months the elder and, intellectually at least, his cousin's equal. Yet Tetrok had always been favored by the Fazrul to be the next Ruler. Was it this which had formed Valton's personality toward the narrow and supercilious, or was it his elders' observation that he was narrow and supercilious that had rendered him only second best? He had risen through capability and hard work to become head of all in-system colonization, but even this did not satisfy him. Short of being the next Ruler, would anything?

Even so, Xeniok thought, the Fazrul will not vote until I die or step down, and I will not step down until my son has returned from the Earth system. It is not yet a foregone conclusion. If Valton were to change his ways, he might yet have a chance.

Would Valton ever change? his uncle wondered. Could he? More to the point, did Xeniok wish him to? His natural prejudice toward his immediate flesh and blood notwithstanding, Xeniok believed there was a certain innate wisdom in the people's favoring Tetrok.

No father can be with his son for every moment of his coming-of-age, and as Ruler, Xeniok had been absent more than most. He had also been, like most fathers, unwilling to know the intimate details of his son's private life once Tetrok had discovered the female of the species.

He could not know that it was Tetrok who had convinced Valton finally that life was less than perfect, and that while some were born to greatness, others had to settle for whatever else was left. . . .

∽

"Your sister's growing into quite the beauty," Tetrok mentioned to Nebulaesa when he was seventeen, she sixteen, to see how she'd react.

"She's a baby!" Nebulaesa had sniffed. "Not even thirteen yet, and with her nose so close to her compscreen she's developed a permanent squint! Though she's my sister and I love her, she's more a bookworm than a beauty."

Tetrok shook his head. "Jealousy's such an ugly trait! It's giving you permanent frown lines. I expect your browridges will meet in the middle someday if you continue on this way!"

Never shy and still the tomboy, Nebulaesa had swung at him then, connecting with his rib cage and knocking the wind out of him. She began to pound him with her fists until, laughing at first, Tetrok had to beg for mercy. The two were straightening their clothes and trying to remember their dignity when they became aware of Valton watching them.

"I think she likes me!" Tetrok grinned, still teasing.

"Then I question her judgment, cousin," Valton said, surprisingly smooth for once, helping Nebulaesa to her feet. The three had recently been skill-scanned for telesper ratings and Valton's was the highest. Krecis had been giving him extra tutoring; it seemed to calm him and give him purpose.

"Will you both stop talking about me as if I wasn't here!" Nebulaesa protested, glaring from one to the other, though she could not glare for long. They were both surprisingly easy on the eye and, she had discovered recently, both found her attractive as well. Which of them, if either, would she choose? Nebulaesa wondered. Though Valton was the tiniest bit handsomer, her eyes kept returning to Tetrok.

They would flirt and tease, all three of them, all through that warm season and well into the cold; Zeenyl would look up from her compscreen occasionally to rub the tip of her nose and marvel at them. She would never act that way when she was older! She would find a sensible mate, one as serious about his studies as she. But then, she didn't care who grew up to be Ruler; these three did.

It was during the midwinter festival that Valton asked Nebulaesa the question that would alter both their lives.

"B'Laesa?" They were in one of the outbuildings feeding the *ngemiil*, which Valton was interbreeding for a science project; the small three-tailed creatures reproduced every thirty-three days, which made them an interesting subject. Close to a hundred of them lolloped about both young people's ankles, mewling and nuzzling each other, vying for attention. "If it weren't a matter of who would be Ruler, would you care for me?"

The poignancy of his question startled Nebulaesa, and for the first time in their lives she saw him in an entirely different light. Gone was the rough companion she had run with, wrestled with, gone rock climbing with, soaring over the treetops together in their light sails, she dipping her wings to glide under his sail, then yanking the lanyards hard to roll up over him, for the sheer pleasure of seeing his eyes widen at her daring. Gone was the ill-tempered boy always elbowing Tetrok out of the way, needing to win at everything else because he could not win at being Ruler. In his place, holding a blue-striped *ngemiil* against his cheek in an incredibly tender gesture, was a desperate young man, desperate for love of her. Nebulaesa's eyes welled with tears.

"It isn't about being Ruler, Valton; it never was. You and Tetrok both have teased me ever since the solstice—who says I have to choose either of you?"

Valton nuzzled the *ngemiil* and let it climb up his sleeve and perch on his shoulder to trill in his ear; he looked crestfallen.

"You aren't answering me, and I know why. It's because you care for Tetrok more than me!"

"That isn't true—" Nebulaesa started to protest, not entirely sure herself. Valton had never expressed such a depth of feeling before. How did she know he was sincere? How did she know this wasn't just another way of competing with Tetrok, with her as the prize? Well, she was no one's prize!

"Valton . . ." She hesitated, reached out and touched his cheek, the one the *ngemiil* wasn't rubbing against. "Perhaps if you explained it in my mind . . ."

He recoiled slightly; he couldn't help himself. Nebulaesa's telesper rating was next highest after his. The work he and Krecis were doing was very specialized, very exacting; there were places in his mind that were rubbed raw with the effort, making him feel vulnerable. Above all, Valton hated to feel vulnerable. Nebulaesa saw him step back and misunderstood.

"Never mind!" she said, threading her way among the moil of *ngemiil,* intent on returning to the main palace. Had she walked any faster, she'd have collided with Tetrok.

He'd been looking for them both to tell them the intercom was out of order and there were extra guests for dinner; their presence was expected, and would they kindly run their hands through the sterilizer after handling the *ngemiil*? Overhearing what they were talking about, he'd stayed just outside the door and listened. Two months later, when Nebulaesa confessed that she loved him, he let nature take its course.

≫

Xeniok, knowing none of this, wondered what it was about Valton that had transformed the self-righteous boy into the supercilious adult. But whatever it was about Valton, his uncle the Ruler made a point of always knowing his nephew's whereabouts, of keeping apprised of his activities at all times. Better the enemy one knew than the enemy unknown.

"Uncle," Valton persisted now, "what do you think he has been doing while he waited for the Earthians to arrive? Does he think us so ingenuous that we believe he merely watched and waited?"

"There are the mining operations to oversee," Xeniok answered vaguely. "The data gathering, the genetic experiments—"

"It's like that grandiose gesture with the crown jewels before he left," Valton persisted, ignoring his uncle's distracted mood. "He would have us believe he refused to accept them because of the dangers of the journey ahead. 'They belong to the people of Fazis, and I will not have them removed from Fazis at my behest.' A populist gesture to placate the grandmothers who trot their grandchildren into the museum to gaze at them!''

Xeniok remembered the occasion exactly. It had held none of the calculated motivation Valton was suggesting. The Ruler observed his nephew with a studied mildness. He was a bit of a dandy, overdressed in a way which, whether he was conscious of it or not, made him appear older than he was. On any public occasion, Valton's voice always seemed louder than anyone else's; he must be noticed at all costs. Tetrok's quiet ability to win the people's hearts offended him.

''Is there something wrong with a populist gesture?'' Xeniok asked now. ''Tetrok made the people happy without harming anyone. They will remember that when he returns and it is time for the Fazrul to vote. I did not write the law, Valton; I merely abide by it.''

Once before, they had had this conversation, when Valton was a child. What Valton had done that time might have caused his uncle to disavow him entirely. . . .

♉

''Father, I have to come home at once!'' Tetrok's high, preadolescent voice had come through the holocom even before his image had completely formed. ''They know who I am!''

The boy was only eight, and quite overwrought. It had taken Xeniok, interrupted in the middle of a meeting with a group of agricultural advisers, some moments to calm him and find out precisely what was wrong.

''Someone has told my teachers who I really am!'' The boy's distress reached his father from the faraway colony world where he had been sent, under an obscure name, to receive the same education as his peers. Now someone had revealed him as the Ruler's offspring. ''The word has reached the entire school. They taunt me. They say I've lied to them, that I am deceitful. They say I'm not one of them. I don't like it here anymore, Father! Please send for me; I want to come home!''

Xeniok had stopped himself from speaking immediately. There were tears in the boy's eyes, an undue display of emotion for a Fazisian of his years, yet significant of his sensitive soul. And reaching his mind toward his son's, Xeniok could feel that there was more left unsaid than was being said. This was a delicate matter, to be handled delicately.

"Have you been harmed by these ... accusations?" he asked carefully. The memory of mud being thrown, staining the back of his shirt, flashed across the boy's mind, quickly suppressed.

"N-no, Father," he answered, controlling his voice, though he was breathing hard.

"And your teachers have not joined the condemnation, surely?"

"Only s—No, Father," the boy said quickly and untruthfully. A teacher could be dismissed from his post for such a breach. Even in his distress, Tetrok would not betray those set to teach him.

"Then this is a small storm, a temporary matter, and you will weather it. And in weathering it, you will show your tormentors whom they are dealing with."

The boy swallowed hard; his tears were gone. "Yes, Father."

Now for the more difficult question, Xeniok thought. The one to which I already know the answer!

"Tetrok," he began carefully. "How do you suppose the truth was made known?"

He had deliberately asked the question this way, to give the boy a choice. Only the Ruler's immediate family and a handful of trusted retainers knew that Xeniok had sent his son abroad to study among his peers, and no adult would reveal such information. Tetrok and his father both knew only one other who could possibly have told.

"I—I suppose I don't know, Father," Tetrok answered with equal care.

"So I see," Xeniok nodded, and with a few further words of reassurance, said goodbye to his son. Then he sent for Valton.

☙

There was no attempt on Valton's part to deny what he had done; the boy freely admitted letting the rumor leak through his access to the interplanetary computer nets. Xeniok left him waiting in the reception hall for almost an hour, ample time to contemplate his indiscretion. This made him no less determined to defend his action once he stood before his uncle.

"It's hypocritical!" Valton announced with some bravado, false or genuine, using a big word he'd only recently learned. "Why should his identity be secret? The people have a right to know who lurks among them!"

"Perhaps that was not your decision to make," Xeniok suggested, holding his patience. His sister had spoiled the brat, and this was the result. Or was it as simple as that? Xeniok had replaced his father as Ruler without obstacle. What must it be like to be in Valton's place, so near and yet so far? Even at his tender age, he must sense this.

"Had you asked me, I would have explained my reasons," the Ruler said, adopting a gentler tone with his aggrieved young kinsman. "It was not so that Tetrok could 'lurk,' but so he could be one with his people, understand them from their midst rather than some elitist vantage. Had you discussed this with me first, nephew—"

"I would have been told once again that if I were true leadership material, I would know these things instinctively, without asking!" the boy finished for him.

Yes, Xeniok thought, he knows! "I did not write the laws of succession, Valton, I merely abide by them."

"If you really wanted to, you could change them!" the boy answered, his temerity amazing in the face of what the Ruler of all Fazis could do to him. "Who is better placed than the Ruler to change the laws? Except you won't, will you, because you want Tetrok to be Ruler. Uncle, I did not ask to be 'almost good enough'!"

He is only a boy! Xeniok reminded himself before he could trust himself to speak. And I cannot fault him for his honesty. Nevertheless . . . "Is being Ruler all that matters to you? Does it not occur to you that your particular gifts might be better used in some other important capacity? You might, for example, someday be as valuable to Tetrok and to Fazis as Krecis is to me—"

The lad's sullen expression had changed to one of open hostility; his colors were high and violent.

"Would you change places with Krecis, Uncle?" he asked

coldly. "When you can answer yes to that, I will accept your argument!"

A less temperate Ruler might have disciplined him severely for this. Perhaps that was what Valton wished, to have the quest for leadership denied him once and for all. But Xeniok let him go unpunished. No external control would change Valton; he would have to find his discipline within.

"Your point is taken, Valton," the Ruler said with the full weight of his office upon him and a dangerous look in his eyes. "But I caution you: I have permitted you your defiance this once, because you are young. Never presume to defy me again!"

∽

Valton's indiscretion meant that Xeniok's experiment was essentially a failure; from then on everyone knew who Tetrok was, and there were those who fawned on him because of who he would one day be. Still, Tetrok was Tetrok, and a natural leader. Perhaps Valton's willful act had not done so much damage after all.

Except to Valton.

"Tetrok has discretionary orders," the Ruler pointed out to his nephew now. "And he has a point. There is more to this matter now than mere economics. We must learn about these Earth beings. Negotiations to remain as a presence in their system, perhaps a treaty. At least an attempt to work together."

"They strike me as inferior beings!" Valton sneered. "What advantage can we derive from working with them?"

Once again, Xeniok suppressed a sigh. No, it seemed that Valton would never change.

"The advantage, at least, that they may not ask us to leave."

# CHAPTER 6

Tetrok and his party might have the tentative support of their government, but Nyota was not to be so lucky.

It was impossible to actually talk to Earth at this distance; videocomm messages had to be sent as single bursts, to which the recipient could then reply. The time lag varied with the relative position of Titan to Earth, but there was always a gap.

In the nineteenth century it was the telegraph, Nyota thought ruefully, sitting with her chin in her hand, waiting. In the twentieth, it was fax machines. Now we twiddle our thumbs waiting for vid-returns. Which means Bydun Wong can pontificate at me for an hour or more and I can't interrupt him; the best I can do is freeze-frame him while I think out my answer, knowing he's drumming his fingers on his desk back on Earth waiting for my reply.

And pontificate was what Bydun Wong did best.

"... while we find your discovery extraordinary," the bland face on the compscreen went on, as Nyota resisted the urge to put him on slo-mo and turn his words into the mush they really were, "nevertheless, the watchword must be caution. Before you or your crew initiate any further action, the ESC requires a full report on these Fazisians, their weapons capabilities, their perceived as well as their stated intentions in our solar system. I need not remind you, Dr. Domonique, that you are solely responsible for exercising the tightest possible security on communications. No one—repeat: no one— is to send any comm to Earth from your position except through secured channels ..."

Yes, Counselor Wong; whatever you say, Counselor Wong! Nyota thought. How am I supposed to provide you with a full report when I'm dangling up here in *orbit?*

Realizing she'd just answered her own question, Nyota motioned to Copeland.

"Give him enough time to think we've listened to the full message, then send this reply: 'Complying fully with your instructions, Counselor. Will answerback when report is complete.' "

"Don't you think you should record that message in per—" Copeland started to say, but Nyota was already on her way below to fetch a hardsuit. Just following orders.

⚳

So it was that Nyota and Langler ended up back on the surface of Titan, as guests of the Fazisians. Up in the *Egg,* Copeland kept Nyota updated every hour on reports coming in from Earth: the ESC had convened a plenary session to discuss the *Lòng Dàn*'s findings, while at the same time trying to notify the other Councils without tipping off the media. Everyone knew how that would work out; it was only a matter of time before the leaks—and possible planetwide hysteria—began.

Nyota tried explaining this to Krecis and Tetrok and the others at dinner.

"I don't know what the reaction is going to be on your planet once you give them the news," she said in careful Fazisian; it was getting easier all the time. "That is, if you haven't already told them."

"Our government is aware of your people's existence," Krecis said carefully. "Discussion is now under way as to how best to inform our people."

"Well, from what I see here, they'll probably be a lot calmer about it than we are," Nyota said diplomatically. Amazed at her own equilibrium, knowing Langler was watching her from across the table where he sat between Phaestus and Zeenyl, she could not believe she was actually seated at a formal dinner with Fazisians, people from another planet!

"Do you have the same kind of . . . information media that we do? Video news programs, computer information nets, that kind of thing?" Luke Choy was asking with great enthusiasm.

Some of it got lost in the translation, but eventually Nyota and Vaax, the two best linguists in the group, got it sorted out.

"Very similar," Vaax replied in careful English. Already he had learned to raise his tone half an octave, to be more accessible to Earthian ears; there had been some discussion at the start of the meal about adapting a kind of hearing aid into the air filters the Earthians now wore around their necks.

At their first meeting, it was the Fazisians who had adapted, filtering some of the methane out of the room's atmosphere. Now that the Earthians were going to be staying with them for a while, they'd been provided with filters which balanced the air they breathed for their own needs. The guest rooms would be almost methane-free at first. It was hoped that the Earthians, if they were permitted to stay, would gradually adapt to the air Fazisians breathed.

Aside from this small distinction, Nyota thought, this could be a dinner party on Earth; Lord knows I've had to sit through enough of them at the ESC's behest. That is, if I accept the fact that this food is real and not something out of a sci-fi movie. What *is* this I'm eating?

It didn't seem polite to ask. Besides, as peculiar as it looked, whatever it was tasted wonderful. Like their colors, Fazisian flavors seemed to the Earthian palate to have a little something extra. Nyota watched Langler mastering the art of Fazisian table manners and had to smile.

"I expect our people will be pleased to know that we are not alone in the realm of creation," Krecis said graciously, when the conversation flagged.

"Don't count on Earth feeling the same," piped up Luke Choy. "They still think God created us as the only intelligence in the universe. This'll knock their socks off."

" 'God'?" Vaax inquired, reflecting the obvious confusion of all the Fazisians present.

Nyota explained. "On Earth we speak of the Supreme Being of the universe as God, if you will."

"Why would anyone consider limitations in the Almighty One?" Vaax asked.

"Wow!" Luke Choy beamed. "You guys believe in God? Wow!"

All eyes turned toward the cocky young helmsman.

"Ah, even so," said Krecis thoughtfully. "Our history's traditional stories relate, and Fazisians firmly believe, that a cataclysmic event took place in our star system about twenty-five thousand orbits ago. We believe that through the intervention of the Almighty One a small contingent of life-forms evolved upon the planet Fazis, and that it is from this contingent that we have all descended.''

"The Big Bang!" Luke Choy blurted out.

Phaestus was finding this bright, brash young man amusing. "Just so, young Choy," he said, incurring Choy's gratitude. "It seems our worlds share much in common."

Nyota mused over this before speaking. "If I understand you correctly, your assumption is that Fazisians and Earthians have *one* belief. It appears we are both in for some surprises."

Krecis and Tetrok exchanged a quizzical glance.

"Please explain, Nyota," Krecis said eagerly.

"Well, Earth history on this matter would seem to be a bit more complicated than yours. First of all, we have a myriad of religions or beliefs among our people, not a single philosophy. They range all the way from a denial of God by atheists, to agnostics who state that they just don't know, to believers in the existence of God derived from a number of different viewpoints."

"From *different* viewpoints?" Vaax asked incredulously, as the emerald of Zeenyl's eyes seemed to fairly glow with excitement.

"Yeah," said Mr. Irrepressible. "Some still believe God created the Earth in seven days instead of the Big Bang."

"How is that contradictory, my friend?" Phaestus inquired.

"Well, you can't have it both ways. One's religion and one's science," Choy proclaimed confidently.

"Did not your God / Supreme One create the Big Bang?" Krecis asked.

"Yes, but . . ." Choy was beginning to fluster.

"Then if his Big Bang created Earth, did not God create the Earth by creating the Big Bang?"

"Well, it doesn't explain Adam and Eve, as opposed to evolution!" Choy was not to be outdone.

"What religion are Adam and Eve?" Zeenyl wanted to know. "Or are they atheists or agnostics?"

Tetrok, who had been quiet for some time, spoke. "And you say you have many . . . beliefs . . . for the believers?"

"Quite," Langler responded. "We have Buddhists originating in the Eastern countries, Jews and Christians and Muslims originating in the eastern Mediterranean and quickly spreading throughout several continents, pantheistic cultures in Africa and Australia and the Americas . . ."

"And they all have a different . . . God?" Zeenyl asked.

"Well, not necessarily," Nyota answered. "But they do approach and worship God from different viewpoints. Christians, for example, believe that the Son of God, Jesus Christ, actually took on human form some two thousand years ago and became a man on Earth, giving his life as the supreme sacrifice to redeem mankind from their transgressions. Of course, there are prototypes for this kind of Messiah in several older religions. Others who believe in a Supreme Being do not believe in Jesus as the Son of God, but do believe in God as the Supreme Being of the universe."

"Doesn't such a plethora of beliefs lead to serious conflict at times?" Tetrok asked.

"You are very wise, my friend," Langler said. "Indeed it has. We have a sad history on Earth of many wars between believers of different philosophies, which have resulted in the senseless killing of thousands upon thousands of people."

"Yes," Nyota added. "We seem to be beyond that point now, as far as wars and killing go at least. But, indeed, conflicts still exist."

"I understand now what you meant when you said the situation was more complex on Earth," Krecis interjected.

"Yeah," put in Choy, getting the last word. "Not even a plethora of legal minds can sort out such a plethora of beliefs."

"Well," Krecis admitted. "My simple mental prowess has been exhausted by this revelation."

"Attorney Luke Choy, you're right!" Nyota laughed. "Of course, I can't help but agree with what one of our wise men once said—'First . . . let's kill all the lawyers' "

She wasn't sure if the words, much less the concept, had translated, but Vaax got the joke first and turned a brilliant gold, making a sound Nyota had come to interpret as laughter. He clarified for the others, who were equally amused. Such a riot of sparkling coloring the awed Earthians had never seen.

"It seems yet another aspect we have in common," Krecis replied. "The nature of law on any world seems to consist of making simple things the more complex."

This time Tetrok laughed. "Krecis is not only Fazis' most respected and celebrated scientist, Nyota. He is also a litigator or lawyer of equal standing in brilliance and respect."

Nyota looked up at Krecis in embarrassment. "I think I've just offended you," she said.

"Quite to the contrary," Tetrok answered, and once again Nyota could feel the other Fazisians' minds brushing against her like a breeze upon her skin. "You and I as scientists must do the opposite: take that which is complex and make it simple."

Nyota had tried to do just that. It began with a bunch of broccoli.

*

The PLUMs were kept in the *Egg*'s lower aft cargo bay; one literally had to traverse the entire length of the ship to get to them. On her way, Nyota had stopped in Hydroponics.

The basic design of hydroponic labs aboard interplanetaries had not altered since the first Mars expedition. Seedlings were planted along the inside of what was essentially a huge hollow drum, which in the old days had had to be rotated constantly in order to create its own artificial gravity in an otherwise zero-g ship. Nowadays the drum principle had been retained, even though they no longer needed to rotate; it was simply the most efficient use of premium space to grow tomatoes on the ceiling as well as the floor.

"It's risky!" Cervantes, the agronomist, told her when she asked what she could bring the Fazisians as a dinner gift. "My hunch is that anything we can eat they can eat, but you can't be too careful. Look at how many allergens we Earthians find in our own foods. Then there's the bean factor—"

"Meaning there's enough methane in the atmosphere already," Nyota finished for him. "So you think maybe a food gift wouldn't be a good idea?"

Cervantes had shrugged. "We also don't have that much left in the way of fresh produce after a year out."

Nyota looked thoughtful. "That might actually make it easier. What have you got?"

"Broccoli," the agronomist replied, "broccoli, and more broccoli."

Nyota sighed. How had she known? The first Mars voyages had taken four to seven months at zero g, and Mission Control had been obsessive about bone loss, monitoring crew members daily to make sure their bone mass wasn't deteriorating to dangerous levels. Calcium supplements were mandatory, and lists of high-calcium foods were posted everywhere. If anyone were to sum up the early interplanetary missions in one gestalt, it would have been: "Eat your broccoli!"

It was almost traditional for long-range spacers to hate the stuff. Even if you didn't, you had to pretend you did. So while Hydroponics staff dutifully cultivated the heavy dark green stalks in lovingly nurtured stands, there was always plenty of it left over for mulch.

Personally, Nyota loved broccoli. She selected a particularly healthy-looking bunch from the nearest bed, expertly lopped off the woodier stalks, washed it under the sprayer, and sealed it in an airtight pouch.

"Nothing ventured!" she told the agronomist, who shook his head and went back to his seed corn.

At the last minute, Nyota ordered Luke Choy to report to the PLUM as well; she wanted the young lawyer's input during dinner. Her delay had given Langler time to report to the aft bay and struggle into his suit without being watched, something else she had planned in advance. The psychologist was grateful enough for her tact to keep quiet for once. They hardly spoke as the PLUM lowered itself carefully through the methane-laced atmosphere; they no longer needed to. Nyota had begun to relax with and rely on Langler. Each could feel the excitement in the other's mind. And Luke, for once, was too wired up to talk.

Tetrok was thrilled with the gift.

"How is it prepared?" he asked immediately, taking it from her hands and marveling at it. How had he known it was food and not, say, a floral arrangement? Nyota had only to look at the sparkle in his eyes to know.

Could he read all her thoughts? No, she decided, but it was

high time she chose which ones she'd let him read and which she wouldn't. A trained esper, she set about closing some of the doors of her mind.

"You can eat it raw," she suggested. "Sometimes we serve it with other raw vegetables—carrots, cauliflower, zucchini, none of which we happen to have available at the moment—as a kind of appetizer. Or it can be steamed and served as a side dish. Maybe you could methane-vapor it."

This time it was Tetrok who laughed.

A sudden flurry among the other Fazisians present resulted in someone's producing a small device and handing it to Krecis, who touched it to the broccoli. Nyota and Langler watched as a series of what were probably numbers scanned down the minuscule LCD on the face of the device.

"Acceptable," Krecis announced, returning the device to Zeenyl, who slipped it into a pocket of her gown. To Nyota he said: "A molecular scanner. To be certain we can digest it. I am pleased to report that we can. Before we ask you to eat any of our foods, we would like to run similar tests. If you could provide us with certain . . . samples . . ."

Nyota frowned, not certain what he meant. "Of course, but what—"

Zeenyl approached her in a carefully nonthreatening manner, another small device in her hand. Touching it to the skin of Nyota's forearm, she watched the readings on its screen. Then she reset the device and applied it to Langler's arm.

*Do you realize how easily they could kill us? If this thing were a weapon, or contained a poison . . . Even their food could be designed to poison us . . .* The thought came unbidden to Nyota's mind, and she prayed no one but Langler could hear it; she was even embarrassed to think that Langler had. But he was her ship's psychologist, and she'd brought him along for just this purpose—to keep the situation in perspective.

Langler didn't answer in her mind. He simply shook his head almost imperceptibly, in a motion Nyota took to mean: Not now; I'll explain later!

At any rate, the damage—if it was damage—had been done. Zeenyl had taken her "samples" and now consulted with Vaax on some linguistic point.

"Blood and skin samples," Vaax explained to Nyota in English. She found herself examining her arm and finding no scratches or incisions of any kind; she hadn't felt a thing. "To analyze your . . . DNA?"

"Ah, yes, DNA," Nyota replied, nodding. "I understand now."

Zeenyl had taken the broccoli and disappeared, apparently to reanalyze the samples against the dinner menu. It was exactly what Nyota would have done if the Fazisians were her dinner guests. Inwardly she breathed a sigh of relief. Everything made sense, so far.

&

MEMO

FROM:       Nyota Dominique, Ph.D.
            Commander Lòng Dàn
TO:         Bydun Wong, L.L.D.
            Chief Counsel/ESC Earth
SUBJECT:    The Fazisians

Sir:

You've asked me for a full report on the beings we have encountered here on the surface of Titan, but asked with the kind of urgency which makes me believe that the sooner I give you my initial impressions, the better. A full report, in my personal opinion, would and will require years of study and interaction. What I'm giving you here is the merest sketch of these extraordinary people we have encountered.

Yes, they are "people," in the fullest sense. They are cultured, intelligent, highly evolved, and more technologically advanced than we are. With their full consent and cooperation, I will append a brief history of their civilization, as soon as our computers are finished translating it. With their permission, I have also provided you with photo portraits of several Fazisians, giving their names, professions, and a brief biography of each.

Note: "Fazisian" is a transliteration of their name for themselves; while it has been fairly easy for Dr. Langler and me, with the assistance of esper-interaction, to assim-

ilate their spoken language, the alphabets are going to
take some time.

Fazis is one of six planets in the Vega Solar System.
Like Earth, it is the only naturally inhabited planet, although Fazisians have colonized some of the other planets and their satellites. Fazis has an atmosphere composed
of hydrogen, nitrogen, helium, oxygen, and about ten percent methane. Its terrain is similar to Earth's, though its
gravitational field is approximately one half of Earth's.
This factor has made it somewhat easier for the Fazisians
to adapt to the light gravity of Titan than it has thus far
proven for us.

The mean temperature in the temperate zones on Fazis
averages approximately 10° C, which makes the Fazisians
far more adaptable to cold than we are. In fact, they have
had to alter the environmental controls in the guest quarters to accommodate us, and whenever we are in the common areas, Dr. Langler and I have taken to wearing very
heavy clothing.

Nyota paused in her report, thinking of the dinner party
earlier this evening, wondering how she could possibly process
the myriad thoughts and impressions roiling through her brain,
much less reduce them to the concise form Wong and the
Councils demanded. The very first contact between Earthians
and a previously unknown species had just occurred, and here
she was reporting on the need to wear sweaters in the dining
quarters! What this moment needed was diplomats, sociolo-
gists, cultural anthropologists, not a handful of scientists rhap-
sodizing over broccoli and Fazisian cuisine.

No, wait a minute—check that! Nyota thought. What this
moment needs is precisely the clearheaded approach of a
group of scientists from both sides determined not to muck
this up the way every first contact between cultures on Earth
has been, the way it's been allegorized in every science-fiction
novel in the past century and a half. It may have been pure
dumb luck that brought us together, but it's got to be scientific
method and cool heads that keep us together. And hopefully,
the fact that they, too, believe in a Supreme Being will be a
positive influence on our peaceful desires, and not a cause of

division as we have experienced it on Earth in the past.

Nyota felt a bit claustrophobic from not being able to view the full landscape of Titan from her quarters because of the nearly constant swirl of methane fog. The inner environment of the Fazisian compound ran on three ten-hour shifts to match the thirty-hour Fazisian day, and by that reckoning it was the end of the third-shift, sleep time for all but essential personnel, almost "morning." Nyota had not slept at all. She was so energized she didn't think she'd ever sleep again. She went back to her report.

> Possibly the most important factor to remember about Fazis is that extra ten percent of methane in the atmosphere. It has affected every aspect of Fazisian biology, from the plant life to the people themselves, their appearance, their mental abilities, even the sound of their voices.
>
> The full range of Fazisian telepathic powers will require years of study, which Dr. Langler has volunteered to undertake. I can only add that the facility with which Commander Tetrok reached into my mind, and the ease with which I was able to understand him, has made it possible for us to communicate in each other's languages quite literally overnight.

And "communicate," Nyota thought, doesn't nearly describe what Commander Tetrok and I have been doing!

⚖

It was Zeenyl who had truly noticed it first. Gifted with such limited telesper powers as to be virtually psi-null, she nevertheless had no difficulty communicating with her spouse. She could not resist giving Phaestus a little mental nudge at the dinner table.

*What do you think, my love?* she questioned him, eyeing first Tetrok and then Nyota. *An unlikely pairing, or a natural one?*

Typically, Phaestus had no idea what she meant: *I don't understand!*

*Tetrok and the Earthian female!* Zeenyl thought impatiently. *Surely you noticed the intimacy of the mindtouch!*

*A necessary tool for ease of communication, that is all.*

Phaestus dismissed it with a kind of mental shrug.

Zeenyl sighed, exasperated. Was the male of every species always so obtuse and single-minded? Or was she reading too much into Tetrok's interaction with the Earthian, hoping he would find some other female of interest, thereby releasing his hold upon Nebulaesa?

Zeenyl had still been a child when Tetrok and her sister had their brief, tempestuous affair; there were far more questions than answers in her mind. But she had seen the way Nebulaesa looked at Tetrok as recently as their sojourn on Outlyer-21. Was he the reason she had never chosen a mate? If he were otherwise preoccupied, would Nebulaesa get over him and choose another?

Without speaking of the past, Zeenyl had brought her observations about Tetrok's intimacy with Nyota to Krecis' attention.

"My concern as well," he concurred. "I have spoken to Tetrok about it, but he sees nothing untoward. Perhaps there are worse ways to initiate contact, and yet . . ."

The OldOne could not finish his thought. Zeenyl, with a kinship born of gender rather than species, determined to speak to Nyota personally.

The eagerness with which each side had agreed to an information exchange was contagious. Throughout dinner it seemed as if they were all talking at once—examining everything from the food to what everyone was wearing, questioning customs and protocol, learning the slang and idiom of each other's languages. More than once Nyota had looked down the table at Langler and rolled her eyes; they were both suffering from sensory overload, and she wondered if the Fazisians felt the same way. It got to the point where every time she looked at Tetrok she could see him looking at her, amusement in those sparkling green eyes. Oh, those eyes!

The somewhat restricted sunlight on Fazis, due to the heavier atmospheric conditions which exist most of the time, combined with the ten percent methane atmosphere, has caused an eye development somewhat different from ours. Fazisians possess light-sensing abilities not only in the Earthian visual range, but also in the infrared range. It is almost safe to say that Fazisians can see in the dark . . .

Not for the first time, Nyota wished she were psychic as well as esper-gifted. If she'd known they would find Fazisians on Titan, she would have packed some of her good clothes. The Fazisians themselves didn't seem to distinguish between work clothes and dress clothes; all of their attire was gorgeous, the fabrics high quality, the colors brilliant, the ornament just right, and every garment tailored precisely to enhance the innate grace and beauty of the individual wearing it. Compared to their hosts, Nyota and Langler in their regulation ESC jumpsuits, even with full rank insignia, looked positively ordinary.

As if reading her mind (well, why not? They all could), Zeenyl had approached Nyota just as dinner was winding down and everyone rose from the table.

"Such delicate bones!" she said, taking Nyota's hand gently. She herself was a full head taller than the Earthian. "And yet I think, among your people, you are considered a beauty?"

Nyota managed to look embarrassed, but Langler, overhearing, had no such compunction.

*Among the most!* he thought so that both women could hear him. Nyota scowled at him. He was getting entirely too good at this!

"Will you permit me to offer you a small gift?" Zeenyl motioned for Nyota to accompany her.

There were actually two gifts. The first was a pendant of finely wrought metal—titanium, Nyota thought—and unfamiliar red gemstones which Zeenyl placed around Nyota's neck.

"Oh, I couldn't!" Nyota demurred. "This is exquisite. And I have nothing to offer in return."

"Perhaps you will, in time," Zeenyl said mysteriously, refusing to take the gift back. Her second gift was a less welcome one. "If I may ask, what were your . . . feelings . . . when Tetrok first touched your mind?"

"Surprise," Nyota said at once. "Esper capability among Earthians is somewhat rare; we've barely begun to study it. Your people's mental abilities seem so effortless."

"Surprise," Zeenyl repeated. "Nothing more?"

"Oh, much more! Pleasure, relief that communication would be so much easier than we'd anticipated—"

"Personally, I mean," Zeenyl prompted.

Nyota had to think about that for a moment. "I was—flattered. Honored, I guess you'd say, that one of your leaders would confide in me so readily. Yours is a very trusting species."

"Not always so trusting," Zeenyl said carefully. "Ordinarily, what Tetrok did would not be permitted as casual contact between individuals. It is usually reserved for more . . . intimate contact."

Nyota understood in a heartbeat. "A courtship ritual," she suggested warily. "Almost a kind of—foreplay?"

Zeenyl turned the concept over in her mind. She made a gesture which Nyota already knew meant yes.

In spite of the chill of the Fazisian common rooms, Nyota felt her face flush.

"That was very presumptuous of him!" she said crossly, tightening her jaw to keep from finishing her thought. Zeenyl gave her a puzzled look.

"You are angry," she observed.

"A little," Nyota admitted, not wanting to offend her hostess.

Zeenyl nodded. "Justifiably so. Nevertheless . . ." She sighed. "I wish you Earthians would turn colors with your moods as we do. It would make matters so much simpler!"

Nyota decided she was being teased and began to laugh. She reached out to hug the Fazisian woman in instant sisterhood.

"I think I must have a talk with Tetrok!" she had said finally, and Zeenyl had agreed.

☙

Now, in the privacy of her very sumptuous guest room at the start of the Fazisian day, Nyota decided she was less angry than she was flattered.

She yawned and turned off the minicomp where she'd been composing her report. She didn't know what to do first: order a cup of tea from the wall servitor, check in with Copeland on the *Egg,* or try out the Fazisian-style shower. While she pondered, she heard a tapping at her door. Running her fingers through her hair and hoping she didn't look as mussed as she felt, she opened the door to Langler.

"Couldn't sleep either?" He greeted her with his wolfish grin, angling himself into the room. In the corridors the gravity was at Titan-normal, easier for him to maneuver in; once inside Nyota's quarters, he had difficulty.

"You and I have some unfinished business," she answered by not answering; she was getting used to his reading her thoughts.

Langler maneuvered himself into a chair and frowned; for once she had him puzzled.

"You made a face at me during the broccoli incident," Nyota clarified. "I had this horrible thought that Zeenyl might have killed us with that scanner device if she'd wanted to. You shook your head."

Langler shrugged. "I didn't want you to blurt out what was written all over your face. Rationally, all we've got to do is remember context. They're outnumbered here. If any of their Earthian guests meets with an 'accident,' they don't know but that the entire forces of Earth could wipe them off the face of Titan. Besides, from what I'm learning of their culture, they're incredibly nonaggressive."

Nyota sat in the chair opposite him. "Explain."

"Their history shows no internecine wars for over three centuries. I know—" He held up his hand to silence whatever objections she might have made. "Histories can be rewritten. But they've come down from the trees, so to speak, at about the same time we did. They've been able to advance beyond us only because they've devoted their energies to space exploration instead of local wars. In a sense their evolution is remarkably like ours."

"That's what you've been doing all night . . . studying the data package we'll be sending back to Earth," Nyota suggested.

Langler nodded. "I'm not saying they're perfect. I tried chatting up Krecis about the ruling family and the political structure and heard a lot of words but very little information.

But they seem to prefer the Machiavellian model to the Darwinian one.''

"What does that mean exactly?" Nyota asked.

"It means their history indicates a fairly unbroken line of succession to the Ruler's throne. However, when a candidate for Ruler is challenged by the opposition, the result is a lot of behind-the-scenes political maneuvering, which may or may not be successful. But for as long as the rulership has been hereditary, there's never been a violent takeover. Not a populist movement or a military coup.''

"How long a period of time are we talking about here?"

"Over a thousand of their years," Langler replied. "Nine hundred of ours.''

Nyota shook her head in amazement. "I'll keep that in mind,'' she said.

"Wish we could be as sure of our own people," Langler said. He nodded toward the minicomp. "What do you think the response will be when they get your report?''

"I wish I knew." Nyota got up and fiddled with the wall servitor, making tea. She raised her eyebrows at Langler, who shook his head. "The worst they can do is panic, scrub the mission, and tell us to come home. That's not going to make the Fazisians go away.''

Langler was skeptical. "You don't think they'd launch a military backup?''

"Which would take over a year just to get here? No." Nyota shook her head, yawning in spite of herself. She sipped the hot tea. Too hot. It burned her tongue; she was awake now. "By their lights, if the Fazisians are aggressors, you and I and the *Egg* are already casualties. The worst they'll do is order us home, and that's not cost-effective.

"Langler, you're the psychologist; you tell me: Which do you think is the stronger human impulse—fear or greed?''

Langler only laughed his bitter laugh.

# CHAPTER 7

Counselor Wong rubbed his eyes wearily. If he had to assess one more computer simulation for interplanetary contact, he swore he would resign. Just how many of these theoretical models were there?

"Effective this date, 2,187," the computer informed him when he asked. "Adjustments and modifications to on-screen model expected to yield at least seven more at the conclusion of present run."

He'd been afraid of that. Was the answer to have the Select Committee study every single one of them and debate the pros and cons of each while the *Lòng Dàn* idled above Titan with her meter running? Or was it a simple matter of taking Nyota Domonique's on-site assessment at face value and assuming these Fazisians were as friendly and willing to negotiate as they seemed?

"Query . . ." Wong said. "Extrapolate odds on possibility species designated Fazisian is untruthful in its expression of peaceful intention, and provide recommendations for action on our part if they were to attempt to invade or attack Earth."

"Working . . ." the computer replied.

Counselor Wong pressed the release button on the thin band adorning his left wrist. It was not entirely decorative. The pressure released painkillers directly into his bloodstream to relieve the beginnings of a terrible tension headache. In approximately ten minutes he was to address the entire Select Committee, some in person, others via telescreen from their various locations throughout the system, to continue the debate he'd been having in his head ever since he'd received Nyota Domonique's report.

Could they or could they not trust the Fazisians?

☙

Crown Litigator Gulibol did not need theoretical computer models in order to assess the situation. The Fazisian government had had an official first-contact policy on file for a full century before any ship had ventured out of the system. Gulibol's concerns were at once more concrete, and more ephemeral.

"If they ask us to leave," Sublitigator Zadora reminded him unnecessarily, as she and her colleagues from the Conclave of Litigators contemplated the holo images of Earthians which had replaced their hypothetical four-species assessments, "we will have to not only abandon the on-site research facilities, but sacrifice access to immeasurable natural resources. It is safe to say that all of our colony stations on the Sol side will have to be abandoned, so dependent have they become on the ore drones."

"We are all well aware of this," Gulibol said, also unnecessarily. Of the dozen Fazisians in the committee chambers, there was not one who did not know precisely how vital it was not to retreat from Titan.

The drones had begun their journey in Krecis' time. Constructed from alloys of native Fazisian aluminum and titanium pirated from Krecis' ship and amalgamated with structural steel refined from the high-grade iron ores the first expedition had harvested on Titan, the cavernous holds of these automated ships were filled with all the mineral wealth that Fazis lacked. The far-flung colony stations, Ruler Xeniok's pride and joy, depended upon the processing and refining of these minerals for their very existence.

And if Titan had to be abandoned, the stations would no longer be self-sustaining. This was just what Valton and the opposition parties needed to hear.

"Sixty satellites," Gulibol mused, accessing an ancillary holo of the Sol System. "The system contains sixty natural satellites! How were we to know the Earthians would aim their ships toward this particular one?"

"Litigator, the question remains," Zadora said, attempting to focus him. "If we refuse to leave their system, will the Earthians attack us?"

&

"This goes way beyond a real estate squabble," Bydun Wong told his assembled committee. "We're talking about first contact with a heretofore unknown species. However grandiose that sounds, it's exactly what we're dealing with. If we screw it up, to be perfectly blunt, it could be the biggest PR blunder in the history of Earth."

"So what are you saying, By?" Summer O'Donegal, Chief Counsel for the Mars Colonies, wanted to know. "As I understand it, we're in about the same position Columbus might have been if he'd stumbled onto a twenty-first-century culture. Wouldn't the smartest thing be to make nice and see what they've got to offer?"

Wong nodded, clearing his throat. His headache was almost gone. "Not only that, but what if they're in contact with still more intelligent species out there? If we don't cooperate with them . . ."

He left his thought unfinished. There was an ambivalence in the room—a mixture of concern about the unknown and excitement over the encounter—which reflected that on the planet at large. It was strong enough to taste. As if to cover it, everyone in the room and on the open radio frequencies to the stations began talking at once. Bydun Wong felt his headache returning.

&

Fazisians had long since conquered the tension headache by means of biofeedback techniques. Nevertheless, Crown Litigator Gulibol had more in common with Chief Counselor Wong at this moment than either man could possibly imagine. While Fazisians rarely raised their voices, the turmoil of a dozen telepathically trained legal minds all speaking those minds at once was enough to give even a Fazisian a headache.

*Surely if they meant to attack they would have done so immediately upon discovering our incursion into their system . . .*

*Perhaps not. Perhaps they wished to study us first, to see what use they could make of us . . .*

*A reactionary view at best. Why can we not assume that their perception is as evolved as ours? What if . . .*

And while the legal debate raged across two solar systems, scientists from both worlds put their heads together on Titan and tried to find the shortest distance between two points.

☄

"Is there a way to do it?" Nyota asked Phaestus.

"Technically, yes. If your people can follow our instructions precisely, it can be done. As to the moral implications . . ."

Here they both turned to Krecis for advice.

"The mere fact of your presence here has altered your species' perception of the order of the universe irrevocably," he said to Nyota solemnly. "I do not see that a little boost in communications technology will do any more serious harm."

The Fazisians set about instructing Earthians on how to build a holocom.

Nyota hailed the *Egg* and instructed Copeland to bring her three top people down in a second PLUM to assist Vaax and his engineers, who were soon beside themselves with as much enthusiasm as a Fazisian could express. Once the introductions were complete (Nyota wondering if she and Langler and Choy had looked quite as goggle-eyed as Copeland and her people did shaking hands with beings who changed color as they smiled and murmured, "So pleased to meet you") and the Earthians got over the fact that the Fazisians now spoke flawless English, with a smattering of Russian and Chinese thrown in for spice, the two teams set to work.

Nyota found herself standing around with her arms folded, watching Vaax crawling beneath a console to tinker like an auto mechanic while Copeland handed him conversion chips with the precision of a physician's assistant. She soon became aware of someone standing just behind her.

"Doubtless they can manage without our getting in the way," Tetrok said quietly in her ear. "Vaax tells me four hours at minimum. Will you come for a drive with me?"

She wasn't sure she'd heard him correctly. "A drive?"

"Krecis suggested I take you on a tour of our mining facilities," he explained formally, though there was that perpetual twinkle in his eyes. "In the interests of full technological disclosure, of course."

"Of course," Nyota nodded. "A drive in the country. Are you going to put the top down? I don't want to muss my hair."

He looked so puzzled she wanted to kiss him. Quickly she explained the Earth tradition of driving with the top down.

"You are teasing me." Tetrok smiled. "Is this customary?"

"In this case, retaliatory," Nyota replied mysteriously, and went to get her hardsuit.

She'd yet to see what Fazisians wore to go out in the environment; as expected, their environmental suits were so elegant as to make her feel positively plain beside this tall, striking peacock of a man. Just as well, Nyota thought, her thoughts locked down for the duration. *If what Zeenyl told me is true, I don't want to give him any encouragement!*

♄

Their vehicle, an enclosed two-seater equipped with terrain-following electro-optics and riding smoothly on a cushion of exhaust gases a few inches above the surface, hovered above a rise overlooking a frozen methane lake. Nyota peered through the windscreen—there was atmosphere inside the vehicle and she'd been able to remove her helmet, gasping a little at the methane content at first, knowing she'd have a sore throat before this trip was over—to try to see the far shore of the lake where it disappeared into the undulating rust-red mist. She found she couldn't. The lake extended for kilometers, its surface a roil of methane-and-water ice deep-frozen in mid-wave countless millennia ago. Clearly that solid mass had once flowed as liquid. Carefully melted under laboratory conditions, it could do so again. Who knew what secrets it contained?

"Down there," Tetrok indicated, pointing to a small aperture at the base of a cliff farther along the shore. "That lode alone can fill an ore drone to capacity in a twenty-day shift."

The opening could have been a natural cave mouth, for all the evidence of activity surrounding it. There was no track on the rock-hard surface, no slag heap, no strip-mining. As Nyota watched, a line of four pilotless trams emerged from the mine adit and moved over the surface to a point approximately one hundred meters along the lakeshore, where they stopped and formed themselves into a hollow square. With a move too quick and graceful to be seen they suddenly slid together, interlocking into a single seamless unit. Nyota swore she could almost hear the snap.

"When one hundred such units have formed, they will be airlifted to the central locus and attached to a power pack," Tetrok explained. "That's all an ore drone is really, a hundred interlocked modules with an ion-converter engine attached. They are coded so that some will be detached at Outlyer-twenty-one while the rest continue on to the other outlyers. Only about twenty percent actually reach Fazis Prime."

Nyota nodded. All of this was in the report the Fazisians were preparing to broadcast to Earth if the holocom experiment worked. She supposed she should be paying closer attention, should ask for an inside look at the mine itself, but she was no engineer, and she was far more interested in the biological research being conducted on the lakes and back in the labs in the main compound, research which Tetrok had so far only hinted at. Besides, she couldn't help thinking there was an ulterior motive for his luring her out here alone.

"What did you mean when you said 'retaliatory'?" he asked suddenly.

They were strapped into bucket seats in the vehicle, isolated inside their individual environmental suits complete with gloves; Nyota supposed he could reach across and touch her if he wanted to, but it hardly seemed worth the effort. Still, she could feel her attraction to this man, and wondered if it was reciprocated.

"Vaax and the others should be finished about now," she said, glancing at her chronometer. "Maybe we should be getting back."

Her dazzling smile indicated she had no intention of answering his question. Somewhat bemused, Tetrok started the vehicle for the return trip.

❦

". . . would appreciate your putting a rush on this," D'Borah Copeland said into the radio microphone. Then she looked up at Vaax with a sigh of exasperation.

"This thing had better work!" she said. "If those bone-heads at Capcom could just learn to follow a simple instruction without having to get three separate authorizations for every relay toggle! Now they tell me they'll have to send to Beijing for enough high-quality platinum for the receptor plates, and they're already complaining about cost overruns. I don't think they really believe this is going to work.''

"I imagine it must be difficult, if one has never seen the technology," Vaax admitted sympathetically. "It seems this will take longer than we anticipated.''

"You can say that again!" Copeland said, watching the incoming board for some indication that her last message had been received and might actually be responded to. When Vaax looked as if he might in fact repeat his observation, she put her finger to her lips. "It's just an expression. I didn't mean it literally.''

"I know," Vaax said. "You'll pardon my saying so, but it amazes me that Earthians have made it into space at all. You are so . . . contentious.''

"As opposed to you Fazisians, who are so polite!" Copeland replied.

It would in fact be four days, rather than four hours, before the holocom experiment could begin.

✍

"Keep scanning for radiation or weaponry of any kind," By-dun Wong whispered to the DefCon phalanx he'd ordered to surround the holocom platform before he would consent to have it activated. He wondered if he could be overheard by the Fazisians, and decided he didn't care. Let them know he and the Earth he represented were both on the alert, in case they tried to pull anything.

Besides, there was enough background chatter among the others in the Council chambers and on comm from the stations to mask his words.

"Incredible! How do they do that? It's as if they're actually in the same room!''

"Holographic technology's been around for centuries!" someone else said, less impressed. "Zoetropes, stereopticons, three-D movies . . .''

"That's not the point. The point is simultaneous broadcast. That's what's impressive.''

Watching and listening from the command center on Jupiter-1, Mark McCord turned to Beth Listrom.

"No," he said. "What's impressive is their giving away their technology for free."

Beth shook her head. "I wouldn't call that impressive. I'd call it suspect."

"Nothing so far, sir," the DefCon chief told Counselor Wong as his team kept their eyes glued to their equipment, glancing up from time to time at the incredible display taking place in the center of the room.

Even the images Commander Domonique had sent back to Earth hadn't prepared them for this. These Fazisians were positively strange-looking. What was even stranger was hearing them speak English, and appear to be standing, completely three-dimensional, in the inner sanctum of the Earth Space Council.

As for how Bydun Wong himself felt, standing alone and unprotected in the center of his own specially designated receptor plate, knowing he could be seen on Fazis in the same way he was seeing Gulibol, wondering if there wasn't some trick involved, some way in which the Fazisians could reach out and grab him, pull him across parsecs of space to hold him for ransom on their homeworld . . . He was a bureaucrat, not a hero, dammit, and there was no provision for this in his contract as Chief Counsel. Inside he was shaking like a leaf, and when this session was over he was going to need an antacid along with his headache remedy. The important thing was not to let it show as far as Fazis.

". . . and, to reduce the excess verbiage as much as possible, Counselor Wong," Crown Litigator Gulibol was saying, the drone in his tone indicating he had no intention of doing any such thing, "it is my understanding that your Earth's common law has a provision for what is known as 'possession being nine-tenths of the law.' As such, an established long-term Fazisian presence on the natural satellite of your fourth, er, excuse me, your sixth planet—the moon which you designate Titan—would suggest . . ."

At the console in the Fazisian control center on that very natural satellite, two teams of scientists watched the holographic confrontation on a small view-cube, simultaneously shaking their heads.

"They'll generate enough hot air to heat Titan to Earth-normal before they're done," Nyota suggested.

"Quite possible," Krecis agreed. "Impractical, however. The logistics of filtering out all that carbon dioxide . . ."

Both teams laughed.

"Litigator Gulibol," Bydun Wong was saying now, stumbling only a little over the pronunciation of the Fazisian's name. "We do not contest the actuality or the longevity of your presence on Titan. We are simply constrained to point out that the satellite lies within the boundaries of our solar system, and as such . . ."

"Krecis?" Langler, far more interested in the course of Earthian/Fazisian social interaction than in territorial imperatives, had no compunction about seeking the advice of the wisest individual on Titan. "What do we do? If we wait for them while they haggle it out, submit it to a vote, send it to committee . . ."

Langler shrugged, unable to continue. Krecis looked to Nyota.

"I for one say, let's get on with it," she said without the slightest hesitation. There were nods of agreement, some less enthusiastic than others, among both teams. "My crew and I are on a mission to explore Titan. There's nothing in my orders relative to the presence of anyone else here. I say we get to work."

&

Compared to orchestrating the holocom hookup, bringing the *Dragon's Egg* down out of low orbit and integrating it into the Fazisian colony compound was child's play.

The *Egg* was designed to soft-land like a shuttle, but, given the uneven terrain and how close they'd be bringing her to the colony, it was decided to back her in like an old-fashioned booster rocket. Technicians from the ship interacted smoothly with their Fazisian counterparts on the surface of Titan, and within a day, the big ship had been retroed to a whisper-quiet touchdown less than five hundred meters from the compound; there a swarm of Fazisian robotrams similar to the ones Nyota had watched emerging from the lakeshore mine gathered around it, while a kind of heavy crane used in the placement of the modular colony structures lumbered out of the main storage hangar and stood ready.

First everything inside the *Egg* was battened down. Then her entire crew was evacuated into the Fazisian compound, hopping across the quadrangle like so many hardsuited kangaroos, as Nyota and her first-contact team had done—incredibly—only a week earlier. Then with an assist from Titan's light gravity, the crane's grapples secured the forward end of the big ship and gently, gently laid her down into the waiting embrace of the encircling robotrams.

Three hundred Earthians and an equal number of Fazisians watched as the trams caterpillared toward them on their all-terrain treads, bringing the *Egg* closer. After some consultation between both engineering teams, the ship's aft starboard airlock was interfaced with the main airlock just outside the colony's biotech laboratories. Adjustments were made, and an all but permanent connection now made the ship an integral part of the colony.

"No alterations have been made to anything but the airlock," Nyota assured her assembled crew at the end of that eventful day. "In a pinch we can be back in orbit and on our way back to Jupiter-one within twenty-four hours. Let's hope it never comes to that."

Crew quarters remained what they had been on the journey here—private living spaces for the crew of the *Egg*. But soon the labs and the greenhouse, the dining hall and all the common areas were populated by Fazisians as well, and more and more Earthians were seen mingling with Fazisians inside the colony proper. Through a kind of cautious sociological osmosis, the integration of the two teams proceeded in small increments—a handshake here, an exchange of pleasantries there, a carefully established working relationship between two groups of scientists eager to learn as much about each other as about their differing technologies. At end of day, Earthians and Fazisians gathered to learn each other's slang, listen to each other's music, watch entertainment cubes together and explain the nuances and in-jokes, exchange small gifts and play lighthearted interactive games that often resulted in uproarious laughter from the Earthians and quiet smiles on the part of the Fazisians. Earthians began to show up for work wearing traded bits of Fazisian clothing, and some Fazisians began to emulate the Earthian custom of wearing earrings to complement their own traditional neck pendants. There was even the occasional bit of harmless flirting.

There were xenophobes on both sides, but they were rare and generally, wisely, kept to themselves in the parts of the ship or the colony where the other species was not likely to turn up. Nyota assigned Langler to work with the Earthians, while Krecis, apparently tireless, took it upon himself to work with his own kind. Of all those involved in this empirical experiment in interspecies relations, Krecis understood best the full significance of what they were doing here.

All was not well on the homeworld. In subtle covert ways, Valton had attempted to form his own opposition party, expending all his energies in an attempt to lure other malcontents into a coalition to challenge the Fazrul's vote on the succession. That Valton clearly expected to enter himself as the opposition candidate against the absent Tetrok came as no surprise to anyone.

But what did Valton want, beyond the obvious lure of personal power? Of all Fazisians, Krecis knew best what Valton wanted, for Valton had once been his best and brightest pupil, but they had failed each other. . . .

❧

The older the foursome grew, the more the hothouse environment of the family gatherings chafed on all of them, except Zeenyl. Oblivious of their life-and-death debates, she sat in the corner by the hearth, occasionally glancing up from her studies when the voices got too loud. Scattered among the colony worlds to finalize their various studies, they now met only at holidays, which made the debates that much more fervid.

"Never mind them, little one," Krecis would whisper to Zeenyl beneath the tumult played out across the dinner table or a game of *jdartha*—the subject might be anything from politics to the precise color of *kleringaial* blossoms following a summer storm, but it was always discussed as if lives hung in the balance. "It's a mercy they will someday be assigned to places as far from each other as possible, in order to distribute all that energy where it may do some good."

"They don't bother me anymore," Zeenyl had assured him once with a smile. "Not since you've strengthened my mental shields so they can no longer easily read me."

It was the least he could do, Krecis thought, to defend this gentlest of his charges against the others' roughshod ways. Looking at her, he wondered why he still called her his "little one"; she was as tall as he and had grown into quite a beauty.

The din the other three were making grew louder still.

"What would you have done, then—left them all to starve?" Valton challenged Tetrok. The two had been reliving the Donema Campaigns all afternoon. "A determination of which colonists would survive the longest on the lowest rations would have saved hundreds more lives until relief supplies arrived. Your decision to do nothing—to 'let nature take its course'—is as idiotic as Donema's idea of choosing those who would die by random selection!"

"Assuming this were more than an intellectual exercise," Tetrok countered, shaking the *jdartha* tiles idly in their small enameled box, "would you be prepared to sacrifice those closest to you if your scientific determination warranted it?"

"Meaning you and me?" Nebulaesa interjected. In Donema's position, she'd have put everyone on short rations according to their weight and metabolism, to give all the colonists an equal chance at survival, but both cousins had dismissed that as impractical. Because it truly was impractical, Nebulaesa wondered, or because neither of them had thought of it? Ah, men!

"Anyone!" Tetrok insisted, still rattling the tiles without shaking them out on the board to make his move. "Including himself, if his research dictated it."

The timer sounded and Nebulaesa took the tile box away from Tetrok, who had forfeited his turn by procrastinating; she shook out the tiles and made her move. Someone had to keep this game going, or they would be here until sunrise!

"Yes," Valton said. "Anyone. Including myself. In fact, I would be the first to volunteer to die, to set an example for the others."

"Ah!" Tetrok studied the board while Valton shook out his tiles, a small smile playing at the corners of his mouth. "So you would sacrifice yourself as an example, leaving the colony without its best leader. What if the survivors decided not to abide by your dictate once you were dead? Not that you would care if anarchy ensued, since you would be beyond its reach. Beyond the reach of guilt for condemning old ones and children to death, too."

Valton drew himself up with dignity. "It has always seemed to me that the mark of a true leader is the ability to accept the ghosts of his own actions."

He glanced at Krecis as he said this. He was still young, still callow and unfinished. He needed the OldOne's approval more than he would admit. Krecis nodded imperceptibly; his best pupil had mastered this much, at least.

*

"Your telesper potential is as high as mine was at your age," Krecis had informed Valton when the most recent skill scans had been completed. Unlike the scattershot approach to mental telepathy which was the norm on Earth, Fazisians took their study of mental abilities as seriously as anything else. "Do you understand what that means?"

"It means there's at least one thing I can do better than Tetrok!" the young man had said at once, regretting it as quickly.

Krecis allowed his statement to fall into what seemed an interminable silence. It was true; Tetrok and Nebulaesa had scored within a single point of each other—even their techniques were in character, Nebulaesa's dogged and thorough, Tetrok's seemingly effortless, because his pride would not allow him to show how much effort he gave to anything—but Valton had surpassed them markedly. It was the narrowness of his perception which disturbed Krecis.

"Is that so important to you still?" he asked finally.

"Krecis, how can it not be?" Valton sprang to his feet, nostrils flaring like the thoroughbred he was, his colors high and his entire high-strung posture evidencing his lifelong distress. "Why is it that the very skill scans which show me superior in MT create gray areas in my leadership abilities?

As a member of the Order, don't you believe that a superior telesper would make a superior Ruler?''

The Order of Telespers had fewer than one hundred living members at any time, Krecis among them. Far better than Valton, he knew the drawbacks of superior mental telepathy or MT abilities.

"I know only that a superior telepath can make a more dangerous Ruler. You do not need me to cite the historical precedents."

"I would not make the mistakes that Klerek and his Terrorists did," Valton said evenly.

"There are far more mistakes to make than Klerek's," Krecis countered. "Valton . . . I invite you to study with me. One on one, apart from your cousins or anyone else. My intention is to someday sponsor you as my acolyte to the Order." He watched the young man's colors before he added: "If you wish it."

Valton's colors ran high for several moments; Krecis read surprise, awe, and a touch of uncertainty before the younger man could gain control of his thoughts.

"Krecis, I—I am deeply honored," he said finally, as all the tension left his body and he sat down to collect himself. "But—"

"You will not be Ruler," Krecis told him with absolute coldness. "This is not prescience but fact. It is time to rid yourself of a young man's obsession and move on."

"What if Tetrok dies?" The words were out of his mouth before Valton could stop them. "Krecis, believe me, I wish him no harm, but—"

"Don't you? Think before you answer, Valton. Remember who it is who can read your thoughts, no matter how skilled you become."

"Hypothetically, Krecis," the young man said with a coldness to match his mentor's. "He's requested deepspace assignment. Accidents happen. I am next in line. Is it foolish for me to stand prepared?"

"It is only foolish for you to pursue this thought to the exclusion of all else. Valton, will you be my acolyte?"

To Valton's credit, he had tried. He and Krecis had explored the intricacies of each other's minds and their interconnectedness with the whole of creation until Valton could easily submit his application, under Krecis' aegis, as acolyte to the Order. Krecis had done all he could to hone Valton's passion toward the good and free him of his obsessive need to rule, but it became obvious to Krecis that it was not enough.

"By the Powers of all the universe . . . I shall rule, not Tetrok!" Valton blurted vehemently.

Krecis and Valton had ceased their private study by mutual agreement. Not even the cousins knew what had happened, nor did they comprehend the true depth of Valton's abilities. As Krecis watched the threesome squabble now over their *jdartha* board, he took Valton's words about guilt and responsibility to heart. Was there anything he might have done differently?

"You're cold-blooded, cousin!" Nebulaesa said, as the tile box once again came into her hands and Tetrok set the timer. "What if everyone here were a member of your colony? If your scientific data dictated it, would you condemn us all to starve? Even Krecis?"

It wasn't a fair question, she thought, even as she asked it. Surely even Valton, even theoretically, could not condemn Krecis.

Valton's answer took everyone but Krecis by surprise.

"Even Krecis," he answered, looking the OldOne in the eye as he said it.

&

Now, a lifetime later, as Xeniok struggled to maintain his power base as Ruler in the absence of his son, Valton's obvious scramble for power made Krecis, who knew him better than anyone, profoundly uneasy. He also could not help wondering if there were those like Valton on Earth.

&

"Conclusions, people?"

Bydun Wong had never felt so wrung out in his life. He couldn't pinpoint the precise moment in the endless negotiations with his Fazisian counterparts when he'd stopped thinking of them as "aliens" and begun treating them as if they were just people. Granted, they were chameleon-skinned people with purple-blue hair and orchid fingernails and voices that put him in mind of cicadas humming in slow motion over a continuo of bass violins, but even that was soothing after a while. He'd noticed the other members of the committee succumbing too. It was hard not to like these people, or was that part of some secret power they possessed?

He kept looking at his own fingers, splayed out on the onyx surface of the conference table, trembling slightly. He almost expected them to start to fade, become translucent and then transparent and finally disappear, as the holocom images of Gulibol and the other litigators had done over the course of the past several days. Wong was amazed to find himself still here; they hadn't kidnapped him back to Fazis after all.

You've been reading too much sci fi, Wong! he chided himself, then waited for those around the conference table to share their opinions.

By mutual agreement, the holocom transmissions had been halted for thirty days so both parties could discuss their conclusions privately.

"They've boosted our commtech by about twenty years," Summer O'Donegal pointed out, nodding in the direction of the now vacant platinum-plated holocom receptors affixed to the floor and ceiling in the center of the committee room. "And they've answered every question we've asked. We could conceivably set down in the capital on Fazis Prime and walk up the steps of the Ruler's summer palace—that's how open they've been with us."

"And that doesn't strike you as suspicious?" Bydun Wong asked, playing devil's advocate.

Summer shrugged. "They know they're stronger than we are. They don't see us as a military threat, except to their immediate colony on Titan. They want to stay on Titan. I don't think we need to look for any motive more complicated than that . . ."

☙

"I wouldn't make that assumption!" Beth Listrom muttered as the transmission from Earth finally reached her and Mark McCord on Jupiter-1.

"Oh Beth, you're just being paranoid," Mark said, not entirely teasing. They were usually a good counterpoint to each other: Beth the hard-nosed military commander, Mark the laidback civilian in charge. "Look at the amount of information they've disclosed. They've virtually given us a blueprint for invasion if we wanted it, right down to the precise location of every one of their outlyer stations."

"How do we know that's all of them?" Beth demanded. "For every one they've shown us on those holomaps, there could be ten more they haven't. And how do we know they're unarmed? Because they say so? Come on, Mark, grow up!"

"Don't take that tone with me, Commander!" Mark said, a little testily. "Summer's right. These people can afford to argue from a position of strength. They know they can whip our collective asses—militarily, technologically, even telepathically—so they don't need to. Hell, if they'd wanted to invade Earth they could have done it twenty years ago!"

"It's that telepathic business that bothers me!" Beth said ominously. "How do we know they haven't brainwashed the whole pack of us through that holocom gizmo of theirs?"

Mark had to laugh at that. "Thought you didn't believe in esper ability!"

"I don't!" Beth countered. "Oh, I've read the literature on it, just like everybody else. And I used to watch those little mind-reading tricks you and Nyota did, though if you ask me, that was more about hormones than—"

"Watch it," Mark warned, always protective of Nyota.

"Sorry." Beth grimaced. "But I'll always be skeptical—of espers, and even more so of telepathic aliens."

♄

Three weeks later, Chief Counsel for the Earth Space Council Bydun Wong and Crown Litigator Gulibol of Fazis agreed upon the final wording of the First Contact Accord:

> . . . and in conclusion, agree that there is no intrinsic harm in, and in fact may be much good derived from, a mutually governed research colony as established upon the surface of the natural satellite of the planet Saturn, which is hereafter to be designated "Titan" by both par-

ties to this Accord. To that end, science research teams led by Krecis (party to the Accord from the planet designated "Fazis") and Nyota Domonique (party to the Accord from the planet designated "Earth") shall be conjoined in mutually beneficial exploratory and research projects as determined by both parties and approved by each respective government. To that end, effective this date, these parties are instructed as follows:

That Dr. Domonique shall, with all due speed, bring her vessel (designated *Lòng Dàn)* to a soft landing on the surface of the satellite designated Titan, whereupon provision will be made by the Fazisian colony to incorporate said vessel into structural conjunction with the physical plant of said colony . . .

Nyota read the Accord over Krecis' shoulder on the viewcube in the laboratory and had to smile.

"Way ahead of you, people!" she said, clapping her hands together lightly, ever so pleased that she'd guessed right.

"Indeed," Krecis agreed.

# Chapter 8

"Every time I'm trying to work in here you hang around this greenhouse like a butterfly in sweet clover!" Nyota remarked. "Milord Tetrok, what do you want?"

She had taken to calling him "Milord Tetrok" because he was so unlike what she'd expected of the probable future Ruler of an entire civilization, despite his natural charisma, the innate aura of authority which sat so lightly on his broad shoulders. He seemed more like something out of a medieval romance—a knight-errant, or a mischievous boy.

Tetrok reached past her to snatch something out of one of the harvest bins.

"Don't flatter yourself that it's you, Dr. Domonique," he replied solemnly, hiding his stolen treasure behind his back. "I only came for the broccoli."

"Oh, you! Give that back! You're worse than a young Navajo on peyote; I swear you're going to make yourself sick with the amount of unfamiliar veggies you eat. Haven't you ever heard of Montezuma's revenge?"

Tetrok shook his head, holding the broccoli at arm's length above his head so she couldn't snatch it from him. "Never. But doubtless you will enlighten me."

"Enlighten you!" Nyota glowered at him; she would not so much as condescend to reach for what he had stolen. "I don't have time to enlighten you. Zeenyl and I are working almost round the clock with both agronomy departments to see how many of our plant species we can adapt to your methoponic farming methods, and all you do is get under my feet. Is it customary for the future Ruler of Fazis not to do any real work?"

Nyota could not believe the words even as they came out of her mouth; she sounded infatuated, a teenager with her first

crush. She had to remind herself she was still furious with
Tetrok for slipping into her mind so easily, so familiarly, that
first time. She pretended to concentrate on the inventory on
her flat screen but gave it up, frowning.

"I need to talk to you, seriously. Put the broccoli down,
please, and pay attention!"

The twinkle left Tetrok's eye and he relinquished his pil-
fered prize.

"I've offended you," he said. "Please tell me what I've
done wrong."

Nyota came right to the point. "Zeenyl told me that what
you did the first time we met—walking around in my mind
like that, without even asking permission—is a breach of your
own protocol. That two people—particularly a man and a
woman—don't usually reach that level unless they're . . .
courting."

"I see," Tetrok said thoughtfully. There was an expression
in his eyes that Nyota could not read. "I made a mistake, then,
and I am sorry.

"What I did was in the nature of—an experiment," he went
on. "What I believe you would call 'a shot in the dark.' There
was no reason to expect your species to have telesper powers
at all. To discover that both you and Dr. Langler were quite
gifted espers was exciting. I thought my action would save
time, and help us to communicate more efficiently. I truly
meant nothing else by it."

Nyota found herself drawn closer to him; they were almost
touching.

"Didn't you?" she asked.

They were no longer alone. Out of the corner of her eye,
Nyota saw Krecis making his way deliberately down the long
rows of vegetation, his hands tucked in his sleeves, his expression unreadable. As if it had been her intention all along,
Nyota scooped the head of broccoli out of the bin and shoved
it into Tetrok's hands.

"Here!" she said coolly. "If it gives you any digestive
upsets, ask Dr. Cervantes for some of those enzymes he's been
working on; they should help. Hello, Krecis," she added, as
if surprised to see him, and with a nod to both men which
indicated she had business elsewhere, she slipped away.

Tetrok did not wait for the elder man to voice his obvious disapproval.

*OldOne* . . . he began, but Krecis refused his attempt at mental communication with a gesture.

"This will not serve," he said aloud. "It would be better for everyone here if you would more often keep your thoughts to yourself."

"OldOne—"

"Be silent!" Tetrok had never seen Krecis angry before. "You may be heir apparent, but I think you forget your place here. My experience takes precedence in some things. You will let me speak."

A wise leader knows when to follow. Damping down his own quick temper, Tetrok bowed to the older man's wisdom.

"There is none in this colony who is not aware of your attraction to this Earthian female, and that is a matter for your own judgment, as informed by what we continue to learn of these Earthians. At least, some of us do. While you engage your leisure time in mating dances and gourmandizing, some of us continue to weigh and study the situation."

Tetrok looked down at the dark green head of broccoli in his hands and suddenly felt like a fool. He set his treasure down and tried to remember his dignity.

Unlike Fazisians, who stored their data on palm-size holocubes, Earthians used less efficient flat disks. The hand Krecis slipped out of his sleeve contained several such disks, labeled in Russian. Tetrok had acquired enough of the written language by now to read the labels: *A Brief History of Extrasensory Perception and Telepathic Experimentation, 1866–2050.*

"They are too new at these skills," Krecis said solemnly, as Tetrok pocketed the disks, indicating that he would study them. "You endanger our entire purpose here by pushing too fast. How much of your communication with Nyota is of the mind?"

The question was pointed and, Tetrok thought, an intrusion into his privacy. Nevertheless, he understood Krecis' concern. There were times when a would-be Ruler's privacy was not his own.

"Not as much as you fear," he tried to assure the elder man. "Consider that while your study of the species is theoretical, mine is no less valid for being empirical.''

"It is not your study but your methodology which I question," Krecis began.

"Her mind is as strong as mine!" Tetrok said with sudden passion. "I know!"

"And she intrigues you," Krecis finished for him. "for reasons not having to do with the mind.''

"OldOne," Tetrok replied, "out of deference for your widowhood, I have hesitated until now to remind you that the mind is the most attractive of all sexual characteristics."

Memories of Zandra clouded Krecis' thoughts for the briefest moment, and Tetrok instantly regretted his words. Before he could speak again, Krecis recovered, his mind more incisive than ever.

"To what end do you pursue this . . . courtship of yours?"

It was the one thing Tetrok had not bothered to think through. He was not even sure enough of Nyota's thoughts to know if his desires were reciprocated.

"It occurs to me that a planet was once united by similar intentions," he replied.

He was being disingenuous, Tetrok knew, in mentioning the Clan Wars of Fazis' ancient past, which had threatened to destroy the entire race until they were resolved by intermarriage. Each clan chieftain's eldest son had been betrothed to the eldest daughter of another. The children who resulted had ruled jointly over new clans structured out of the old, and their children had also married outside their birth clans. Within five generations all of Fazis had been united into a single "clan," whose Ruler was thereafter chosen not by blood but by the people's vote. The system had worked for over a thousand years.

Krecis looked at Tetrok thoughtfully. Only the young could presume to know so much. He thought of what he had come to know of Nyota—independent, centered, and just as likely to dismiss Tetrok out of hand as to welcome his advances. Indeed, Krecis thought, Tetrok was correct about one thing: her mind was as strong as any Fazisian's. It seemed to Krecis she could almost *be* a Fazisian. Some things were better left to take their course.

"You are presumptuous," Krecis remarked, and Tetrok

managed to look chagrined. "But, as you will. It is not my place to tell the future Ruler how to run his affairs."

"Isn't it?" Tetrok asked mildly. "It seems to me that is exactly what you were doing."

Krecis folded his arms back into his sleeves, inscrutable.

"As a matter of cultural exchange, the experiment interests me," he said. "And of course, in this instance, there can be no thought of offspring."

❦

The Earth Space Council simply forbade human reproduction during space exploration without the formal consent of the Council; such exceptions had been made, for example, for families in permanent residence on the space stations. Since they had never had contact with other intelligent life before, it was always understood that this Council ruling applied only to all Earth expeditions. The discovery of Fazisians had put the entire situation in a new light.

Tetrok and Nyota weren't the only ones who had felt an attraction. And the Fazisians, in particular, had learned too late the dangers of any form of reproduction in an alien environment.

❦

Phaestus told Nyota the story one evening after dinner.

"The planet was one of the least hospitable in our system, but its cultivation was deemed necessary because of the havoc we were wreaking on Fazis Prime at the time."

"How long ago was this?" Nyota asked quietly. She was seated near what to the unpracticed eye seemed to be a roaring fire. It was, in fact, a hologram of an open hearth superimposed over a methane-fueled radiant heater. There were many of these scattered about the common buildings now, out of deference to the Earthians, who still had difficulty tolerating what Fazisians defined as room temperature. Even knowing that the heater distributed its warmth evenly and the "fireplace" was an illusion, Nyota could not resist warming her hands at it.

"Three generations ago. Approximately four hundred of our years," Phaestus replied. "We had not yet accepted the fact that natural resources were finite. Rare was the day when the sun shone through the hydrocarbon haze we had wrapped around our homeland. The first-growth forests were all but gone, the waterways were rank with industrial effluvia . . .''

Nyota nodded sympathetically. She knew—oh, she knew! Did every civilization have to go through such a greedy adolescent phase?

"We had begun the colonization of Fazis Second and Third, but felt we needed more, always more. This planet was to have become Fazis Fourth, until the horrors struck.

"It was one of the outermost planets in our system, its maximum daytime temperatures in the range where nitrogen liquefies, not too unlike here."

Nyota shivered involuntarily.

"Yet we discovered volcanic activity beneath the crust and were able to harness this to heat the environmental bubbles we constructed near the equator. It was hoped that, with our apparent talent for creating greenhouse gases, we would eventually succeed in heating the entire planet."

"And then what?" Nyota prompted.

Phaestus looked embarrassed for a generation of Fazisians who had died before his own parents were born. "Precisely. We did not sufficiently think it through. Ironically, however, we never had the chance to discover our error on that monumental a scale.

"To our amazement, we discovered that the permafrost contained not only microorganisms but indigenous chlorophyll-based plant life as well. Had this world once been as warm as our homeworld? We never had time to find out. The excitement of our discovery led to a fever of cultivation. Expeditions came back daily with exotic flora which we defrosted and set to growing in our greenhouses—carefully segregated from the plants we had brought with us, of course, but soon burgeoning with an incredible tropical lushness, more like your Earth than our own cooler Fazis. There seemed no end to the species we could find beneath the ice . . .''

Nyota stretched like a cat in front of the fire. Most Fazisians, she had observed, were multitalented, and Phaestus was a poet as well as a scientist. He chose his words precisely, weaving them together in the manner of a practiced storyteller. The oral folk tradition was as strong on Fazis, apparently, as it had once been on Earth. Now that she had grown accustomed to Fazisian voices, she could listen to Phaestus for hours.

"You will have noted there are no children on Titan," he said suddenly, breaking his narrative. "Without rigid habitat controls and express permission from the Fazrul, none in the Offworld Services may bear offspring. Even given permission, most of us hesitate. This is the legacy which haunts us from our gravest error, Fazis Fourth."

Zeenyl and Langler joined them then, the Fazisian woman slipping into the storytelling circle to sit silently beside her spouse, clasping one of his hands between her own. Langler, navigating with difficulty as always, settled slowly by the "fire" with Nyota.

"A natural disaster?" he suggested, having caught the last of Phaestus's words. "Or some sort of genetic accident?"

"We were not so careless," Phaestus said mildly. "Nor so trusting of circumstance. The colony had been established for over a decade before there was any hint of the disaster to come . . ."

The other three, even Zeenyl who knew how the story ended, remained silent after that.

"We began testing our new world in careful increments. For all our excitement at finding so many new species, we tested each to the submolecular level to see if it could, first, coexist with our own flora and, second, be crossbred. If there was the slightest doubt about the hardiness or safety of a particular subject, it was instantly rejected. We also set about adapting the flora we had brought with us to their new environment."

"Just as we're doing here on Titan," Nyota suggested.

Phaestus acknowledged this. "Thereafter—and we are speaking of time periods encompassing several growing seasons; nothing was done in haste—we began breeding hybrids. Some were successful, some not . . ."

Afterward, Nyota couldn't say exactly when Phaestus's voice shifted from outside to inside her mind. Even the usually perfectionist Langler couldn't be precise. Knowing his audience was as mentally gifted as he, Phaestus made the shift quite smoothly, inviting the Earthians to see what his mind could see. . . .

*♋*

*In her diaries, published one year after her death, Garissa, the Governor's daughter, mentioned a sense of foreboding long before the morning she found that all the leaf vegetables had succumbed to a mysterious ailment.*

"*It was as if they had been melted, dissolved by some strong acid; they were literally liquefied, reduced to foul-smelling puddles leaching into the soil which only the night before had fostered row upon row of healthy plants,*" *she wrote.* "*Strangely, I was not shocked. I had sensed . . . as if I had expected this. My feeling of dread, which the elder women attributed to the hormone imbalances of early pregnancy, now had a cause.*"

*Analysis of the puddles showed that the hybrid plants had mutated literally overnight.*

"*It is not a parasite or plant disease which destroys our food supply,*" *Garissa wrote,* "*but something about our very presence on this world itself which has altered the natural order of things. It serves no purpose to isolate the affected plants from the rest of the greenhouse, for the 'contagion' exists at the genetic level and, even as the rest of our crops succumb, there appears to be no way to stop the destruction in time. Within ten planetary rotations, we estimate, we will have nothing but emergency rations to eat.*"

Through Phaestus's eyes, Nyota and Langler watched Garissa and her fellow colonists move helplessly through one crisis after another as the animal experiments also succumbed to mutation. There were no indigenous animals on Fazis Fourth; the only animals bred there were those which had been brought as embryos from Fazis Prime—milk herds, egg-laying fowl, and the occasional pet.

"*Where only days ago the milk was safe, it now evidences the rapid overgrowth of virulent carcinogens,*" *Garissa reported dispassionately in her diary.* "*The fowls' eggs are weak-shelled, cracking open to decay even as we watch. At first we wondered how long it had been dangerous to eat these things. Now we know . . .*"

*Nearly all the colonists began to develop rapid-growing and particularly nonresponsive cancers; the youngest children and adults past half-age died quickly. The breeding stock produced stillbirths or freaks—offspring with extra limbs or heads and atrophied inner organs—none of which lived more than a few hours. Eventually all the adult animals developed leukosarcomas and had to be destroyed.*

*"The Fazrul had at first ordered us home," Garissa wrote. "Now they have reversed themselves and ordered us quarantined here, as if the cancers which devour us are somehow contagious. And in a particularly bitter irony, we young women, who came here expressly to rear a generation of strong, healthy children beneath an unsullied sky, find ourselves in terror for the pregnancies we carry."*

✍

"Within days of this final entry, Garissa and several other women miscarried." Phaestus concluded his sorrowful tale aloud. Nyota started slightly at the transition; her mind had been with Garissa. "The fetuses were found to be severely deformed.

"Denied the right to return to their homeworld, their food supply running out, medicines depleted and cancers eating them alive, the colonists of Fazis Fourth resorted to a suicide pact. No one has set foot on their world since.

"It was later determined that the deadly phenomenon was unique to the environmental circumstances we discovered on Fazis Fourth and the result of our too rapid heating of the atmosphere and the release of heretofore unknown carcinogens. However, the experience has made us fearful of the unknown and untested."

"As a consequence," Zeenyl said, speaking for the first time, "the instant Krecis reported your first radio transmissions to the Fazrul, a plenary session was called and a statute passed: No matter who you were, how like or unlike us, how many generations we spent in interaction with you, or how many new species we might encounter elsewhere, no Fazisian would reproduce with a member of any other species."

"The penalty," Phaestus concluded solemnly, "is exile to a penal moon, with one's offspring, for life. No other crime carries such a penalty. Even murderers are punished individually, not through their offspring. Since the entire species can be endangered by the process, there are no exceptions to this rule.''

Phaestus and Zeenyl sat holding hands in silence for a long moment after this. Langler stared into the "fire." Nyota, uneasy with the silence, sought some diplomatic way to break it.

Her first thought, carefully shielded from her companions, was: I wish I'd known this sooner! The instant it flashed across her mind, she wondered why. What kind of scientific method was this? Bad enough her own feelings toward Tetrok kept surprising her; she still had no idea if his chronic teasing was simply a scientific method of his own—a form of xenopsychology far less formal than Langler's—or if he felt the same way. And here she was regretting the fact that she'd never be able to have a child with him!

Get a grip! she chided herself. You've lived this long without ever considering having a child with anyone. What the hell's come over you?

Whatever it was that made her shiver this time was nothing a fire hologram could cure.

"What a terrible tragedy!" she said softly. "Yet your people have been out in space without any further difficulties for four hundred of your years."

"Exactly why the Fazrul made such restrictions," Phaestus countered. "Perhaps that's the reason we've survived four hundred years without further difficulties."

"I understand that, but it was your own people reproducing among yourselves!" Langler protested. "And it was the food supply coupled with the contaminated atmosphere which created the cancers. The situations aren't the least bit analogous."

"Your point is well-taken," Phaestus acknowledged. "However, logic as we scientists practice it is frequently not the foundation of a governmental edict . . . at least not on Fazis."

Everyone simultaneously broke out in laughter, recognizing Phaestus's sardonic humor.

"You Fazisians have no corner on that market," Nyota said. "On Earth we had laws for centuries that forbade the mixing of races and classes. It wasn't logic that set these restrictions; it was a myriad of reasons which could be boiled down to bigotry or some superior gene theory."

"It seems Fazisians and Earthians may be more alike than any of us imagined," Zeenyl contributed.

Nyota addressed Zeenyl, woman to woman. "Do you think the prohibition might be . . . reexamined—once we've been here long enough?"

Zeenyl made a negative gesture. "The Fazrul rarely changes its mind."

Nyota nodded in sympathy. "Yes, I'm afraid the same is true on our side."

As a scientist, Nyota had to be satisfied with the parameters for experimentation she'd managed to wangle out of her own government. She'd been on Bydun Wong's case before he and Litigator Gulibol had even arranged their first holocom meeting, insisting that not only should the crew of the *Dragon's Egg* be allowed to experiment with the embryos and cryo-frozen DNA strands they'd brought with them but, if possible, they should be allowed to attempt to crossbreed them with Fazisian species.

Some months before, all the Titan explorers had celebrated when both governments reluctantly agreed to allow elementary experiments, including submolecular crossbreeding, but only in highly controlled laboratory environments. This was the opening they had all waited for. But was it as far as they would be permitted to go?

≈

As he neared three-quarters age, Krecis required less sleep than he had in his youth. While he followed the Titan colony's accepted diurnal rhythms and was as active as any of his peers in the daytime, he was also known to work or study far into the night.

Fariya and the other females attributed it to loneliness, and more than one had offered him the comfort of her arms to pass the long nights, but Krecis had always and graciously declined. No one questioned where he went or what he did on his long nocturnal walks throughout the colony compound. This night, as on many nights, Krecis made sure he was alone before he passed into a part of the colony most of its inhabitants didn't know existed.

He had designed this secret chamber from the earliest days of the settlement; even he could not say why. The trusted workers who had aided him had long since departed for Fazis or the outlyers. Thus, at this point, he was the only one on Titan who knew of the secret labyrinth. It lay beneath his laboratory, reached only by activating a silent air-cushioned elevator, hidden behind an all but invisible door, obscured by a ceiling-high stack of storage cubes. Krecis manipulated an innocuous-looking handle on the center cube and the entire stack moved aside on silent hinges. Optical sentries caused the unit to close automatically once he had passed within.

There was no need for lighting in the passageway; a Fazisian's infrared vision grew keener with age, and Krecis could move literally in the dark. A light came on in the chamber below as he entered, bright enough for the work that transpired there.

On an immaculate laboratory table, several meticulously arranged rows of shallow vessels held the graduated results of an ongoing experiment. As he did every night, Krecis made note of the progress of the contents of each vessel, logging it in a small hand-held computer. Then he adjusted the light above one vessel, the temperature below the next, left the third untouched, and so on. Looking for all the universe like some primeval denizen of Earth—part druid, part shaman, part alchemist, part mad scientist out of an old B-movie—he rolled up his long, flowing sleeves and retrieved an oversize carafe of some murky, roiling liquid from a nearby cryo-unit and began to feed carefully measured doses of this mysterious nutrient to the life-forms in the vessels.

When Nyota Domonique told him that she had been sent to Titan to determine if there was life in the frozen lakes, Krecis was grateful he already knew she was a telesper. Above all, he did not want any stray thoughts about his work to slip out into her mind. If Earthians were to learn what he already knew, all his work might be in jeopardy.

Yes, there was life on Titan, at least a score of anaerobic algae, locked in the ice for millions of years. Meticulously harvested, carefully thawed under laboratory conditions, refined and cultivated, they had extraordinary properties. Some could heal wounds, others could increase the mental abilities of lower life-forms. Still others served merely as vitamin supplements or skin lotions—unbeknownst to them, every Fazisian on Titan had been ingesting these in a Garpozin-based protein supplement that all spacers took to compensate for calcium loss and environmental toxins—but each algal form was in and of itself a miracle drug.

What would Earthians do if they discovered this? Having learned their languages from what they'd thought were "safe" comm transmissions, Krecis had a fair idea. They would overrun Titan, secure it as a military base, and doubtless, tell Fazisians to go home. He must not allow this to happen.

Krecis studied his handiwork for some moments, slowly rolling his sleeves back down over his wrists, then moved away from the laboratory table to a small reading niche at the far end of the minuscule chamber. An ergochair, a cup of strong *grinish* heated over a lab burner, and the perfect degree of light for reading embraced him as he settled in for study. His subject tonight was the Earthian legal process, from Hammurabi to Bydun Wong. He must understand these beings thoroughly, in anticipation of what was to come.

He had found an unusual ally in the *Dragon's Egg*'s young helmsman, Luke Choy.

"My degree's in space law, sir. I shipped out before I could practice, but I've got a photographic memory, and if I don't know something, I at least know where to look it up. I'd be glad to help."

Krecis had considered the young man's offer solemnly. He had not seen such alacrity, such an eagerness to please since he had been a much younger man, and tutor to the ruling family.

"I would be grateful for your assistance, Ensign Choy," he responded, and Luke had gutted the *Egg*'s law library to give him what he needed.

Krecis read until nearly dawn. Then he checked his experiment again. Satisfied with the night's accomplishments, he returned up the secret airlift to the realm of the living.

# CHAPTER 9

Genetic engineering was Nyota's stock in trade. Wielding any of a select array of "molecular knives," she could snip and splice a double helix in her sleep. In fact, she often did. Most of her more successful experiments had been preceded by detailed "dress rehearsals" in her dreams.

Why, then, had her dreams suddenly become nightmares?

"It is because neither of us has done this with an offworld species before," Tetrok suggested, finishing her unspoken thought as they worked side by side. Nyota no longer considered it unusual for him to do this.

Tetrok was having trouble sleeping as well.

"Is it the ghost of Fazis Fourth which haunts me?" he wondered aloud. "We have agreed to work with the simplest lifeforms, to terminate all experimentation should anything go wrong. Why do I waken barely an hour into each sleep cycle with a screaming in my mind?"

"I don't know," Nyota replied. "But I feel it too."

They seldom spoke aloud anymore. They were together almost constantly in the biotech lab, supervising a staff of Earthians and Fazisians engaged in everything from simple *E. coli* carrier experiments to boost the protein content of certain strains of bean plants, to complex feats of molecular engineering which, among other things, would make it possible to grow broccoli on Fazis, Fazisian *kerltha* on Earth, and both varieties on Titan. By now their mental abilities were so attuned that they could converse all day without saying a word.

The work was a joy, the success rate encouraging. Why the nightmares and the interrupted sleep? It was not until Nyota, sleepless for what seemed the tenth night in a row, took to roaming the corridors and ran into Krecis that she was able to put it into words.

Krecis seemed not at all surprised to see her. "Walk with me," he invited, and Nyota fell into step beside him. As with everything else about him, Krecis' pace was measured, deliberate, and got him where he needed to go.

"It's a matter of two factors," Nyota said after a long silence, knowing she didn't need to preface her remarks with any kind of explanation; Krecis would know exactly what she was talking about. "One, how far should we go? Two, how far will our respective governments allow us to go before they order us to stop?"

"Perhaps one should not worry about the latter unless and until it affects the former," Krecis suggested. "Given the inherent inertia of any government, one should have ample time to formulate a policy for the former."

"That's just it!" Nyota said. "Tetrok and I both agree the next step should be animal experiments, but do we stop at diatoms and observe them for a hundred generations before we progress to, say, planaria? Or do we initiate both experiments simultaneously only to discover we've created a mutant flatworm big enough to eat the entire colony?" She ran her fingers through her thick black hair in frustration. "I've never felt this . . . uncertain before."

They walked in silence for some moments after that. Krecis noted that Nyota no longer wore the air filter around her neck; she had adapted to Fazisian atmosphere sooner than most of the other Earthians. Nyota was aware of a quiet warmth, a gentle reassurance lapping at the edges of her mind; Krecis was working some of his unobtrusive mental magic. She was smiling up at him when another presence entered her mind. Tetrok. He was also awake, also pacing the corridors not far from them. In a matter of minutes they would intercept each other. Nyota stopped, her hand on Krecis' arm.

"I think I'm going to go back to my room now."

Krecis covered her hand with his own in a very Earthian gesture. "What is it that you fear?" he asked incisively, seeing the emotion pulse around her like an aura.

"I—" Nyota stopped. He knew, or at least sensed, what was troubling her. Why not say it aloud? "Krecis, I—I think I'm in love with Tetrok. That's the most unscientific observation I've ever made in my adult life, but I have no doubt of its accuracy and its validity. The problem is . . . I don't know what to do about it.''

Krecis had also sensed Tetrok's presence in the corridor, even before Nyota did. He removed her hand from his arm, giving it a little avuncular squeeze.

"If you were asking my scientific opinion, I'd suggest you tell him," he said, stepping back just as Tetrok rounded the corner ahead of them.

"But—" Nyota turned. Krecis was gone, vanished like the mage he was. She turned back to confront Tetrok, who looked as drawn and haggard as she felt. *Poor baby!* she thought, not caring if he heard her, and went to him.

*ॐ*

Something about Valton's tone had put Nebulaesa immediately on her guard.

"Surely you and your sister communicate regularly," the OffWorld Commander suggested casually. Too casually, Nebulaesa thought. "I only asked what you gossip about. Zeenyl must have endless stories about what it's like to live and work with these . . . Earthians.''

"As if only women gossip!" Nebulaesa chided him, buying time. As her superior officer, Valton received regular reports from her on the status of Outlyer-21 and reports forwarded from Titan. What else did he want to know, and why? Nebulaesa had not forgotten her childhood's lessons.

She had found Tetrok honest to a fault, even when it cost him punishment for some prank or accidental breakage. Valton, on the other hand, although always acknowledging his acts when confronted or caught, seemed immune to blame either external or internal, able to rationalize his way out of anything. Yet in ending their early love affair Tetrok had hurt her deeply, while Valton, she was certain, still loved her. As a consequence, Nebulaesa had always wondered whom she'd ally herself with should the two ever find themselves on opposite sides politically as well as personally.

This far into adulthood, commander of her own outlyer station, she still could not decide. Nevertheless, she was always careful to address Valton in a distant professional or a light-hearted sisterly manner. Valton was not always so constrained.

"Gossip . . ." Valton seemed to be weighing the merits of the word he'd chosen. "Perhaps I did not mean anything quite so trivial. Subtext, then. Tell me in your own words, Commander, what the official reports do not say."

"Commander!" Nebulaesa thought. That's certainly distant enough! Her holo image, close enough for Valton to reach out and touch, made a dismissive gesture.

"There seems to be a great deal of enthusiasm for the conjoined project. Zeenyl and Phaestus both report they enjoy working with their Earthian counterparts. With double the personnel, the work proceeds in half the time. The energy experiment alone—"

Nebulaesa stopped, aware that her color had gone high, letting Valton know that she was temporizing. She would have to control her EC, her emotional colorizing, better around Valton. His image leaned closer to her, so close she had to force herself not to pull back.

"You know what I'm asking," he said, his own color warmer than it should have been—and he a master of EC control—if this were really nothing more than a casual conversation between old friends. "Two intelligent species who find each other unusual, perhaps exotic, working in such close proximity . . . Surely scientific research is not all that's going on."

"If you're asking about intergender conjunctions, Valton, why not say so?" Nebulaesa said, more sharply than she needed to. "The answer is: I do not know. Zeenyl is happy with Phaestus; it's not something she has mentioned to me."

"And knowing Zeenyl," Valton said, remembering the shy little bookworm who nevertheless missed nothing, "if it were going on, she would have mentioned it."

"Exactly," Nebulaesa said, growing tired of the effort it took to keep this conversation neutral. "Is there anything else?"

*Yes, there is!* Valton wanted to shout into the depths of space. *B'Laesa, tell me why you've never chosen a mate! Tell me why you requested assignment on Outlyer-twenty-one, in order to be as far away from Fazis—and from me—as possible! Tell me if you've gotten over Tetrok—and if so, if I could swallow my pride, would I have a chance?*

ॐ

She had toyed with them both, playing one against the other,
for an entire season, hoping perhaps that both would go away
so that she need not make a choice. She was far too young
and footloose, intent upon her own career, to commit herself
to any male just yet. What if she chose Tetrok and he became
Ruler? Would she be free to roam among the stars, or must
she, like Xeniok's spouse, content herself as co-Ruler? As for
choosing Valton, his superior telesper powers—which awed
her—combined with his obsession about becoming Ruler,
frankly frightened her. Either way, she would be co-Ruler and
the most powerful woman on Fazis. If Valton hadn't refused
her mind-contact that afternoon in the *ngemiil* enclosure, might
she have trusted him? It was all so long ago. Why did she
continue to pine after Tetrok when Valton could be hers for
the asking?

*Ask me, Valton!* she thought to him across parsecs of space.
*Ask me again as you asked me when we were both very young.
I do not honestly know what I will answer this time!*

If Valton heard her, he did not respond. Above all else, he
had his pride. His image leaned back away from hers; he
yawned. "Is there anything else?" she had asked him.

"Not really," he said, entirely too ingenuous, and signed
off.

ॐ

Nebulaesa sat staring at the empty chair where Valton had
"sat" during their holo visit. Outlyer-21, part mining colony,
part frontier town, lay on the outer rim of Fazisian space.
Nothing much happened here, and commanding the station
had proven to be more drudgery and less challenge than Nebulaesa had hoped. She longed to return to the capital, if only
for a little while, to catch up on court gossip, perhaps request
a rotation home and a chance for promotion to a better post.
Who better than Valton to advance her goals? And while she
did not share his passion, she did enjoy his company. That
could prove useful. She would keep her ears open.

ॐ

Mark McCord gave Beth Listrom a quizzical look. "You've certainly changed your tune."

Beth grinned at him, all innocence. "Flexibility is the watchword of intelligent command, Mark; you know that."

Mark shook his head, not fooled for an instant. "Oh, yeah, sure! A couple of months ago you were foaming at the mouth about how dangerous it was to interact with Fazisians on any level. There goes the neighborhood, wouldn't let your daughter marry one—"

"I don't have a daughter, Mark."

"Don't play cute with me, Elizabeth. Why are you suddenly so gung ho about the Titan project?"

"There's a simple answer. The more we learn about them, the easier it will be to protect ourselves against them if we ever have the need."

"And the complex answer?"

"I'll save that for Wong and the Council when they ask for my opinion."

*

Beth Listrom's attitude was shared by many on Earth. Opinion among those opposed to the Fazisians ranged from that of the lunatic fringe who fed on direct video transmissions to personal receiver cubes, which had long ago replaced the printed tabloids, and who insisted they were a hoax perpetrated by the government—dark-skinned Earthians decked out in purple feather wigs and green contact-lens implants, whose skin tones only appeared to change color by means of video "morphing"—to a carefully worded xenophobia among the intelligentsia, which usually expressed itself as conservatism. "They seem too good to be true," was the consensus among this group. "What aren't they telling us?"

Except in certain backwaters, there was hardly a concerted "Fazisians Go Home" movement, but even the most liberal Earthian gobbled up every datum the media made available from Titan by way of Jupiter-1. The Earthian thirst for information was, ironically, abetted by Fazisian holocom technology. With this glut of information, Earthians were enraptured, excited. Yet, an hour without it and they were fearful, suspicious.

By now every official Earthian settlement within the Sol System had a fully operational holocom installation; it was not only possible to communicate simultaneously from Earth to Selenopolis to Mars to the stations and back again, it was equally feasible for anyone with official commlink clearance to interact directly with members of the government on Fazis Prime itself! An Interplanetary Friendship Society had recently been formed; its members played computer chess and ran an E-mail newsletter in five languages.

The official debate continued between solar systems. Barely a month went by that Bydun Wong and Crown Litigator Gulibol didn't have a little chat; when vital communication between them was called for, they mutually altered their daily routines to accommodate each other. In the ultimate irony, Gulibol and Wong, watchdogs assigned to the preservation of their own species over/against the other, found themselves in almost complete accord most of the time.

"You know how it is with these scientists, Litigator," Wong would begin his lament. Anyone watching the exchange between the two could almost expect them to put their arms around each other like two old friends sitting side by side on a park bench. "They think that just because they're billions of miles beyond our direct control, they can make their own decisions with impunity. I have to keep yanking the reins to remind them there are command decisions involved here, that the Council is in charge, and there can be no room for negotiation or insubordination."

"Well, precisely, Counselor," Gulibol would reply with a slight sniff, implying that he and his Earthian counterpart operated in a more rarefied atmosphere than mere scientists and explorers.

Neither Wong nor Gulibol was merely a lawyer. Each had a substantial background in history and sociology, as well as in the psychology of their own species, now augmented by as much as each could learn about the xenopsychology of the other. However, lawyers will be lawyers the universe over— hidebound, humorless, and given to straining at gnats. If a third party had entered into this conversation to point out, "Gentlemen, you're entirely in agreement with each other!" they would both have missed the point.

"They simply do not understand the long-term ramifications of their headlong experimental enthusiasms!" Gulibol cried, wringing his hands in a dandified gesture that got on Wong's nerves. Bydun Wong nodded sagaciously.

"I understand entirely, Counselor," he would interject from time to time, letting Gulibol do most of the talking.

Wong considered himself at an advantage, having Langler and Luke Choy in place on Titan. Langler provided him with monthly reports on the psychology of Fazisians as he was studying it in the field. As for Lieutenant Choy . . .

Wong sometimes wondered whose side Choy was on. The young man was certainly bright enough, and a very good lawyer, and under Krecis' aegis, was proving to be an able administrator. It was the fact that Choy deferred to Krecis in most matters that made Wong uneasy. The kid seemed to have a bad case of hero worship, and it made his loyalty suspect.

Not only that, Wong thought, but don't tell me the Fazisians don't have agents in place studying us even more thoroughly than we're studying them! And we don't even know who they are . . .

Gulibol was still talking.

"And my task, as you can imagine, Counselor, is further complicated by the fact that not only is Krecis unimpeachable, but the principal in my case is the heir apparent." Gulibol did not add that insubordination was encoded in Tetrok's very genes.

"You have my sympathy, Litigator."

"Please, call me Gulibol . . ."

⌘

Would the citizens of Earth be surprised to know that their views on Fazisians were mirrored almost exactly among their counterparts on Fazis?

There was an ancient saying: Put any two Fazisians in a room together, and within an hour you'll have two equally valid arguments and three new political parties. True democracy—one Fazisian, one vote—had reigned on Fazis since the Reformation. Voting tended to be more on issues than candidates, which meant that on any given day a Fazisian was free to vote on something—a proposition, a referendum, a modification or amendment to an existing law—with computer tallies being added up continuously. The system seemed to be cumbersome but it was fair, its major disadvantage being a tendency to spawn opposition parties like cold germs. Most such parties lived and died on a single issue or group of related issues, but occasionally some leader possessed the subtlety to form coalitions of these scattered parties.

Valton was precisely that kind of leader.

"We are not so foolish as to object to the interaction of our people with Earthians," he would begin a typical speech. "After all, it is we who first crossed the boundary into their star system. Nevertheless we urge caution, more caution than the current Fazrul rulings seem to exercise . . ."

Politicians talked and litigators debated. Militarists like Beth Listrom watched and waited, flexing their muscles idly, while opportunists like Nebulaesa looked for their chance. Media services boosted their ratings and holocom technicians enjoyed continued job security. Meanwhile, on Titan, the real work went on.

✑

Krecis allowed the catlike creature to climb up his arm and twine itself around his neck, settling finally on his shoulders like a living fur stole. Its golden eyes blinked at Tetrok and Nyota with only mild curiosity.

"We have virtually dozens of embryos and isolated DNA strands in the freezer," Nyota said. "Everything from mice to dolphins. We were expecting to perhaps populate methane lakes with dolphin clones and use selected genomes to modify other existing species. That changed, of course, when we bumped into you. But I was thinking . . ."

She was thinking that this was the next logical phase, to advance to mammal experiments before either the ESC or the Fazrul pulled the plug. The more complex the species, the longer the experiment would take, and the less likely its genetic programming would be compatible with anything that had evolved in a different solar system. A flatworm could be chopped up, its DNA mixed with any of several species of Fazisian *grin't,* and the offspring observed within a matter of days, with an anticipated high success rate. Any mammalian species, even mice, would take weeks to months to breed true, and there would be fewer successes.

Normal gestation for the creature contemplating Nyota from Krecis' shoulder was eleven weeks; its offspring would not be fully mature for nearly a year. What Earth species' traits would best complement its strong points? While its outer appearance was that of a cross between a rhesus monkey and a domestic house cat, Nyota had felt the power of its mind.

In the course of her career she had held extended conversations with Cape gorillas fluent in Ameslan and conducted sophisticated underwater experiments with dolphins. She recognized protointelligence in whatever form she found it. The intelligence this creature projected was more cetacean than feline. If she were to stir a few dolphin genes in with its DNA, what wondrous combinations might result?

"Wondrous?" Tetrok wondered aloud. "Or potentially horrific?"

Nyota shook off her own apprehension. "We won't know unless we try. Krecis?"

As always, the two younger scientists deferred to the scientific genius of their elder statesman. By way of answer, Krecis uncurled the catlike creature from his neck and placed it in Nyota's arms.

♄

Ultimately, along with the planaria and the mice and several dozen species of fish—a staple of the Fazisian as well as the Earthian diet—and the ubiquitous *E. coli,* which served as the carrier medium for so many of the crossbreeding attempts, there were to be two higher-mammal experiments. One involved cloning the cat creature's genome following alteration with select dolphin traits. The other consisted of injecting DNA from the cortical tissue of a prototelepathic Fazisian species called a *vririki*—which, from the way Krecis described it, was apparently a sort of highly intelligent monkey—into some cryo-frozen eggs from a most unusual source.

"Can you use these?" Langler asked Nyota, handing her a mysteriously labeled cryocontainer from the very back of one of the biotech freezers.

" 'Canis familiaris "Vikki," ' " she read. "I don't remember our requisitioning any canine materials."

"We didn't," Langler said. "That's my own personal contribution."

"Who's Vikki?"

"My dog." Langler looked suddenly shy. "Best friend I ever had, before or since. She died when I was a kid. We'd been meaning to breed her, but she developed this rare form of cancer. Environmental, not genetic; the eggs are clean— I've had them checked out. A colleague of my mother's at the lab managed to salvage them before they . . . put her down. He said when I got over my grief I could clone myself another Vikki someday. But I never did. Seemed to me there'd only ever be one Vikki. Don't know why I've kept those all these years; the storage alone has cost me a small fortune . . ."

His voice trailed off, and Nyota wondered if he was going to cry. Why, Frank Langler, you old phony! she thought. You do have a heart after all!

"What kind of dog was she, Frank?"

"A miniature dachshund," he said thoughtfully; if he'd heard what Nyota was thinking, he did not acknowledge it. "No bigger than a football, but she was all heart. You could pick her up with one hand, but you knew she'd kill for you. She had these big, melting eyes, and I swear she understood every word I said. It was how I discovered I was an esper, communing with Vikki . . ."

He did actually blink away a tear then, and Nyota touched his shoulder.

"Thank you, Frank," she said quietly, placing the cryocontainer in her own high-security section of the freezer. "We'll see what we can do."

☙

Vikki's son developed *in vitro* in the main biotech lab.

The fetus floated in a blood-warm amniotic bath in a Plexiglas container, fed through an umbilical on a Garpozin-based liquid Krecis had carefully formulated to meet the nutritional needs of all three of his parent species. He grew visibly with each passing day.

"Originally we'd hoped to actually clone Vikki once we'd

augmented her cortical DNA with genes fifty-four A and fifty-six C from the *vririki,*" Nyota explained to Langler; she had invited him into the lab ahead of the others, who would be arriving shortly to witness the "birth." "But they didn't take. So we've had to inject fifty-four and fifty-six into the haploid of a second Fazisian species, something called a *mur'ti,* which—"

"Whoa!" Langler leaned against the countertop and raised his hand in protest. "Back up and explain all that, slowly. Use nice short words. I'm only the shrink, remember? I never got past Bio one-oh-one."

"I doubt that very much!" Nyota said, but she explained anyway.

What she had done was to take a strand of DNA from the cerebral cortex of the *vririki* and, using a specialized enzyme which acted as a "molecular knife," isolated and snipped out the two very specific genes—54A and 56C—which determined prototelepathic capabilities in a species which communicated via ultrasound, transmitted and received through a pair of highly sensitive antennae set above its complex, infra-red-receptive eyes. While she had been performing this incredibly delicate microscopic surgery, Tetrok had been busy "splitting" an entire DNA helix from the sperm of a *mur'ti,* a small, silky-furred six-legged canine which had been used as a lap pet on Fazis since ancient times. Using the same enzymatic cutting technique Nyota had employed, he then snipped out the two corresponding genes on the *mur'ti* haploid or half-helix, discarding them. The *mur'ti* was not telepathic. At least, it hadn't been until its genetic material had been brought to Titan.

Working together, the two geneticists had spliced the *mur'ti* haploid onto a haploid Nyota had earlier split from a DNA strand derived from one of Vikki's egg cells. The splice had taken successfully, and the creature floating in the four-liter container under warm amber heating cells was the result.

"He'll look more like the Fazisian species," Nyota explained. "A *mur'ti* with *vririki* antennae. But he'll have Vikki's personality."

"Son of Vikki," Langler murmured with a catch in his voice. "Got a name for him?"

"I thought we'd do what the Fazisians do," Nyota said. "Wait until after he's born and he tells us what he wants us to call him."

As she said this, the others began to arrive—Tetrok, Phaestus, Zeenyl, and lastly, Krecis, who paused to examine the second major experiment in progress elsewhere in the lab. In a second Plexiglas container the catlike creature's offspring floated, almost fully developed; if all went well, it would be ready to be induced within the next ten days. Krecis never let Nyota or Tetrok know that he had spiked the embryo fluid in both containers with one of his algae-derived concoctions.

The OldOne had joined the others to officiate at the birth. Carefully he altered the temperature gauges on the heating cells, gradually reducing the temperature. At his signal, Tetrok injected a hormone cocktail from a syringe into the umbilical running from the nutrient pack into the creature's abdomen, while Nyota activated the tiny pump that would slowly drain the amniotic fluid away, replacing it with a methane-enriched oxygen mixture. Running her hands and forearms through the sterilizer beam and unsealing the lid of the container, Zeenyl prepared to be the midwife.

Phaestus and Langler watched. As its environment altered, the creature's movements altered as well, from a languid floating to a definite struggle to move on its own. As Zeenyl lifted it out into her arms, swathed it in a sterile blanket, and wiped its face dry it began first to whimper, then to howl. She handed the creature to Krecis, who stopped its howling in the most practical way possible, by feeding it.

"We will have to conduct exhaustive tests," the OldOne announced solemnly, watching the little furball sucking mightily on the nutrient bottle he held for it. "I will, of course, also manage to eke a monograph out of this in order to impress my fellow scientists on Fazis. Nevertheless, on purely empirical evidence, I believe we may consider this experiment a success."

Langler laughed out loud and clapped the OldOne on the back; everyone gathered around to marvel at the tiny creature and stroke its incredibly silky soft fur.

The small, frenetic furball with the melting dachshund eyes and antennae that sparkled in different colors with his ever-changing moods became known as Mushii. The telepathic feline with the sleek golden fur, clever simian hands, and long, foxy tail who emerged from her own carefully controlled environment some ten days later was called Catlyke. The two began to commune with each other while still maturing in the lab. By the time they were weaned, they had also linked minds with Krecis, becoming his constant companions, following him like a wizard's familiars on his moody nocturnal perambulations, or perched on his desk while he worked. What they talked about no one knew.

Occasionally one or the other of the animals would declare temporary fealty to someone else in the colony: Catlyke could be found draped around Nyota's shoulders as she visited the greenhouses, and more than once the usually wry Langler was caught in a contemplative mood, his long fingers stroking a contented Mushii's fur as the creature sighed and settled to sleep in his lap. In the shadow of Saturn, life went on.

# Chapter 10

"If we cannot sleep," Tetrok said, his arm around Nyota's shoulder as they watched a rare Saturn-rise break through the methane clouds of Titan, "we might as well not sleep together."

Nyota laughed; she couldn't help herself. "I don't think you realize what you've just said!"

Tetrok sat back at a distance so he could study her high-cheekboned face, his colors blushing into a soft rose beneath his everyday bronze. Was he embarrassed? His smile never wavered. "Enlighten me," he said.

How had they come to this? Nyota wondered. The transition had been so gradual, so effortless it was as if they had known each other all their lives. She felt more comfortable with Tetrok than with any other being, Earthian or Fazisian—so comfortable she was afraid to let their friendship go further, become a relationship, which, in her experience, was the first step toward disaster.

Meanwhile, she wondered if it was healthy for two beings—any two beings, much less two from such disparate origins—to come together so naturally, without so much as a difference of opinion. If they were to become lovers, would that change? She remembered how she and Mark used to shout at each other, their earlier passion transmogrified in the end into passionate anger against each other. Would that happen if she and Tetrok took the next step? Nyota breathed a silent prayer against it. A not so silent prayer, for Tetrok heard it in her mind.

"How can we quarrel when we agree on everything?" he wondered aloud.

"Please!" she said, touching her fingers to his lips as if to still them. "Don't . . . spoil it. Let's leave it where it is for now. I don't understand it, but I'm afraid to examine it too closely."

"A very unscientific viewpoint!" Tetrok teased her, taking her chin in his hand. Did he mean to kiss her? Nyota did not give him the opportunity.

"Don't ruin what we have!" she whispered, then suddenly became all business. "I'd better go. We have a briefing with our crew in less than an hour."

In little more than a month, she and Tetrok would be leading an expedition to the Sea of Ethane.

❧

It was the single most distinctive feature on the face of Titan, a cold stew of frozen elements, a virtual chemistry lab as big as Lake Superior teeming with untold riches in pure elemental form. Now that it had been proven that Earthians and Fazisians could work together in harmony, the joint venture on Titan was expanding its parameters. While Tetrok and Nyota labored on the far side of the moon harvesting the riches of the Sea, Phaestus and Zeenyl, with a select crew chosen from both species, would be expanding upon a complex and dangerous energy experiment not far from the colony.

Even as Nyota, her thoughts in turmoil, left Tetrok to return to her quarters, Phaestus and Zeenyl lay unsleeping in each other's arms.

*It won't be long now,* Phaestus thought to his bride, feeling her discontent as he had almost daily since the Earthians had arrived. *The results of Krecis' most recent tests have been promising. He will find the solution to our problem; he must!*

"How long is long, my love?" Zeenyl asked aloud. "I think working with these Earthians and their shorter life spans has made me more conscious of time. I so want to have a child!"

"And so we shall," Phaestus assured her. "But we must remain on Titan until Krecis' experiment is successful. After that, we will apply for permission to settle on Outlyer-twenty-one. Nebulaesa will be only too happy to expedite our transfer, if only to have her little sister close to her."

"It would be so simple if we did not always need the Fazrul's permission just to reproduce here!" Zeenyl lamented.

"It's intrusive, an invasion of our privacy. As if they were lurking under the bed, watching us!"

"Zeenyl . . ."

"We have tamed this environment!" she lamented, knowing it sounded like whining. "At least within the confines of the compound; it is no more hostile than any on Fazis Prime. Why can we not have our child here?"

Phaestus keyed the windowport from opaque to transparent so that they could see the roiling methane fog which was a constant beyond.

"Would you truly want to raise a child here?" he wondered. "And alone? A child needs other children to grow with or it will grow . . . strangely. I would not wish to rear my child here. On the station there are families . . ."

"All right then, how long?" Zeenyl wondered.

Phaestus activated their private holocom unit, calling up the theoretical model for the energy experiment. Begun under Krecis' administration, the small power plant harvested methane directly from the atmosphere as well as from the frozen lake beds, converting it to ethane, acetylene, and ethylene, combining it with nitrogen to create hydrogen cyanide. Expanded to full capacity, the plant not only could provide fuel for an entire fleet of transports running full-time between Titan and the outlyers, but could, with the permission of the Earth Councils, warm the entire planet. Once the errors of Fazis Fourth were guarded against—which was where Tetrok and Nyota's research in the Sea of Ethane would come in—there was no reason why Titan could not become another Fazis, another Earth, or some happy medium in between.

Working with such volatile gases was hazardous but, as the computer model showed, the risks fell within accepted parameters, and the project had received high priority from the Fazisian government. Bringing it up to full capacity would surely have its rewards.

The only reward Zeenyl and Phaestus wanted was a chance to settle somewhere where they could raise a child.

"Soon!" Phaestus assured the woman he loved, enfolding her in his embrace. "A year to complete the project, a matter of months for all the clearances to be processed. In that amount of time, Krecis' experiment will surely bear fruit, in the truest sense. Within two years, my love, I swear to you, you will have your heart's desire!''

❦

Krecis contemplated Nyota somberly once she finished speaking.

"Truly," he said after a long moment, "this is your heart's desire?''

Nyota did not have to look at Tetrok to know it was his as well.

"Yes," she said. "It's what we both want. It's the next logical step. And it will serve both our worlds.''

Krecis considered this last aspect. How much did Nyota know of the political turmoil Valton was generating on Fazis even now?

"Enough to know that the divisive factions could pose a serious threat to Xeniok's rule if they're not placated,'' she said aloud.

Krecis had not meant to leave his thoughts open, but Nyota's request had startled him, and he'd grown careless.

"What we're proposing''—Nyota took Tetrok's hand in hers; he had not spoken, but she presumed to speak for him— "would be the final proof that our two species are not alien to each other, that if we can bring into existence a child who is the best of both worlds—''

"Nyota," Krecis interrupted. "We have spent many hours together discussing our beliefs in the Almighty One—in your terms, God Almighty. Is your proposal in consonance with these beliefs?''

She hadn't foreseen this line of questioning from Krecis and was momentarily dumbfounded. Tetrok came to the rescue.

"Of course we discussed that most important issue. We concluded that we would not be violating any sacred rule.''

"I see," Krecis replied with a tinge of skepticism. Nyota, recovering from her shock, looked deeply into Krecis' eyes.

"It's a very good question, WiseOne, as usual coming from you. We have indeed discussed it and feel strongly that God, the fountain of love, would not forbid the creation of this child of love, even under these unusual circumstances.''

''Well stated, my child,'' Krecis said, as he squeezed Nyota's hand. ''And neither shall I forbid it.''

The three of them joined hands, and with melded minds offered one another the solidarity of love.

❧

''Absolutely not!'' Bydun Wong slammed the desktop emphatically. ''Are they out of their minds? Never!''

''Counselor, you knew it would be the next logical step in the process,'' Beth Listrom said evenly.

''The commander is correct,'' Crown Litigator Gulibol added. ''We all knew it would come to this.''

Thanks to the wonders of modern holocom technology, the three sat cozily around the same conference table, even though each was anywhere from millions of kilometers to multiple parsecs from the others. Those Earthers who needed regular recourse to holocom in order to get the job done had gotten over their initial phobia and eliminated the need for separate receptor plates and sometimes separate rooms in which to conduct their communications; it was possible to set the receptors down anywhere now, and hold a holo conference at arm's length.

''And why not?'' argued Beth. ''Dr. Nyota Domonique is a brilliant microbiologist. This is her field, and from what I understand about this Tetrok character—''

''Tetrok possesses the highest degree accorded Fazisian scientists and would not enter into this lightly,'' Gulibol stated firmly, coloring slightly.

''Exactly!'' Beth continued, determined not to lose Gulibol with her brusque cut-to-the-chase attitude. ''And Nyota represents the best of Earth. Besides,'' she added, hoping to lighten the mood, ''she's got cheekbones to die for, damn her!''

She only succeeded in causing a confused raised eyebrow from Gulibol at this last remark. In a sardonic aside, Beth said: ''Private joke. Tell you 'bout it later.''

''Hold it!'' Wong raged. ''You two are quibbling over the strengths of intergalactic genes and missing the whole damned point!''

Neither Beth nor Gulibol had expected this outburst. Wong

folded his hands on the tabletop, trying to compose himself before he continued.

"I have a minimal understanding of the science of this, but I do know that crossbreeding species is fraught with dangers—freaks, monstrosities, whatever we choose to call them. Not to mention that this nonsense positively smacks of miscegenation . . ."

The word rocketed through space and struck Beth's ears like a thunderclap. My God, she thought, what is he saying?

"Miscegenation?" Gulibol inquired.

"Not important." Wong quickly dismissed it. "The answer is no. An unequivocal no."

"Indeed. It is much too risky," Gulibol agreed.

Recognizing an ending when she heard one, Beth conceded. "So be it."

♐

From the time they first knew they were of one mind, Tetrok and Nyota had hounded Krecis for days.

"I agree," the old mage said. "It is the next logical step. But we are dealing with moral issues. The creation of a sentient life, the creation of a life-form which has never before existed in the universe, formed out of both species. A possible political pawn which factions on either or both of our worlds might wish to exploit."

"Only if they discovered the truth of the child's origins," Tetrok suggested.

Krecis was taken aback. He knew precisely what Tetrok was suggesting.

"My research indicates that a child so created would almost exclusively resemble the Fazisian parent, at least in appearance. Are you suggesting we disguise this theoretical child's parentage? To this I will not consent!"

"Then you have researched it," Nyota said softly, more than a little alarmed at the OldOne's fervor.

Krecis seemed surprised that she would be surprised. "Of course. It is—"

"The next logical step," she finished for him. "Then you agree with us."

Krecis chose his words carefully. "I agree that the time will come when the universe will welcome children intermixed of the best of Fazis and Earth. I do not know if that time is now. And even as I put your request forward to the Earth Council and the Fazrul . . .''

Nyota squeezed Tetrok's hand and beamed at him.

''. . . I must present all sides of the argument.''

꿈

'' 'Miscegenation'!'' Beth Listrom hissed at Bydun Wong. ''I can't believe you used that word in the context of our discussion with Gulibol!''

''What the hell are you ranting about, Listrom?'' Wong demanded.

Beth was livid. Knowing she was already on redline for insubordination, she was going to tell the boss exactly what she thought anyway. None of her superiors had ever been able to keep Beth Listrom on the safe side of the line.

''Oh, c'mon, Bydun. If you don't know, you should know!''

''Continue your lecture, Commander, but get to the point!'' Wong offered testily.

''Surely you are aware, Counselor, that the concept of miscegenation implies that a superior gene pool is 'mongrelized' by an inferior one. Gulibol is probably learning that even as we speak. And which gene pool do you think he will believe you were referring to as the superior one?''

''That's not what I meant—'' Wong defended himself.

''It is what you said,'' Beth interrupted. ''And from where I'm sitting, it sounds like you just insulted the man and his entire species!''

Wong was not about to admit that much. ''I'll clear it with Gulibol the next time I speak with him,'' he said grudgingly. ''Is there anything else, Commander?'' he said with exaggerated politeness.

''Yes,'' Beth said, ignoring the sarcasm. ''Just one more thing. It's not something I can put my finger on, sir, but . . .'' She wished the thought made more sense to her so she could explain it better. ''If you were asking me—and I know you aren't—there's something in what Nyota and they are proposing that could be to our advantage. Something to do with their esper powers combined with ours. Something . . . of possible

military value, even . . . I don't know. My recommendation
would be to at least hear them out.''

"And so we shall, Commander. Your opinion has been
noted." Even if I intend to totally disregard it! Wong thought.
"Wong out."

Beth glowered at the empty chair in her office on Jupiter-1
where Wong had been sitting only a moment before. Poor
chump! she thought. You don't know Nyota like I know Nyota. Don't be surprised if even if you say no, she goes right
ahead without you!

♄

Krecis vanished for the next several days, immersing himself
in the philosophies of both worlds and studying precedents in
both Earthian and Fazisian law for the proposal he was about
to make.

"At least he's eating," Fariya reported, monitoring the activity of his food servitor from the main computer. "But he
refuses to come out of that . . . cave of his. Does anyone know
what he does down there?"

"Has anyone but Krecis ever been down there?" Vaax
wondered. As two from the original expedition, he and Fariya
felt a proprietary interest in the OldOne's welfare.

"I think we should leave him to his privacy," Nyota suggested. She too had been surreptitiously watching the monitors
to make sure Krecis ate regularly; it was the only way any of
them could check on his activities once he sealed himself off
in his underground sanctuary. "He feels very strongly about
this, and it's courageous of him to present our case for us."

"Are you sure that's what he's doing?" Tetrok demanded.
Never in all the time he'd been on Titan had he so wished he
could countermand Krecis' authority. "He said he intended to
present a balanced argument for both sides. In short, he's remaining completely uncommitted. I cannot believe—''

"Can't you?" Nyota asked. "Then maybe you don't know
him as well as you think you do." As well as I have come to
know him, she thought but did not say.

The OldOne finally emerged from his cave less than one
sleep-cycle before the deadline both the Fazrul and the Earth
Council had set for his address to them. He looked haggard

and seemed unsteady on his feet, yet there was fire in his eyes.

"I will rest now, I think," he announced hoarsely, holding in his long fingers the few notes he would commit to memory before the holocom broadcast. "But I wanted each of you to know that when the time comes, my thoughts will be complete."

"We never doubted it—" Tetrok began, but Krecis was already gone.

∞

"We're on the tightest possible beam," Gulibol assured Bydun Wong only hours before the broadcast. "Be assured that this transmission is absolutely secured."

Wong made no secret of his relief.

"Thank God! Although, Litigator, I don't know that there's anything further to discuss. I believe you and I are both of the same mind on this issue."

"Absolutely," Gulibol agreed. "However persuasive Krecis may prove to be—and I caution you, Counselor, his powers are formidable—there is no question but that their request must categorically be denied. Or have I mistaken you? Your private conference with Commander Listrom—"

"Has not altered my position one iota. I'm with you, Litigator. Request denied: categorically."

∞

Never had this corner of the galaxy been so full of listening ears. Concerned citizens from Earth to Selenopolis to Mars to Jupiter-1, from all the Fazisian worlds and all twenty-one outlyer stations, watched transfixed as the spare, dignified figure of Krecis appeared on their two- or three-dimensional transceivers.

No mean actor, Krecis had judged his audience well. His usual everyday garb—a plain lab uniform in traditionally luxurious but unadorned Fazisian fabrics—had been replaced by the full regalia of his rank and office. Every honor and decoration he had ever received shone resplendent across his chest, and the pendant of the Order of Telespers hung about his neck. He held himself regally, and only the road map of care etched on his craggy face gave any indication of his age.

The richness of his deep, mellow voice soon drew the attention of two worlds to a focus on the neutral ground of Titan, and held it fast.

"My friends and colleagues," Krecis began simply. "You are all aware of the work we have accomplished in this place. We have informed you of our failures as well as our successes, and you are as aware as we that in science, even as in life, the only certainty is that nothing is provably certain . . ."

"This guy could have taught Barnum a thing or three!" Beth Listrom remarked.

"Quiet!" Mark McCord snapped, listening intently.

On Outlyer-21, as if in mirror image, Nebulaesa listened also, the holo image of Valton sitting beside her.

"He will argue for Tetrok's wishes; he must!" Valton announced between his teeth. "Could Xeniok's oldest friend do otherwise?"

"You're so certain," Nebulaesa said, who was less so.

Valton spread his hands in an accommodating gesture.

"Let him! The experiment will be a failure, the fetus a monstrosity which will have to be terminated, and the ill it will create between our kind and this mongrel species will be a thing wondrous to behold."

*Silence!* Nebulaesa thought, not daring to say it, as she tried to hear Krecis instead.

As it turned out, the OldOne surprised them all.

"There is much to say in favor of any scientific advancement in and of itself, but an advance which, in the long view, appears to benefit so many, while at the same time having no perceived deleterious repercussions, is a rarity indeed . . ." He spoke slowly, measuredly, assuredly; there was no external indication of the turmoil and uncertainty roiling in his mind.

He had, less than an hour before, received a personal transmission from Xeniok, a last-minute plea from his old friend—ironically, carried on a subsidiary wave just under the transmission from Gulibol to Wong:

"They hem me in from all sides, my old friend. Not since the Great Division has there been such controversy. It is not personal vanity that necessitates I maintain control, but sheer terror of what will happen if the coalitions seize it from me, vote Valton in, then self-destruct under their own internecine quarrels.''

"I understand entirely,'' Krecis replied. Well that the Ruler had evoked the specter of the Great Division of a thousand years past; it had been on his own mind as well.

"When you speak to the Fazrul and the Earth Council,'' Xeniok said earnestly, looking older than old, "you must speak for me as much as for the young ones and their wishes.''

"My dear friend, I hope to speak for us all,'' Krecis had answered, wondering even as he said it how he was to do that.

"Nevertheless,'' he said now, addressing the people of both worlds, "it is not necessary to remind the scientist that every action has an equal and opposite reaction. Consequently, there are as many reasons not to create life out of both our species as there are reasons to do so . . .''

"Oh, spare us the devil's-advocate routine!'' Beth muttered under her breath. Mark was no longer paying any attention to her at all. "We know where your real feelings lie!''

"Biological parameters indicate that there is a less than twenty percent chance that an *in vitro* embryo resulting from the fertilization of a human ovum by Fazisian sperm will not be viable,'' Krecis explained. "As this risk is no more than we might expect from either a human or a Fazisian embryo so nurtured, we deem it acceptable.''

"I told you!'' Valton hissed in Nebulaesa's ear.

"However,'' Krecis continued, "preliminary research indicates that any embryo which survives the initial phase has one chance in three of resulting in a sport or so-named 'monstrosity,' which in conscience cannot be brought to term. Are we as creators of life prepared to end such a life?''

"You were saying?'' Nebulaesa asked Valton quietly.

"Yet it can be argued that since most *in vitro* experimentation begins with no fewer than four embryos, electing only one of the four to complete gestation, this risk may also be considered acceptable.''

Nebulaesa did not have to so much as glance at Valton to know that he was smirking. Parsecs distant, so was Beth Listrom. Only a few feet away from where Krecis was speaking, Nyota reached for Tetrok's hand.

"Having thus, I trust, presented an adequate overview of

the scientific concerns," Krecis said, "I will now attempt to address the macrocosm in which this proposed microcosm would take place . . ."

Pity! Bydun Wong thought, caught up in Krecis' words in spite of himself. You're knocking yourself out for nothing, OldOne; we will not be moved!

"A child born of two species which have discovered each other as we have, possibly alone out of an empty universe, cannot but be the best of both worlds. Arguably, such a child might constitute an equation which is greater than the sum of its parts. Certainly such a child's existence may serve to strengthen the bond between our two species. However, even as no child asks to be born, much less into what manner of world it will be born, the burden lies heavy with those who give life to that child, and a child which carries the legacy of both worlds can be seen to carry twice the burden . . ."

Alone in his private chambers at his own request, Ruler Xeniok listened in admiration to his old friend's eloquence. He was strongly in favor of the experiment, but his was one voice against a multiplicity of voices in the Fazrul. Xeniok was surprised to find tears coursing down his face. Was it only because, knowing his son, he knew this hypothetical child would be his grandchild?

Using his holocom console to scan the entire conference room from which Krecis was speaking, he found Tetrok and saw too the darkly beautiful Earthian female beside him. Filled as much with wonder as with sorrow, Xeniok knew the Fazisian decision must come from the people. Then, of course, there was the Earthian decision, however that would be arrived at. He did not hold much hope for a final affirmative answer.

"Can any here today know what circumstance will bring to either of our worlds within the life span of this child?" Krecis' long hands gripped the edges of the podium from which he spoke, as if he needed something sure to cling to. "What if our species quarrel? What if the work we have done on Titan comes to naught and either or both of us are called home? Where, then, can such a child call home?"

"Good point!" Bydun Wong said aloud. Gulibol, beside him but not beside him, gave him a curious look.

"Technically the child need only achieve its twentieth year

in order to be accepted as a full Fazisian citizen . . .'' Gulibol began, but trailed off. Not that it would make the slightest bit of difference, but where was Krecis going with this argument anyway?

''Yet it can be pointed out,'' Krecis continued, his breath coming shorter now, showing the physical as well as psychic toll this proposition was taking on him, ''that children have been born in times of war and economic turmoil, in times of flood and famine and grave uncertainty, because the species must continue. How better to assure the continuance of both our species in harmony and progress than by the creation of this child?

''What we ask here today is not merely permission for yet another scientific experiment, but a chance to join our two worlds in a single living being, whom we hope to be a prototype for many such beings, the creation of a third species never heretofore known, a species for the future! Councillors, we will do the work, but the decision rests with you!''

With not a little flair for the dramatic, Krecis suddenly vanished. At his signal, all holocom from Titan had been abruptly terminated, leaving audiences in two solar systems alone with their thoughts.

''What the—'' Bydun Wong demanded, pushing comm toggles impatiently. ''Capcom, get them back! What the hell does he mean by cutting us off like that?''

''Hailing, Counselor,'' came the anonymous voice from Comm Central. ''Please stand by . . .''

The holo image came back up to reveal an empty podium; Krecis was nowhere in sight.

''Titan Central, what the hell was that all about?'' Wong demanded. He calmed down a little as Tetrok took the podium, with Nyota Domonique beside him.

''My apologies, Counselor. Krecis has said all he wishes to say. He suggests Dr. Domonique and I pursue the finer points with you and Litigator Gulibol.''

''Agreed!'' Wong and Gulibol said almost in the same breath.

The debate would go on for hours more, before all holocoms faded to black so that the two governments could reach their final conclusion. Only Krecis absented himself. Like Xeniok, he knew what the answer would be.

# CHAPTER 11

"No!?" Nyota cried, voicing the reaction of everyone on Titan. "How can they simply say no?"

Even as she asked it, she wondered how she could be so naive. She'd fought the bureaucracy for her entire career; why should this be any different? This one hurt on a personal level, though. It wasn't about science or even economics, but about ancient Earth prejudices and recent Fazisian politics. Nyota didn't know which infuriated her more.

Work went on as usual, but people seemed to have more time to congregate in the common rooms, as if seeking consolation in numbers. Now that they'd hit the glass ceiling and been told they could go just so far and no farther, it was hard to muster any real enthusiasm for the government-approved projects. Their entire purpose on Titan had been to prove that Earthians and Fazisians could reach an accord. It was beyond irony to learn that their governments could only agree to disagree with them. Suddenly everything they had accomplished seemed so unimportant, so uncertain. How long before either or both sides were called home?

"They treat us like children!" Zeenyl said crossly. "What would they do, I wonder, if we were to proceed without permission? How could they stop us? Even if they called us home, the experiment would be well under way before they could enforce the order. They can hardly 'terminate' the child once it is born. What's the worst they can do?"

"Merely terminate our careers," Phaestus suggested, calmer than his spouse, wondering how much of her distress was due to Tetrok and Nyota's hypothetical child and how much to their own. He looked to Krecis for advice. "Uncle? You have not spoken at all."

"Nor will I," Krecis answered thoughtfully. Nyota was surprised; neither Krecis nor Phaestus, who was actually his grandnephew, had ever referred to their kinship in her presence until now. "Unless and until I have something to say."

Tetrok was far less restrained. "This is all about politics. In truth, it's all about Valton. I know he influenced the Fazisian vote. Promises, bribes—he'd do anything to secure his position."

Krecis looked at him mildly. "An interesting speculation, from someone an entire solar system distant. I was not aware that the ancients' gift for transmigration had reemerged in you."

Tetrok managed to look chagrined. The uneasy silence that followed might have gone on indefinitely if Nyota hadn't cleared her throat.

"You've lost me. 'Transmigration'? What's that all about?"

"In ancient times, or perhaps only in legend, some few rare Fazisians supposedly had the ability to project their minds beyond their bodies," Krecis explained. "In your culture, you might call them saints or mystics, those who were gifted with a . . . metanoia . . . which transcended the life of ordinary mortals."

Nyota nodded, though she could not for the life of her imagine what a Fazisian might consider "ordinary."

"One might seem to be sitting here, conversing with the rest of us," Krecis continued, "but part of one's mind would be projected elsewhere, to see and hear what transpired in another part of the world or, were one to possess such a talent in our times, another part of the universe. It was said that lovers, especially, could commune with each other over great distances. The tale of Kaalath and Metilla, for example, who were separated for twenty-three years by the Gerilek War . . ."

His voice trailed off and they all pretended not to notice. Even Nyota knew by now of his undying love for his long-lost Zandra. *By war or time or distance,* she thought to the OldOne, *but not, apparently, by death.*

"Alas, no!" Krecis said aloud, recovering himself, favoring the sulking Tetrok with another of his mildly ironic glances. "My point, through all of an old one's meanderings, was to accuse our future Ruler here of spying on the opposition even at this distance. Anyone so gifted need not fear the machinations of a mere Valton.''

Only Krecis could have said it and gotten away with it. In spite of his anger, Tetrok laughed.

"We'll wear them down!" he announced. "We will continue with the approved work; perhaps we can even push their deadlines, exceed their quotas, dazzle them with our enthusiasm. Then we will resubmit our application.''

There were nods of agreement, and the work resumed.

*

"We all know it will never happen!" was what he said instead when he and Nyota and Krecis were alone. "Has any government, in any of our experience, ever reversed itself on so visible an issue?''

Nyota and Krecis shook their heads in unison.

"We are scientists! We will not be dictated to like children!" Tetrok, in the full flight of his Ruler's eloquence, was unstoppable now. "Even children are given a fairer hearing, at least on my world. This is the next logical step; it has to be attempted sometime. Are we to be denied our place in history?''

Krecis narrowed his eyes at this. "And is this not a political statement?''

"OldOne, be careful!" Tetrok warned. "It is they who have reduced the matter to the mud puddle of political considerations. It must be done, and it is we who must do it.''

Nyota had had enough. She stepped between the two towering males, her hand on each one's arm.

"Stop it, both of you! Next you'll start butting heads like a couple of bighorn sheep!''

" 'Bighorn sheep'?'' Krecis and Tetrok asked in unison.

"Yes.'' Nyota began to explain. "A species of horned mountain animal on Earth. The males have a penchant for . . . oh, never mind!

"If this is really about the search for truth,'' she told Tetrok, "then it's got to be approached calmly, rationally, and without any concern for what's going on in the smoke-filled rooms on your homeworld.''

"Smoke-filled rooms? I do not—''

"Oh, hush a minute; I'll explain later. And you—" She turned her attention to Krecis. "Is it ambivalence, WiseOne? Perhaps even fear? Or only that you're so unassailably honest you don't have the capacity to defy them or sneak around on them?"

"It is all of that," he admitted, covering her hand with his own, his eyes smiling at her. He seemed to reach a decision then. "Nevertheless, cowardice avails nothing. And as governments are not noted for their honesty, is it so great a transgression to withhold an occasional truth from them?"

❧

It was decided. They would proceed without permission, in defiance of the dictates of both their worlds and, of course, in utter secrecy. And while Krecis was and would always remain ambivalent, Tetrok and Nyota found surprising allies elsewhere.

"How will you do it?" Phaestus came to Tetrok alone, speaking in a quiet undertone in the middle of a conversation about the energy experiment barely a week after the official denial. Tetrok did not have to ask him what he meant.

"Exactly as we intended had we been given official sanction," he replied in the same tone. "An Earthian female gamete fertilized by a Fazisian's sperm with the expectation of several successful embryos, the optimum of which will be nurtured *in vitro* in a water-based nitrogen/oxygen mixture augmented with methane."

Phaestus listened solemnly, noting how Tetrok carefully managed not to mention the names of the donors.

"That's it, then? The fetus would mature entirely *in vitro*? Why not a host female to carry it to term?"

"Absolutely not." Tetrok made a negative gesture. "Why draw attention to ourselves? Far too dangerous for all concerned."

Phaestus considered this. "Not if the female were one known to desire a child of her own."

"Zeenyl," Tetrok said unnecessarily. "Did Krecis ask you to come to me?"

Now it was Phaestus's turn to make the negative gesture. "Zeenyl wants a child, our child. You are aware that my uncle has made the sterility gene his particular study.''

Tetrok nodded.

"Did you ever have cause to wonder who his subjects were?''

Tetrok considered this. Krecis' articles in the scientific journals made it clear that he was a carrier of the so-called 'sterility gene' which had been isolated only within the past two decades. It explained why he and Zandra had never had children. But Tetrok had not considered until now that the OldOne's grandnephew might also be a carrier.

"All of my uncle's research has been applied in my case,'' Phaestus explained. "Because of Zeenyl's eagerness to have a child I was only too happy to volunteer. But the results thus far have been . . . uneven.''

"Not all problems have been solved, even by Fazisians, even in these times,'' Tetrok suggested quietly.

"Indeed,'' Phaestus agreed gravely. He hesitated, steeling himself for what he was about to say next. "My uncle has one further experiment to try. If it fails, Zeenyl will in all probability require a—donor, in order to conceive. In the ancient tradition, we had thought to ask you.''

Tetrok found himself deeply moved, but Phaestus was not finished.

"But now that you and Dr. Domonique have decided to go forward with your experiment, Zeenyl and I would like to offer ourselves as the host parents. Our own desire for a child will make a good cover story.''

Unable to speak, Tetrok touched Phaestus's shoulder in a companionable gesture.

"Phaestus, I thank you,'' he said at last. "Nevertheless, for the safety of the experiment, it is probably best to nurture the fetus within the laboratory. But once it is born, it is logical that you and Zeenyl be the 'parents' of the child.''

Nyota had to blink away tears when Tetrok told her. She hugged Zeenyl and Phaestus both.

"Thank you! Thank you so much! I can't tell you how much this means to me—to us!'' she kept saying again and again, leaving her thoughts open to the warmth of theirs.

They might all have sat around for days in a self-congratulatory haze had Krecis not suggested they begin the final preparations. And so, well aware that the universe was watching but that it wasn't really paying all that much attention, the five conspirators took their chance.

⚭

In all Krecis' years on Titan, the methane clouds prevented the majestic sight of Saturn far oftener than not, yet it shone through that night. As a scientist, he could explain the precise chemical and climatic conditions that resulted in this phenomenon; as high priest, he considered it an omen.

He and Nyota stood alone before one of the colony's rare viewports inside the body of the *Dragon's Egg* and watched the Saturn-rise.

Beside him, Nyota sighed contentedly. "It's times like this that make me feel closest to God."

The statement puzzled Krecis. "Please explain. How is it possible to be closer to, or farther from, that which is all? In my studies of Earthian law, I encountered frequent references to 'religion.' " He said the word in English. "There is not even an equivalent word in Fazisian. I must admit after our dinner conversation that first evening, I am even more confused, Nyota.

"Define 'religion,' " he challenged her.

Nyota chose her words carefully. "It's a system of beliefs . . . in a god, or sometimes several gods or, some would say, several manifestations of the same god. Out of this system of beliefs evolves a moral code, a way of distinguishing good from evil and, ideally, practicing the good."

"And is it necessary to subscribe to a religion in order to practice the good?"

"Not at all. Many people live exemplary lives without subscribing to any particular faith."

" 'Faith'?"

"A belief in things unseen," Nyota supplied.

"Such as subatomic particles," Krecis suggested. "Or God."

Nyota smiled. "Now you're getting it!"

"Yet if, as Dr. Langler says, more people have died of religion than of the flu, this implies a history of . . . oppression, persecution, execution?" Krecis asked carefully, not wanting to offend. "At least, so my reading in legal matters—the frequent reiteration of a need for 'religious freedom,' for example—seems to indicate."

"Well, yes, but—"

"Is it common, then, for Earthians to kill each other in the name of the particular manifestation of God which they choose to represent their religion?"

"Well, not anymore, but—"

"And would it be acceptable to say that these manifestations are in fact aspects of the same god?"

"Krecis, I'm a scientist, not a theologian! What you're asking me—"

"Then why is it necessary to have religions?"

Nyota was completely nonplussed. "Krecis, I honestly don't know!"

They contemplated the rings of Saturn for a long moment without speaking.

"Maybe if you told me what Fazisians believe in . . ." Nyota suggested finally.

Krecis spread his hands in an eloquent gesture. "There is nothing to believe in."

His statement unaccountably upset her. "You mean you're atheists?"

Again, she had to say the word in an Earthian tongue; there was no counterpart in Fazisian. That in itself should have tipped her off to what Krecis was about to say next.

"Nyota, do you believe in air?"

"I see what you mean. God is all. God is in everything, because God is everything. It's only Earthian vanity to try to put God in a box."

"Just so." Krecis smiled. "You are becoming quite Fazisian."

As they watched, the methane clouds began to gather again, sliding across the face of Saturn, threatening to obscure the golden beauty for who knew how long—years, perhaps decades. Nyota sighed again.

"I don't suppose Fazisians believe in astrology, either?" she asked.

"Is this also a religion?" Krecis asked.

"More of a custom, a way of looking at life."

She explained the rudiments of it.

"Interesting," Krecis observed thoughtfully. "Never having considered such a possibility, I will reserve judgment," he said graciously, adding: "And which of the twelve signs is yours?"

"I was born under Capricorn," Nyota said. "And so you see, Saturn is my ruling planet. Secretly, I've always considered myself to be Saturn's child."

✍

Her seeming calm in Krecis' presence was a sham. Now that they had done what they had done, Nyota was fraught with second thoughts.

Two days earlier, she and Tetrok had provided Krecis with the necessary donor specimens. The experiment had been initiated; there was nothing to do now but wait, hope, pray. That didn't mean one didn't also worry.

Nyota retired to her quarters. Sometimes hot running water was the only cure for what ailed her. She undressed slowly, setting the Fazisian-style shower for the hottest temperature she could tolerate, touching the fragrance-release buttons set into the shower wall; the scent of Fazisian healing fragrances soon filled the room, utterly intoxicating. Setting the spray for needle-fine, Nyota stood in the steamy water for a small eternity.

Stepping out, she toweled off, wrapped herself in her favorite purple satin robe and stretched out on her green velvet–covered sleeping mat. The shower hadn't helped; her thoughts still raced at panic speed. For all the dangers she'd survived to get this far, she'd never believed the part about one's life flashing before one's eyes in times of stress, because it had never happened to her. Until now. She tried all the meditation techniques she knew. Nothing worked. Her mind kept returning to the test tube in Krecis' secret lab.

✍

For all his Fazisian training, Tetrok was no better off. Alone in his own quarters, he had had the same thought as Nyota, though the warm flowing mixture of herbal juices he preferred caressed and cleansed his body but did not soothe his thoughts.

Was he more afraid the experiment would fail or that it would
succeed? At any rate, it was too late now.

Drying himself and swathing his supple, muscular body in
a fur wrap, he decanted a goblet of berry wine, sipping it
slowly in the luxury of his overstuffed chair. Suddenly, a
strange and unfamiliar feeling enveloped him. Neither a telepathic impulse nor an effect of the wine, it was nevertheless
incredibly pleasant. Intrigued, Tetrok stared into the depths of
the wine, giving himself over to this magnificent sensation.

♄

She knew when she looked up she would see him.

What had been the blank wall of her sleeping chamber,
familiar after all the months she'd lived here, was transformed
into a long, shining corridor. Tetrok materialized before her in
brilliant light, standing there in regal majesty, his fur robe
framing his magnificent body, flowing open from his shoulders
to his toes. Nyota felt drawn to him, irresistibly.

♄

He knew when he turned she would be there. He had set down
the wine and glanced in his tiring-room mirror, to see her rise
like a goddess from the sea. Her purple robe enhanced the
chocolaty richness of her flesh; her coal-black hair and flashing
eyes attracted him as they never had before. Why had he never
seen her this way until now?

They approached each other, their robes dissolving into
nothingness; they stood transfixed, guiltlessly observing the
wonder of each other's bodies for the first time.

Nyota marveled at Tetrok's body hair, a perfect interweav-
ing of green, purple, and silver strands running down the center of his chest to a kind of natural protective thong, arching
up from there along the curve of his hips, meeting at the juncture of his round, firm buttocks. She saw too that he had no
nipples, which both fascinated and disturbed her. Some men's
nipples were as sensitive as a woman's; lacking them, was
Tetrok that much more sensitive elsewhere? Even as she pondered this, she reveled in the way his eyes devoured her.

Her skin is so smooth! he thought, grateful for once that it
remained the same luxurious color all the time; it would feel

like silk beneath his fingertips, he knew. He marveled at her lack of body hair, except for that small, alluring triangle. Hers was a perfect symmetry, a perfect geometry of Earthian beauty, and he longed to touch her. Simultaneously they reached out to touch each other's faces.

He isn't really here! Nyota thought with the small part of her brain that was still rationalizing, but it no longer mattered. She "felt" his fingers caressing her cheek, and closed her eyes and sighed. Their minds touched in greater intimacy than she had heretofore imagined.

For the briefest instant they shared a common image, the image of the minuscule embryo—no more than a cluster of cells thus far—which held both their destinies. Then their minds merged, his stronger telesper abilities engulfing every neuron in her brain. They became a living hologram, their bodies merging in virtual reality even as their brains entwined, meeting like clouds in a warm spring sky, softly, gently. Neither could tell where one ended and the other began, and neither cared.

Sounds and colors meshed and interchanged inside and outside them; angelic choirs and auroras twinkled and flashed in auras all about them while rainbows hummed and tinkled in their minds, the music both alien and familiar. At once floating blissfully in the depths of space and hurtling through the void at breakneck speed, they clung to each other, their separateness vanished; they were one.

∞

At that very moment the tiny embryo began to vibrate strangely, to radiate as if it were a tiny star. Alarmed, Krecis had to force himself to tear his eyes away from the phenomenon in order to check his readings. Strangely, everything was within normal parameters, yet the embryo continued to radiate. Krecis watched until, as suddenly as they began, the radiation and vibrations began to fade. When it was quiescent again, he transferred the embryo into the glowing globe. As Nyota and Tetrok loved, Krecis had labored.

Even to Fazisian eyes, the light was strange here. In the center of the small separate laboratory where only five scientists were authorized to enter—if anyone else in the colony knew what transpired there, it was not spoken of—infrared and ultraviolet lamps bathed a large globular container in alternating soft glows. By carefully calculated prearrangement, the lamps sometimes shut themselves off and there was no light at all.

Umbilicals branched out of the top and sides of the globe like so many vines, connected to auxiliary containers holding nutrients, vitamin supplements, and complex chemical soups calculated to ensure this embryo's optimal development. Only Krecis knew precisely what they contained. Still further connectors reached out to aerators which would provide a precise balance of nitrogen, oxygen, and methane even as they siphoned off carbon dioxide and other organic wastes. Once the embryo was "implanted" in the globe, meticulously calibrated monitors would take constant readings of its heartbeat and all autonomic functions.

A delicately balanced audio system would provide a "mother's heartbeat" for the embryo to feel, set at a rate midway between Earthian and Fazisian normal. Even the natural process of a pregnant female's everyday physical motions would be simulated by a wave machine, which would keep the amniotic fluid surrounding the embryo in constant gentle undulation. The designer of all of this, Krecis had thought of everything.

Lastly, there would be music tapes, soft pleasing sounds from the noted composers of both worlds. These were Nyota's touch.

Once he'd transferred the embryo from the test tube where it had been created into the globe, Krecis studied it through the lens of an acoustic microscope. He added one final infusion of his most refined algal preparation just before he made the transfer.

The embryo floated tranquilly in its nurturing bath, seemingly at peace with the universe. Krecis smiled. What a magnificent genesis!

♉

It was simultaneously more erotic and more exhausting—physically, mentally, and emotionally—than any corporeal sexual encounter either had ever known.

In the days that followed, both seemed to be sleepwalking. Their work in the labs and their preparation for the Sea of Ethane continued apace, but their conversation was monosyllabic, and only pertaining to the work at hand.

Neither had ever surrendered complete control before. Was it possible, Nyota wondered, that this was more embarrassing than the physical sensations they had shared? Whatever it was, neither could look the other in the eye. How were they ever going to survive the Sea of Ethane? She would take it as it came, she decided, her mind once again straying to the still-invisible protolife flourishing in Krecis' secret lab.

∞

Krecis watched his fellow conspirators with growing concern.

The decision to create the embryo had visited upon him far more ambivalence than either Tetrok or Nyota could suspect. There was, quite simply, so much to fear. Official discovery of the experiment could destroy all their reputations and careers, could send Tetrok and the child into lifelong exile, could rob him of Titan and all his work here, could damage irreparably the rapprochement between Fazis and Earth. Could the interests of pure science justify all that?

He had consented to the experiment when Tetrok and Nyota were acting upon scientific logic, but that situation had changed. Something had happened, something which had left both of them in a state of raw, fevered emotion, and neither of them would speak of it. Krecis alone was able to keep his perspective. What was he to do?

He would not, could not destroy the embryo. But he would not stand idly by while the two whose child this was passed each other like ghosts. Profoundly beset, Krecis contacted his old friend Xeniok.

The transmission in itself was not unusual. Like all his private transmissions to the Ruler since his arrival on Titan, this one was sent at the usual interval, and on the special wavelength he had designed so that no one else could access it. Only the content was a little untoward.

"Are you certain this is wise?" Xeniok asked with a frown when Krecis had made his request.

"I fear so, my lord," Krecis answered thoughtfully. "It is
time . . ."

&

Not long after, he summoned both couples to his cave. As all
five watched, the month-old embryo, no larger than an oppos-
able thumb, made tiny swimming motions in its amniotic bath.
   *See?*
   The thought-impulse came from somewhere around Nyota's
ankles. The five scientists were not the only ones present. Catlyke and Mushii, allowed the run of the colony now that they
were almost mature, housebroken, and being taught to communicate on a dolphinlike telepathic wavelength, had a tendency to follow Krecis everywhere. As soon as they'd entered
the lab, Catlyke had leapt with feline grace onto the countertop
beside the heartbeat monitor, where she could fold herself up,
groom herself with her talented fingers, and watch the proceedings at close range. Mushii, with his six short legs,
couldn't reach.
   *See!* he repeated with greater urgency, scratching at Nyota's
boots and nudging her ankle with his cold wet nose when she
didn't respond immediately. *Want see!*
   "Oh, all right, you little pest; wait a minute!" she said,
scooping him up in her arms, nuzzling his soft, silky fur, kiss-
ing the top of his head. "There now, you can see. Satisfied?"
   The creature's antennae twinkled gold at her; he was very
satisfied.
   "How soon will we know the sex?" Phaestus inquired.
While he had the basic biology background of most Fazisians,
he was primarily an engineer, and needed occasional enlight-
enment on the fine points.
   "We already do," Krecis replied with a twinkle in his eye,
a twinkle that disguised the chronic misgiving in his soul. "It
is female."
   "What shall we—" Nyota began, before she remembered
that Fazisians, like many Native Americans on Earth, did not
name their children until after birth. Besides, it was so soon.
Any number of things could go wrong in this first trimester.
   Fussing slightly, Krecis checked and double-checked all the
monitors yet again. Even when the lab was unattended, the

monitors were tied in with a pager he carried with him at all times. He alone would be in charge while the other four were gone, and he would not rest until the child was born.

Phaestus and Zeenyl would be working at the energy plant nearby, staying in the barrackslike living quarters there to save themselves the tedious process of suiting up for travel back and forth from the main compound every day. Still, they could be notified to return within a few hours should anything go wrong with the experiment which required their decision. Nyota and Tetrok, however, would be a full day's journey distant on the Sea of Ethane and, barring emergency, would not return for almost three months.

Objectively, it was all for the best. Any suspicions Valton or either government might still harbor would be dispelled as the two couples went about their assigned work far from the labs of the main compound. And surely no one would suspect Krecis, who had argued so eloquently for all sides, to be part of any conspiracy.

Ironic! Krecis thought. Had Valton remained my acolyte, he would know me better than any living being. Would that make him my ally in what we do here, or my most formidable foe?

*

Three months to the day later, Zeenyl notified her sister, Nebulaesa, of some wonderful news. Nebulaesa was not entirely surprised; the couple had sought and been granted permission from the Fazrul months before. Nebulaesa relayed the news to the proper authorities on Fazis Prime.

"So you are to be an aunt." Valton's interest was far too acute, his reaction far too immediate. Did he monitor every incoming transmission from every outlyer, Nebulaesa wondered, or only hers? "How delightful. When is the child due?"

Nebulaesa told him.

"Extraordinary," Valton observed. "Considering Phaestus's . . . special situation, Zeenyl can doubtless tell you the very moment it was conceived."

"Doubtless she can!" Nebulaesa retorted, wishing immediately that she could recall her words. Her coloring went high. Every time she spoke to Valton she was haunted by his youthful confession of love for her; it made it difficult to speak to him, much less to recall that he was her superior. She should know better by now, but her emotions betrayed her every time.

"Don't be embarrassed, B'Laesa," Valton said tenderly. "I am familiar with Krecis' reports to the journals on his work with infertility. I am aware that he and Zandra never had children, and that, as his grandnephew, Phaestus may very well carry the gene. You haven't betrayed any family secrets. Or have you forgotten that I am family too?"

"I have not forgotten," Nebulaesa answered, thinking: Though you don't know how I wish I could!

"It only seems to me," Valton said ingenuously, "that given what else has been stirring up the turgid atmosphere of Titan, your sister's pregnancy might strike one as a little too . . . coincidental, don't you think?"

"My sister has wanted a child since she and Phaestus were wed," Nebulaesa replied, by way of not replying. If she did entertain Valton's suspicious turn of mind for so much as a moment, he would be the last to know.

"The first child of ruling lineage born on Titan," Valton mused.

"Ruling lineage?" Nebulaesa echoed him. "Is that so important?"

Valton made an expansive gesture. "You are next in the ascendancy after me. Zeenyl, however reluctant she might be to even consider rulership, is next after you, and her child is included in the succession. And I have always considered Krecis' line to be of the ruling class. At any rate . . ." He broke off his musing and became all business again. "The pregnancy is quite an event. We must have holos, interviews with the fortunate couple, perhaps a commendation from the Fazrul for their efforts . . ."

"There will be ample time for that after the child is born," Nebulaesa replied before terminating the transmission.

An announcement was made to Earth authorities as well, but given little attention there. Aside from a brief "People in Space" item, news about two Fazisian citizens' private lives was not considered all that important.

☙

Later on the night that Phaestus and Zeenyl departed, Krecis visited the secret lab alone, or at least in the absence of anyone but his two familiars. The day had been spent in seeing off the crew bound for the energy plant; having farther to travel, Tetrok and Nyota and their team had already left for the Sea of Ethane two months earlier. The main colony compound, divested of nearly half its population, seemed ghostly. Was it possible that it had been this empty before the Earthians had arrived?

Krecis moved about the lab once more, checking monitors he knew to be on line, all but obsessive about the contents of the glowing globe in the midst of all this. The two creatures observed him from their vantage on the countertop—Krecis had lifted Mushii up automatically, and following a brief skirmish over who would sit where and who had the better vantage point, they had settled in beside each other, Catlyke's long twitchy tail draped sociably around Mushii's neck—picking up the distress that ran like static through his mind.

*Upset!* Mushii observed to Catlyke, his antennae sparking blue.

*Know that!* Catlyke retorted impatiently, watching the Fazisian intently; she liked to pretend her powers of observation were more acute than Mushii's, when in fact they sometimes ended at the tip of her tail.

"Indeed," Krecis said aloud, "I am upset. And if you two will kindly keep your thoughts to yourselves, I need not be further upset."

Chastened, the two creatures hunkered down, making themselves as small as possible. They watched as Krecis framed the glowing globe in his two long hands, like a soothsayer consulting an oversize crystal ball. If they listened very carefully, they could hear his thoughts.

*You are already more than the sum of your parts,* he thought to the minuscule protolife floating in its deceptively safe, warm bath. *For if you are discovered too soon to be what you are, it will mean destruction for both your parents, a tragedy for two worlds. Tetrok is nascent Ruler as much by way of genealogy as by skill, but she who is your mother will walk in natural greatness all her life . . . if. If you, and my part in creating you, do not endanger her . . .*

Krecis removed his hands from the globe, folding them into his sleeves. Well aware that the two presentient creatures were listening to him, he buried his next thoughts in the deepest recesses of his inner mind:

No one and nothing must threaten either the experiment or those who had initiated it. He was an old one who had already lived a full life. If his best work was behind him, so be it. He and he alone would accept the consequences of what happened next.

# CHAPTER 12

Cloud cover above the lakes was usually thicker than over land, but occasionally it lifted, the ubiquitous fog of rusty methane flakes clearing unexpectedly. As Tetrok and Nyota bobbed in the little hovercraft they'd set down on the surface of the super-cooled Sea, it did so. As if fate had decreed it, they were given a glimpse of Saturn and her rings. Overcoming her shyness in his presence at last, Nyota tapped at Tetrok's mind and he looked up through the porthole without speaking.

*Beautiful! Like you . . .*

"Hmmm . . ." Nyota remarked aloud, trying to keep it light. "Is that what I mean to you? Rock and dust and gas and ice? I think I've been insulted!"

*No. You are . . . home. Safe haven. A jewel in the night sky. The beginning of something wondrous. The most important person in my life.*

"I'm glad!" Nyota said, though she stopped herself from saying all of those things about him. At first she'd wondered if only she had experienced the strange, erotic encounter, but Tetrok's skittishness around her meant he had experienced it too. She was just on the verge of speaking to him about it, but could not.

This relationship continued to puzzle her, even worry her. So much of it now hinged upon what transpired in the globe inside the secret lab. If the experiment failed, if their child failed to thrive . . .

She shook her head. She contacted Krecis daily, sometimes several times a day, to make sure everything was all right. There was nothing else to do but to wait, and hope. Beside her, Tetrok felt her thoughts. He squeezed her hand. She shook her head again.

"I'm tired. Gloomy," she said, rubbing her eyes. "So's the rest of the crew. Morale's down. We've all been out on the ice too long. What say we take a few more readings and head back to camp?"

"Agreed," he said.

Despite the cryo-temperatures, there were places where the Sea was actually liquid. The phenomenon had puzzled scientists since the first Voyager readings were attempted; at that time it had been dismissed as interference from the methane in the atmosphere and faulty instrumentation. Now, however, with the pontoons of their hovercraft lapped by waves of liquid ethane, this particular group of scientists was coming to terms with the actuality.

"Nyota?" Tetrok rarely spoke her name, and never with such puzzlement in his voice. He was scowling at the sample he'd just sucked off the sea floor with one of the craft's "tentacles" and run through the analyzer. Nyota peered over his shoulder and frowned too. The readings made no sense, unless . . .

"That can't be!" she said. "Take a couple more samples, over there away from that shallow area." She pointed to the site she meant on the scanner grid. "Maybe there's a heat vent? Some kind of volcanic activity?"

"We would read that from here." Tetrok pointed to the dynoscanner, which showed no extraordinary energy flux. "I will take readings elsewhere, but that greenish substance is consistent everywhere in this area."

Green? Nyota wondered. It looked gray to her, but Fazisians did see more colors than Earthians. She watched the analyzers closely this time. No matter where Tetrok gathered his samples, the results were the same. They were reading living matter.

"Algae," Nyota said finally, when test after test had yielded the same results. "Or the closest analogue. At these temps it should be impossible. Not to mention that it's anaerobic."

"Is that so unusual? When you mentioned volcanic activity, I was mindful of similar organisms which feed on sulfur on the ocean floors of Fazis Third."

"And on Earth," Nyota concurred. "But the combination

of lack of oxygen and the low temp . . . Beats me, but there it is. We've found it. Life on Titan.''

She said it as if it were to be expected, as if it were the whole purpose of her expedition, as if it were the most exciting discovery—after Fazisians, of course—in the entire solar system. She'd save the elation and excitement for later. There were countless small details to take care of first.

''Let's collect as much of it as we can safely store, and see if we can duplicate these conditions back at base camp. If we can keep it healthy until we get it back home . . .''

It was as simple and as low-key as that. And she hadn't realized until that moment that she'd begun to think of the colony as ''home.'' Was she crazy? Had she actually thought the ESC would allow her to stay here forever? And what was she supposed to do if—when—Tetrok was called home to be the next Ruler?

Stop speculating! she told herself. This is the most important moment of your career and you're mooning over eventualities. Stop it this minute!

Except that it wasn't the most important moment of her career. That wouldn't happen until her child—her daughter—was born. And the most important discovery of her life was that she could love a Fazisian, and give him a child. Compared to that, finding life on the surface of Titan was, well, anticlimatic.

♄

Still, reports had to be filed. While everyone else at the base camp joined in spontaneous celebration—as much because they could now return to the relative luxury of the main colony and not have to spend their lives in pressure suits, Nyota suspected, as because they'd found what they'd been sent for—she contacted Krecis on her portable videophone.

As she began her report, Krecis seemed inordinately busy. He kept his back turned toward Nyota, presenting her with the disadvantage of not being able to see his face as she told him their news. He was silent for so long after she'd concluded her report that she checked the console to make certain she hadn't lost the connection.

''Interesting,'' Krecis said at last.

"Interesting?" Nyota echoed him, trying to read she knew not what into the neutrality of his voice; behind her in the cramped little temporary barracks, the team was celebrating the find with as much noise as a group of Earthians and Fazisians could make. "Is that all you've got to say?"

"For the moment," Krecis replied. "Perhaps it would be best if we discussed this further when you return. I would also ask that you tell the rest of your crew to maintain confidentiality on this discovery."

"I—I don't understand," Nyota said. "OldOne, this is possibly the biggest find on Titan since—since even your crew arrived here." Even as she said it, she wondered if that was the problem. Krecis, jealous of what the younger generation had accomplished? She dismissed the thought as unworthy even as she thought it. There would be some other, eminently logical Krecis-reason for his caution. "All right. I'll admit I don't get it, but we'll keep a lid on it until we get back."

"Excellent," Krecis said, again in that maddeningly neutral tone. "What is your ETA?"

"Tomorrow at about thirteen hundred."

She could see him nod with satisfaction. "We will await you. There is much to discuss."

"I agree. By the way, how's the—experiment?"

He had severed the connection, without so much as a sign-off. Nyota felt her heart sink into her shoes. Had something happened to the child? The second trimester had begun yesterday; having crossed that mysterious boundary, she had been falsely lulled, assumed all would go well hereafter. In the excitement over the algae, she hadn't made her daily call until now.

Nyota raised a hand to hail Krecis again, then hesitated. Was it better to know now, or to wait and hear the truth in person?

"What's wrong?" Tetrok was beside her, having sensed something from across the room and left the party of celebrants to see to her. He rested his hand on her shoulder; she cradled it against her cheek and kissed it.

"Nothing," she lied—the only time she had ever lied to him. "But I'd like to see if we can boost our departure time a little. I'm eager"—she had almost said "anxious,"—"to get back as soon as possible."

Had she known what awaited her, she might have been far more anxious.

*ↄ*

They had barely unsuited before Krecis called a meeting of what Nyota had taken to calling the Gang of Five. She hadn't expected him to summon Phaestus and Zeenyl back from the energy experiment. Whatever this was, it was deadly serious. She felt a psychic chill which had nothing to do with the room temperature.

"This . . . substance is not unknown to me," Krecis began, after the algae had been presented to him, its properties analyzed to the submolecular level and listed on the outside of the hermetically sealed containers it had been collected in. "On our very first expedition to the lakes some seventeen years ago, I discovered small amounts of it in a runoff near the main ore mine . . ."

Nyota nodded, remembering the time Tetrok had brought her there.

"I assumed it was extremely rare, surviving only because the ice had liquefied owing to volcanic activity."

"That was our first thought . . ." Nyota began, then let her voice trail off before it began to tremble. She'd tried to read something from Zeenyl or Phaestus when she'd first come into the room, but the couple's minds were as closed to her as their faces, their very skin tones. *What was wrong?*

"Now, however, I see it exists in vast quantities," Krecis finished, as if she hadn't even spoken. He looked at her solemnly. Did she only imagine great sorrow in his eyes? "Did you never wonder at the source of the nutrients I have treated you all with since you came here?"

"You said they came from a Fazisian colony world," Nyota began. "I assumed . . ." She put the entire thought together and smiled in spite of her anxiety. "OldOne, you're entirely too clever for anyone's good! So everything—the protein and vitamin supplements, all the medications—is derived from algae that you've harvested right here on Titan?"

Krecis nodded. "There is yet another laboratory below this

one, where I have conducted experiments of a private nature ever since I discovered the substance, or rather, substances, for there are several. In certain combinations, their properties are remarkable. Ingested as a high-protein nutrient, a few freeze-dried ounces can provide an adult with a full day's nutrition. Applied as a topical dressing, it heals burns and abrasions most miraculously, and provides a sterile environment for healing more serious wounds. These aspects you have experienced.''

He paused for effect. ''What you do not know is that it is impervious to extremes of heat and cold and all known forms of radiation, and that none of the bacterial or viral samples in either Earthian or Fazisian lab inventories seem to have any deleterious effect on it. I am currently working on an injectable form which can function as an anesthetic and, I believe, release the body's natural endorphins in a manner of self-healing.''

As fascinated as she was by Krecis' revelation, Nyota was not entirely mesmerized. He's temporizing! she thought. There's something more. What *isn't* he telling us?

''The knowledge that it exists in plenitude is . . . gratifying.'' Krecis almost seemed to smile. ''Yet I believe it might be wiser not to share that knowledge with our respective governments as yet. It might raise unrealistic expectations of a 'miracle cure,' even become the impetus for launching further expeditions which might draw undue attention to what we do here.''

That was it! Nyota thought, as immensely relieved at this moment as she had been terrified the previous one.

''Undue attention to the child,'' she said.

Too late, she saw Zeenyl's eyes fill with tears. Too late she saw Krecis' shoulders sag as if with a terrible burden.

''My dear Nyota,'' he said with barely controlled distress, ''our grand experiment has failed.''

☍

It didn't seem possible to grieve any more.

Inasmuch as there was anything to explain, Krecis explained.

''The fetus simply ceased to thrive. Monitors began to show imbalances in electrolytes and blood gases. Compensation was made, but further imbalances evidenced, more rapidly than could be corrected. Finally it was clear that the fetus was in distress and, as we all agreed, no heroic measures were applied. It was . . . allowed to die.''

He paused for a moment, then went on.

''Postmortem indicated a spontaneous mutation in several ribosomes.'' He pointed to them on the holo image rising out of the center of the table in their midst; while Nyota and Tetrok leaned forward to examine them closely, Phaestus and Zeenyl seemed barely to glance at the image. ''Without the ability to manufacture certain key proteins, there was no possibility of survival.'' Krecis shut down the holo. ''Apparently, with our present level of knowledge, any further attempt to hybridize our two species will meet with similar failure.''

Nyota hugged herself, keeping her voice steady. ''Then there's no way we could have anticipated this?''

Krecis made a negative gesture. ''Unfortunately, no.''

''We will want to review your findings.'' Tetrok spoke up for the first time. Did he only imagine he saw a covert look exchanged between Krecis and Zeenyl?

Krecis indicated the holo controls. ''They are, as always, accessible to you.'' He dropped the clipped neutral tone he had adopted from the beginning. ''Tetrok, Nyota, this grieves us all. Never had so much hope been invested in a single experiment, a single life—''

''We knew the risks, and now we must accept them!'' Tetrok said, too sharply. Only Nyota knew it was his way of grieving, but when she tried to meet his eyes he looked away. ''Enough! We must not meet in this way again; it draws too much attention.''

He did not wait for their acknowledgement or Krecis' permission, but stormed off, confident that in this one matter his word would be obeyed.

''Excuse me!'' Nyota also slipped away when the silence had gone on too long. She needed Tetrok, needed to be with him. Forbidden that, she needed to be alone.

It didn't seem possible to grieve any more. And because their grief must be kept to themselves, it was that much more difficult to bear. Once Zeenyl and Phaestus returned to the energy experiment, Nyota was alone.

✍

"Langler, I mean it. Leave me alone. That's an order!"

He'd come to pound on her door after she hadn't shown up for work in three days and he'd noticed it on the duty roster. She'd also refused to take his calls. He knew she wasn't ill; she'd have reported to MedSec if she were.

"I'm taking a few days off," she told him now, holding the door open just enough to speak to him, refusing to let him enter her quarters. "I think I'm entitled. In fact, I recommended it for everyone who was out on the Sea. It's no big deal; don't make it one."

Langler shifted his weight uneasily on his crippled legs. She knew he couldn't stand out here indefinitely. Her mind was completely closed to him, for possibly the first time in their precarious professional friendship. Not so her face; he could tell she'd been crying.

"Yes, I'm upset about something. No, I don't want to discuss it," she said, reading his thoughts, which he'd made more accessible. "Yes, I know it's your job as counselor to at least make the inquiry, and you've done so. Logged and appreciated. Now go away!"

"I can override you, you know," he said quietly, remarkably compassionate for once.

"But you won't," she said, mustering one of her dazzling smiles. "Will you?"

Dissatisfied, Langler left her alone. The whole thing smelled fishy. Like everyone else in the colony, he'd heard the scuttlebutt about the mysterious substance the expedition had found on the sea floor; they might have a security lid on outside contacts, but it was impossible to keep the secret here. It should be a reason for rejoicing. So why were Tetrok and Nyota both avoiding everyone else in the colony and, come to think of it, each other? Why the abrupt and unannounced return of Phaestus and Zeenyl from the energy plant, and why had all of them vanished into some secret confab with Krecis when they were barely out of their pressure suits?

Langler's esper rating was actually higher than Nyota's, but he'd never gotten as close to Krecis as she had and knew better than to try to read the OldOne. Still, he'd flourished in his time here, learning to read other Fazisian minds. He'd even put in a request for a posting on Fazis Prime, if diplomatic relations were initiated and Earthians assigned to an exchange program. Barring that, he hoped to stay on Titan indefinitely, working with both species. The Fazisians had promised him a null-grav room on either world.

So how come all the top-level minds on Titan were suddenly closed to him? What the hell was going on?

As if in answer to his question, an official holocom arrived within the hour, summoning Tetrok home.

∞

The fully crewed ship which was to escort the new Ruler home had been dispatched while Tetrok was still out on the Sea of Ethane. Tetrok contacted his father at once, demanding an explanation.

"I have held Valton off since you and the Earthians discovered each other," Xeniok said immediately. "His argument then, as his argument now, is that their presence in the system vitiates the initial purpose of your mission, and therefore there is no reason for you to remain on Titan. At this point I am forced to agree. There are other missions closer to home which can profit from your expertise."

"Father, I have said from the moment we first encountered the Earthians that contact with them was far more important than any mere exploratory expedition. At the time, you seemed to agree with me. Further, there are countless experiments under way here on Titan—"

"All of which can continue uninterrupted under Krecis' able administration," Xeniok interrupted, not addressing the whole of his son's objections. "You are needed elsewhere."

I am needed, Tetrok thought, to appear on Fazis as often as possible in order to keep Valton and his factions at bay! This is not about my work as a scientist, but my role as someday Ruler! It could be another half-age before I rule. What is the urgency?

"As Ruler, you can override the head of the Offworld Services," he said to his father.

"So I can," Xeniok acknowledged. "But then Valton can go to the Fazrul and request a hearing. It's messy and counterproductive. Besides, I concur with Valton. I wish you to return to Fazis.''

This caught Tetrok completely off guard. There was more to this than Xeniok could tell him on holocom. Besides, with the experiment failed, the child dead, how could he stay on Titan any longer?

Tetrok set his jaw. "I might have been informed before the ship was sent."

"Would that have caused you to decide differently?"

Tetrok didn't want to answer that, though the play of colors on his face did so for him. While he knew that the incoming ship would also bring needed matériel and replacement personnel for those on Titan who wished to return home, its principal purpose was to escort him back to Fazis. He felt coerced. All the same, to refuse would be self-indulgent, and Fazisians were not fond of self-indulgent Rulers.

And above all else, Tetrok wanted to be Ruler.

"Where is the ship now?" Tetrok asked Xeniok. His father must know none of what transpired in his mind—not his reluctance to leave Titan, not his relationship with Nyota, most certainly not what had transpired in the secret lab against two worlds' strict orders. However tragic the event, perhaps it was meant to be. Tetrok was no philosopher, nor was he interested in telling his troubles to a therapist. Work had always been his therapy; it would not fail him now.

"Approaching Outlyer-seven," Xeniok informed him, his canny face showing a bleak approval of his son's unspoken decision. "ETA Titan in thirty-six orbits."

Tetrok accepted the inevitable. "I will be prepared."

♄

I have failed! Tetrok thought. In all respects.

There was no one nearby to hear his thoughts. Like Nyota, he kept to himself whenever he was not working, trying to come to terms with the coldness clutching his heart. He did not blame himself for the failure of the experiment; Krecis had said it was unavoidable. But was it? Tetrok had examined the records again and again, looking for something he might have missed, some molecular signpost which might have warned him not to risk this. Was he not at least partially to blame for not seeing it?

Certainly he was entirely to blame for the headstrong attitude which had made him insist they go forward in spite of the prohibition. Had the experiment been discovered before its time, four other people would have suffered the consequences with him. Tetrok knew only too well the fate of Fazisians who violated this particular law; how dare he expose his loyal comrades to the risk of lifelong exile? As for Nyota . . .

As for Nyota, he doubted her government's penalties would have been so severe, yet how dared he endanger the woman he loved? Was it because he did not truly love her?

The coldness penetrated Tetrok's heart. What was he to do now? He had said he would return to Fazis; he had not said alone. By what right could he ask Nyota to surrender her career and her homeworld, to go with him?

By what right had he presumed to fall in love with her at all?

If the child had lived, would he even be having these doubts?

☞

They continued to work together for the time remaining—side by side, often elbow to elbow, rarely speaking unless it related to the work at hand, two ships passing in the night. Nyota wondered how much longer she could bear it. It was as if, in closing off his mind to her, Tetrok had rejected her as much as the fetus had rejected its chance at life. Or so it seemed to her as the days lengthened out and the silences grew heavier.

Did she think it would have ended any other way? How had she presumed to fall in love with a man who first and foremost was a Ruler, and who could not risk that destiny to choose an Earthian woman? She tried to envision herself beside him as he ruled Fazis, and could not. Was it only because he'd never given her a chance? Not until now had she realized how cold Fazisians, like their climate, could truly be. Tetrok's eyes, meeting hers as he handed her a sample or a data-cube, were the eyes of a stranger.

She wanted to speak to him, shout at him, plead with him to talk to her, reach into his mind and pull his thoughts out, restore the precious intimacy they had shared, which she would never share with another. Instead, as stubborn as he, she let her silence lengthen into his.

She also contacted the ESC and requested a transfer.

✍

"OldOne, I'm sorry, but I can't honor your request on this. It's too important. My world needs to know."

Given all the secrets he'd been harboring, Krecis had to acquiesce to her on this one. It hadn't been difficult to persuade Tetrok, but Nyota was adamant.

"We're looking at a wonder drug," she insisted. Tetrok said nothing. "There are countless applications for something like this, Krecis. We can't just let it sit here."

"I disagree," Tetrok said, his voice as quiet as hers but with an edge to it of—what? Anger? At least immovable stubbornness. Nyota could not meet his eyes. "OldOne, I will abide by your request for now. No one on Fazis will hear of this."

"Until you need it as your trump card against Valton!" Nyota hadn't meant to say it aloud. What difference did it make? She'd been thinking it, leaving her thoughts open to him; if he hadn't been so damnably stubborn he could have heard it there. Still, she covered her mouth with the back of her hand, as if she could recall the words.

The look Tetrok gave her was frosty. "Perhaps so."

Silently Krecis watched the uneasy interplay between them before giving his attention to Tetrok.

"Ultimately you will do as you choose. It matters little to us, who have recourse to Garpozin and related healing agents. My thought was to give Earth a year or more in which to utilize a resource they require far more than we."

"Toying with the fate of worlds, OldOne?" Tetrok's tone was bitter. "That isn't usually your style."

"Nor is cynicism yours," Krecis countered.

"As you will!" Tetrok said at last, as if the whole discussion wearied him. Again, he seemed to have difficulty remaining in Nyota's presence overlong.

"I've put in a request for a transfer," she told Krecis breathlessly after Tetrok was gone. "My thinking is that if the ESC doesn't want to send a shuttle, I can modify one of your fusion engines to boost the *Egg*'s aux shuttle and fly back to Jupiter-one on my own. There are a few Earthers who'll want to go with me while the rest stay here. It shouldn't take but a couple of months.

"The algae need to be tested under Earth-normal conditions," she urged, "under as many different environments and variants as we can devise. My people need this, Krecis." She hesitated. "I need it."

The OldOne did not speak. Given what else had been taken from her, could he deny her this? She was of Earth; he had no authority over her in any case.

"Let me—" Nyota's voice faltered as she fought back tears. "Let me try to salvage something from this . . . situation, please?"

Krecis nodded, accepting.

∽

Dr. Nyota Domonique and Major Copeland, along with the handful of Earthians who'd never felt comfortable with Fazisians, and a few who had obligations to return to on Earth or Mars or Selenopolis, were to depart Titan in a longrange shuttle hybridized from the most compatible elements of Fazisian and Earthian technology. It didn't seem possible to Nyota that this little ship, barely big enough for the fifteen people aboard her, could make better time to Earth than the *Dragon's Egg*.

"Believe it, Commander!" Luke Choy assured her, running his hand over the helm controls admiringly like a kid with his first car. "I wish I were driving her home, but looks like I've got my work cut out for me here."

Following a recommendation from Krecis, the ESC had appointed Choy provisional commander of the Earthians on Titan in Nyota Domonique's place. Bydun Wong had admitted it was an unusual move.

"He's very young, and not a little green," he told Nyota in a private holocom. "Still, he does have a degree in space law, from what you tell me he gets along with everyone in the colony, and Krecis can't speak too highly of him."

"And his grandfather is head of the consortium that built the *Egg*," Nyota pointed out unnecessarily.

Bydun Wong cleared his throat and refused to answer.

"Besides, Langler's staying on to keep his nose clean. And I hear he's got a girl," she'd added. "Choy, I mean."

It wasn't anything official, but Luke Choy seemed to spend all of his free time with a Fazisian woman named Arikka. She was one of the youngest Fazisians on Titan, and supervised the automated mine trams. On her free days, she and Choy would go off into the hills in a flyer or spend hours playing virtual reality games. If anyone had ordered Luke back to Earth he'd have been heartbroken.

"You're awfully young to be given this much responsibility, mister," Nyota lectured him, as they made the transition. "Don't let it go to your head."

"No danger of that!" Luke assured her, grinning at the whole thing. "Krecis has promised to be my mentor. Anything I lack in experience, he's got ten times as much."

Nyota marveled at the pairing. Krecis was an innate nurturer, and had taken the young Earthian under his wing as if it were the most ordinary thing. What was odd was the way Luke, usually such a smartass, fairly idolized the OldOne.

"I don't think there's anything he doesn't know about!" he told Nyota, sheer awe in his voice. "Since I started out giving him the lowdown on Earth law, I swear he knows more than I do. I'm beginning to think he's lived forever. He looks like Merlin; maybe he really is."

"Whatever!" Nyota had shaken her head in amazement. "As long as it works!"

Frank Langler's reasons for staying were somewhat different.

"The truly wonderful thing is the telesper work I'm doing here," he'd told Nyota only the night before. There was a fire in his eyes she'd never seen before. "You know what it's like to be one of the top espers on Earth, and I'm even better at it than you."

Nyota simply nodded. It wasn't an ego thing with Langler, just a statement of fact.

"There's no challenge," he was saying, almost talking to himself. "You spend half your life damping down your thoughts so you don't scare people. Here, among Fazisians, I'm only a beginner. I can spend the rest of my life learning."

"What else, Frank?" Nyota asked, knowing him too well by now to think there was ever a simple answer. He looked down at his near-useless legs before he answered.

"I'll never be able to function in normal g again. The gravity here is almost light enough to where I'm not exhausted just sitting upright. There's talk of my visiting Fazis someday, if relations between our worlds continue in this vein. They have the technology to keep me floating free, so I can be with people, live in cities again . . ."

He didn't finish his thought, didn't have to. Nyota nodded, glad he was staying behind.

She had to bring the algae with her now. It would be her future, maybe her ticket to return to Titan someday, if she ever got over the memories; possibly, like Langler, she would be invited to visit Fazis too. For now, she owed it to her people and the Fazisians to research this phenomenon for the sake of both their futures.

✍

How did you watch a part of yourself climb into a Fazisian ship and depart for another solar system, most likely never to return? Even as she did it, Nyota didn't know the answer. She watched the departure monitors through a haze of silent tears, going over and over last night's conversation in her mind.

At least Tetrok had come to see her before he left. Was she supposed to be grateful? She wanted to be angry but could not.

"It was all just a ploy, wasn't it?" she challenged him before he could even speak. Let him take the full brunt of her anger; she had nothing left to lose. "Find the most likely Earthian female, father a child by her, bring them both back to Fazis as some sort of triumph—"

"Nyota . . ."

"Buy yourself an alliance through marriage. We used to do that in medieval times, when women were chattel, something to barter with—don't you touch me!"

He had meant to take her shoulders, stroke her cheek, try to gentle her; her voice flung him back more effectively than a blow.

"All you wanted was to accomplish something no Fazisian

had ever done before, blow Valton and his factions right out of the water. There was no love in you at all!''

''Wasn't there?'' he said, when finally she was silent.

She flew at him—she thought, to pound him with her fists, spend her anger against his strength and that infuriating stoicism. Instead she found herself clinging to him, sobbing against his chest.

''I'll never love anyone else the way I loved—the way I love you,'' she whispered, surprising herself as she said it. ''Damn you; why did I ever let you touch my mind?''

He cradled her head against his shoulder. ''For the same reason I let you touch mine? Because we are incomplete without each other?''

She looked up at him. His eyes were familiar again and—she had never seen a Fazisian weep, had not until this moment even known if they could—tinged with tears.

''Are we? Then how can you return to Fazis without me?''

''In the same way you can return to Earth without me.'' He took her chin in his hand, kissed her brow, left his mind open to her in soft, wordless embrace. ''Because we must. Because we are leaders among our people who must labor—separately, for now—to bring them together. We thought to do that with the child. Now we must find other ways.''

Tears coursed down her face; she barely felt them.

''Don't promise me anything!'' she said. ''I couldn't bear to have you tell me—''

''Tell you what? That there will never be anyone else? That I will live for, labor for the day when we can be together again? Very well, then; I won't tell you any of that at all.''

They had parted on that note. She watched the monitors until the ship was out of range. And several days later a hybrid longrange shuttle shot out of the light gravity of Titan like a bird in flight, heading first for Jupiter-1 and, ultimately, for Earth.

☙

Some days later, far into the colony's night—not that it mattered anymore to the old mage, whose days and nights were as intermixed as those on the methane-clouded surface of this world that had been his home for all these many years—Krecis

entered the no longer secret laboratory where he had nurtured
the remarkable algae since he'd first discovered it. Certain he
was alone—he had not even brought his familiars, Catlyke and
Mushii, with him, to their vociferous objections—he touched
the palm of his hand to a place on the far wall of the subterranean cavern. To the unpracticed eye it was no more than the
rough-hewn surface of indigenous Titan rock. Doubtless every
Fazisian in the colony could declaim at length upon its min-
eralogical composition, down to the last fleck of mica schist.
And yet, it moved.

The seemingly solid rock slid away slowly, revealing Krecis' last secret.

This innermost chamber was lit by a strange but familiar
light, the light of infrared and UV lamps gently bathing a
wombsized orb suspended in a movable frame which mimicked the motions of a pregnant woman as she walked, sat,
breathed, slept, woke to move again. Within, a five-month fetus floated languidly, flourishing.

# Chapter 13

*The very first thing she remembered was his face.*

*"It is not unusual for a Fazisian child to recall the details even of her own birth," Krecis would tell her when she was old enough to ask, old enough to understand. "But given the unusual events surrounding your birth, it is perhaps best that this wrinkled visage is your first memory. Surely it taught you to fear nothing else."*

*Saturna would laugh because she knew he wanted her to, but always with a sadness around her eyes.*

*"Don't say you're ugly, Krecis-mine. To me you will always be among the most beautiful of men!"*

*Krecis would touch the feathery brightness of her hair. "That is only because you are young yet."*

*Did the memory of his face extend back to the moment of her birth? Surely her first awareness had come not long thereafter, for his face, his presence were her entire world then. His gentle hands ministered to all her needs—feeding, bathing, comforting; his resonant voice provided knowledge, explanations. He spoke to her as if to an adult, providing answers to all her questions, even the unspoken ones, reciting odd bits of poetry, occasionally even singing. His mind wrapped around hers like a blanket—not intrusive; there were very rigid protocols involving unschooled minds—but sheltering, safe-keeping. His spare body became her refuge, holding her close as she slept, being there for her when she woke.*

*As the oldest child on Titan (encouraged, perhaps, by her birth, three other women had birthed within the year, several more thereafter), she had ample time to observe the usual course of family life. She had also seen holovids depicting family life. She knew that children had parents—a mother, a father. Often these parents lived apart temporarily or per-*

*manently, and all the children but she eventually left Titan for Fazis or one of the outlyers, but each of them had two people who could be designated "my mother, my father."*

*Krecis had told her quite clearly that he was not her father. Grandfather? she had asked then, knowing one child of Titan who had been sent to live with grandparents on Fazis Second while his parents remained behind, and thinking with her child's mind that perhaps her case had been the opposite. No, Krecis had told her. Say, if you will, that I am your great-uncle. To be simpler, and because it pleases me, call me Krecis.*

*From that point on, she did; adding her own possessive, he became "Krecis-mine."*

*She never knew her parents. Sometimes as she grew older and the adults in the colony forgot how well she, gliding silently among them, could hear with ears and mind, she would catch stray bits of information about them. Apparently, they'd been something like heroes.*

✍

"It's for the best, believe me." It was Zeenyl who offered Krecis comfort, contacting him by holocom daily from the energy plant. "Whatever the short-term consequences, history will thank us."

"Though Tetrok may not," Krecis suggested.

"Dear WiseOne," Zeenyl comforted him, "you know full well how headstrong Tetrok and Nyota are. They would have revealed the truth as soon as the child was born. And you also know full well how devastating that revelation would have been to them *and* the child."

Krecis knew all of this. It was why he had done what he had. Only in the small hours of the morning—he'd forgotten what it was to sleep—did what he had done knock against his skull and whisper terror.

"I should not have implicated you and your spouse," he told Zeenyl now.

"How else?" the determined young woman demanded. "The child needed surrogate parents to hide her true identity, and it is well known that Phaestus and I wanted a child. Now all of Fazis knows it, and Nebulaesa pesters me constantly, insisting I return to the station to give birth. She has even threatened to get an official order from Valton, lest her niece suffer some unspecified danger from being born in this hostile environment. Obviously I cannot risk being seen by her. Am I to suffer a convenient 'miscarriage' this close to term? How will you explain the child's existence then? Or do you propose to hide her until she reaches adulthood?''

Krecis had no answer to any of this.

''Phaestus and I considered the possible complications from the onset,'' Zeenyl went on, trying to reassure the OldOne. ''I will admit, keeping the truth from Nyota was . . . difficult. We neglected to comprehend how truly sensitive these Earthians are. I doubt she will ever recover from the 'death' of her child.''

''She is a scientist,'' Krecis countered. ''She knew the risks.''

''Now you sound like Tetrok.'' Zeenyl realized too late how harsh this sounded. ''Am I not a scientist too? OldOne, forgive me, but we must see this through, now more than ever. It has even been suggested I step down from the ethane experiment because of the dangers, in my 'condition.' ''

She had perpetrated the ruse to the nth degree, wearing loose clothing to accommodate her ''pregnancy.'' Fazisian women carried smaller than Earthians, but as far as Zeenyl's co-workers could see, she was indeed quite happily pregnant.

''Who would presume to make such a suggestion?'' Krecis asked mildly, knowing how strong-willed Zeenyl could be. Further, no one else involved in the energy experiment outranked her.

''Phaestus,'' she said. ''No one else would dare.''

''Then perhaps for the sake of domestic harmony, you should take him up on his suggestion,'' Krecis said. ''How soon before you have full power on line?''

''The engineers are running the final models through now. We'll fire up the mains in a matter of minutes.''

Krecis continued to labor over the enigma of the infertility gene. He was close, so close. He knew he must publish soon to cover Zeenyl's pregnancy before Tetrok and Nyota questioned the discrepancy in the timing of her ''delivery.'' Likewise, there were only a few plausible months to play with in which to cover the double deception.

As the days grew into weeks and the weeks into months, Krecis contemplated the flourishing fetus in her glowing globe, adding carefully calculated amounts of Titan algae to the nutrients feeding into the synthetic umbilical cord. Catlyke and Mushii, having long since grown bored with the object of the OldOne's obsession, lay curled together on his reading chair. Until the creature in the globe was as telepathically evolved as they, there was no point in expressing the slightest interest.

It was Catlyke who felt it first. Wild-eyed, she leapt out of a sound sleep, every hair on end, and flew across the room, digging her strong fingers deep into Krecis' shoulder, tugging frantically at his hair. The OldOne winced, but did not drop the nutrient bottle.

"What—" he demanded, but the creature's primeval terror overrode his words.

*DANGER!!!*

He was unhooking her grip, petting her to try to calm her, when the tremor shook the room.

In fact, it shook the entire compound. Alarms shrilled; the sounds of hurrying feet greeted Krecis as he reached the corridor, the two animals at his heels. He knew, everyone knew, what had happened.

"The energy experiment," Vaax announced unnecessarily, headset at his ear, even as Krecis crossed the threshold of central control. "The power plant . . . We can't raise them . . . Seismic readings indicate a deep-core implosion . . .

"It's gone," Vaax finally reported directly to Krecis, a stunned expression on his face; he put the headset down. "Wide-band indicates nothing but burning debris. If anyone's alive, there's too much radioactivity to tell from here. The auxiliary power reactors must have blown up too!"

Stricken, Krecis hurried to go with the rescue crews. No one tried to stop him.

Unattended in his secret lab, the substitute for the sterility gene took.

∞

They found Zeenyl at the outermost edges of the debris. She had been farthest from the core when it imploded, monitoring readouts from the shielded control center by her husband's dictate. Though they were of equal rank, his wishes had prevailed this time.

"For the child's sake," was all he said, and Zeenyl had acquiesced. The others, had they lived, would have remarked on the tenderness with which the two had cared for each other and the unborn.

But the others were gone. Phaestus, all of them, vaporized in an instant when some imbalance in the ethane/methane flow—it would take months to run the data through again and again to determine exact causes—had flared over redline and started the chain reaction. In nanoseconds—Zeenyl could not so much as draw breath enough to warn them—it was over, and not enough left to claim, to scrape off fragments of shattered walls or twisted metal for a memorial service. Earthians, notified of the tragedy, would think of the permanent shadows on the walls at Hiroshima, immortalizations of what had once been living beings.

But Zeenyl, five levels above the core, had been thrown clear, partly buried under the clear-steel shell of the command center; the thickness of the metal, added to the irregular waves of radiation, had confused the rescue party's readings until one of them almost stepped on her. A fragile pocket of atmosphere had been trapped as well to allow for her shallow breathing; she was hypothermic, comatose, barely alive.

It was Krecis who with trembling hands swathed her in an enviro-cocoon to stabilize her until they reached the compound, Krecis who picked her up bodily, cradling her gently as he carried her to the rescue pod.

☞

"Krecis, why am I different?" she had asked him when she was very young.

Zeenyl had always been set apart from the two boys and her sister, not only by age but by temperament. Quieter, less impulsive, more observant, she was also, according to the skill scans which had shown Valton to have superior telesper abilities, virtually psi-null. She could shield, she could receive from a highly trained telepath, but she could barely send at all.

Many Fazisians were equally limited; it was not considered a flaw, merely a variation, as being tone-deaf or color-blind might be on Earth, and such individuals frequently showed superior abilities in other areas. But, already disadvantaged by the triumvirate's being older and more vociferous, Zeenyl was troubled by it.

"Each of us is unique, Zeenyl . . ." Krecis had begun, only to be stopped by those knowing child's eyes; she was too intelligent to be placated by a doting adult's alibi. "I think— and this is simply one Fazisian's opinion—that your mind is closed to the rest of us because you were meant to keep important secrets."

Krecis did not know where that thought had come from, but it satisfied the child.

"I like that!" she responded with a quiet smile, then pulled her minuscule compscreen, her constant companion, out of the pocket her father had designed in her overtunic especially for her. "Will you help me with my calculus?"

"Only until such time as you can help me," Krecis answered.

☙

Important secrets indeed! Krecis thought bitterly, clearing the med section as he laid Zeenyl's ruined body out on the table beneath the monitors.

"I will see to her!" he told the colony's official healer, dismissing her abruptly.

"She will not live," the healer was constrained to tell him. Something about the readings, quite aside from the gravity of Zeenyl's injuries, had made her frown.

"I am aware of that," Krecis replied grimly, activating the sterifield, rolling up his sleeves, locking down his emotions; this was Zeenyl, his little one, as much his child as any of the four had been. "I cannot save her, none can. But this is about more than her life . . ."

Once again the healer frowned. Krecis had medical credentials, and most Fazisian women could deliver their own children if need be, but Zeenyl had allowed only Krecis to examine her from the onset of this pregnancy. The healer was Fazisian, hence above such petty emotions as wounded pride, yet something about this situation had disturbed her from the beginning. If only, she thought, she had the authority to override Krecis . . . but she did not. She dared not.

"Her epidermal tissue is profoundly contaminated," she said in parting, already surrendering the field. "You'll want to take precautions."

"All the more reason why, as I am already affected, I wish to spare anyone else the danger," Krecis said tightly. Zeenyl's skin was beginning to slough off in places like third-degree burns; careless handling could cause radiation sickness in anyone treating her. "If you will allow an old one the freedom to work . . ."

Dissatisfied, the healer left, though as an afterthought she left the room's recording monitors on; she would review their findings later.

Krecis had assumed she would. He left the audio untouched but, with magician's fingers, arranged for a timed malfunction on the visual. It would result in a gap of several moments before the backups kicked in. It would be all he needed.

Only a Fazisian could think so clearly in the midst of chaos and disaster.

Zeenyl came to consciousness only once. Oblivious of the condition of her now almost fleshless fingers, she seized Krecis' hand.

"The child . . ." she gurgled, struggling to be heard, her breath bubbling from damaged lungs. She was still aware enough to know that the room was monitored, and would keep to their conspiracy with her last breath. "My child . . . You . . . only you . . . will rear her . . . as yours, Great-uncle."

"I will," Krecis vowed, covering her hand with his own, more so she could see than feel it; there was no sensation in those blood-slicked fingers. He willed himself not to imagine the prickle of isotopes invading through his pores, knew he would be severely ill later, when he could spare the time. He knew Zeenyl's will, and Phaestus's, contained a clause naming him guardian, but should Nebulaesa contest it, claiming right as next of kin, who would be cold-blooded enough to override a dying woman's wish?

Zeenyl managed a tremulous smile before she lapsed into merciful unconsciousness, from which she would not awake. Krecis barely paused before busying himself with the only life he could save.

Even as the video monitor winked out, the audio recorded the bleep and pulse of respirators, the squeal of a heart-rate monitor on redline, and a thin but lusty indignant wail.

Saturn's child was born!

⌘

He called her Saturna, a glowing tribute to the mother planet as named by the Earthians. Nyota, he was sure, would be pleased, and Tetrok would concur. It pained him that they would never have the opportunity to agree.

He would never have wished for the tragedy that obscured the true circumstances of her birth. Nevertheless, as time passed, Krecis realized how fortunate he had been.

The destruction of the energy plant prompted continuous investigation, reports to and from Outlyer-21 and Fazis Prime, a cautious notification of the ESC on Earth; fortunately for the sake of interplanetary relations, there had been no Earthians working on the energy experiment.

Had Tetrok asked him directly, Krecis would have told him the child was Zeenyl's, which under the terms of foster parentage was true enough. In an extraordinary twist of fate, the fertility experiments had begun to show positive results; Krecis had been at work on a monograph for the scientific journals the very day Zeenyl died. If necessary, he would make some reference to the success of his research, and out of respect for the dead, surely Tetrok would not inquire further.

But Tetrok did not ask.

Tetrok was still in space, while on Fazis Prime, the news of Krecis' medical breakthrough was all Fazisians could speak of. And to think Krecis' own great-nephew was the first successful recipient. Tetrok felt a wrench of pain and envy as he read the holocom. Yet he could only feel joy for Phaestus and Zeenyl. They, who would have raised his child, would now not be denied their very own.

Nyota, too, was still in space when she got the news. Her hybrid shuttle was tethered in Jupiter-1's repair dock for three months, being tuned up by admiring Earth engineers. Although she realized Krecis' success with fertility genes would be a great boon to people on both Fazis and Earth, she could not help but feel ambivalent about Zeenyl's good fortune. Would Zeenyl have put off getting pregnant now . . . had the experiment been successful, she wondered. Probably, she was that kind of woman, Nyota decided.

"You look like hell," Beth had greeted her, skipping the wine with dinner and ordering them both a double vodka. "Want to talk about it?"

"I'm tired, Beth; I'm just so tired," was all Nyota would say as they touched glasses in a wistful toast.

"Maybe you'll perk up by the time you get home," Beth said.

Home? Nyota thought ironically. Where was home?

"Maybe," she said, just to close the topic. "The discovery of these algae is an extraordinary piece of luck and I want to give it my full attention, but right now I'm just tired."

Beth nodded, humoring her, knowing better. "Who was he?" she asked, as only an old friend could.

Nyota began to cry. Eventually she would tell Beth about everything. Everything except the child.

By the time Tetrok and Nyota reached their home planets, news of the tragedy had been announced. Their grief for their friends was palpable, relieved only by the news of the survival of Zeena's child. The irony was not lost on either.

She was almost as big as if she'd gone to term; her vital signs were optimal, with no trace of the radiation sickness which might have been expected, given the supposed circumstances of her birth. Krecis himself had been less fortunate. Despite an immediate injection of a megadose of an algae-based serum he had not even had time to test completely, he was rewarded with several days of vomiting and a severe skin rash for trying to prolong Zeenyl's life.

"Will you be all right?" the healer had asked, even as she suited up for the journey to the energy plant; she had offered him standard counteragents, but he refused, treating himself with infusions of the mysterious substances he developed in his private lab until the vomiting stopped. The healer sometimes wondered if her presence was extraneous. "It disturbs me to think of you relying solely on those witches' brews of yours.''

"As I am responsible for the child, I shall have to be,'' Krecis replied, dabbing at his lips with a sterile cloth as he emerged from the toilet, his skin a uniform ashy gray, and that was that. Before the healer returned from the energy plant, he would be entirely restored to health.

&

The child was beautiful.

All Fazisian children are beautiful, but Saturna was Saturna. Ill as he was at first, Krecis could not take his eyes off her, would not even set her down in the soft cradle he had specially designed, but carried her everywhere, in his arms when he was strong enough and his hands unoccupied, in a sling against his chest the rest of the time. She slept tucked in the crook of his arm at night, so that at the first whimper he could soothe her with words and warm milk. Fazisian men were as nurturing as their women, and Krecis doted on his charge. No one in the colony disapproved.

"Perhaps it was not a mate he needed after all,'' Fariya was heard to observe. "At last he has found someone to set beside Zandra in his heart.''

Eventually Saturna would totally claim his heart. As with most things of great value, this would come at a great price.

For now, he had only to contend with Nebulaesa.

&

"With all due respect, my dear Krecis, it isn't healthy. She should be here, with her next of kin, with other children. We have tutors, a nursery, everything she could possibly need.''

"I will provide her with everything she needs,'' Krecis replied quietly.

Nebulaesa was struck by an image out of her own childhood, of Krecis' special attentions to each of them, her cousins and her sister. She had especially cherished their telesper training.

"Let me, Krecis! Oh, let me!'' she would plead every time he asked for a volunteer for a particularly difficult puzzle. He would nod his permission and she would concentrate her entire

mind, trying to ignore Tetrok, who with his usual indifference
to competition merely sat back and watched her struggle. She
would forget all about Valton, until he solved the problem a
split second before her.

"It's a *flibbiflit*!" he would announce, triumphantly, of the
image Krecis was holding in his inner mind, to see if Nebulaesa could find it. "Specifically a blue one with yellow wings.
The left-hand—no, the right-hand—wing is torn from being
blown against a crown-thorn bush. You saw it this morning
during your presun walk."

Nebulaesa's face would crumple in disappointment.
"You're a bully, Valton! That wasn't necessary! Krecis, I saw
it too, only I thought it was the right-hand wing that was torn.
I only didn't have a chance to speak."

"I know," the WiseOne said, his gaze leveled on Valton,
who did not look away. "It was the right-hand wing. I held
two images in my mind, Valton; you found the easier one,
Nebulaesa the truer one."

If Valton was as disappointed as Nebulaesa, he showed it
less. Tetrok, watching, suppressed a sigh.

"Your cousin thinks he is doing you a service by goading
you to quicker performance," Krecis had suggested to Nebulaesa. "He does not count the cost to himself."

♄

What a race they'd run the WiseOne after all! Nebulaesa
thought now. How he tried to balance the equation, compensate for their flaws and spoiled, self-indulgent little person-
ages! Was it healthy for them to have grown up as they did?
Would it do the child harm to be reared in a more tranquil
environment, with the best of teachers? If she was as intro-
spective as her mother, Zeenyl, perhaps so. Nevertheless . . .

"Can you provide her with a sky full of stars?" Nebulaesa
demanded, and the question stung. The sky surrounded Out-
lyer-21; there was no view outward that did not contain stars
and even galaxies by the handful. On Titan, an occasional
glimpse of Saturn's rings through rusty methane fog was the
only view.

"Not at this time," Krecis admitted. "But given your indulgence, I can honor her mother's wish."

Nebulaesa tapped the holocom console uneasily, forgetting that Krecis could see her. In truth, she dreaded the thought of turning the child over to Valton, or of having to raise her herself. But there was something here she could not put her finger on, something that made her uneasier still.

"You'll not deny me visitation rights," she said.

Krecis spread his hands magnanimously; the child, having been held up to display for her aunt on holocom, had with a newborn's disdain for official proceedings grown bored, and slumbered in the sling on Krecis' chest, her thumb in her mouth and her forefinger rhythmically rubbing her small nose.

"Of course not, my dear Nebulaesa. Come to Titan whenever you wish, stay as long as you like as my guest. The child needs to know her kin. But by her mother's wishes, and as Phaestus was my nephew, I will raise her here."

⌗

"You must persuade him otherwise!" Valton insisted. "You were his next-best pupil after me; surely you can reach into his mind and find some weakness to appeal to. You are the child's next of kin. It is your right!"

"Is it not also my right not to exercise that right?" Nebulaesa demanded, weary of the entire matter. Visions of her sister's horrific death haunted her waking hours as well as her dreams; to have the infant with her, to search that nascent face for traces of Zeenyl's features, was more than she could bear. Why was Valton so insistent?

The news of the explosion had filled Valton with a perverse satisfaction; even at this distance Nebulaesa could feel it resonating in his mind. It frankly repulsed her. How could she ever have entertained any pity toward this man and his unrequited feelings for her?

Unaware that his thoughts were so blatant, Valton had completely rationalized his reaction to the tragedy: The deaths were understandably regrettable, and it took great power of will to repress fond memories of his childhood playmate in the face of death, but surely there was some way to use this against Tetrok and to his own advantage. Still, what was this child to him?

"I only meant to use my office to appeal to the Fazrul,"

he said now. "To facilitate your obtaining what is rightfully yours. If it's what you want."

"To rear my sister's child, with all my other responsibilities? Not really. Besides, were we to contest Zeenyl's dying wish, the child would be grown before the courts could settle it."

"Saturna . . ." Valton mused. "An unusual name. Presumably derived from the Earthlings' name for the mother planet, Saturn. I wonder why. Was this also Zeenyl's dying wish?"

"I have no idea!" Nebulaesa said, too sharply. She wanted time alone to grieve for her sister, to puzzle all this out. As commander of Outlyer-21, she hadn't the luxury. "What difference does it make?"

Instinctively, Valton knew he'd gone too far.

"You're right, B'Laesa; it's not important. As you wish, then. Let the OldOne raise the child, at least until she's of citizenship age. You'll want to look in on her long before that."

"That I will."

⌀

Nebulaesa would brood over it, turning the facts she had at her disposal over and over in her mind until the child reached three years. Only then would she pay a visit.

Meanwhile, the final reports came in on the energy experiment: accidental implosion. No implication of faulty materials or improper deployment, nothing that indicated Fazisian or computer error, though further research was needed to determine ways to avoid such an accident in future. Earthians might have cited Murphy's Law. Fazisians mourned their dead and retrenched, halting further exploration of Titan to rebuild.

Valton could not resist flaunting this at Tetrok virtually the moment he arrived in the capital.

"Twenty families in mourning," he observed ruefully, almost as if Tetrok were in some way responsible, accosting him on the steps leading up to the audience hall where he would give his official report to his father and the Fazrul. "Perhaps the greatest offworld tragedy since Gremar's, when your father first began his reign. What perverse fate is it, do you suppose, which haunts our family's rule with accidental deaths?"

"I do not believe in fate, cousin," Tetrok replied, eyeing him narrowly. The two still looked enough alike to be brothers. Even their gestures were similar. Only a perpetual squint of cynicism around Valton's eyes distinguished them. As they mounted the steps together, both walked with their heads down, their hands clasped behind their backs. So much alike in form, so utterly different in spirit. "Only in accident."

"Phaestus was the best engineer our generation produced," Valton went on. "It was unlikely he overlooked anything. I have seen the preliminary reports, and while they suggest nothing unusual, I am constrained by the lessons of history."

"Are you?" Tetrok listened carefully to see where this line of reasoning was going. He had not trusted Valton since his cousin had revealed his identity to his classmates when they were children. "And what do they teach you?"

"That scientists and engineers, those who do the actual work, are too often at the mercy of their superiors, whose goal is always greater productivity, even to the limits of safety. Sometimes those with ambitions to rule may lose their perspective in their drive to succeed . . ."

Valton did not need to finish his thought. His words could no longer provoke Tetrok to anger as they had when they were boys; except for a tightening of the jaw and a heightening of his color, he kept his mind locked down, his thoughts to himself.

Valton never lost his cooler color. He knew his words had struck home.

"As head of Offworld Services, I intend to study this accident to the last atom," he concluded, as they reached the top of the broad staircase.

"Do you? How compassionate of you!" Tetrok replied with some sarcasm, regaining control of his colors. "Then, as someone familiar with the site, I will be happy to assist you."

He turned away to enter the audience hall, not waiting to see what color Valton might have turned.

The commander of an outlyer, unless she already had a spouse when she assumed command, slept alone more often than not. Protocol dictated against choosing one's companions from subordinates, and while there were always new acquaintances to make from the constant traffic of ships on layover at the station, their presence was by definition transitory. This night, as most nights, Nebulaesa slept alone.

When she slept. Twice she had awakened with a cry, the bedclothes tangled about her limbs, her body feverish. Over and over she dreamed of Zeenyl, and the last conversation she had ever had with her sister.

"You're so thin!" Nebulaesa had fussed, walking all around the holo image of her sister to study her, just entering the third trimester of her pregnancy, her work clothes altered to accommodate her burgeoning figure. But aside from the obvious expansion of her waist, Zeenyl looked no different. There was no fullness to her face, no bloom; she looked much as she always had. "Are you eating enough? What does the healer say about your condition?"

"That all is well. That I am healthy, and so is the child, and all is progressing normally," Zeenyl had answered serenely. Carefully, though Nebulaesa could not know this. "You always make too much of me! Is that the burden of the elder sister?"

"Always!" Nebulaesa had said, managing a laugh. Did she notice that Zeenyl's mind was closed to her? If she did, she attributed it to some holdover from childhood when, bullying as elder siblings will, she had teased Zeenyl mercilessly by reading her mind aloud, prefacing her pronouncements with the taunt "I know what you're thinking!" until Zeenyl learned better mindskills and, thereafter, seldom let her sister read her thoughts.

How often thereafter would Nebulaesa regret that childhood bullying!

For now, she simply enjoyed her sister's presence, wishing it were actual so that they could embrace, and share a meal together, instead of simply visiting on holocom.

"You don't know how I miss you!" Nebulaesa said. "I know I've argued myself hoarse about the benefits of rearing your child here instead of on that murky rock, but surely you can visit with me once she's born?"

It was Zeenyl's turn to laugh. "I most assuredly will! Perhaps I will even share a secret with you, a most amazing experience . . ."

"Tell me!" Nebulaesa urged, in the tattletale voice of their shared childhood. "Am I supposed to wait until your daughter's old enough to travel? Unthinkable! What secret? Tell me now!"

Zeenyl had laughed outright. "You always were impatient. Some things never change! I shall tell you when I'm ready, not before. And threats will get you nowhere."

"As I so well know!" Nebulaesa had said, remembering her skinny, stubborn sibling, always struggling to keep up with the older children, never giving in. "Very well, I shall find some suitable revenge when the time comes!"

They had both laughed.

Now Nebulaesa cried out in her sleep. Revenge? Her dreams took revenge on her nightly. What was Zeenyl's secret? Did it have to do with the child? Had she taken it with her into death? Sleepless, Nebulaesa watched the stars and wondered.

Had she known Valton had been listening, having intercepted Zeenyl's holocom, spying on them both, she would have been even more sleepless.

# CHAPTER 14

"I will answer one thousand questions and no more," Krecis told his young charge solemnly when she was three. "Thereafter you must find the answers yourself."

Saturna pondered this with a three-year-old's special seriousness, cocking her head and peering at her mentor out of the corners of her eyes as was her habit.

"I will not need one thousand questions," she announced once she'd thought it through.

"Truly?" She had distracted him from his work for the twentieth time that morning, yet Krecis smiled. "I expected you to be far more curious than that."

"I am very curious!" she assured him, her chin in her hands, her elbows resting on her plump knees as she perched on the edge of a high stool, the better to watch him work; he was doing something mysterious with a beautiful piece of diamondlike Titan crystal, which threw rainbows of color onto Saturna's face as its facets caught the light.

"Then how will you be satisfied with fewer than a thousand questions?" It seemed to the OldOne as if she asked at least that many in the course of a single day.

This crystal had occupied most of Krecis' attention in recent days, and even his joy in Saturna was proving a distraction. Found during a preliminary inspection of a newly opened ore shaft, the strangely faceted specimen had no counterpart on Fazisian worlds nor, as Krecis' careful inquiries among Earthian geologists indicated, anywhere in the Sol System except Titan. Further, he had been unable to find its like anywhere except in that particular mine shaft, and even there it was rare enough so that this chunk—as large as Saturna's small fist—was the biggest single specimen obtainable.

Thus far it had evidenced interesting transmitting properties, but Krecis was convinced there was much more. In spite of Saturna's chattering, he remained absorbed in it.

Saturna hopped down from the stool and began to dance lightly about the laboratory, humming to herself. "Because I will really, really only ever ask one question."

"And that is . . ." Krecis prompted, shutting the crystal away in a special box, though he already knew.

Saturna stopped dancing and grew very still. *"Why?"*

It was in fact the question she asked most. Why was the sky red? Why were holocom people not really there? Why did bathwater spin in circles as it went down the drain? Why were fingernails orchid? Why, in fact, did one have fingernails? Why did Catlyke twitch her tail in her sleep? Why could she clean herself with her tongue while Fazisians couldn't? Why did this food taste spicy and that one sweet? Did her hair grow while she was sleeping? Why must she go to bed when she wasn't tired yet? Why did she dream?

Krecis sighed, feigning resignation. "You have a point. 'Why?' really is only one question, isn't it? The single question which opens to us the secrets of the universe. You are entirely too clever for me!"

Saturna took him literally and tugged at his sleeve until he clasped her hand.

"Don't be sad, Krecis-mine! I have a plan. First you must teach me everything you know. Then I will teach you everything I know. Then we shall both be clever!"

Krecis freed his hand from hers to rest it on the brilliant indigo of her silky hair.

"It sounds like an excellent plan, Saturna. But might we not begin after lunch?"

"Lunch!" the child cried, tugging at his hand and skipping lightly, her excitement rousing Mushii, who began to dance about her feet. Catlyke, asleep on the highest shelf and far too sophisticated for such antics, opened one eye, sighed, and went back to sleep. "Lunch is an excellent plan!" Saturna announced, mimicking Krecis' words as she pulled him along with her. "Let's go!"

Skipping and chanting "Lunch, lunch, lunch, lunch" all the way down the corridors—Krecis had taken to teaching the child Earthian languages along with her native Fazisian, to the other colonists' amusement and amazement—the two rare companions arrived in the commissary, spreading smiles everywhere in their wake.

The population of the Titan colony had altered considerably in Saturna's lifetime. For one thing, the few Earthians who did not feel comfortable living and working with Fazisians had returned to Earth on Nyota Domonique's vessel. In addition, Fazisian cargo ships arrived at regular intervals several times a year, and many of them carried passengers to and from the Titan colony. Saturna always had new faces to add to the ones she already knew.

Her favorite human, she had to admit, was the melancholy Langler. She knew the story of his shattered legs and spine, but this deformity had never gotten in the way of the loving conversations between these two strange companions. Saturna with her extraordinary telesper ability was one of his favorite subjects; Saturna as a winsome child was one of the few people in the universe who could make Langler smile. He smiled as she sat beside him at the commissary table now.

"OldOne, I do believe she's making you younger," Fariya observed. The tragedy surrounding the child's birth had faded somewhat as everyone around her rejoiced in her presence.

"Only on my better days!" Krecis remarked, remembering his dignity. "Yet I must confess she does inspire more such days than I thought I had remaining to me."

"C'mere, Squeak!" Luke Choy said, using his pet name for her as he gave Saturna her daily hug before going back to his office. In response, the child dug into a pocket of her jumpsuit and presented him with a highly polished blue stone.

"For Arikka," she explained. "She found this zoisite in the new quarry and gave it to me for my geology project. When I finished, I thought I'd polish it and give it back."

Luke kissed the top of her head. "I'll make sure to give it to her," he said.

Everyone loved Saturna. Was it possible the child had grown to such an age without ever having seen a frown, or heard a sharp word of disapproval? While she had a naturally sunny, lively disposition, it was fostered by the nurturing and attention all around her. All the universe's children should have been as blessed as Saturna.

Only Krecis' thoughts were sometimes clouded when he looked at her. How much longer could he keep her secret?

His greatest difficulty arrived with Nyota Domonique's frequent communiqués from Mars. Both Tetrok and Nyota had kept in touch with Krecis in the years since they'd left Titan, and each sent small special gifts to "Zeenyl and Phaestus's" child. Neither seemed to suspect that Saturna was anything other than what she was purported to be. But while Krecis had no qualms about keeping Saturna's secret from her father, communicating with Nyota brought with it a special sorrow intermingled with the joy. And Nyota frequently asked him to send her a holo of the child for a memento, and he managed to conveniently "forget."

There had been no further expeditions sent to Titan, and while the Fazrul saw to it that communications between Earth and Fazis remained open, most were held at the highest levels—principally between Crown Litigator Gulibol and Counselor Wong.

The Fazrul communicated with Krecis via Nebulaesa and Outlyer-21; Krecis and Xeniok kept up their private correspondence as well. This too presented Krecis with a moral dilemma. While there were many secrets he had kept from his old friend over the decades—there were some things a Ruler was better off not knowing—to conceal from him the fact that he had a granddaughter was troubling.

The ESC required Commander Choy to report on developments on Titan at least once a month, and revised his orders as the situation warranted it. But there was no official communication between Krecis and anyone on Earth, or Luke and anyone on Fazis. It wasn't that it was forbidden; it was simply understood that it was not to happen. Krecis was able to learn far more from his friendship with Luke Choy than from any official source. Yet somehow he managed to know more, from his seemingly remote outpost on Titan, than anyone else from either homeworld. Under Krecis, Titan seemed the center of the universe.

He knew that Nyota's revelation of the Titan algae had caused great excitement on Earth. Her reward had been appointment to a fully staffed lab facility in which to experiment with the substance. Within the past three years her research had yielded a spate of pharmaceuticals, nutritional supplements, environmental cleanup agents, even animal feeds and soil enhancers. The impact on Earth had been profound. A recent communiqué from the ESC announced the appointment of Dr. Nyota Domonique as Governor of the Martian colonies. She would continue her research there.

She is content, Krecis thought. She has been amply rewarded for her accomplishments, and she has chosen to have no further contact with anyone from Titan but me. When she and I speak, it is only about our work. That is as it should be, for now.

"Who is?" Saturna, her mouth full of food, demanded from where she sat swinging her legs idly across the table from him. Startled out of his reverie, Krecis merely looked at her. "You were talking in your mind again. I listened. Who is content?"

The child's esper abilities were innate, powerful, sometimes frightening. Was this a result of her mixed heritage, or of lifelong infusions of methane and refined algae? Krecis could only hope to discipline that curious mind before she grew much older.

"Perhaps I was talking in my mind to avoid the necessity of talking with my mouth full," he chided her gently. Saturna giggled and swallowed the half-masticated mess in her mouth. "Have you forgotten that one does not listen to another's mind without permission?"

The child looked chastened. "I did forget. I'm sorry!"

"When you are grown enough to remember without being reminded, I will tell you whom I was thinking of."

Saturna gave him a sidelong look. When Krecis wore that stolid expression, there was no wheedling him. She finished her lunch in silence, knowing without even probing him that his thoughts would be more carefully guarded in her presence from now on.

As they ate together, he studied her exquisite features. Mercifully she showed no outward physical signs of her Earthian ancestry, except for her eyes. While they possessed the characteristic upward-slanting shape of Fazisian eyes, there was a golden cast to them, less the brilliant emerald green of most Fazisian eyes than a greenish-gold hue, like chrysolite. But only someone expecting to find such a difference would notice

it, Krecis hoped. A healer examining her might find her heartbeat slow for a Fazisian, but he had been her physician from
the moment of her birth and there was no danger of detection
as long as she remained in his care. Earthian antigens in her
blood might be the most overt giveaway, but that secret, too,
was safe with him.

But for how long?

Then there was her personality, which was more exuberant
than that of most Fazisian children, but even that could be
explained away. Saturna was Saturna, the first child born on
Titan, a very young soul entrusted to the care of an old one.
She was allowed to be unique.

Occasionally Saturna easily interacted with the younger
children on Titan, but mostly she preferred the company of
Krecis and her familiars. To compensate, Krecis had surrounded her with every form of education and entertainment
suitable to her mental ability. She had her own computer, complete with holo programs, which could take her instantly from
the Mountains of Kalindra on Fazis Second to the Australian
outback on Earth. With its help she could swim the oceans or
walk in space, consult with the holo images of living Fazisians
from every walk of life or visit with those long dead, become
a cloud or a slime mold or a flying *gilda* beast. She seemed
never to feel alone.

When she was older, Krecis meant to arrange for her to
have pen pals, friends her own age on Fazis and the outlyers
and perhaps even on Earth, friends sometimes as solitary and
in need of contact as she.

∂

Catlyke's and Mushii's esper abilities, evolved before Saturna
was born but limited by their presentient nature, augmented
hers in infancy and then leveled off as, almost daily, she surpassed them. Not only could she already mindtalk with any
adult Fazisian, but she could communicate with either of the
animals on a wavelength not even Krecis could hear. Whenever anything was broken or missing, whenever too many
sweets were ordered from the servitors, there were only three
possible suspects. More often than not they were all in it together, and all three had perfected a near-identical expression

of injured innocence which made even Krecis smile. It was difficult to discipline any of them.

Saturna and her furry co-conspirators inhabited a secret world within the world of Titan and she seemed content to have them as playmates, even more so than her peers. This too made Krecis watchful. How would she react if her entire universe were to abruptly change? There were many possible reasons why that might happen.

Having been absorbed in matters on Outlyer-21 for far too long, Nebulaesa had announced that she was paying Titan a visit.

✍

There was no point in pretending that the commander of Outlyer-21 was merely here on a social visit. Nebulaesa's first request surprised no one.

"I wish to see all reports pertaining to the accident," she informed Krecis when he met her at the airlock. "And I wish to be taken to the site."

"Of course," Krecis assented. The site was no more than a mass of twisted structural metals and a pile of rubble, its radiant leakage contained within an environmental bubble, untouched by Valton's order and Krecis' acquiescence following the initial investigation. Sealed in a hardsuit and observing proper precautions, Nebulaesa could root about there to her heart's content; every fragment had been sifted and resifted and there was nothing further to find.

"Very well," Nebulaesa said, perhaps surprised that her carefully veiled demands had been so easily granted. Surely Krecis knew their impetus came from Valton. "Now you may take me to the child."

Krecis had thought it best to bring Nebulaesa to Saturna rather than the other way around. The child had never met a stranger—everyone on Titan had been there since before she was born, and she even knew the passing freighter crews by name—and he wanted her to be relaxed, in a comfortable setting, for this most important confrontation.

He escorted Nebulaesa to the schoolroom where Saturna spent the greater part of her day.

What Nebulaesa encountered as she crossed the threshold

was a jungle. An elaborate holo program of exuberant green-
ery created a suitable backdrop for a host of strange-looking
animals. A large, tawny feline with a ruff of coarse hair framing its massive head stalked a herd of ruminants with starkly
striped hides as they milled about a water hole. Nebulaesa all
but recoiled at the sounds and smells, the sheer torpid heat of
the place. It was nowhere on Fazis.

"Computer?" A small voice issued from the center of
things, not yet as deep as an adult Fazisian's, almost piping.
"Show me a termite nest in the same environment. I want to
go inside."

"Saturna . . ." Krecis said softly.

The small figure manipulating the holo controls had had her
back to them; now she swung her chair around to face them.
Nebulaesa saw two animals with her, one in the child's lap,
the other curled about her shoulders like a stole. Both looked
vaguely Fazisian, but alien as well. Were they actual, or part
of the holo program?

Even as Saturna turned to contemplate her visitors, the program shifted. The jungle vanished, replaced by a mass of roiling, scrambling arthropods as big as the child herself,
emerging from rough-hewn tunnels opening out of the walls,
teeming everywhere about the room. Nebulaesa had to steel
herself in order to stand fast.

"Saturna, end the program please," Krecis said patiently.
"You have a visitor."

Nebulaesa caught a tendril of disappointment from the
child's mind as she complied. Not until that moment had she
realized that this three-year-old had the mental control of an
adult. Most Fazisian children's minds were a welter of uncon-
trolled impulses at this age—undisciplined, easily read. Extraordinary! Nebulaesa thought, as the holo program did not
end precisely but froze in midframe, leaving the insects goggling at her with their multifaceted eyes as the child hopped
down from the chair and came to them.

"Did you know that some termite nests are bigger than this
room?" she asked the newcomer solemnly. "And that's only
the part that's aboveground. There are more than a million
termites for every person on Earth. I learned that from my

xenobiology program. That's where this program's from, from Earth.''

Having finished her speech, she smiled and held out her hand for the stranger to touch, as Krecis had instructed her.

Saturna knew who Nebulaesa was; Krecis had told her that, too. The OldOne hadn't said exactly that her aunt would try to spirit her away from him, but when asked directly, he hadn't denied it either. Saturna knew it all depended on how she behaved.

Years later, Nebulaesa would wonder if it was only coincidence that the child was studying Earth that day.

''You're very beautiful,'' was the first thing Nebulaesa said, resting her hand on the child's hair, as few could resist doing. Even as she said it, she frowned. She could see nothing of Zeenyl in the child's features, nor of Phaestus either. What she thought she saw disturbed her profoundly.

''Thank you,'' Saturna replied politely, also as she'd been instructed. The combination of the compliment and the frown confused her momentarily, and she tried to read her aunt's thoughts in spite of the taboo, finding them firmly shut against her. ''So are you,'' she added after too long a moment. This was not going well. She tried to think of something else to say. ''I was hoping you'd wear your green dress, though. The long, flowing one that matches your eyes.''

Nebulaesa was momentarily taken aback. The dress was formal and only worn for receptions with visiting dignitaries; to her knowledge she had never worn it during official hours, to make holocom broadcasts, the only time the child would have seen her.

''I—I did not bring it,'' she heard herself saying. ''I thought this visit would be more relaxed, that I would wear more comfortable clothing. But I will wear it for you when I return to Outlyer-twenty-one and send my next holocom broadcast. Perhaps I might even have the replicators make one for you in your size,'' she added, not sure what the child intended, other than to dazzle her with her telesper abilities, which she had.

Saturna seemed disinterested. ''Thank you, but I don't dress up that often,'' she said. ''When I'm grown, perhaps I will.''

She looked as if she was about to return to the computer program waiting for her on the walls. She did not bother to see the mild amusement in Krecis' eyes, much less the disturbed look in Nebulaesa's.

"I will leave you to your . . . studies," Nebulaesa said uneasily, the outsize insects on the walls disturbing her almost as much as the child's so casually plucking the image of her favorite green dress out of her carefully shielded mind. "Perhaps we will talk at length later . . ."

"When you have rested," Saturna suggested for her. "Krecis tells me space travel is tiring."

The child is uncanny! Nebulaesa thought, not staying to watch her reactivate the termite program. Nor to see the silent glance Saturna gave her mentor which said clearly: *There, that ought to make her think twice!*

It did not take a mind reader to understand that Saturna did not want to leave Krecis, not for anyone.

"You do look fatigued," Krecis suggested, showing Nebulaesa to the guest quarters.

"So I am!" she admitted, allowing him to leave her there alone. Though not for reasons of space travel, OldOne!

She had come to Titan with an agenda and, having just met its object, she did not know how she was to fulfill it. Perhaps if Valton had not ended his last communication with her in quite the way he did . . .

∽

She had put off visiting Titan for as long as possible. Some of her reasons were legitimate—an excess of ships passing through Outlyer-21 now that new mining operations had been initiated in a nearby asteroid field, the upgrading of the station's holocom capacity, a spate of personnel changes, an accident involving an ore ship and an access pylon which had shut down an entire wing for months for repairs—but she was also marking time, studying events on Fazis Prime. Less than a year after his return from Titan, Xeniok had announced that Tetrok would spend the next two years inspecting the science stations on each of the satellite colonies. As soon as he returned, he was assigned to rehabilitate the colony on the dreaded Fazis Fourth. Xeniok was in his prime and seemed to have no intention of stepping down as Ruler; he wanted his people to know his son as a scientist and explorer before they considered him as their next Ruler.

It was a precarious dance, in that Valton's coalition might win further support in that amount of time, but the aging Ruler wanted his son to assume power from a position of strength. Nebulaesa wanted to wait and see how it all turned out.

But Valton had grown impatient with her procrastinating.

"Your instincts are the same as mine," he told her. "We both know something isn't right about the mess Tetrok left behind of Titan."

"Mess?" Nebulaesa repeated. "A record increase in mineral production, some extremely impressive technological breakthroughs, the initiation of relations with a new species and access to their biotech—not, with all due respect, what I would call a 'mess.' "

She was cautious of her tone, if not her words, reminding herself that the arrogant brat whose hair she used to tangle with twigs whenever she found him asleep under a *frii*bush was now her superior. Wondering too if the feelings of the adult Valton for her were still as passionate as they had been in their youth.

"The energy experiment was an accident," she insisted for what seemed like the hundredth time. "Even I, whose loss was far greater than yours, can acknowledge that."

Valton dismissed it with a gesture. "What about the algae? He deliberately kept its existence secret from us for well over a year, while allowing the Earthian female to bring its benefits to her world first."

Valton no longer referred to Tetrok by name; it was always "he," third person, their common foe.

"I wondered about that myself," Nebulaesa said carefully.

It had caused her considerable soul-searching. If she did not still see herself as Tetrok's future spouse, co-Ruler with him someday, would she have been so forgiving?

"There, you see!" Valton said triumphantly. "Who knows what other secrets he has kept from us, and for what purpose. You will go to Titan, ostensibly to visit with your niece. While you are there, you will discover whatever else you can."

"Is that an order?"

Valton's tone softened. "It doesn't have to be. Nebu-laesa . . ."

He did something out of character then, out of keeping with his office; he reached his holo fingers out as if to caress the image of her face from so far away.

Nebulaesa had to force herself to neither lean toward him nor retreat.

"What if, in some hypothetical universe, I were Ruler?" Valton asked, his tone gentle, seductive. Nebulaesa had been too long alone. "Could I make you forget Tetrok, even for a little while?"

Nebulaesa would never know what instinct formed the next words in her mouth.

"I am a pragmatist, Valton. I've never done well with hypotheses."

Valton as Ruler, she as his wife? The permutations of that had wearied Nebulaesa all the way to Titan.

𝒮

"Your behavior toward your aunt was . . . decorous, for the most part," Krecis told Saturna as he tucked her into bed, waiting while Mushii and Catlyke arranged themselves—one under the covers, one on top. "But the termites were excessive, I thought."

Saturna giggled in spite of herself.

"That was naughty," she allowed. "But I wanted to see. I think Nebulaesa wants to take me away with her." The child stuck her lower lip out. "Catlyke and Mushii don't like her either."

"Saturna, the emotions of presentient creatures are hardly a criterion—"

"I don't want to live on a station!" the child cried plaintively, her colors high. "I don't want to leave Titan. I don't want to leave you!"

"Nor do I wish you to," Krecis assured her. "But surely you and I together can bring our persuasive powers to bear on Nebulaesa without being . . . naughty from now on, don't you think? Also, it would be wise to avoid such blatant displays of your telesper abilities."

"What do you mean?" Saturna sat up in bed, all innocence, though Krecis knew better.

"The green dress?" was all he said.

"It wasn't telesper," the child stated. "And I didn't see the harm."

Krecis was puzzled at the first remark, but continued.

"The harm, my child, is that if you make yourself too interesting to Nebulaesa, she will want you to return to the station with her all the more." He waited for her eyes to widen with fear. "I will argue for your wishes, of course, but you must be more—grown up, I think, as long as your aunt is here."

Knowing he was on her side was all Saturna needed.

"I'll try!" she said. Reassured, she snuggled beneath the coverlet and went immediately to sleep.

*

"You should take your rings off," she advised her aunt the next morning when they met for a game of *kangi*ball. "Jewelry always gets in the way."

Nebulaesa had pondered all through breakfast, which she insisted on sharing with the child and Krecis, trying to find some common ground upon which to interact with her niece. She didn't have much time. Within a day or two of her arrival she could expect a holocom from Valton demanding to know if she'd been out to the accident site yet. Whatever she was to learn about Saturna she must learn soon.

Only as they were clearing the dishes away did she hit upon the child's passion for *kangi*.

"Do you play?" Saturna cried enthusiastically; Nebulaesa had merely mentioned the Fazis Global standings to Krecis in passing and the child had suddenly become animated.

"Why, yes, occasionally, though I'm not at all proficient," Nebulaesa replied, surprised, seeing the fire in the child's eyes.

"Good! Then I shall be able to beat you," Saturna announced. "Most of the adults here are still too good for me, and the children are too young to play yet."

As if she were not still a child herself! Nebulaesa thought, marveling.

"Sometimes Vaax lets me win, but I can always tell," Saturna went on. "And Krecis does not play at all. Though," she added loyally, "it's his only failing."

"Hardly!" the OldOne contributed dryly; he had been watching the interplay between aunt and niece with silent amusement for some time.

"Will you play me?" Saturna requested, making an effort to be persuasive, as Krecis had suggested. If she could show her aunt how complete the facilities were here on Titan, it might work in their favor. "It's very different here, because the ball courts are set at normal Titan gravity. Or we could set the court for Fazis g or even zero-g if you want; the Earthian Langler and I play that way sometimes."

Nebulaesa hesitated. This was exactly the sort of opportunity she wanted. But let the impetus come from the child.

"Please, Auntie? I promise you a good match."

"Of course, Saturna," Nebulaesa said at last. "I'd be happy to."

⌖

She might have removed the rings—the official commanders' signet and a smaller ring, the gift of a long-forgotten lover— if the child hadn't mentioned them. Now that she finally had Saturna alone, it was time to remind her that there was a difference, still, between her and an adult.

"I will keep them on, thank you," she said primly, more to remind the child of her place. "They've never gotten in my way before."

Nor did they this time. They played three rounds, Nebulaesa losing badly in the first because she was unaccustomed to the gravity. She won the second handily. As they began the third round, she thought of holding back but decided not to. Saturna, she decided, was far too used to getting her own way.

Nebulaesa took the third round by a single point, and not easily.

"You play well," Saturna told her graciously as they were catching their breath, then went to retrieve the ball where it had lodged in the net. Nebulaesa's last save had tangled it quite thoroughly, and she had to struggle with it. "It's stuck!"

"Here, let me help you—" Nebulaesa offered.

"I can do it!" Saturna said, asserting her independence.

Their hands worked at cross-purposes for a moment, until the child cried: ''Ow!''

A sharp point on the commanders' signet had scratched Saturna's wrist, breaking the skin. Nebulaesa recoiled in horror. As soon as Saturna had wrested the ball free of the net, she took the child's hand and examined the wound.

''The healer ought to look at that.''

''It's nothing,'' Saturna assured her. She laughed then, and Nebulaesa looked to see what she was laughing at.

As she watched, the wound closed of itself, and disappeared.

# Chapter 15

"It's the algae," Krecis told her matter-of-factly when she came to him in a flurry of demands for explanation. "Surely you have read my monographs to the science journals by now."

"Monographs reporting on research begun virtually the first year you established the colony here," Nebulaesa reminded him crossly. "Why did it take you so long to report on something as valuable as this?"

Krecis seemed surprised at her attitude. "As a scientist, surely you understand the importance of repeated trials and retests. Some of my experiments literally took decades to verify. Consider me a perfectionist, but I wished to be certain of all the properties of the substance I was studying before I published. Besides, realistically, this substance is nothing more than a more potent Garpozin."

Nebulaesa gave him skeptical look. "Garpozin! Garpozin accelerates the body's natural healing capacity; it does not make a wound whole in a matter of seconds. Garpozin is an old folk remedy compared to this!"

Krecis gave her the Fazisian equivalent of a shrug. "I suppose I have been working with the substance for so long that it is no longer miraculous to me."

Nebulaesa was still skeptical. "Is that why you swore Tetrok to secrecy for an entire year? Why you gave the algae to the Earth woman to bring to her government before you shared it with your own kind?"

Krecis sighed. "Tetrok understood my reasons, and gave them to Xeniok and the Fazrul, where they were accepted. I saw no urgency. We have advances enough on Fazis, and it was not as if we were in competition with Earth, which needed the discovery far more than we."

"Valton doesn't see it that way. Valton believes you meant Tetrok to use it as a ploy, a way of garnering more support at the last minute should he need it—"

"Valton!" Krecis said impatiently, a rare tinge of anger in his tone. "I have known Valton since before he was weaned, and I say now for your ears—and for his, as I know you have them—that his was a narrow turn of mind even in childhood, and he has not improved with age!"

"OldOne," Nebulaesa said gently. "I too accept your explanation. I only wanted you to be aware of the 'official' position. Valton will question you further; you know that."

"Let him ask his questions!" Krecis snapped, but his anger was spent.

"So it is the algae which give the child her extraordinary capacity to heal?" Nebulaesa said slowly. "That was not mentioned in any of the journals. Tell me how it works."

"When I first discovered the algae and began to understand its extraordinary properties, it seemed to me precisely what we needed to survive here on the frontier," Krecis began carefully. "After testing it on many of the animals I have since sent back to Fazis, I began ingesting it as a nutritional supplement for several years. This is in the journals, as is the fact that eventually all of us on Titan, even most of the Earthians, have come to rely on the algae to keep us well and counteract any deleterious effects of prolonged exposure to this environment."

Nebulaesa nodded. She had read all of this.

"In addition, Zeenyl agreed to take injections of a strengthened form of the nutrient during pregnancy," Krecis went on. This was a partial truth; such a conversation had in fact taken place, prior to a pregnancy which had not. "I also added judicious amounts of the substance directly into the amniotic fluid during gestation. I did not presume to such radical techniques until I had tested this method not only on lower lifeforms but on myself for over fifteen years. As you have noted, its effects on the immune system are conspicuous."

"Would you have told me about the healing if I had not witnessed it?" Nebulaesa demanded.

"My research is not yet complete," Krecis replied, not entirely answering the question.

He rolled up his sleeve then and, choosing a sterile curette from the autoclave, scored his own flesh with it. Where Saturna's wound had healed almost instantaneously, his took several minutes.

"As you can see, the efficacy of the treatment diminishes with the subject's age," he said thoughtfully, rolling his sleeve down.

"What other extraordinary gifts have you given Saturna?" Nebulaesa asked.

"Whatever her gifts, they are Saturna's. Her parents' legacy, not mine."

Nebulaesa frowned at this. "Curious. You well remember from her childhood that Zeenyl's telesper skills were never strong, and Phaestus's family tells me his were only average. Yet the child—"

"Is exceptional."

"I would say frighteningly so."

Krecis smiled faintly. "There is no mystery, Nebulaesa. Phaestus and I were kin, and I am of the Order. Some gifts are recessive. And in the absence of her mother, I communed with the child virtually from birth."

"You have trained her, then?"

"Just so."

Dissatisfied, Nebulaesa pondered this, idly turning the signet ring on her finger. On a sudden impulse she returned to her quarters and removed the ring, locking it in its own compartment in her jewel case. If asked, she would say she did not want it in her way on her inspection of the accident site. In truth her motive, like Krecis' explanations, was more complex than that.

♄

The accident site yielded nothing beyond what previous inspections had revealed. Nebulaesa's final report to Valton was remarkably brief. She fully expected him to be furious, but no matter. She hoped to bring him news of a different nature which would make him forget all about the energy experiment.

The signet ring had gouged Saturna's wrist rather deeply; Nebulaesa was certain there were traces of her blood on the sharp facet that had cut her. Enough to run a DNA scan? The possibility had obsessed her the entire time she was away at the accident site. She could barely wait for the rest of the colony to retire before accessing one of the labs the night of her return.

What else was there about Saturna that Krecis had failed to tell her?

Furtively, Nebulaesa sneaked into a deserted lab, using her commanders' access code. She felt foolish sneaking about like this. No mean scientist in her own right, she had full authorization to commandeer any of the labs to conduct a private experiment of her own. Yet she did not want Krecis to know what she was doing; there was something so profoundly strange here that Nebulaesa found herself on the defensive for simply trying to find out what it was.

The blood sample proved adequate for a scan. Nebulaesa waited impatiently, tapping her long orchid nails against the lab table while the computer did its work. When the full scan came up on her screen, she called up Phaestus's medical file for comparison.

She knew his medical history, and had known of Krecis' research into the infertility gene long before the OldOne made his findings public. Had Saturna been the first successful outcome of Krecis' work? Was this the secret Zeenyl had not had time to tell her?

It was easy enough for someone of Nebulaesa's rank to access the DNA scan of a deceased relation; she had also obtained Phaestus's family's permission. As the computer brought Phaestus's pattern up alongside the sample taken from the ring, even a first-form student could see the differences.

Saturna was not Phaestus's child!

Nebulaesa was too shocked to scream. Yet somehow she was not at all surprised. Would the computer let her have further information?

"Computer? Provide scans for all adult male colonists past and present," she instructed. "Scan one at a time on voice command only."

The screen beeped: *Unable to comply.*

Nebulaesa frowned. "Explain!"

*Access codes protected under privacy laws.*

Nebulaesa's frown deepened. It wasn't as if she hadn't expected this; Fazisians were fastidious about their privacy. What disturbed her was that the next thing she intended to do was patently illegal. Would Valton thank her—more to the point, would he protect her against legal action—if she found what she was looking for?

With nervous fingers, she tapped in an access code she had no business using.

"Complying." The computer, in the absence of any moral dilemma, immediately gave her what she wanted.

Once she had it, she was no longer sure she wanted it.

*"Tetrok!"*

She hadn't meant to say it aloud, and wondered how carefully her thoughts were controlled, lest any casual stroller passing the lab at this hour—however unlikely that might be—should overhear her. She gathered her wits about her.

"Computer," she instructed it, keying in one final illicit code. "File current screen to my personal comp. Then wipe all evidence of this transaction."

🙟

Zeenyl and Tetrok . . . Nebulaesa's mind reeled with permutations. Was it as simple as Tetrok's being the sperm donor, or as complex as their having an adulterous affair? The latter was far more serious for a future Ruler than for an ordinary citizen, particularly where it yielded a child who might also want to be Ruler someday. What would Valton do with the information, if he knew? What would happen to the child?

Simultaneously shocked, angry, and confused, Nebulaesa wrestled with her soul. What was she to do with the information she had just uncovered? Confront Krecis, who had to be at least aware of what had transpired, if not an active part of it? Give the secret to Valton, who would make what use of it he might, assuring her power in the process? Or keep the secret to herself, using it against Tetrok, or Valton, as she chose?

Could she tear the emotions she still felt for Tetrok out of her heart? Could she bear the thought of being Valton's accomplice? Again, what would become of the child in any case?

Nebulaesa shut down the lab, erasing all traces of her presence, and returned to her quarters, which closed in about her like a prison cell. Not knowing what to do, she would do nothing, for now.

Nothing but bear the brunt of Valton's anger for not giving him more leverage from the accident site! she thought bitterly, as her eyes refused to close in sleep. Let Valton rage. His anger could not touch her, really, not with what she knew.

She departed from Titan abruptly and with little fanfare, pausing long enough to say goodbye to Krecis and the child, who came to see her off. With a small child's frankness, Saturna did not bother to pretend she was sad to see her aunt go.

Ah, little one! Nebulaesa thought, unconsciously using Krecis' pet name for her departed sister. She touched Saturna's cheek, forgetting how strong her mind was. You have not seen the last of me!

Saturna said nothing. But her strange eyes, eyes the color of chrysolite, narrowed slightly, and their message was clear: *I know who you are!* Nebulaesa heard in her mind. *And I'm not afraid of you!*

❧

Where did the years go after that? Krecis was a scientist; he knew the precise parameters of real time, yet he was at a loss to explain how it seemed that one moment Saturna was a small, precocious child and the next she was a young woman, old enough at twenty Fazisian years, eighteen Earth years, to request passage to her homeworld in order to declare her citizenship. Was it only his desire to cling to those wondrous growing years, to postpone the inevitability of losing her, that made them slip through his fingers, teasing at his memory, as if in accelerated time?

Saturna was the miracle of Krecis' later years, the one thing following the death of his beloved Zandra that could make him believe there was more to life than work, duty, and more work. Watching Saturna grow, learn, and mature, he found there were days when he did not think of Zandra at all. At first he was appalled, but then he understood. That which does not grow must die. As long as Saturna was part of his life, Krecis need not even think of death.

And he had found a safe repository for Saturna's entire history in a most unlikely place.

The glowing crystal he had found as if by accident, pocketing it for its beauty if not its inherent properties while on an inspection tour of a newly opened mining site, had proven an extraordinary find. After years of study and many failures, he had with dogged determination managed to construct within the crystal an electro-optical memory circuit. The memory bank could be accessed only with a light frequency that exactly matched the vibrational frequency of certain molecules unique to this particular crystal.

Within this ornamental sepulcher—which he had cut to a cabochon face on one side while leaving the naturally asymmetrical crystalline shape on the other, complete with all the rifts and crevices natural forces had created in it—Krecis had recorded Saturna's entire history, beginning with the first encounter between Tetrok and Nyota. He updated her life history daily. When it was time for Saturna, at twenty Fazisian years, to journey to Fazis to declare her citizenship, he would give her this beautiful ornament, without revealing its inner secret until the time was right.

Until then he would only watch and wait, continuing to study the young woman as he studied the crystal that contained the story of her unique life.

Obviously she was intelligent, and she was endowed with the special gifts of both her heritages. But as he watched her grow, Krecis discovered that Saturna had gifts which were hers alone.

All Fazisians had infrared vision which made it seem as if they could see in the dark. But the methane/ethane environment to which she had been exposed *in vitro,* combined with the algae's special side effects, made it possible for Saturna to virtually "feel" with her eyes. Krecis had discovered this during the games they'd played when she was very small.

"Hide anywhere and I will find you!" the child had announced, mischievous, challenging him. At first Krecis had hidden in small, contained areas like the laboratories or the living quarters, putting out the lights and concealing himself, despite a growing stiffness in his bones, in the most improbable spaces, silent as only a Fazisian could be, shutting down his mind, barely breathing. Saturna found him every time.

"I can see you breathing in the dark," she would explain to him.

"You mean you can hear me," he attempted to correct her, but she was adamant.

"No, I see you," she explained. "It's warmer where you are. My eyes tell me the difference. And when you're excited or out of breath—like the time we ran into the holovid room and you hid beneath the seats—you are even warmer. You tried to hold your breath, but it did not fool me."

Krecis looked thoughtful. He began to test her abilities in ever-larger spaces like the commissary, finding that she could "see" another living being over great distances. He recruited Catlyke and Mushii in these games as well. Saturna could distinguish between them even in the dark.

"Catlyke usually gets bored and falls asleep," she explained. "So if I'm looking for her, I look for a quiet warmth and slow breathing, usually high up, or in the most comfortable place in the room. Mushii's easier because he cannot resist moving around and because he never keeps his thoughts locked."

*Try to!* the creature protested indignantly, but it was true. Mushii's mind was like his small six-legged body, keeping up a running commentary on everything he encountered, from a leftover crumb on the carpet to his mistress's conversation.

"I know, little one," Saturna said, picking him up and cuddling him, nuzzling his silky fur. "But, admit it, your mind's like a compost heap, always fermenting, never still."

*Better than sleeping always!* he pouted, glowering at Catlyke, who yawned in his face.

*How would you know?* the feline inquired laconically, resettling herself on her perch above all their heads.

"Don't fight, you two!" Saturna admonished them, aware that Krecis observed everything. Aware too that he could not hear the creatures when they talked to each other, but she could. It was another of her talents.

There seemed to be no limit to the range of her infrared vision within a confined space. There was no way to test it outdoors on Titan, and for the first time Krecis regretted keeping her here. Then he discovered a still more disturbing talent in her.

"It's not fair, really!" Saturna lamented one day. Eight years old, she was bored with hide-and-seek, and explained why. "I can find you so easily, but half the time you can't find me!"

Krecis shrugged. "I haven't your talent for seeing in the dark."

Saturna's eyes danced. "What if I hid in plain sight?"

"Please explain."

She got up and went into the next room, the creatures following her. "I'll show you."

In a moment she called him inside. It was a sitting room adjacent to one of the greenhouses, where one could enjoy the foliage through a window-wall while being spared the humidity of the main room. There was piped-in music, leftover from Nyota Domonique's tenure, more for the plants than for the people. Krecis stepped across the threshold, his eyes automatically scanning under chairs and behind potted plants for the small figure; he saw Catlyke ensconced in the deepest chair and Mushii assiduously investigating the plants, his front paws scratching at the window-wall, but he did not see Saturna anywhere.

Then he saw the neat pile of her clothing, everything she had been wearing, folded in a small heap on the floor, her shoes beside it.

"Saturna?" he called, thinking she might have gone beyond into the greenhouse itself. Instead, he heard her voice practically at his elbow.

"I'm right here!"

Startled, Krecis took a step backward, narrowing his eyes. If he stared very hard at the place the voice had come from, he could see a slight distortion of the surrounding air, like a heat shimmer, but nothing more. "I cannot see you."

"Maybe this will help."

Krecis watched as Catlyke seemed to take wing, rising out of her chair with the typically disgruntled expression she wore whenever she was disturbed out of a comfortable position. Then she seemed to float in midair, at about the height of

Saturna's shoulders, as if she were draped about them, also typical.

"You're getting heavy!" he heard Saturna scold the creature. "What have you been eating lately?"

He found the animal thrust into his arms by invisible hands. Then Saturna's clothing seemed to float up off the floor, assuming the shape of their wearer. To Krecis' absolute astonishment, Saturna slowly materialized before him, smiling triumphantly.

The OldOne's pulse quickened with excitement. For generations Fazisian scientists had attempted to take the body's natural color-changing abilities and enhance them into a practical invisibility, a chameleonlike ability to blend with one's surroundings. Every attempt had proved futile; entire careers had been squandered upon this minor obsession. Yet a child had mastered it.

"How—?" Krecis sat in a chair with Catlyke in his lap, unsure of his legs, much less his voice. "How did you do that?"

Perhaps concerned that she had frightened him, Saturna stroked his shoulder affectionately.

"I'm not sure. I just think about it and it happens."

"You can do it at will, then?"

Saturna shook her head. "Not always. Sometimes I'm too tired or distracted. It takes a lot of energy, and concentration. I can really only do it for a few minutes before I start to slip back into visibility."

"Will you promise me something?" Krecis said carefully after a long moment. "Two things, really."

"You know I'll promise you anything, Krecis-mine."

The OldOne nodded, barely reassured.

"First, that you will not demonstrate this ability for anyone else."

"I promise."

"Second, that you will tell no one else about it."

Saturna looked worried. "I promise, of course I do. Krecis, is it something bad? Do you mean I shouldn't do it anymore?"

He touched her hair lightly. "No, it's not bad in that sense. I will want to make sure it has no detrimental effect on your health, but no, it is not bad. In fact, as it is your unique gift, it is good. But . . .''

Saturna wished it were she, not Catlyke, who was sitting in Krecis' lap; she felt a sudden need for comfort.

''But what?''

Krecis lowered Catlyke to the floor and put his arm around Saturna's shoulder.

''It's very difficult to explain, but it could be dangerous. There are people who would not understand, who might treat you differently because of it, try to teach you to use your talents for . . . harmful things.''

''You mean I'm like Catlyke and Mushii,'' Saturna said with sudden seriousness. ''That's why you must keep us all here.''

Long ago Krecis had explained to her that while most of the animals bred on Titan were sent back to Valton on Fazis, Catlyke and Mushii were the first creatures to be crossbred from Earth species, and consequently belonged as much to Earth as to Fazis. Further, they were the only telepathic creatures, and it was important to keep them in a controlled environment until their full capabilities were known. Krecis started visibly, locking down his thoughts.

''That is not—'' he began, but Saturna was too quick for him.

''Am I, Krecis? Am I a hybrid like the creatures?''

Krecis did something dishonest then; he smiled.

''How do you arrive at such a conclusion? A hybrid of what? Two Fazisians? I have told you again and again of your parentage. Do you doubt me?''

Saturna wrestled with that thought for what seemed an eternity. If her beloved Krecis had been dishonest with her, was anything safe in all the universe?

''Nooo. I only wondered—''

''I think that is enough wondering for one day.'' Krecis rose from the chair imperiously. The animals, sensing his mood, fell into lockstep behind him, jostling only a little to determine who would go first. ''As you have said, your talent for invisibility requires a great deal of energy, and learning of it has most assuredly taxed my strength.

"We will study this phenomenon further, together," he told her. "But for now . . ."

Saturna nodded, squeezing his hand. "I promise, Krecismine!"

Krecis had learned a great deal that day. He could not know that there was far more about Saturna to learn.

♄

The Gregonian could not pinpoint the precise occasion on which he'd first heard the tiny, plaintive mindvoice—more an inchoate cry than an actual voice—tickling his subconscious from the vicinity of the Sol System. Being a precise man, he found this unsettling.

What had confused him at first was that in addition to his meditations, he had also been absorbed in an intensive study of the literatures of his world at the time. It was one of his talents as Justice to be able to multitask so skillfully, accomplishing more in an average day than most of his fellows did in two. But sometimes he got his mental wires crossed and, much to his solon's dismay, he blurred the line between what he knew to be real and the vaster realm of the uncertain.

"One of the paradoxes of nature," Niklosa would explain patiently for what seemed to her the thousandth time, "is that when a force as powerful as Imagination Communication is employed in unknown or unproven circumstances, one must diligently explore all possibilities and proofs before a definitive statement can be made regarding reality or fantasy."

Isidros, who had been studying with Niklosa since he was weaned, would as a small boy rub the central auditory receptor on the top of his head, as if it would make him hear better, and even more, understand what his solon was telling him. Now, a half-century later, he did finally understand, but as Niklosa was wont to observe, it made him no less impatient for results.

So even though he'd been in one of the deeper levels of IC when he first heard the small voice, he'd thought at first that she was just an overspill from his studies, some fictional character speaking in his mind down the generations from the time the great epics were written. Since Gregonian study methods were so auditory in nature, this was a frequent occurrence.

There were many child-heroes in the rhymed historical novels of the Platinum Era, and Isidros had thought the girl child one of them.

That she never gave him her name, because she lacked the skill to, was his first indication that she was not a figment of his imagination. Ever since then, he'd tried to regulate his communications with her, tried to teach her to "speak" to him from the far side of the galaxy. Still, he could not prove that she was real, nor had he yet learned her name.

Ridiculous! he thought. Worse than ridiculous; it's downright silly for the Justice Dispenser of Gregonia to be so enraptured with a child, a child who may not even exist. Maybe I should just write an epic of my own and make her the protagonist; that would certainly enhance my stature with the academy!

Instead he found himself reaching out to study her, and to reveal small bits of information about himself and his world in her most receptive mind with ever-increasing frequency.

He had begun by doing what every Gregonian had wanted to do since they had first discovered their IC capabilities two thousand years before: showing this child the planet where he lived, through IC.

# CHAPTER 16

When Saturna was very young, Krecis had taught her how to access the alpha waves that created the best dreams. He had also taught her how to rewrite her own dreams—to analyze the elements in them that puzzled or frightened her, to eliminate the stuff of nightmares. She could create fairy castles or termite caves as easily in her dreams as in a holovid program. But from the time she was fourteen, whenever she lay in bed at night in that twilight state between waking and sleeping, she began to experience something which was not a dream.

Throughout her young life, Krecis had observed as she exhibited one wondrous ability after another, but even he did not suspect her ability for Imagination Communication.

She did not know how she knew that the place was called Gregonia; she only knew that she knew it, and that it was no dream. Whenever she sent her mind there, thinking it was a dream, she found for the first time that she could not alter the scenery at will.

But what scenery!

Clearly this was a world which had been at peace for millennia, longer even than Saturna's ancestral Fazis. A quick overview of the planet showed no burned-out abandoned cities, no refugee camps, no defoliated forests or ravaged croplands, none of the debris of war which on younger worlds often took centuries to clear. Instead, sprawling metropolises of pastel stone and gleaming metals displayed themselves in muted luxury along the banks of pristine rivers, where fish leapt amid indigenous plants and pedestrians walking the arched stone bridges above could see clear to the depths of the riverbed. Still other, older cities, remnant perhaps of an ancient warlike time, clung to the sheer sides of mountains, overlooking terraced gardens and orchards, and valley floors planted with lush irrigated acreage as far as the eye could see.

It was obvious that Gregonians prided themselves on their love for natural beauty. Their architecture was replete with natural artifacts encompassing all aspects of growth. Living trees and rock outcroppings were frequently used as part of the basic structure of homes and even public buildings; there was as little distinction between indoors and outdoors as the planetwide temperate climate would allow.

Wildlife shared the streets of these cities with their sentient denizens. Horned and antlered quadrupeds strode the streets unmolested, while winged and feathered raptors nested in the high places, their cries piercing the early-morning air as they sought their small prey.

Saturna could hear the sounds the birds made, as she could see that the Gregonian sun was brighter than the sun on Fazis, and a different color from that of Earth and Titan. She could smell the morning scent of the vining trumpet flowers clinging to the house walls and spilling over windowsills into the interior of rooms, and had learned to distinguish it from the night scent. She could smell the luscious yeasty odors from the numerous bakeries in the lowland cities where Gregonians bought their breakfast bread. If she tried very hard, she could even taste that bread, hot and fresh and reminiscent of something not quite cinnamon, but not precisely ginger, either. Dreams did not have taste and smell; Gregonia was no dream.

Nor were its people. Saturna had an active imagination, but she could not have imagined these people if she'd tried.

They seemed somewhat smaller than Fazisians, though within the normal range for many Earthians. When she'd first realized that, Saturna had literally sat up in bed and thought about it so hard that the image of Gregonia vanished entirely from her mind. She had switched on her bed lamp and sat cross-legged, her chin in her hands, puzzling over it.

If she was looking at Gregonians in the context of their planet—judging them relative to the height of the trees, the size of the gentle hoofbeasts grazing their grassy gardens so meticulously they never needed pruning—how could she tell their size? What if everything on their planet grew to gigantic size, and a Gregonian could hold a Fazisian in the palm of her hand? Then again, what if Gregonia was a planet in miniature, and Saturna could pick up one of its citizens like a toy?

These thoughts had banished sleep entirely, and Krecis noticed her yawning and nodding over breakfast. It was not until some weeks later that she got her answer.

She had frequently had dreams in which she was an active participant, walking among people and landscapes either familiar or strange, but in those dreams she had always been aware of her body—could, for example, hold her hand in front of her face or glance down at the clothing she was wearing. When she found herself "visiting" Gregonia, she was aware of her own presence there, but could not see herself, as if she had rendered herself invisible the way she had demonstrated for Krecis. No one on Gregonia noticed her, and she was able to walk among them, making note of their height relative to hers, discovering that even at fourteen she was taller than many adult Gregonian women.

If anyone asked her, how would she describe them?

Superficially, she would have to say they looked more like Earthians than Fazisians; their skin did not change color with their moods, but they came in more varieties of color to begin with. Most were blue-toned, ranging anywhere from a deep slate to a kind of turquoise, with large black-irised eyes, fringed with thick amber lashes, set wide in their overlarge heads. A minority, perhaps ten percent of the beings Saturna could see on the streets and in the shops, seemed to have more green tones to their skin, an almost universal muted jade. Their eyes were nearly white, the pupils slitted like a cat's instead of round, and they had no eyelashes. Then there were beige ones, such as Isidros, with chocolate-black hair and thick black lashes over large black eyes.

Gregonians in general seemed to lack facial hair, and the hair on their heads ranged from thick and coarse to scant and silky, sometimes lying flat and sometimes floating in the gentle breezes, exposing the auditory receptors which were their most interesting feature. Gregonians had no ears, in the way that Fazisians and Earthians had vascular fleshy protuberances set symmetrically on the sides of their heads. Instead they had three equidistant bumps arrayed on the tops of their heads which could only be sound sensors. Saturna had deduced this from observing very young Gregonians incline their heads toward the source of sounds.

And while she didn't understand a word of their language, it sounded to her like singing. Always a quick study, she began to learn the Gregonian language-songs, humming them to herself.

"It's a pretty melody," Krecis noted, catching her unaware one day not long after she had shown him how she had taught herself to disappear. "But I do not recognize it. Did you compose it yourself?"

"No," Saturna answered warily. When had she begun to be wary around the only person in the universe she really loved? "It's the way people talk on Gregonia."

"Gregonia?" It was the first time she had mentioned it to him, to anybody. "And where is that?"

She told him, not everything but as much as she thought he would find interesting.

"You have a very vivid imagination," he suggested. The legacy of your Earthian heritage! he thought but did not say. Sometimes he felt as if he would burst with the knowledge he was unable to share with anyone. "Perhaps you should write fiction."

"Gregonia is not fiction, Krecis-mine. It's quite real."

This gave the OldOne pause. Indulging Saturna's fantasies was one thing, but if she began to take them too seriously, what might that mean?

"Is it? Then how is it that you come to it through a dream? Can you find it on an astrogation chart? Have you ever met any of its inhabitants?"

"No, of course not!" Saturna chided him, as if he ought to know better. "But just because I haven't doesn't mean they don't exist."

Krecis considered. "Valid enough. But show me where it lies on the charts so that I may verify your findings."

"I have a better idea," Saturna said. "Why don't you test my knowledge by having me describe some other worlds I've visited and you tell me how much is my imagination?"

It became their latest pastime. Saturna would concentrate, going into a kind of trance. When Krecis spoke to her directly, it was clear that she was still present in the room, but her

responses were dreamy, as if her voice was working in slow
motion in comparison to her mind. And not all of that mind,
clearly, was still in the room with Krecis.

"I see a world . . ." she would begin, her eyes closed, her
eyelids fluttering slightly, "covered with cloud, so thick the
sun never reaches the surface. It is warm, very warm, and
moisture drips continuously from trees so large I almost can't
see the tops of them from the ground . . ."

Krecis found it curious that she should view the planet from
ground level rather than from out in space, but said nothing
except, "Go on."

"There are plants with flowers the size of my head, insects
as big as Mushii with iridescent wings . . ."

Mushii, having heard his name, looked up at her expec-
tantly, chirruping in his throat, his antennae twitching curi-
ously. When he felt what she was thinking, he tucked his head
between his two front paws and shuddered.

"Fish so huge they could swallow me in a gulp," Saturna
went on, "swimming in seas so shallow they have learned to
walk on land . . ."

When she emerged from the trance there was a sheen of
perspiration on her face and she was suddenly very thirsty.
Between swallows of a cooling drink, she gave Krecis the
coordinates of this primeval world; he cross-referenced them
against the latest dispatches from the Offworld Services, reporting on the exploration of yet another solar system. His
hands began to tremble.

"Saturna . . ." he began carefully, mindful that she was still
a child and he must not be overharsh with her. "Surely you
know that anything addressed directly to me from the Offworld Services is for my eyes only."

"Of course I know that," the child answered, puzzled.

"You did not—accidentally, let us say—happen to read
such a dispatch?"

Saturna shook her head vehemently. "Even if I'd wanted
to, I don't know how to descramble them."

Krecis had to stop himself from smiling. Saturna was entirely too clever, and he had been entirely too lax in letting
her have the run of his private office, especially as she grew
older. Yet he knew she would not lie to him. How had she

been able to so exactly describe a world so newly discovered the Fazrul had not even given it a name?

"Perhaps you found the description of this world in my mind?" Krecis suggested.

Again Saturna shook her head, frowning. "Now that you mention it, I can see it there. But no, not until this moment."

The last dispatch had mentioned a second planet in the same system. When a follow-up report on the search team's initial readings arrived at Krecis' terminal, he did not descramble it immediately.

"Tell me about the twelfth planet in the same system as your jungle world," he challenged Saturna.

She did.

"It's much farther from the central star and should be very cold," she said slowly from the depths of her trance, her voice and movements lugubrious. "But it has six moons, which play havoc with the tectonic plates, causing almost constant earthquakes, and breeding hundreds of volcanoes. The largest of these is near the equator, and makes Olympus Mons on Mars look puny . . ."

When she returned from this trance, Saturna looked ill. She shivered violently and, unsteady on her feet, went to get an extra overtunic to warm herself. Krecis, concerned for her, had also been watching the behavior of the animals whenever she went into some of these trances. Catlyke reacted aggressively, lashing her tail and growling, her hair standing on end as she stalked the corners of the room, restless and wide-eyed. By contrast, Mushii huddled close to his mistress, trilling angrily, as if to protect her in spite of his own fears.

By the time Saturna returned, rolling the cuffs of her tunic up over her delicate wrists, Krecis had descrambled the new dispatch. His eyes were bleak.

"How do you do that?" he asked in a voice grown wintery with dread. "How are you able to see?"

Saturna shrugged, wondering why the OldOne seemed so disturbed. She had actually stood on the surface of the worlds she described and had felt only wonder, not fear.

"I don't know. I simply put my mind to it, and I'm there. But do you believe me about Gregonia now?"

"Tell me where it lies," Krecis repeated quietly.

Saturna thought about this. "Only if you swear to me to keep it secret. I don't know why, but it's important. I feel— This is not scientific, but something tells me they don't wish to be contacted; they only want to communicate through my mind."

Krecis weighed this. It might be Saturna's way of disguising her own doubts about the reality of the world she described. Was it a sign of her growing maturity that she wished to keep secrets from her mentor?

"Very well," he said at last; certainly she had kept enough of his secrets for him to grant her this. "I promise."

She told him where to find Gregonia.

It lay on the outer reaches of the galaxy, approximately equidistant from Earth and Fazis. Its primary and the precise position of its attendant planets were exactly as Saturna described them. The distance of the planet she referred to as Gregonia from that primary, its mass and the angle of its orbit, everything, suggested precisely the climatic conditions she described; its age and that very temperate climate made it a likely candidate for the evolution of intelligent life.

But Gregonia, if that was in fact the planet's name, was too far from either Fazis or Earth to make exploration practical. Optimal conditions for the evolution of life did not prove that such life existed. In spite of Saturna's conviction, Krecis did not believe. But he continued to be curious.

"Tell me more about Gregonia," he would urge the child, as if it were she who told him the bedtime stories, now that she was older. She provided him with detailed descriptions until he asked: "And what is the name of your special friend?"

But here Saturna refused to indulge him. Her eyes wore that wary look again.

"That's a secret I must keep to myself alone," she answered evasively, and Krecis did not press it. If anything, her reluctance confirmed his doubts. Nevertheless he recorded this, as he did everything about her life, in the heart of the crystal ornament.

♄

She did not know why she felt so protective of Isidros, didn't think it at all strange that a teenage girl should feel protective of a grown man. But as her mental skills increased, she had been given glimpses of Isidros's life that she knew she must not share with anyone else.

Krecis had a point, in that she could not prove the reality of either Isidros or his world. Her "special friend" tended to communicate with her only in times of stress, or on the verge of sleep, times when she was receptive to mental impulses from any of several sources. She could not summon him at will, though she often tried. There was a kind of separation between them, an almost tangible mental screen which she could never quite overcome. Saturna found this very frustrating. Yet whenever she was being "visited," which only happened when she was alone, she could not refuse or turn away.

She watched Isidros move through his days, saw him rise in the morning and step into the bath. A Fazisian by culture and not burdened with the prudishness of Earthians, she was not shy about studying him and seeing how his body was similar to those of the males of the two species she knew, as well as how it differed. She especially admired the way the long, lean muscles of his back and shoulders moved beneath the unchanging color of his golden-beige skin.

She watched him dress and meditate and read the day's weather from the direction of the wind and the number of clouds in the sky. She stood invisibly beside him on the balcony of his breakfast room as he fed the remnants of his meal to a hoofbeast in the garden, the creature delicately raising its great antlered head and taking each morsel directly from his hand with velvet lips. She admired Isidros's gentleness most of all.

Having finished his meal, he would go to his study and receive the day's reports from his computer, send and receive communications, all in a calm and orderly manner. At mid-morning he would walk in the garden, sometimes swimming in the natural pool diverted from a bubbling hot spring which flowed through his property and beneath his house, warming it before flowing on to the neighboring estate. Then he would report to the Courts of Justice. Most often he walked; occasionally, if he was hurried, a flitter marked with some manner of official seal would arrive on autopilot and whisk him through the skies.

When he walked, people greeted him. As he strode up the steps of the justice building and into the tiring room to don his official robes, everyone seemed pleased to see him. Gregonians were, in Saturna's observation, a serene and open people, yet Isidros seemed to inspire in them, male and female alike, a special degree of warmth; he seemed universally loved.

Yet Saturna had never sensed such loneliness in anyone but herself.

Isidros's spacious home was decorated with delicate three-dimensional works of art, almost all of which included a holo image of an absent friend or family member. Some of these twenty or so children and adults bore a striking familial resemblance, some did not; some were of the minority ethnic group whose members Saturna had noticed on the streets. From the way Isidros studied these holos, sometimes addressing those dear to him as if they were actually present, she knew that they were important to him, and that he missed them. Why was a man who was so universally loved always alone?

And why didn't he have a mate?

Saturna found herself blushing to a tawny bronzish gold as she suppressed that thought. What if he could "hear" her through their so frustratingly one-sided communication? She'd observed Gregonian custom long enough by now to understand that every adult could choose as many as three mates, sometimes all at the same time. How this worked out if any or all of one's mates decided to choose up to three mates of his or her own she was not sure, but she barely understood the mating customs of Fazisians or Earthians, so she let it go. But while he acknowledged the smiles and friendly gestures of the women around him, Isidros treated them all equally, never singling any of them out for special attention.

Had he once had a mate and lost her? Saturna wondered. Or had he simply never found a mate in the true sense of the word—a match, a peer, an equal? As she crossed the threshold into adolescence, she dared wonder: How would he respond if he were to encounter her?

Again she blushed, and faltered at the quantum physics equations Krecis had assigned her to complete before lunchtime. She heard Catlyke purring in her mind.

"I beg your pardon?" she said aloud. "How much of my mind are you reading now, Your Impertinence?"

*Enough to know!* the creature answered, kneading her mistress's knee with her little prehensile fingers. As Saturna had grown older and her telesper skills increased, her constant companions' had as well. She could communicate with Catlyke and Mushii almost as well as with another Fazisian.

"Enough to know what?" she demanded, deliberately speaking aloud in order to remind Catlyke of her place. Unperturbed, the creature began to groom her golden mane and gave her mistress a knowing look.

*Heat!* Catlyke purred. *In my species, what you're feeling is called being in heat. How will you mate with him from so far away? Better to choose a closer mate.*

"Don't be ridiculous!" Saturna scolded her. "You have no idea what you're talking about. And get off my lap; all this fidgeting is distracting me!"

*Hmmmm!* Catlyke responded, slithering to the floor in a fluid motion and returning to her grooming, watching Saturna smugly with her long-lashed eyes.

"Heat!" Saturna thought, her computer chiding her as she made yet another miscalculation in the equation on her screen. As well call it that as call it "love"; she could understand the first where she could not the latter. Animals' mating drives were based on measurable chemical changes in the blood; so were Fazisians' for that matter and, she supposed, Earthians', too. What was this "love" business, anyway?

Objectively she could observe it in others. Krecis still loved Zandra, though she'd been dead for decades now. Love as a kind of homage to a dead person was something Saturna had tried to understand, even though she had studied the holos of her parents for hours without ever feeling anything for them but a sadness that they'd had to die. Was that love? Even if it was, what did it have to do with her fascination with Isidros? Catlyke was right about one thing: What could she do about it from so far away?

Dreamy and distracted, she made several more computational errors before she shut down the program crossly. She would go to the exercise compound and work up a sweat, try to get this out of her system, tell Krecis she would finish her physics another time. What was the rush, anyway?

&

Watching her, Krecis wrestled with despair. What had he done?

The more Saturna's unique talents continued to surprise him, the more he wondered if he and all her parents had done the right thing. He recalled the hysteria surrounding the attempt to create a cross-species child and wondered if the hysterics had been right. What, in truth, had he created?

Her dreaminess could simply be a phase, an aspect of her Earthian heritage Krecis had not considered. Would it make her seem strange, even frightening, to other Fazisians? Would they become suspicious of her ancestry when she journeyed to the homeworld to declare her citizenship? He had hoped all speculation concerning the child's origins had been laid to rest with Nebulaesa's visit; still, he remained uneasy.

His uneasiness grew when he discovered Saturna had also spoken to Langler about Gregonia.

"And what do you make of this . . . fantasy of hers?" the OldOne asked the Earthian psychologist cautiously.

"I wouldn't be in a hurry to categorize it as a fantasy, OldOne," Langler replied. "I've studied the history of your people's ability to transmigrate mentally—"

"Our *ancient* history," Krecis reminded him.

"True enough. But if it was a legitimate skill and not just a literary conceit from the old legends, it's a skill that still exists. Modern Fazisians may have simply lost the ability to tap into it. I'd take Saturna's fantasies more seriously if I were you, my friend."

Warily, Krecis continued to test his charge, asking her to use what she had taken to calling "imagination communication" or simply IC in order to "visit" places more easily verified than the two—no, three, if one counted Gregonia— planets she had already described.

"Tell me something specific about Outlyer-twenty-one," he challenged her on one such occasion. He knew Saturna had watched routine holocom between Nebulaesa's station and Titan all her life, but such broadcasts were almost always generated from the communications center or Nebulaesa's quarters, leaving the rest of the station a mystery to Saturna. The child (was she, at fourteen, a child? Krecis wondered) had never set foot off Titan, and he himself had not been to Outlyer-21 for decades before she was born. Surely there was some detail Saturna could not know about unless her IC was genuine.

She did.

"They've redecorated the commissary," she reported, as if she were watching the renovations take place. "Changed the shape of the viewports—they were oval, now they're more a deltoid shape. There are the strangest flowers in the table settings. Someone brought them on a passing freighter; they vibrate softly when you speak near them, creating their own background music. And the third of the six food synthers has a glitch in the programming. It makes everything taste like *ferij*root."

She and Krecis both grimaced at that.

"They've shut it down until it can be reprogrammed," Saturna finished, trying not to look smug. "Do you believe me?"

"It's plausible enough," Krecis replied mildly. "When next I speak to Nebulaesa, I shall ask her."

✿

Before he had the opportunity, something untoward happened.

"You know, OldOne, you might accomplish twice as much if you weren't always picking animal hair out of your experiments!"

The speaker was Arikka, one of the youngest Fazisians on Titan, which gave her the same right Saturna had to tease the old mage. She and Commander Choy had also chosen each other, and this gave her a degree of privilege. But everyone teased Krecis about the two animals constantly milling about his laboratories.

"Hardly proper scientific procedure," Fariya added. She and Krecis had known each other for over a century, which gave her the right to say anything to him. She and Arikka, who had become fast friends, loved to torment the WiseOne.

Mushii, lacking a Fazisian sense of humor, growled and sparked his antennae at the two women. Even Catlyke opened one eye and raised the fur along her spine until she saw Krecis was amused and not threatened by the two women's words. She went back to sleep on her high shelf.

Krecis did not react at all, except to scoop Mushii off the countertop and set him on the floor, where the recyclers kept a constant flow of fresh air moving to whisk away pet hair and all other debris. This was answer enough, and the two women went away, leaving him to his work. Assured he was alone except for the creatures, Krecis retrieved the crystal from its secret repository, preparing to update the memory.

It would take only moments; there was no need to terminate a molecule-extraction experiment using Titan algae, which was already in progress. He completed the entry into the crystal, then set aside a few smaller pieces he had recently retrieved from the same vein in the ore mine; if they proved as high-quality as the larger stone, he would use them to store lesser records as well. As he removed the algae solution from the centrifuge, he heard Catlyke hiss and Mushii begin to growl.

"I have barely finished defending you two against charges of disruptiveness," he said mildly, not even glancing up from his work. "Kindly do not discredit me so soon."

Who knew what they were fighting about? It rarely took much. One would jostle the other, take umbrage at some breach of personal space, filch a particularly savory bit of food (it did not matter that there was plenty more where that one came from). Sometimes their fights were over nothing at all, as this one was. In a tiny corner of his consciousness, Krecis was aware of the skirmish taking place behind his back, but paid it no mind. He poured his algal solution carefully into the prepared beakers, his hands steady.

Catlyke had backed into a corner, her most dangerous position, though after a thousand such battles Mushii had still not learned. He charged her, growling and bristling. She swatted at him with one hand, her claws retracted, a warning: *Back off! Leave me alone!* Mushii stood his ground, stiff-legged, and charged again. His nails skidded on the stone floor and he crashed headfirst into Catlyke, who exploded. Puffing herself up to three times her normal size, she lashed out with her

powerful tail, slapping Mushii on the head, hard. He let out a
frightful yelp, and Krecis, who had barely set the vial down,
started slightly, knocking it over.

It was not a disaster. What remained in the vial was over-
flow; he had already treated the substances in the beakers. But
the two animals froze in midfray and slid apart. Their fur deflated back to normal, their ears and tails drooped as they
watched the old mage furtively. He was staring transfixed at
the fragments of crystal sloshing in the spill. They heard the
gasp as it exploded in his mind.

The solution had engulfed the fragments of crystal on the
lab table. Krecis began to mop it up, but not before he rounded
on the two cowering creatures.

*"Out!"* he said, so harshly that there was no argument.
They slunk through the small door at the base of the larger
laboratory door and went to find Saturna.

The crystals were reacting chemically to the solution which
still bathed them; a barely visible light green radiance emanated from them. Quickly scanning them for dangerous radiation, Krecis could barely contain his excitement. His
adrenaline surging, he touched one of the crystals. The light
green radiation changed color to a deeper green!

Krecis recoiled, fear rushing through his body as he brushed
the same crystal with his fingers a second time, watching the
color of the beam alter from deep green to a soft blue.

A crystal which, when treated in this manner, radiated different colors with the mood of the person touching it? The
implications were magnificent. Krecis calmed himself and proceeded, removing the largest of the crystal fragments, still ra-
diating blue, from the solution with laboratory tweezers and
cleaning it. The radiation ceased at once. The OldOne placed
the crystal back on the table's surface and gently nudged it
into a remaining puddle of algae solution. Once again a dark
green beam emanated from the crystal.

Meticulously Krecis cleaned each piece of crystal, and returned them to the box where he kept them hidden. It was
enough for one day. A glance at the chrono told him it
was time to check in with Nebulaesa for his ten-day report. He must remember to ask her about the renovations to
Outlyer-21.

✍

Nebulaesa frowned when he asked, but answered everything in the affirmative.

"You're suddenly very interested in the daily routine of my little universe," she observed. "Who told you?"

"Rumors." Krecis dismissed it. "Long-term spacers complain about everything. Word gets around."

Nebulaesa did not seem convinced. "Or Saturna," she said. "It's the green dress scenario all over again."

Krecis was silent, confirming her hypothesis.

"I should have thought you'd be more interested in the news out of Earth. They are sending another expedition your way."

"Are they indeed?" Krecis banked down his surprise. Why now, after all this time? "Why was I not informed?"

"You are being informed now, OldOne; I am informing you. Commander Listrom of Jupiter-one informed me less than an hour ago."

✍

What she did not tell Krecis was that she and Beth Listrom had been communicating privately for over one Earth year, their communications bypassing Titan entirely.

Bydun Wong and the Earth Councils had been watching their people's progress on Titan; Luke Choy, now Governor Choy, had been providing them with detailed monthly reports on every aspect of the colony's development ever since he'd taken office. Despite the tragic failure of the energy experiment, operations had quickly recovered and the colony continued to expand. Ore production, hydroponics, and the countless scientific experiments begun long before the arrival of Earthians proceeded apace. It had always been assumed that someday more Earthians would come to Titan.

That day was now or, at least, however long it took for an Earth ship to arrive, and Krecis had not been directly informed. Luke Choy got his orders forty-eight hours later.

"Son of a gun!" was all he could say. Nothing the ESC did could surprise him anymore.

*∂*

"It's procedural," Nebulaesa assured Beth Listrom, when she first initiated the holocom with the Earth woman who commanded Jupiter-1, her virtual mirror image in the system. "Krecis may be autonomous on Titan, but that is where his authority ends."

"I hear you!" Beth said, studying the Fazisian woman's coloring carefully to try to guess her mood and motivation. Whenever she was dealing with these people, she always had the feeling that there was more to them than met the eye.

The two women sat conversing at arm's length from many parsecs' distance. To preserve the pretense that they were actually in each other's presence, Nebulaesa had suggested they have tea together.

"I'm a coffee drinker myself," Beth had responded, refusing to give an inch. Still, she'd gone through the motions, setting her featureless disposable coffee mug "beside" Nebulaesa's elaborate tea service on the low table beside her chair. Pity she couldn't reach through the holocom and grab one of those little tea cakes or whatever they were! Beth thought wistfully; they actually looked quite tasty. "At any rate, let's get down to business. The ship we're sending was launched from the Mars shipyards three weeks ago. She'll make stopover here before confirming your government's okay to proceed to Titan."

"I assure you that 'okay' will be forthcoming, Commander," Nebulaesa said graciously, choosing a tea cake and nibbling genteelly at the corners; she could not help noticing Beth watching her greedily as she ate, and it amused her. "You'll send me the proper manifests and crew lists?"

"Of course," Beth promised, making a note for herself. "As soon as we finish here. I'd have sent them sooner, but some personnel signed on at Mars, while the rest transferred from Earth and Selenopolis, so I wanted to wait until we had a confirmed list."

Including, she thought but did not say, a particular choice of my own!

"Understood, Commander." Nebulaesa finished the tea cake, dabbing at her lips with a napkin before she continued.

"May I ask you a personal question? You were friendly with several of the crew of the *Dragon's Egg,* were you not?"

"Still am," Beth admitted with a frown, wondering where this question was coming from. "Spacing's a small world; everybody knows everybody else. And Nyota Domonique and I were roomies at the academy, if that's your question."

Nebulaesa smiled. "You're very perceptive, Commander. That was precisely my question. You see, it's my belief that you and I have a great deal in common. I've always thought that women, particularly women in command positions, possessed a kind of solidarity which transcends species . . ."

"Go on," Beth prompted when she hesitated.

"You and I also have in common the fact that we were both witnesses to a certain holocom some years ago. A holocom in which the scientists on Titan requested permission for a certain—biological experiment. I'd wondered if you could shed some light on those years, from an Earthian perspective. Perhaps provide some insight from your long acquaintance with Dr. Domonique of which I might not be aware . . ." Again she hesitated. "Anything which might smooth the way for the new ship's arrival and help its crew adjust to their new home more readily," she added quickly.

"Nyota and I used to be very close," Beth said emphatically. "Only the fact that we're locked into different commands and hardly ever see each other has made us less close. Don't ask me for gossip or anything tacky like that, because you won't get it."

This interview was not going as Nebulaesa had hoped. She must find a way to ease out of it without tipping her hand. She leaned back in her chair, adding an extra few inches to the parsecs between her and Beth.

"I would never dream of doing any such thing, Commander," she said coolly. "My thought was to prevent the kind of advance and withdrawal your government seems to have considered a logical procedure for space travel since its inception. To the Fazisian mind, it seems wasteful. I can't abide waste, Commander."

"Neither can I, Commander," Beth assured her; she didn't trust this woman, and she was sure the feeling was mutual. "I'll give you this: we do have one thing in common. We may both be frontline commanders, but we're still beholden to the paper-pushers back home.''

∽

Back home on Fazis, Valton the master of comminterception, consulted his Earthian/Fazisian lexicon for the definition of "paper-pusher." He was not happy with the answer he received. Still, the insult only partially dimmed his extreme pleasure in knowing that his continued monitoring of Nebulaesa's communications had given him access to Beth Listrom's as well.

∽

"Are you angry with me, Krecis-mine? I know it's my fault the creatures made such a mess in your laboratory, but I've scolded them both. What else can I do to make it up to you?"

The OldOne had virtually disappeared into his lab for days; several people had remarked on it, but it affected Saturna most of all. Krecis hadn't realized how much his obsession with the crystals had absorbed him.

"What did the creatures tell you exactly?" he asked, knowing they communicated with Saturna in ways even he did not understand. No one, especially not Saturna, must know about the crystals now.

"Only that their fussing made you spill something. I questioned them thoroughly, though of course each one blamed the other, so I never got the story straight. Was it serious?"

Krecis made a negative gesture. "Not really." In fact, it was most extraordinarily serendipitous, though I can tell neither you nor the creatures that! "It is only that Arikka and Fariya had barely moments before chided me for giving the animals the run of the laboratory. I suppose I . . . lost my temper."

"Most unlike a WiseOne!" Saturna chided him now, patting his shoulder. "Then that's not the reason you're angry with me? What is it? Tell me!"

"I am not angry, Saturna, merely . . . preoccupied. And I have been thinking," he announced, by way of changing the subject. "You have begged me since you were very small to let you have an overlander to explore Titan, and I have heretofore refused you, saying you were too young."

"Yes?" Saturna's eyes glowed with eagerness. She'd driven virtually every vehicle on Titan, but only for short distances. She wanted to see the entire planetoid. Was Krecis finally about to give her permission?

"I think it is time," the OldOne said dryly, as if it were a minor matter. "But," he said, at the young woman's excitement, "only if you bring someone else with you."

"Of course, anyone—oh, Krecis-mine, thank you!" She hugged him, ecstatic, barely listening.

"For one, the creatures." Krecis itemized them both on his fingers. "They must get used to space travel eventually, and a low-orbit flight to the overlander site is a good beginning. And also Dr. Langler."

Saturna did not ask why Langler? He would have been her first choice, after Krecis himself anyway. But Krecis felt compelled to explain.

"Dr. Langler wants to further his study of your, what do you call it, IC? And it will be good for him to leave the colony compound. He so seldom does."

"It will be wonderful!" Saturna announced, hugging Krecis again.

It will indeed, Krecis thought. For you, for Langler, and for my work on the crystals . . .

♄

There was only one thing more he had to do, and that was to contact Xeniok on their locked-down wavelength. Whether it was pure coincidence or not, Xeniok issued a formal announcement on that same day.

The Fazrul, as it did every year, had sent Crown Litigator Gulibol to the Ruler to inquire as to whether he intended to rule for another year, or to name a successor to be submitted for their approval. Xeniok chose the occasion to break precedent:

"I name as my successor my only-born son Tetrok," he declared. "Nevertheless, I ask the Fazrul's leave for a five-year moratorium before he is subjected to the vote. My own father, as you will recall, died suddenly, and I was thrust into the role of Ruler without adequate preparation. That I have ruled at all adequately is the result of the advice and assistance of many able persons. My son may not be so fortunate. Therefore I ask the Fazrul's indulgence, that Tetrok may be prepared.''

Some said the move was foolish. What if Tetrok devoted the next five years to preparation only to be turned down by the Fazrul? Conspicuously silent in that particular debate was Valton.

"Let him take all the time he wishes," he told Gulibol in confidence, all the while thinking: It will give me an equal amount of time to prepare!

♉

Meanwhile, on an Earth ship making its way toward Jupiter, Harley Block looked up from his bank of computer monitors, blinking myopically. The chronometer informed him it was time to eat again. It seemed to Harley as if he'd barely finished eating. He sighed and touched the Save toggle. Oh well! If he didn't eat he'd get sick, just as he'd lose bone and muscle mass if he didn't exercise to compensate for zero g. It all seemed like such a waste of time. To Harley everything was a waste of time, except his work.

# CHAPTER 17

Harley ("Call me Hack; I really hate 'Harley'!") Block was to be Beth Listrom's agent-in-place.

If the commander of Jupiter-1 hadn't practically drafted him, Hack would have been perfectly content to stay on Mars for the rest of his life, living inside his computer. He stayed on Mars because he'd been born on Mars, and had never felt a desire to travel anywhere else. In fact, the very idea of space travel made him sick to his stomach. He'd only survived the journey from Mars to Jupiter-1 by rearranging the ship's state-of-the-art computer array so that it exactly resembled the one he'd left at home; that way he could pretend he'd never left home.

"I'm not doing this for the money, you know," was what he told Commander Listrom when he reported to her, stumbling off the ship into the unfamiliar gravity of the station. Was it only his imagination, or were the walls of her office closing in on him? He hated this place, hated any new place, hated having to talk to people in person instead of on voice mail or, if absolutely necessary, holocom. "Money means nothing to me."

"I realize that, Hack," Beth said, not unkindly. She'd taken an almost immediate dislike to the little twerp, but she had a job to do. "Even so, I didn't notice you blocking your account when I tried to make the transfer."

Harley shrugged. "It's just numbers on a screen. I never spend money on anything, except to upgrade my equipment. Now I don't even have to do that. That's the only part of your deal that appealed to me, by the way, the upgrade level. 'In perpetuity' was the way it was worded in the contract. I can request upgrades on my equipment at any time, for any reason, even after this assignment is history, in perpetuity. I really liked that part!''

"As long as you remember that the assignment, and only the assignment, is history," Beth pointed out. "Any conversation you and I are having at this moment, in fact, never took place."

Hack looked momentarily confused before the light dawned and he started to nod. "Gotcha! . . . Commander," he added as an afterthought.

Beth sighed. She had to keep reminding herself that Harley was Jubal and Marissa Block's only son, and that she and Jubal and Marissa had served together for ten years before the two had married and settled on Mars. Was it the light gravity that had made Harley such a sniveling, hunch-shouldered nerd, or was he some kind of evolutionary throwback? He seemed incapable of looking anyone in the eye. He had both his parents' intelligence and then some, but at the cost of their vibrant personalities. It was hard to say if Harley had any personality at all. Oh well, it was only his intelligence Beth needed.

"Harley, while you're here, I want you to enjoy yourself," she suggested. "The nightlife on this station is the best in the system. We've got first-run movies, a live theater, two casinos, a wonderful cabaret with some of the top entertainers . . ."

Harley shook his head. "I'm not interested in any of that stuff."

"There's also the library—"

"Interlinked with the systemwide on the ship," he finished for her; he was rude along with everything else. "Nothing special."

"Our university extension, then," Beth tried. She needed to keep the kid on her side. Was there anything he wanted? "We have lecturers from some of the most prestigious—"

"If they're lecturing on computers, I can teach them," Harley cut in. "If it's anything else, I'm not interested."

Beth counted to ten before she spoke again. "What are you interested in, Hack?"

"Finding out why you specifically asked for me on this trip to Titan. I'm no spacer."

You certainly aren't! Beth thought. The commander of the ship that had brought him here had complained about his refusal to get with the program since they'd eased out of space-dock over Mars.

"No, but you're the best computer hack on Mars," Beth said plainly.

"Best in the known universe," Harley corrected her, absolutely without irony. "So what? Our system on Titan's standard. Anyone with a top rating can handle it."

"What about the Fazisian system?"

Harley laughed, a sound like disdain. "Even easier. They're more logical than we are, more organized. When they purge they purge clean. No ragtags and glitches like our systems. They're also bugproof. You know, tapeworms."

"Are they?" Beth said with genuine interest.

Socially inept though he was, Harley sensed something then—a change in her tone, a gleam in her eye she didn't manage to entirely suppress. He leaned forward and put his nail-bitten hands flat on the surface of her desk.

"Why don't you tell me what you're looking for, Commander? If there's anything I do like, it's a challenge."

He watched Beth Listrom touch a toggle just under the edge of the desk; anyone else might have missed it, but Hack's skin began to crawl with the subliminal vibration of subsonic scramblers.

In her own office? he thought. This must be really hot!

In a few moments, Listrom had told him just how hot.

*

Among the most dangerous things for a woman to do is to give too much of herself to her career. Too late, Nebulaesa pondered this as she waited for Valton to summon her.

What had she done, or failed to do, to merit recall from Outlyer-21? Valton's message had been terse in the extreme: "Required Fazis Prime. Return at once."

As far as Nebulaesa knew, the summons was without precedent. When she had first assumed command, it had taken the better part of a year to reach Outlyer-21 from Fazis Prime; commanders were only called back to the capital when they were ready to retire. But today's advanced technology made even the old Wingcrafts seem antiquated. Therefore it was possible, if unlikely, for a commander to be summarily summoned home.

Nebulaesa had little choice but to obey. She'd tried to reassure herself on the journey back that such a direct summons could not mean reprimand, but rather promotion. At least commendation rather than dismissal, surely. Still, Valton had not coded his message to her, had not even sent it on a private channel, but on the common carrier wave where anyone could read it. And it was audio only, lacking even the personal touch of a holocom. And it summoned her home—a time- and resource-consuming process even Valton would not resort to unless the matter was serious—without telling her why. What did it mean?

✍

"You were dreaming," Valton told her. His fine-chiseled face had been the first thing to swim into her vision beneath the clear sky punctuated by windswept trees.

"Was I?" Nebulaesa murmured, sitting up. The day had been warm; they'd been wind-sailing until a sudden calm took them down into a valley they'd never seen before, where they'd sat in the shade to eat their picnic lunch and wait for the wind to pick up again. Nebulaesa did not remember drowsing off, but here she was, resting in the crook of Valton's arm, feeling his long fingers brush the hair back from her temples. "I wonder what I was dreaming about."

"About a quarrel you and your sister had over a holobook when you were nine," Valton said airily, flaunting his knowledge; he was chewing a bit of *grana*weed and watching the clouds to see which way the wind had shifted and whether they would have to walk back to the flitter. " 'The Tale of Nerithit,' I think it was. Zeenyl won the argument, and you were lectured about being the elder and how you ought to know better."

Nebulaesa sat up abruptly, the dream returned to her in vivid imagery. "That was half my lifetime ago. You 'listened' to my dream while I was sleeping!"

Valton saw too late the look of violation on her face. "I meant no harm. We've known each other all our lives, B'Laesa; it's not as if I'm a stranger. The dream was right on

the surface of your mind; if you'd spoken it aloud it would
not have been easier to pluck it.''

''If I'd spoken it aloud''—Nebulaesa was on her feet,
brushing twigs and bits of *grana* off her clothes; she would
walk back to the road if it took till sundown, rather than remain with him—''it would have been yours for the taking.
What you did was dirty!''

''B'Laesa—''

''No!'' she shouted. ''It's like the way you used to tickle
Zeenyl when she was little, just because you were the stronger.
Your mindlock is stronger than mine; you have no right to use
it against me!''

☞

Decades later it came to her that this was why she had rejected
Valton, because she did not trust him. Tetrok's telesper abilities were always a shade less than hers; therefore she could
afford to love him.

For all the good it will do me! Nebulaesa thought now,
waiting in the antechamber to learn what Valton wanted. At
least she would be mindful that Valton had not changed overmuch in the years she'd been away. He would resort to almost
anything in order to unbalance anyone who had something he
wanted. All Nebulaesa had to do was find out what that something was.

Valton had wasted no time, but had her report directly from
her ship. Nebulaesa would have liked to rest first, gather her
thoughts, perhaps even check in at one of the better hotels in
the capital for the night at least. Valton's summons did not
even allow her the luxury of a bath.

She entered his inner sanctum to find herself already there.

Without a word, Valton played back for her the conversation he had intercepted some months earlier between her and
Beth Listrom. Nebulaesa watched herself pouring tea, watched
as a few stray crumbs from the tea cake lingered in the corner
of her mouth as she tried to wheedle information out of the
Earthian female, who merely stonewalled her. She became obsessed with watching her own mouth move, wanting to reach
into the holo image for the napkin lying on the tea tray, actually breathed a sigh of relief when her image at last wiped

the crumbs from her mouth. What an idiot she must have
looked to Commander Listrom! Now she turned on Valton
with the outrage of old acquaintance.

"Very amusing! Have I been summoned all this distance to
be lectured on my table manners? How many such communiqués do you intercept as a rule?"

"All of them," Valton said mildly, terminating the holocom, watching the play of colors on Nebulaesa's face and neck
as she fought back shame; even her hands looked embarrassed.
He smiled complacently. "Though I don't—as a rule—do
more than scan them as they come in. Only certain communications merit my complete attention, and this was one of
them." His smile faded. "Tell me what you were trying—
unsuccessfully—to learn from the Listrom woman."

"Is that the only reason you've sent for me?"

Valton laced his fingers together behind his head and swung
his chair idly, Earthian gestures he'd learned from years of
monitoring the very communications Fazis had taught Earthians to use. Did he have so little to do with his time? Nebulaesa
wondered.

"Maybe. Maybe there are other . . . matters . . . I will over-
look if you tell me what I want to know."

Nebulaesa fought to keep her colors under control. She'd
always planned to tell him about Tetrok and Zeenyl and the
child—if she told him at all—while operating from a position
of strength. Now he had her at a disadvantage. Had she waited
too long? Did he know everything already and need her only
to confirm it? What if she pleaded ignorance? Did he have
other sources to prove she'd been withholding valuable information, sources which could destroy her?

Or did he know nothing at all? As she wrestled with her
thoughts, Valton did something she could not possibly have
anticipated. He rose from his chair and took her in his arms.

"You see . . ." he breathed into her hair, and she could feel
his heart beating faster—or was it her own? "I believe that
there should be no secrets between two who love each other."

"W-what—" was all Nebulaesa managed to say before she
succumbed to her own tumultuous emotions.

It was not entirely to Valton she succumbed. Ever since
they'd all been children together she'd been struck by the un-

canny physical resemblance between him and Tetrok. She remembered in fact thinking that while, objectively, Valton was the handsomer, she would always love Tetrok in spite of his imperfection. She'd been fifteen at the time. Was she any wiser decades later?

"You've never taken a mate," Valton murmured between kisses. "Surely it can't still be Tetrok after all this time. Do I mistake you, or was there another reason?"

Nebulaesa clamped down on her thoughts before she spoke.

"Y-yes. Yes, there was," she breathed, thinking: It was this very thing, that you would overwhelm me, make me lose control, use me for your ends!

If she knew that was his intention, could she not maintain control?

Nebulaesa studied Valton intently. His colors were high, evidencing extreme agitation. Did he still feel so strongly for her after all this time? Why not, when her own passion for Tetrok was undiminished? Something in her wanted to say, *No, this is too pat, too contrived; this is not the Valton I have known all my life!*

But what of it? she wondered as they clung to each other. She would never have Tetrok; he had said as much. As a means to an end, could Valton be so bad? Let him think she loved him, so long as it kept her in power. Could she not close her eyes and pretend that he was Tetrok?

"Tetrok and I parted decades ago. Why did you never say anything until now?" she murmured.

"Ask you to give up your command to be with me? Or was I to surrender my position to live on Outlyer-twenty-one as your consort?" Nebulaesa tried to speak but he put his fingers to her lips. "Even that I might have considered, if we did not both have the greater good to serve. No, it was the fear that you would once again reject me. Or worse, say yes because you feared for your command if you said no."

"Then why speak now?" Nebulaesa asked. "And why so urgently? What has happened after all this time to so suddenly change your mind?"

Valton dropped his hands then with a wry smile.

"You know me too well, my dear Nebulaesa. You're right, I have what Earthians would call an ulterior motive. It is,

however, the same as yours. The same which caused you to
question the Listrom woman. Tell me, Nebulaesa. Tell me
about Saturna.''

Well? Nebulaesa thought, why not? It was out of her mouth
before she could help herself.

"She is Tetrok's child.''

Valton feigned a lack of surprise, but the rapid changes in
his skin color revealed the truth. He sat slowly on a nearby
sofa as if he did not trust his legs to hold him.

"Are you certain? How do you know?''

Nebulaesa sat beside him and told him about the fortuitous
accident with her ring, the DNA testing. Valton listened
thoughtfully.

"You have known this for some time, then.''

Nebulaesa nodded.

"Why have you not told me until now?''

"Because I thought you might . . . use it against Tetrok.''

"And you were, foremost, loyal to Tetrok,'' Valton suggested. "Yet you tell me now. I have not coerced or threatened
you. Where is your loyalty now?''

Nebulaesa smiled winsomely, thinking: Poor Valton! My
loyalty is the same as yours—to myself foremost, then to those
who will get me what I want!

"My loyalty,'' she said slowly, "is to the one who loves
me above all others.''

In his egotism Valton misunderstood her, as she'd hoped he
would. "Tell me everything you know about the child.''

She did, speaking of Saturna's uncanny ability to heal herself, of her powerful mind and telesper abilities surpassing
most adults'. Of her disturbing maturity even as a young child.
Of her extraordinary beauty, though she bore no resemblance
to either of her supposed parents.

Valton seemed to reach his decision almost instantly.

"She is almost of age. Before she arrives on the homeworld
to declare her citizenship, Xeniok and the Fazrul must be
told.''

Nebulaesa became suddenly agitated. "Do you realize what
you're saying? What it will do to Tetrok's reputation, and
Zeenyl's?''

"I will keep Zeenyl's name out of it—'' Valton began.

"Ridiculous! How are you going to do that?" Nebulaesa demanded, wringing her hands and beginning to pace. "And Tetrok's career, his very life—an accusation of adultery is one thing for a private citizen, but for an incipient Ruler, whose offspring automatically accede to the line . . . Damn Tetrok! How could he—"

She could not finish. Valton shrugged expansively.

"Tetrok should have thought of that before he succumbed to impulse." Seeing Nebulaesa fighting back tears, he came to her, stood behind her, put his hands on her shoulders and kissed the nape of her neck. "B'Laesa, no one's going to impugn the reputation of the dead. Zeenyl is a hero; she will remain one. In our statement we'll suggest that she was an innocent victim, seduced perhaps by Tetrok's greater power of mind. Zeenyl's telesper limitations—"

"No!" Nebulaesa sobbed, shrugging his hands away, turning on him. "I will not be the cause of this!"

You already are! Valton thought, a secret smile slithering briefly across his face; Nebulaesa, her eyes clouded with tears, did not see it. Valton took her face between his hands and opened his mind to her.

*B'Laesa, my beloved B'Laesa, how long have you borne this secret alone? Let me remove the burden from your weary shoulders, let me share with you the responsibility for what we do next. This child may be the key to all our futures, if we use our knowledge wisely. You are right: to reveal her parentage now would destroy Tetrok, and who knows what it would mean for Saturna's future? As much as I seek to rule, there are limits even to my ambition, dear B'Laesa! Can we in conscience do this to our childhood companion and friend, much less to your niece, an innocent child?*

*Let us keep this secret together, until the child appears before Tetrok to declare her citizenship. Then we will know what to do . . .*

As he took his hands away, Nebulaesa calmed herself. She felt an inner calm she had not known since she first learned Saturna's secret. As for Valton, he was suddenly all business.

"I am relieving you as commander of Outlyer-twenty-one—temporarily," he announced. Before she could protest, he added: "I need to have you close to me, and not only for command reasons."

He smiled as he said it, his colors warming, and Nebulaesa smiled back. Truly, she had been alone too long; this would not be so bad.

"What will I do on Fazis?" she wondered. Having already given too much of her life to her career, she did not know how to stop.

"You will need to be debriefed regarding your tenure on the outlyers," Valton said thoughtfully. "There is also the matter of a replacement for Mereet, who is retiring as head monitor of all outposts. I would like you to assume his place. Eventually you will have to make an inspection tour of all the outlyers, but not immediately."

"And how long do you estimate you will need me to remain here on Fazis?" Nebulaesa asked ingenuously, admiring the curve of his brow, remembering the gentleness of his touch, scarcely thinking of the promotion he had just offered her. Truly, this would not be so bad.

Valton pretended to consider this. "At least an orbit . . ."

"Until Saturna arrives," Nebulaesa finished for him.

"Even so," Valton said, thinking: And now I know exactly how to bring Tetrok down!

✍

*I suppose the Earthians sent their best people on the first expedition!* Saturna observed on a wavelength only Krecis and Langler could hear. They had greeted each of the newly arrived Earthians personally, and Harley Block in particular left Saturna singularly unimpressed. *Are there many on Earth who are like this Harley person?*

*There are as many on Earth as there are doubtless on Fazis!* Langler teased her. *Each of us is unique, and entitled to our idiosyncrasies. It's well for you that the Harley person is psi-null!*

Saturna managed to look chagrined.

The Harley person's reaction to Fazisians was no more charitable.

"Freaky!" he announced to the computer array he'd had laboriously transported from the ship to his private quarters just so he could feel at home. "They change color all the time; I keep wanting to adjust the contrast! Weirdest-looking thing I've ever seen!"

He always talked to his computers because they couldn't answer back. Harley liked it that way. He settled himself in his customized ergochair in the center of the array, arranged the virtual reality helmet over his jug ears, and cracked all of his knuckles twice.

"Okay, kids," he announced, rubbing his bony hands together in anticipation. "Let's go to work!"

*

She was twenty Fazisian years of age, eighteen years in Earthian terms, an adult in either society. In twenty days a Fazisian freighter would join the newly arrived Earthian ship in orbit above Titan, on its regular run. It would bring her as far as Outlyer-21, where she would hop a faster, sleeker colony-runner. Among the runner's many functions as it described an endless loop among the outlyers and the colony worlds was to gather up all the young adults Saturna's age who wished to appear before the Ruler on Fazis Prime to officially declare themselves as citizens of Fazis.

She had never been anywhere but Titan. She was beside herself with a mix of excitement, joy, and grief.

All her life she had devoured every datum about Fazis that the computers could provide her. She had lived for days inside virtual reality holos that set her down in the midst of her homeworld, reproducing the hum of cities and sigh of oceans, the smells and tastes and colors and textures of a world she could not help being drawn to. True, she had visited Fazis via her IC ability, but now she wanted to actually walk among its people, visit its halls and museums and sacred historical places, wanted to feel its soil between her fingers and its breezes on her face, wanted especially the pomp and ceremony of appearing before the Ruler, his son, and the Fazrul to declare in her clear and confident voice: "I am called Saturna, and I name Fazis as my home!"

She did not want to leave Krecis.

"Come with me, please?" she pleaded with him. "How long has it been since you left? Don't families sometimes accompany their children on such a special journey? You're the only family I've ever really known; come with me, Krecis, please?"

The OldOne demurred. "This is your rite of passage, a journey you must make alone. I am needed here."

"As if Titan couldn't run itself without you, at least for a little while! Krecis-mine . . ."

He stopped his work and looked at her, a look which brooked no further argument.

"I will not go with you. However, I will give you something which will always remind you of me."

He disappeared then into one of his inner chambers—it seemed he added new twists and turns to his labyrinth with each passing year—returning with a beauteous object which he placed almost reverently in Saturna's waiting hands.

It was a large crystal, as big as the palm of her hand, whose properties she could not begin to analyze. Was it synthetic, something Krecis had created himself, or some rare element found only on Titan, as only Krecis could find such things? Its many-faceted surface gleamed and teased at her senses, its colors as mutable as a Fazisian's skin, sometimes changing with her mood, sometimes as if it had a mood, almost a personality, of its own. It hung from a finely wrought chain just long enough to slip over her head, allowing the crystal to rest naturally in the curve where her breasts began, as if it were meant to be there.

"Oh, Krecis-mine, it's beautiful!" Saturna said, cupping it in her two hands even as it hung about her neck. Oddly, it felt warm to her touch, not cold and mineral at all. Knowing Krecis, she had to wonder. "It's more than just decorative, isn't it? What other purpose have you designed it for?"

Krecis did not answer. How could he? There was no way to explain the crystal. Like Saturna, it was unique in all the universe.

⚈

For nearly seven years, ever since he had accidentally spilled the algae solution on a fragment of the crystal and watched it glow with inexplicable radiation, he had labored to transform this natural phenomenon into an extraordinary device. In addition to the memory circuits stored so carefully they could not be detected by any kind of scanner, there were added facets to this crystal, so to speak.

For nearly seven years the colonists of Titan had tolerated Krecis' somewhat peculiar experiments. Some had even volunteered to be his subjects. Krecis had chosen among the volunteers carefully, making sure they were not likely to compare notes with one another. He did not want anyone to know the full extent of his experiments.

He had done the same with the construction of his subterranean labyrinth. Each section had been constructed by a different engineer who, more likely than not, would transfer off Titan on the next outgoing ship, on the way to the next assignment. Hence no one but Krecis knew how many rooms there were and which passages led where.

So with his research and application to the crystal. The first phase had been to devise the undetectable memory circuits. Then came the serendipitous accident with the algae and the seeming "magic" that came out of that.

From the algae molecules, Krecis had "birthed" a seemingly indestructible living microorganism which could actually translate biological information to the crystal circuitry. Simultaneously this encoded information could be beamed out of the crystal via a unique chemical reaction between the molecules of the crystal and those of the algae. Once the theoretical model had been developed in the laboratory, it was time to test it in the real world.

That was where the volunteers came in. When Krecis asked for a subject to test a simple physical interaction, Luke Choy was the first to volunteer.

Having discovered that the Earthian nervous system was quite similar to the Fazisian, Krecis stood behind a seated Choy and touched his thumb and first two fingers to the pressure point at the juncture of the young man's neck and shoulder.

"This will not hurt," he assured Choy. When he squeezed gently, Choy dropped like a rock, saved from a fall only by Krecis' strong arms catching him.

"Wow!" Luke announced a few minutes later when he came to. "You know what you just did? You Spocked me!"

"I beg your pardon?" Krecis asked seriously.

"Don't tell me you don't know!" Luke was amazed. "He's a character in one of our Earth legends. Right up there with Merlin in the Arthurian legends, if a little later. Only in the last century, in fact, there was what started out as a little, unheralded TV show, and it soon became an epic. There were movies and novels and—"

Just then Krecis performed the second part of this experiment. As Luke continued to babble, the OldOne slipped a fragment of crystal out of its box and aimed one facet toward a predetermined locus on Luke Choy's skull. Activating the crystal's beam, Krecis "Spocked" his victim a second time.

"Gee, if you wanted me to shut up, all you had to do was say so!" Luke pouted, when he came around the second time. "I didn't even feel you touch me that time."

Krecis did not bother telling him he hadn't. He had confirmed what he suspected—that the crystal had the power to short-circuit the brain just as effectively as what Luke referred to as the "Spock pinch." The first phase of his experiment was a success.

Naturally Luke had to tell everybody in the colony about Krecis' trick—he had never seen the crystal—and some were more curious than others.

"Is it wise to render our Earthian Governor unconscious?" Vaax inquired. "While I will admit he is sometimes too talkative, there are more diplomatic methods of silencing him. I thought I might intervene, OldOne, before you create an interplanetary incident."

Vaax was being ironic, of course. Krecis answered him in kind.

"Therefore as the second-most-verbose individual in the colony, you have volunteered to be my next subject," he responded.

"Perhaps." Vaax smiled.

"Very well." Krecis offered him a comfortable chair, poured him a cup of *grinish,* and asked him what he thought of the recolonization of Fazis Fourth.

"You should know better than to ask me that!" Vaax said somewhat sharply. Anyone who knew his ancestry and the fact that he had lost several branches of his family to that long-ago disaster realized it was a sore point with him. Nevertheless, he and Krecis became engaged in a rather heated, hour-long debate.

". . . and what is most infuriating is the Fazrul's response!" Vaax concluded, all but foaming at the mouth. He had long since left his chair, to pace wildly about the laboratory. "Or should I say, lack of response. To leave the survivors to starve to death was the height of cowardice, absent any scientific method . . ."

So engrossed was he in his tirade that he did not notice the gentle beam of radiant light touching his brow from the crystal Krecis held cupped in the palm of his hand. As Vaax grew more violent in his speech, the OldOne began to stroke the crystal gently, as a therapist might massage the back of a patient's neck to induce hypnosis. Suddenly, Vaax's words trailed off.

"And if the survivors had been allowed to return to the homeworld, only to find later that they carried some undetected virus with them that could destroy the entire population of Fazis Prime?" Krecis queried gently.

"Ridiculous!" Vaax half shouted. "That theory has been put forward more times than I can count. It's . . . It's . . ." He stopped, looking profoundly puzzled. "It's . . . possible, OldOne, that you may have a perspective I never considered before."

The two continued the debate for some time thereafter, and Vaax never grew angry again. While he did not concede his entire point, he did listen to Krecis most seriously, allowing that the OldOne could be at least partially correct.

Alone, Krecis contemplated his newfound "weapon." Had those who first split the atom felt this way?

☙

Over the next several years he would choose many more subjects, discovering that the crystal could hypnotize, cause muscle spasms, even initiate temporary paralysis. Each new discovery simultaneously pleased and frightened him. What manner of weapon could this be if it came into the wrong hands?

From the moment he first discovered the raw crystal in the

mine, he had determined to give it to Saturna as a gift when she came of age. Now, inculcated with all its hidden powers, it might prove the most valuable object she could possess.

As a last precaution, he devised one final "talent" into the jewel, by programming it to respond only to Saturna. This he accomplished by incorporating an ingenious "signal gate" within its internal circuitry, controlled directly by a sample of Saturna's DNA, which he had stored in the cryobank since she was born.

Yes, it was a weapon, a weapon Krecis hoped profoundly that Saturna would never have to use. Yet if he were to send his young charge out into a dangerous universe, he wanted her to be prepared. But when she asked him to tell her the crystal's secret, he demurred.

"Wear it always, whenever you travel away from me. Someday, when you most need it, it will tell you what it's for."

Saturna shook her head. "And you call yourself a scientist! You are a mystic, Krecis-mine, before you are anything else."

He seemed to consult his inner timesense. "Shouldn't you be packing? The freighter is already in departure mode; once all the requisite manifests have been signed, you will be cutting it close indeed. There is also the matter of preparing the animals . . ."

Catlyke and Mushii were going with her; there had never been any question of that. Both creatures were in a state of high agitation, whether because they were feeding off each other's fears of the unknown or Saturna's was hard to tell. The young woman spent most of her time before departure getting them settled into her quarters and trying to calm them.

Catlyke ranged restlessly about the entire cabin, marking every fixture with her whiskers, trilling uneasily, her tail fluffed out and lashing from side to side. Mushii, usually so frenetic, had the opposite reaction. As Saturna set him down on the floor of her cabin, all six legs shot out from under him and he collapsed in a heap.

Saturna called it "rugging out." Mushii had done it to make her laugh ever since she was small. It had the same effect on her now. Giggling and fighting tears at the same time, she scooped the little dust mop up under one arm, the long, lean

Catlyke under the other, and sat on the floor with both creatures in her lap.

"Stop it, please, both of you!" she said, two perfect tears
falling from her chrysolite eyes to trickle into their thick fur.
"This is hard enough; do you have to make it worse?"

*Sorry . . .* Catlyke crooned on their special wavelength, and
Mushii chimed in: *Yes, yes, soooo sorry!*

The three clung to each other, communing, and the melancholy passed. When Krecis came to see Saturna off, she was
a model of self-control.

*∽*

The freighter's few passengers had been shuttled up to one of
its airlocks and off-loaded as it hung ponderously in docking
orbit. The same shuttle brought a lone passenger, Krecis, back
to the Titan surface. The freighter's retros fired in sequence,
and the big ship lumbered out into space.

Saturna stood at the aft port until first the largish rusty moon
and then its ringed and golden mother planet became mere
pinpricks of light, then disappeared into the fabric of the star-
scape. From there on, she looked only forward.

*∽*

Tetrok needed some advice.

For twelve years he had abided by his father's wishes, jour-
neying on countless missions to every world and satellite and
station in the Fazisian system, familiarizing himself with every
aspect of this realm he would someday rule. For nearly seven
years more he had remained on Fazis Prime, committing the
laws and constitutions to memory, sitting in on endless ses-
sions of the Fazrul, learning protocols, preparing himself.
When Xeniok had first asked for a five-year moratorium it had
seemed like an eternity. As five years lengthened into seven,
Tetrok began to wonder if there was such an advantage in
being Ruler after all.

Returning to Fazis had cut short his work on Titan when it
had barely begun. His original mission to explore the Earthian
system was no longer mentioned. Even the extraordinary first
contact with the Earthians had begun to wane in importance
as the years passed.

Tetrok was not idle. In addition to intensive study of every aspect of his planet's governance, from law to sociology to geography, he still kept his hand in space exploration, signing on to every in-system mission that would have him. Xeniok dared not let him venture farther. Offworld travel was still dangerous. What if there was an accident, and the future Ruler never came back?

But how long was he to wait? Tetrok wondered. There was no graceful way to say, *Father, you're getting old and tired. You have summoned me home; now give me the role for which I have trained for my entire life.* Tetrok needed advice, and not only on this.

Having reported to the Fazrul upon his return two decades earlier, he no longer spoke of Titan at all unless directly asked. Most assumed it was because of the tragedy of the energy experiment, and his mourning for Zeenyl and Phaestus. No one on Fazis could possibly suspect the truth.

No day went by that Tetrok did not turn his thoughts to Nyota. He had followed her career through the shared Fazisian/Earthian scientific journals, but they told him only what he already knew: that this woman he had known and loved was a brilliant scientist, and that she continued to enjoy success in her work. But what of the woman herself, the woman who had touched his soul? Did she ever think of him?

He had asked her once if she would consider coming to Fazis as his mate; she had never answered him. Since Fazisians first ventured into space, no Ruler had ever left the homeworld once he acceded to the Rulership. What would Tetrok do, how would he live, if he never saw Nyota again?

In all this time he had not dared communicate with her; there was no knowing how secure a holocom transmission was. And what was he to say to her? *Nyota, do you still love me?* This was not a question for a holocom.

The thought of being Ruler without Nyota held no enticement for him; if anything it made him heartsick. Tetrok began to comb through volumes of Fazisian legal precedent, looking for an answer. When he thought he had enough background to at least ask the right questions, he went to Gulibol.

The Crown Litigator was a lawyer before all else, and lawyers were the same the universe over. Gulibol knew his place was to be the power behind the throne, and he intended to keep that place no matter who sat on the throne. He made it a point, therefore, to be ever accessible to the Ruler's son.

It was he, in fact, who gave Tetrok the opening to ask his questions.

"It has been noted," he observed, as the two of them strolled through the Offworld Museum, where Tetrok had invited him to view the latest plant specimens brought back from a colony world, "that Valton has summoned Nebulaesa back from Outlyer-twenty-one and is grooming her to replace Mereet. It has been suggested by some—mere gossip, no doubt"—Gulibol watched Tetrok's colors closely as he said this—"that theirs is an association . . . not entirely of a professional nature."

"No doubt," Tetrok said, his answer ambiguous, his colors unvarying. "We all grew up together. Whatever 'associating' Valton and B'Laesa choose to do is a natural outgrowth of old acquaintance."

"Were they to join—hypothetically, of course," Gulibol suggested tentatively, "their offspring would be added to the succession."

Tetrok gave the equivalent of a shrug. "Obviously. Just as my offspring—my *hypothetical* offspring at this juncture, Litigator, for as yet I have none—would disrupt the line, usurping Valton's place, unless of course the Fazrul objected. If you're suggesting I rush out and choose a mate in order to secure the places behind me for a position I have not yet been permitted to assume—it's ludicrous. Gulibol, why are we having this conversation? Have you an unmarried sister you'd like to introduce to me?"

Gulibol spread his hands in an expansive gesture. "You are jesting with me. Twenty years away from Earthians, yet you retain their concept of humor."

"What makes you say that?" Tetrok asked, guarding his colors carefully.

"You forget I still communicate regularly with Counselor Wong of the ESC. Through him I have 'met' many other Earthians. Humor is one of their most notable characteristics."

Tetrok seemed satisfied with this answer. "They are an interesting species," he acknowledged, leading the conversation where he wanted it to go. "The vanguard, one hopes, of many future encounters. Which raises some interesting legal questions."

"Such as?"

"Also mere gossip, but there are reports of Earthians forming liaisons with Fazisians on Titan. Rumor has it one such couple has even requested permission to marry."

Gulibol did not ask Tetrok how he knew this. "Indeed. The request is in my computer even as we speak."

"What do you intend to do?" Tetrok asked. He was not looking at Gulibol, but was studying a display case full of soil samples with inordinate interest.

Again Gulibol made his expansive gesture. "One should not presume to legislate love."

Tetrok glanced at him in surprise. "That's a remarkably liberal attitude!"

"I was going to add: 'In the face of interplanetary relations,' " Gulibol said dryly.

Both men laughed—a polite, restrained Fazisian laughter.

"Litigator, I am surprised," Tetrok confessed, as they continued their peregrinations through the museum. "Next you will tell me you would not object to someday seeing a Ruler choose a non-Fazisian mate."

Gulibol clasped his fastidious hands before him as they walked. "There is nothing in the law which forbids it. And it has always been my philosophy not to create laws where none are needed."

As it has also been my philosophy, he thought without saying it, to say less than I know!

What Gulibol knew was this: There were almost as many reasons why Tetrok would not automatically become Ruler as there were reasons why he would. Gulibol did not especially care; his mistress was the law. Whoever became Ruler, Gulibol intended to remain Crown Litigator.

Ever accessible to the Ruler and his son, Crown Litigator Gulibol had also made himself accessible to Valton.

# CHAPTER 18

None of the holos had even remotely prepared her for this.

"It affects everyone this way the first time," the colony-runner's pilot told her as he waited for final clearance to bring his ship into berth. "Even we who are born here, the first time we go offworld and look back, we're overwhelmed. It still moves me every time I return, and I return every few orbits of our beautiful planet. I can only imagine what it must be like to be in your place."

Saturna opened her mouth but no words came out; her colors—swirling up from her toes to the roots of her hair—spoke for her. Finally she shook her head and just stared.

"It's a wondrous planet," the pilot said unnecessarily. He was a man of few words who had seen many worlds; in saying so little, he had said it all.

Clouds of conventional water vapor so bright they hurt the eye were interspun with orange-pink threads of methane cloud, the whole a loosely woven blanket swathing a pristine orb of indigo seas and golden shores, of plant life that vary with the time of day as Earthian trees altered only with the change of season, so that a Fazisian tree might sport spring foliage with the dawn and autumnal reds and browns with nightfall.

The shuttle which brought the runner's passengers to land skimmed too high and fast over the wilder places for Saturna to see any animals, beyond a cloud of flying lizards. Bright crimson and no bigger than her index finger, they navigated by ultrasound, their unheard cries bouncing off the shuttle's exterior, warning them just in time to veer off in precise formation. Watching them, Saturna clasped her hands together in delight.

There would be time to see the animals, she thought, prying Catlyke's tail from around her neck before the high-strung creature succeeded in strangling her. For now, all her attention was taken up by the cities.

Constructed of the same iridescent metals as the colony compound on Titan where she'd grown up, they seemed strange to her here beneath a sunlit sky. How strange it was to begin with to actually be able to see the sun! Again, though she had scanned countless holo images, there was nothing to quite equal the actual feel of sunlight on her eager, yearning skin.

She stood for the longest time on the shuttle pad, relishing the sight of an unclouded sky, breathing fresh, unprocessed air, basking in the sun. Setting the two creatures down to fend for themselves, she began to run toward a nearby sward of herbs and trailing flower beds. Before she could think about protocol or who might see her, she had slipped off her shoes and begun to walk, careful not to crush the flowers, feeling the soil of her parents' native land slide warm and loamy between her toes. Yes, she had done this in the greenhouses on Titan, but it was not the same.

"Saturna?"

She turned to see her Aunt Nebulaesa waiting to greet her. She slipped back into her shoes.

"I'm acting like a child," she said, chagrined.

Nebulaesa smiled. "It's a frequent reaction among colony-dwellers three times your age. For all the artificial environments we create for ourselves, nothing quite equals the feel of home."

*Titan is my home!* Saturna wanted to say, but stopped herself. Not only would it seem ungracious, but why had she come to Fazis, after all, if that were true? Before she could say anything, she began to sneeze.

"It's the pollen," Nebulaesa said, at the young woman's astonished look. "When you've never breathed anything but processed air, there's always at least one allergen to make you sneeze. You'll adjust in a day or two, or we can have a healer boost your immunities. Come. My house is not far, but I thought I'd set the skimmer to tour the city first. Unless you're really tired . . ."

Saturna shook her head, her eyes shining. "Not at all. I can't wait to see—well, everything."

Nebulaesa smiled at her ingenuousness. She liked the twenty-year-old Saturna far better than she had the three-year-old. Gone was the small child's need to impress, especially now that she was out of context, in a world which was not yet her own. A world, Nebulaesa thought, rife with more plots and subplots than such innocence could possibly imagine, all of them impinging on this young woman's fate.

"Have you thought of what you'll do with yourself in the time before your ceremony?" Nebulaesa asked, as they dined in one of the many gardens which formed the outer rim of the capital. From here they could see the gradual rise of the hills which formed the Center City, the Fazrul, the Ruler's winter palace, and, of greatest interest to Saturna, the Hall of Audiences.

But the young woman seemed equally interested in the movements of the soft-footed servers bringing them food in the garden, setting down ever-new dishes of steaming, savory delights on the stone-topped tables even as they cleared away those from previous courses. She was accustomed to fetching her own meals from food processors; the concept of being served, and the subtle choreography of those bringing her countless new things to taste, clearly fascinated her. Learning that all able-bodied citizens took turns performing these functions—serving food, tending the public gardens, clearing the dust from the streets—fascinated her all the more. The very image of her elegant Aunt Nebulaesa with a broom in her hand made her smile.

"I'm sorry!" she said, smiling now, fingering the berry wine goblet delicately, as if wondering if she dared ask for more. "I didn't hear the question."

"You're overwhelmed," Nebulaesa suggested. "There is so much to see and experience. Which is why I was going to suggest a way of acclimating you. You certainly have enough time."

The usual procedure was for all young people born in the same month to appear before the Ruler and the heir apparent in a grandiose ceremony replete with processions and a banquet afterward. At the appointed time, each candidate would step forward individually beneath the eyes of family, friends, and well-wishers and take the oath of fealty to Fazis, promising also to honor the ideal of exploring the galaxy through peaceful means.

Candidates were asked to arrive in the capital at least ten days before the ceremony in order to learn the protocols. In Saturna's case, however, because she was the first child born on Titan, a special individual ceremony had been prepared for her. And because she had arrived well in advance of the ceremony, she was free to do whatever she pleased in the meantime. If she chose to travel anywhere on the planet, she would find every home on Fazis open to her, for all Fazisians were one family.

She had in fact planned something like that, and was about to tell her aunt, when Nebulaesa said:

"How would you like to come with me on a tour of our planet?" Before Saturna could answer, she went on: "Yes, I know you'd like to rough it, hiking the back routes and stopping at random, but the fact is, you won't be anonymous. Your very name will tell people who you are, and you may not welcome their curiosity. Besides, I can show you places you might never find on your own."

Saturna considered this. Wasn't it best to travel in the company of a knowledgeable companion?

"I think I'd like that!" she announced, and it was done.

✍

And not a moment too soon. Even as they finished their berry wine and debated the relative merits of several of the desserts, a message from Valton relayed itself to Nebulaesa's private 'com, asking to meet with the new candidate for citizenship, daughter of his late friend and kinswoman Zeenyl.

As soon as Nebulaesa had shown a sleepy and grateful Saturna off to bed, she replied to Valton's message, with regrets. She and her niece, she explained, would be leaving the capital on the morrow. Perhaps when they returned in thirty revolutions, they could both honor the Offworld Commander's gracious request.

✍

Not unexpectedly, Valton took offense. Did he not have the right to meet Zeenyl's daughter, regardless of who her father

was? Had he not reassured Nebulaesa that he would protect
the child, even if he decided to accuse Tetrok? Why was she
keeping Saturna from him?

There was no point in expressing his outrage to Nebulaesa.
Let her leave the capital with her young charge, then. Valton
had other plans.

When he had checked with his sources and confirmed that
Nebulaesa had in fact requested a thirty-rotation leave, logged
a flight plan for her personal skimmer, and departed the city,
he requested an audience with Tetrok.

✍

"A personal matter, cousin. I would prefer a private meeting.
You're a difficult man to catch unattended."

Something tugged at Tetrok's instincts even as Valton said
this. Valton might be the superior telesper, but he himself was
the superior leader. Something about Valton's request, to bor-
row an Earthian phrase, smelled fishy.

"We can speak here, cousin," Tetrok offered to Valton's
holo image. "This is a secure channel. I regret I can't receive
you personally this afternoon, but as I'm certain you know, I
have departure orders for Fazis Third. We launch in less than
an hour. In fact, were this anyone but you, I wouldn't have
stopped to take the message."

Valton feigned gratitude at Tetrok's graciousness, but he
took little comfort in any of this. Risk saying what he had to
say on a holocom channel, or countenance a delay until Tetrok
returned to the capital?

"I appreciate your making an exception for me, cousin, but
I prefer to meet with you in person," he said with all the
control he could muster. "How long before you return from
Fazis Third?"

"Barring complications—and there are always complications on Fazis Third—about thirty rotations."

Valton weighed this. He'd hoped to confront Tetrok before
Nebulaesa's return. Then again, he had studied holos of the
adult Saturna; anyone with eyes could see that she was not
Phaestus's child. Would close proximity to Tetrok prove she
was his? What could be more dramatic than to be able to

produce the child herself once he had confronted his cousin with his crime?

The image of Valton shrugged. "It's not that urgent. I will await your return, cousin."

Sometimes, Valton thought, it was better to let matters take their natural course.

Sometimes, Tetrok thought, it was better to take matters into one's own hands. Even as the comm officer notified him of his ship's imminent departure, he logged two time-delayed outgoing messages. When he met with Valton, he wanted Xeniok and Gulibol to be there.

*

She cannot be anyone but Tetrok's child! Valton decided as he studied Saturna's features almost to the point of obsession. The delay turned out to be to his advantage; it gave him the opportunity to weigh every aspect of his plan before he acted on it.

How had it happened that Krecis' "little one" had attracted the attention of the future Ruler? Valton wondered, turning the possibilities over in his mind. Was it his own oversight that had not seen the youngest of their childhood foursome turn into an exquisitely beautiful woman? Beauty or not, still she had no fire. Had their little bookworm been seduced by the ever-self-confident Tetrok, or had it been the other way around?

Valton knew the pitfalls of long-term space travel, the constant daily proximity to the same people, the little quirks and tics and annoying character traits that got on others' nerves no matter how carefully the experts balanced the personalities of those on board. Alternatively, shipmates thrown together in such close quarters quickly got to know each other very well, on a level of intimacy which might take years or never develop at all in another context. Shipboard romances, conducted with a bit more formality and restraint than on, for example, Earthian ships, nevertheless did occur.

But not usually between a married woman, whose spouse was also on board, and an unmarried male who would be Ruler.

How had it happened? Valton wondered, then finally concluded: It does not matter how, only that it happened. Zeenyl is dead and can neither defend herself nor admit her culpability; it serves no purpose to tarnish her reputation. It is Tetrok alone who must answer for what happened!

*

It was the most wondrous adventure of Saturna's life.

With her Aunt Nebulaesa as her guide and companion, she flew on a sailboard among colorful *llwelowin*-birds on the updrafts over the Kinsali Mountains, and hiked the pristine trails through the Gnerro Valley. Clutching an air bubble exuded by the *arajik* reeds along the mouth of the Dmerizzk River, she swam for hours beneath the surface and far out to sea, stroking and being stroked by the pods of prototelepathic sea cows who adopted her and gave her an ancestral pod name. She lived for two days in a self-sufficient undersea environment, and for two days more in a telespers' retreat on a mountain so high its peak never emerged from the methane-laced cloud. In the wilder regions, she watched flocks of wild *z'zling,* once hunted almost to extinction, swarm over entire hillsides. As the shadow of a hunting *glurfen* flew over them, they turned color in an instant, each individual furry creature assuming the precise coloration of the rock or bit of foliage it was crouching on. Saturna remembered everything. But most of all, she remembered the people.

She loved the cities, and not only for their wealth of treasures to browse among and buy, the museums and galleries and restaurants and concert halls, the gardens and fountains and libraries and open-air schools, the judicious symmetry of modern architecture constructed in harmony with the very ancient, the sights and sounds and scents of Fazisian life. Beyond all that, she loved the Fazisian people.

They embraced their kinswoman as if she had always been part of the fabric of their lives. Everywhere she and Nebulaesa traveled her story seemed already known, but nothing sensational was made of it. Every Fazisian was unique, and every individual's story was equally of merit. Saturna felt welcomed and loved. Only one thing puzzled her.

"Hereditary rule?" she questioned Nebulaesa after a particularly hectic day, their last in the northern hemisphere before they returned to the capital in the south. "I understand the history of it, and I can see how it's worked all these centuries, but I sometimes wonder . . ."

"What do you wonder?" Nebulaesa asked fondly. She'd been amused at the young woman's reaction when she explained the succession, including the fact that, as Zeenyl's daughter, Saturna was fourth in line.

Whereas, as Tetrok's, you would be second, before all of us! Nebulaesa thought, careful not to let any of her thought slip through to this highly telepathic child. Has Valton in his obsession considered that?

"Well, naturally I wonder what it would be like to be Ruler," Saturna admitted. "But I also wonder what it must be like to be from a nonruling family and realize one might have skills equal to the Ruler's, but never have a chance. If the Ruler were just a figurehead, like the old kings of England on Earth, it would be one thing, but . . ."

"Surely you know there's a provision in the law for just such a contingency," Nebulaesa suggested. "When the heir apparent is brought before the Fazrul for the vote, anyone else of equal qualifications may also submit an application. Why, in Xeniok's grandmother's time, it took seventeen votes before—"

"Before Xeniok's grandmother was chosen Ruler anyway," Saturna interrupted with the impatience of youth. "Allowing . . . commoners . . . to apply is only a formality; the Ruler's offspring always wins."

"There are no 'commoners' on Fazis," Nebulaesa chided her gently, though it wasn't entirely true, and the young woman had a point. "You're young, and perhaps you don't understand the system in its entirety, but it's served us for a thousand years."

"Still . . ." Saturna began, an uncharacteristic frown creasing her beautiful face.

"What, then?" Nebulaesa asked. Never let it be said that maturity could not learn from youth. "What would you suggest in its place?"

"I've read a lot of history," Saturna said. "Earthian history as much as Fazisian. Earthians also went through millennia of rule by tyrants, as we did, and emerged with nonhereditary rule.''

''Are you suggesting Earthian democracy is any more democratic than ours? Do Earthians have the universal right to vote daily on countless referenda which directly affect their lives? Has the Earthian transition from tyranny to democracy been as bloodless as ours? As a student of history, Saturna, you tell me: How many wars for freedom were fought on Earth before they finally got it right?''

''Then if we have the perfect democracy, why do we still need a Ruler?'' Saturna asked with a hint of petulance, not entirely answering the question. ''A thousand years seems an awfully long time for any system to remain unquestioned. Change is the order of the universe.''

''Spoken like a scientist!'' Nebulaesa praised her. ''However, as a scientist you also know that change for the sake of change can lead to chaos.''

''Just as the refusal to change can result in entropy?'' Saturna countered.

''Once we return to the capital and you have a chance to observe the Fazrul and the Ruler in action, perhaps you will see things differently,'' Nebulaesa suggested; this time it was she who was not entirely answering the question. ''And once you have performed your ceremony, the wisdom of what we do may become clearer still.''

Saturna was skeptical, but she kept her skepticism to herself. In her mind she'd been comparing the Fazisian system to the way things were run on Gregonia. Now she stopped and thought about that.

She had not really thought about, or ''visited,'' Gregonia since she had come to Fazis.

Was Krecis right? Was Gregonia no more than a young girl's fantasy, a substitute for the real world she had experienced these past weeks? Or was Isidros, her special friend, still part of her life, silently ''listening'' to her mind across parsecs of space, knowing she lacked the skills to answer back?

Isidros was doing precisely that.

His interest in Saturna had grown with the years, and he was well aware of her current journey to her homeworld. While he respected her privacy and did not "watch" her, he knew her thoughts, reveled in her experiences as much as she did, and kept a proprietary watch over her, a single tendril of his Imagination Communication reaching out from his world to Saturna on hers.

*

Somewhere in between, on a largish moon called Titan, ordinarily among the most peaceful places in the galaxy, a small internecine brush war was taking place.

"I'd like to commission a special ship just to send him home in irons!" Luke Choy was raging. "To tell you the truth, Krecis, I'd like to toss him out in the atmosphere in his underwear and never look back. He stands to ruin everything we've established here!"

The object of Commander Choy's rage sat in a makeshift detention cell looking smug and unrepentant. If his jailers knew his insides were quivering at the thought of being separated from his computers, they'd have him! Harley thought. But he wasn't going to give them the satisfaction. Instead he wrapped his scrawny arms around his concave chest and glowered back at the fuming Choy.

"Perhaps the damage is not so great as that," Krecis suggested, studying this poor specimen of humanity thoughtfully. "I see no reason to allow this matter to spread beyond Titan."

"Maybe neither of us will let it out on official channels," Luke said, "but where there are Earthians, there are bound to be leaks. I clamped the lid on 'com as soon as we caught him, but at least one of my people's sure to have slipped under the wire and phoned home to tell a friend, if not the media, that we found this weasel rummaging through classified files."

Even as Krecis mentally translated Luke's slang—he especially liked the "weasel" metaphor, though, to his way of thinking, Harley Block's activities were more those of a ferret than a weasel—Harley was beginning to doubt himself.

Hack, old friend, he thought, this time you may have gone

too far! When, when will you learn to stay at your console where you belong?

Beth Listrom's orders had been specific: Find out everything he could about Earthian/Fazisian interaction on Titan, especially anything "off the record"—data that were stored out of the loop, kept on Fazis rather than being broadcast out to either homeworld. Hack had discovered early on that Fazisians were even more meticulous about record keeping than Earthians, and it had been entirely too easy to keep several searches running simultaneously.

Officially, he was here to keep every computer on Titan operating at peak performance, particularly those that interfaced with offworld systems on Jupiter-1, which were naturally fed back into the mother system on Earth. It was kindergarten stuff to Harley Block. He'd even managed to impress some of the Fazisian operatives—that is, if he was correctly interpreting the nods and solemn glances they gave him and each other when he accomplished some particularly razzle-dazzle feat—and none of the Earthians could touch him for speed, accuracy, and innovation. Hack was an artist. Still, he'd managed to compress and upgrade the entire system in less than two weeks, and could easily have packed up and gone home, if only there'd been a ship to take him there.

Hack hadn't bothered to think it through, but the fact was that he was stuck on this rock until the ESC decided to send another ship, and that could be a year or more. Commander Listrom had sweet-talked him over that part. As she saw it, Harley lived inside his virtual reality headset anyway; what difference did it make whether he worked from Titan or from Mars? But Hack could feel the difference, and he wanted to go home.

Maybe that was why he'd ventured out into the "real" world of Titan. Better to go home in disgrace—he had ESC immunity, so there wasn't much they could really do to him—than never to go home at all.

At any rate, in and around what he'd been officially sent here to do, he'd also run Beth Listrom's secret agenda, scanning every bit and byte of information on *everything,* from how many tons of silicates were left over from ore refining before each Fazisian ore drone left orbit, to how many packets of *grinish* the OldOne Krecis consumed every hundred days. It was boring, and Hack was bored. Even scanning the reports on the energy experiment—which he did as thoroughly as Valton and Nebulaesa had done before him—turned up nothing. As for the other big project, the one his hacker's instinct told him was the real reason Listrom had sent him here, "Forget about it, Commander," he'd told her. "They did that one by the book. They said they wanted to create an interspecies child, both governments said no, they canceled the project. There isn't a single loose end lying around to indicate otherwise."

"And doesn't that strike you as peculiar?" Listrom's holo image frowned. "Isn't it just a little too neat?"

"We're talking Fazisians here, Commander. They've got the patent on neat." Harley went scrabbling for something on one of his screens. "Okay, you want closure, here's closure. A memo in his private journal from the head honcho, Tetrok, indicating they've shut down the project. Period, end of report. You want me to run a translator program?"

"Not necessary," Beth said, her frown deepening. "You actually accessed his private journal? How the hell did you do that?"

Hack grinned evilly. "Does Macy's tell Gimbels? Let's just say I've capitalized on the fact that Fazisians have a different take on privacy than we do."

"Sounds like you're learning," Beth said, meaning it as a compliment; she'd been expecting more reports on Harley's "inability to integrate," but there had been none so far. As long as the little toad was busy, he didn't have time to offend anyone.

"Just doing my job."

"Oh, I doubt that very much!" Beth Listrom said, signing off.

Here where no one could see him, Hack's grin widened. He hadn't told the boss about the one aspect of the Fazisian system that really bothered him: There were no lockdowns. He could access any file from the day Nyota Domonique and her crew first set foot on Titan to this very afternoon; there were no special codes or passwords, nothing. It was too easy, and it irritated him.

The only files he hadn't been able to break into—so far—
were those directly from Krecis to his own government, and,
for security reasons, that made absolute sense. Hack could just
imagine the uproar if the Fazisians were ever crazy enough to
try tapping into ESC internal files. It was generally accepted
that the Fazisians were too honorable to even consider such
a thing. Hack always figured it was a matter of pride. Why
would the Fazisians even bother tapping the files of a technologically inferior species?

Hack, of course, had no such compunction. He had his own
professional pride, which dictated that any classified document
was only sacrosanct until someone figured out how to crack
it. He had cracked Krecis' code and was scanning merrily
along, when he missed one little trail marker that triggered a
whole series of alarms and shutdowns. Harley had finally
come up against the one person in the universe who was better
at his job than he was, and, tangled up in his own hubris, he
was caught.

*

"Why were you attempting to read my personal files?" Krecis
asked Harley mildly, his tone masking considerable inner turmoil.

The matter disturbed him far more than he would allow
Commander Choy to suspect. There was no precedent for it
in Krecis' experience. For one thing, this was the first instance
in which an Earthian had violated the essential etiquette upon
which the joint government of Titan rested. For another, Harley was unreadable. Not only did his skin remain a uniform
Earthian monochrome, revealing none of his moods, he was
also psi-null; the nuances which would aid Krecis in reading
a fellow Fazisian were not in Harley Block's programming.
And his transgression was so childish by Fazisian standards
that it was difficult to address in any legal, much less interplanetary, context.

This is in addition, Krecis thought in the innermost recesses
of his mind, to the fact that had he been more successful in
his "hacking," he might have exposed my files on the algae
and Saturna and my secret communications with Xeniok . . .

For the first time, he was grateful that the most important person in his life was not on Titan.

The OldOne's face revealed none of this, did not even reveal impatience when Hack refused to answer his question.

"Why were you attempting to read my personal files?" he asked again.

Hack's answer was a sullen silence.

"You'd better say something, mister!" Luke Choy seethed. "Before I waive your immunity as an Earth citizen and leave you to answer to Fazisian law."

Choy was bluffing, but Hack didn't know it. The simple truth was that Fazisian law no longer covered this sort of malicious mischief, since there hadn't been a recorded instance of it in generations. And if Krecis refused to press charges, there was nothing Choy could do but ship the miscreant home, which was probably what Hack wanted in the first place. Still, there was some satisfaction in watching Harley's eyes widen and his jaw drop.

"C-can you do that?" he stuttered, imagining all sorts of horrors.

"Just watch me!" Choy threatened.

Harley's brain reeled. This was too real. Maybe they'd ship him off to Fazis to stand trial. Maybe they'd imprison him for life. Even the thought of living freely on a planet full of these weird iridescent beings with their secret mental powers was enough to turn his knees to water. What if they cut him off from his computers? What if they never let him go home? Harley swallowed, thinking fast.

"Jeez, you know, I really think you're overreacting here. You missed the whole point of what I was trying to do."

His response threw Choy for a minute.

"Explain," he said tightly.

"My assignment was to leak-proof the entire system," Harley explained, gaining confidence now. "That includes the Fazisian side. When I saw how easy it was to get into some of the personal files, I thought: Hack, old buddy, it's your duty to warn these people about security, to let them know that Earthians think differently, and that maybe someday some . . . unscrupulous person might start poking around in your files. Okay, I picked a dramatic way to demonstrate it; so sue me!"

He sat back in his chair, looking smug. "You've got to admit I got my point across!"

Krecis touched Luke Choy's shoulder lightly before the Earth commander lost his temper.

"A moment, please," he suggested, and the two went into an anteroom to confer.

"He's lying!" Luke said through clenched teeth.

"Apparently," Krecis replied.

"And that doesn't infuriate you?" Luke demanded. "I'd like to rip his liver out! Either he's working for someone, or he's just some puny hacker with a big ego trying to show us up. Either way, he has no idea what his little prank could do to the entire Titan mission."

"Only if we allow it to," Krecis observed.

For as long as he'd known the OldOne, Luke couldn't believe his composure.

"Are you suggesting we just let him get away with this?"

Krecis spread his hands in a magnanimous gesture. "Does that not seem best? If it was just a prank, then we have deflated his ego by catching him. If he is in fact working for someone, and we dismiss him unscathed, one of two things happens: either his superiors continue to assign him further clandestine activities, in which case we come closer to discovering who they are, or, because they know he's been questioned, his superiors will no longer trust him."

"His cover will be blown," Luke suggested.

Krecis had read an Earthian spy novel or two in his time. "Precisely."

Luke turned it over in his mind. "So if you fail to press charges on behalf of your government, I can send him home on the pretext that his work here is finished anyway, and neither of us needs to say anything about catching him with his hand in the cookie jar."

Krecis nodded. Luke sighed.

"OldOne, I think we may have struck the first plea bargain on Titan." He clapped Krecis on the shoulder. "As a lawyer, I should be proud of myself. As Earth Commander of Titan, I'm left with a bad taste in my mouth."

Krecis agreed.

❧

Harley was released and put under virtual house arrest. While there were no security guards per se on Titan, he was assigned a babysitter, someone to stand outside his door when he was in his quarters, and accompany him on the rare occasion when he left. Mercifully there was an Earthian ship, an unmanned freighter, stopping by within the next sixty days. A team of engineers would adapt an empty storage bin into a habitat to ship Harley and his hardware home. In the meantime, Krecis would personally monitor all his computer work.

Watch me all you want, old man! Hack gloated. None of you realizes I've gotten everything I want. And I didn't even have to play my trump card . . .

It was one of those flukes that sometimes came out of nowhere when you were tinkering with something entirely different. Harley had been working on a gamma-wave booster, trying to improve the signal on some of the Titan-to-Earth data feeds and cut back the lag time on low-grade transmissions— the kind of unglorified scut work that could at least earn him extra credits, if not qualify as a breakthrough if he could get his patent application in ahead of anyone else—when he'd detected what at first seemed to be a glitch.

It was just weird enough to attract his attention. Hadn't quarks been detected by accident? Harley had wondered with the minuscule portion of his brain that still attached itself to real life, and important things like history. When he cleaned the static out from around this particular funny little wavelength, it began to look even weirder.

What could it be? he wondered. At first it seemed to be aimed—if "aimed" was the word—exclusively at Titan, but when he expanded his search parameters he found some of it streaming toward Earth as well. On a hunch, he'd been just about to include Fazis in his search, when Commander Choy had broken in on 'com to tell him to report to his office *now*. Hack had left his recorders running the entire time Choy and Krecis had been grilling him. Now, confined to quarters, he scanned what he'd picked up, then shut the recorders off.

Harley was no astrophysicist, and he had no idea what he'd recorded, but something about the signature suggested it wasn't a random, natural phenomenon at all. If he'd had a chance to work on it further, he might have been able to trace it back to its source, but no way was he going to keep tinkering with it with Krecis breathing down his neck. If they'd really turned the screws on him, he might have thrown it at Choy, suggesting it was some kind of secret monitoring device, maybe issuing from Fazis, maybe from somewhere else. It would have gotten Choy and Krecis off his case while they went searching for something else. Hell, if they'd found the source, he might even have turned out a hero. But it hadn't been necessary, and for the moment, Hack intended to keep his little discovery to himself.

Who knew? It might be just space noise. Or it might be his ticket to ride.

# Chapter 19

The sight of the capital had a disquieting effect on Nebulaesa. She would have to act soon, and as yet she did not know what she would do.

She had hoped the tour with Saturna, which had extended through a complete orbit of Fazis Second, would give her time enough to gather her thoughts and decide what course to take. But as the skyline rose around their descending skimmer, returning her to the city of the man she loved, she was more uncertain than ever.

Yet never let it be said that her uncertainty showed through the professional facade. The skimmer had barely touched down before Nebulaesa became a whirlwind of activity.

"After your ceremony," she told Saturna, who watched the preparations with bemusement, "you will be presented to virtually every important personage in the city. I thought to acclimate you gradually. We will host a small dinner party for Valton, the Ruler's kinsman and mine, and head of the Offworld Services."

Saturna nodded. Of course she knew who Valton was, recalled a coldly handsome face on official holocoms, a face which for reasons she could not define made her uneasy. As she scooped Mushii off the floor to get him out of the way of the automated rug cleaner, she felt him shiver, sharing her uneasiness.

"Why Valton?" she asked her aunt.

"Because he is interested in you. Primarily because you are a kinswoman but also because Valton is interested in everything which transpires under his command. As the first child born on Titan, you intrigue him," Nebulaesa said ingenuously. "And also because I think you'll find him charming. It's a good place to begin."

☞

Valton had thought so too. Yet it was he who felt uneasy in Saturna's presence, not the other way around.

He had not expected such self-assurance, or such exceptional beauty, in one so young. There was something almost regal in her carriage as she entered the room in a gown the color of malachite and the texture of lush velvet, something in the way she presented herself and took his hand as if they were equals.

Around her neck hung an exquisite pendant the like of which he had never seen before. He found himself staring into her eyes, intrigued by their unusual color, more golden than the Fazisian emerald. Valton the scientist tried to recall if anyone in either Tetrok's family or Zeenyl's might have had such eyes; the more he looked into Saturna's, the more certain he was that no one had. Still holding her hand in his, he could see Tetrok's legacy in her all too clearly, but the beauteous Zeenyl's? By what leap of genetic variance could this child be Zeenyl's?

Still holding her hand, Valton the gifted telesper tried to brush her thoughts lightly with his own and found himself soundly rebuffed. There was no casual access to this one's mind. In spite of himself, Valton frowned.

"Cousin Valton?" Saturna's voice was melodic, disturbingly so. Her own frown mirrored his. "Have I upset you?"

Had she blocked his thoughts so effortlessly that she was actually unaware of it? Valton wondered, finding he'd better look to his own thoughts lest they betray him.

"You're very beautiful," he temporized, unconsciously using the precise words with which Nebulaesa had greeted the three-year-old Saturna when they first met on Titan. Nebulaesa, fussing over some last-minute detail in the table setting, watched the interchange with great interest. "Almost unsettlingly so. Forgive me; I did not mean to frown. I was thinking of your parents."

"A tragedy," Saturna said solemnly, echoing what everyone said when referring to Phaestus and Zeenyl.

"Even so, my child. They would be so proud of you," Valton said, regaining his composure. "That is a most unusual and lovely jewel you wear,'' he went on, escorting her to her seat.

Saturna smiled. "A gift from Krecis-mine . . . for my birthday,'' she said, as she touched it lovingly.

Valton was not to keep his composure for long. In addition to Saturna, he had to contend with the animals.

Valton had been surrounded by animals all his life. Of all the experimental creatures Krecis had sent back to Fazis, only these two took an instant dislike to him. And it was clear to Valton from the atavistic way the hair on the back of his neck prickled that they possessed some manner of telepathy with which to commune with their mistress.

The feline one, Catlyke, draped herself around Saturna's shoulders as she ate, her tail—once she stopped lashing it and glaring in Valton's direction—wrapped around the young woman's slender neck like a fur stole. Her strange little prehensile fingers began to pluck and fidget with Saturna's hair, and she made high-pitched trilling noises to which her mistress would occasionally murmur a response. It was as if an entirely different conversation was transpiring beneath the one taking place across the dinner table. If nothing else, Valton thought, Tetrok's daughter can be quite rude!

Even before dinner he'd tried warming up to the other creature, Mushii. The beast had reacted by bristling all his fur at him and growling in his throat, his antennae sparking furiously. Valton continued to pet him in spite of his hostility; at a silent command from Saturna as she stroked her pendant absentmindedly, the creature relaxed somewhat, his fur smoothing beneath Valton's gentling hands, but the occasional muttered growl meant he was allowing such familiarity, not acquiescing to it.

Now he sat in Saturna's lap, peeking just above the edge of the table at Valton at the far end, his unblinking stare implying that this stranger bore watching.

"Krecis is well?" Valton asked Saturna, helping himself to steaming *kolarajsh* and passing the serving dish to Nebulaesa.

"He was when I left him,'' Saturna answered politely, though she seemed to be paying more attention to Catlyke than to Valton. Nebulaesa passed her the serving dish. "I sometimes think Krecis will live forever. At least, I hope he will. I can't imagine the universe without him.''

Valton managed a faint smile at her enthusiasm, remembering his own when he was her age.

"Nor can I. I miss the OldOne. He was my mentor when I was younger than you. There was a time when I thought I might follow him into the Order of Telespers, but I—made a different choice.''

Nebulaesa glanced at him in surprise. This was an extraordinary confession from anyone, but for Valton to admit to anything like indecision, much less poor judgment, particularly in front of one as young as Saturna . . .

It's a ploy! she thought. His way of being disarming, seeming to be flawed, regretting a youthful indiscretion. He knows that sort of thing has tremendous appeal to the young.

"Yes, I know,'' Saturna said, her tone neutral where it might have been smug. "Krecis told me.''

Now it was Valton who was taken aback. "Did he truly? Does the OldOne frequently discuss the personal lives of highly placed officials with you?''

His tone was sharper than it should have been. Alarmed, Saturna clutched her crystal and stared at Valton, wishing he'd change the subject to something less emotionally charged. Almost immediately, Valton's coloring cooled down.

"Forgive my harsh tone, dear Saturna. It was not my intent to frighten you.''

Nebulaesa could not believe her ears. She slowly released the breath she had been holding.

At some point while the food was being served, Mushii had slipped off his mistress's lap and proceeded to wander about the room, his short legs carrying him under most of the furniture. He chose this moment to nudge Valton's ankle with his cold nose. Absently, Valton reached down to stroke the creature's fur; a sense of calm flowed over him. The instant Valton touched him, Mushii let all six legs shoot out from under him and "rugged out.''

"What—'' Distracted, Valton stared at the animal, who had suddenly transmogrified into an inert wad of fur at his feet. "Is he ill? I barely touched him . . .''

Saturna did not intend to laugh, but she couldn't help herself. She unwound Catlyke from her neck and went to fetch Mushii.

"Stop that!" she commanded, tapping him on the nose as he came back to life. Covering her mouth with her hand, she managed at last to suppress her peals of laughter. "Cousin, forgive me, but he's done that to get attention ever since I was a child. I didn't mean to laugh."

"It's quite all right!" Valton assured her with great dignity, but it wasn't and they all knew it.

The dinner continued in a chill silence punctuated with the most desultory small talk, and Saturna and her menagerie had the good grace to retire early.

♄

Krecis was pleasantly surprised to hear from Nyota Domonique again. As usual, the subject of her holocom was mostly related to her work.

"The last supplies of algae you sent me are almost depleted, OldOne. As you know, we've been accomplishing wondrous things here on Mars, but I thought I'd hit you up for some new stock."

She smiled winsomely as she said it, and Krecis always marveled at how her beauty only improved with the years. She seemed ageless, like a Fazisian. Her face was unlined, and only the fetching streak of gray in her dark hair reminded him of how much time had passed. Her radiant smile was as dazzling as ever.

"Surely you've been cultivating new growths out of the two shipments I sent you," he temporized, if only to prolong her holo presence in his solitary life.

"You know I have," Nyota almost scolded him. "But you also know the algae sometimes become less viable under laboratory conditions. It's been over five years since your last shipment. Besides, if I know you, you've scrounged out a dozen new species since I left Titan."

"Closer to two dozen," Krecis replied dryly, savoring her surprised reaction. "I will see what I can do. It will take some time, of course."

"Of course." Nyota smiled.

"And perhaps . . ." Even as he said this, Krecis did not

know why he said it. ''Perhaps I can think of some favor you can do me in return.''

''Anything, OldOne!'' Nyota said fervently. ''Anything that's within my power; you know that.''

They talked for several moments, picking up the thread of a conversation undiminished by time.

''I take it Zeenyl's daughter is well?'' Nyota asked. ''She must be quite a young woman by now.''

Did he only imagine a hint of sorrow in her eyes as she spoke of Saturna? Krecis wondered.

''She is quite a beauty, Nyota!'' Krecis enthused. ''You would be so proud of her. As would her parents have been, of course,'' he added, covering himself quickly.

''Krecis . . .'' Nyota said finally, then hesitated. ''How is Tetrok?''

''He is well,'' the OldOne answered. ''His father still has not stepped aside to let him assume Rulership, but—''

''Yes, I know!'' Nyota nodded. ''I try to keep up with events through the newscom, but things are so hectic here. If you speak with him ever . . . tell him I think of him.''

''I will.''

&

''She deliberately brought those creatures with her to create a diversion!'' Valton fumed. ''I have been insulted by experts, Nebulaesa, by egotistical local governors and insubordinate outlyer commanders, but never by an upstart, a child barely into womanhood, and her trained minions!''

''I don't think she meant to insult you, Valton,'' Nebulaesa said soothingly. ''Though she certainly disconcerted you immeasurably. It is quite out of character for you to show such a range of emotion. She had you coloring from fury to serenity in seconds,'' she teased. ''Still, I was impressed with how quickly you controlled yourself at the end, Valton dear.''

''Well, she is just a child, overindulged by the OldOne for too long!'' Valton reasoned. Still he wondered at the strange calm that seemed to come over him just as he had wanted to wring Saturna's arrogant young neck.

''Those animals!'' he seethed now, changing the subject.

"There's something odd about them. Since when has Krecis been breeding prototelepathic species?"

"Since he bred those two, obviously!" Nebulaesa snapped, instantly regretting her words. No one was more dangerous than Valton when he was angry.

"They were never mentioned in his reports! He meant to keep them secret, for his own purposes, because he has Xeniok's leave to do as he chooses on that planetoid of his . . ."

"And perhaps he never mentioned them because he never intended them to leave Titan," Nebulaesa suggested. "You can see by their behavior that they're pets, as overindulged as their mistress. It was probably she who pleaded with Krecis to let her take them with her."

"There's more to it than that!" Valton declared, almost triumphantly.

"Perhaps Krecis is working in league with Tetrok and he sent the animals to spy on you," she suggested ironically, hoping to put the matter in perspective with a little humor.

"Perhaps he is!" Valton said with deadly seriousness. He forcibly calmed himself then, and Nebulaesa could not help but notice that it took considerably longer than it had earlier. He took her in his arms. "How fortunate for me that you can see things from my perspective. I no longer need to feel alone."

He is obsessed! Nebulaesa thought. Almost out of control. Dangerous in any event.

"I will speak to Saturna about her behavior tomorrow," she promised him. "That is all it is, Valton—bad manners, nothing more. Promise me you'll put the incident behind you."

Valton kissed her between the upslanting browridges, watching her skin warm at his touch.

"As you wish." He kissed her again, but Nebulaesa could tell that his agitation was still high. "I have requested a meeting with Tetrok. I think it is time to confront our would-be Ruler with what we know. You will come with me?"

He *was* dangerous, Nebulaesa decided, and more than a little mad! Instead of answering, she covered his mouth with her own, and they kissed long and passionately.

"Must you always talk business?" she murmured, when they paused for breath.

"Not always!" Valton allowed, wishing he could be content with just this woman, if not with his place in the scheme of things. Could he not, for this night at least, be content with this woman alone?

He and Nebulaesa kissed again.

The following evening, Nebulaesa presented herself to Tetrok.

☙

In all honesty, he had not thought of her as other than a distant relative, an able outlyer commander, a distant memory, since Nyota Domonique had entered his life. To be confronted by her after all this time, her somewhat brittle beauty arrayed to its best advantage—Nebulaesa had always known how to adorn herself—was unsettling. Yet, while he would hold Valton at arm's length until he determined what he was up to, Tetrok was never too busy to see Nebulaesa.

"I need to talk to you!" she said breathlessly and without ceremony as soon as they were alone. Tetrok had disembarked only this morning from his mission to Fazis Third. Veteran spacer that he was, he suffered no ill effects from in-system travel; nevertheless, he was somewhat fatigued, and had he thought this anything more than a social call, he might have put it off until morning. He frowned at Nebulaesa's urgency.

"I'd hoped you might bring Saturna with you," he said. "Given her special circumstances, I would like to meet with our newest candidate for citizenship before her ceremony. But there is time yet."

How dare he! was Nebulaesa's first thought. How dare he broach the topic so immediately, as if defying me to confront him with it? Then she collected herself, and, her telesper gifts as always slightly more acute than his, scanned Tetrok's peripheral thoughts, finding no duplicity, only honest curiosity about what had brought her here.

Is it possible he doesn't know the child is his? she thought then, but Valton's mind-set had begun to infect her, and she dismissed this thought as quickly as it presented itself. Tetrok was merely shielding his thoughts from her, challenging her to tell him what she knew before Valton did. She would not be so naive.

"I will bring her next time," she promised, thinking: Except that there will not be a next time; Valton will see to that! "For tonight, I wanted us to be alone. Valton means to discredit you."

It was the last thing Tetrok expected her to say. He had seen the fervor in her eyes, the high colors infusing her flesh, and had braced himself for an outpouring of old feelings, feelings that for him were long since cooled, a youthful memory, but for Nebulaesa were still undiminished. The mention of Valton threw him completely off guard.

"What do you mean?"

"This private meeting he has requested with you tomorrow," Nebulaesa said. "Have you no concept what it is about?"

Tetrok made a negative gesture. "I assumed Valton would tell me when he arrived. How is it that you know about it?"

Nebulaesa dismissed this with a gesture of her own. "That doesn't matter. What does is that he claims to have evidence of certain . . . improprieties during your tenure on Titan."

A flicker of something—guilt? At least uncertainty—passed across Tetrok's eyes and, for an instant, heightened his colors before he contained it. Yes! Nebulaesa thought. He knows! And he knows what I have risked to warn him.

But Tetrok had recovered himself and smiled at her—almost, Nebulaesa thought, patronizingly. Poor B'Laesa, his smile seemed to say, overreacting to something which is nothing at all, just as she did when we were young and thought we were in love!

"Valton may claim what he likes," Tetrok said evenly. "Is that the only reason you have come here, B'Laesa?"

If he hadn't called her that, would she have succumbed? Nebulaesa would never know. But she opened her thoughts to him, dropping her mental shields, offering herself to him as she had not since they were very young.

*I love you, Tetrok! I love you still. In spite of everything, I love you no less than the day you left me; if anything my love has grown, deepened, matured in all the time we've been apart. Let us try again, my love; you will never regret it. There is more at stake here than you can know!*

*I never wanted to hurt you!* Tetrok replied in kind. They

were clasping each other's hands suddenly, their minds pouring into each other. *But above all else, B'Laesa, I must be honest with you. My love for you was never felt as deeply•as you felt, when we were together. We were so young then! To try to resurrect the past now would be a terrible mistake, more terrible perhaps than our first love!*

"So that's all I was—a mistake!" Nebulaesa said aloud, pulling out of his grasp.

"Not you, B'Laesa, never you! Only what we did, what I did. Had I known your feelings would run so deep, and for so long—"

"Oh, spare me!" she snapped, and, before she lost her composure completely, left him to his fate.

As she hurried down the stairs and across the plaza to her waiting skimmer, she forcibly reminded herself that this was the man who had seduced her sister. How could she have lowered herself to offer *him* her life? By what perversity could she possibly retain the slightest positive feeling toward him? As long as Valton could guarantee that no harm would come to Saturna, she would cast her lot with him and let history take its course!

♄

As a precaution, Tetrok made two special arrangements. One was to request that Xeniok and Gulibol be present at his meeting with Valton. He was not overly surprised to see that Nebulaesa had arrived with Valton.

"I'd thought we would meet alone, cousin," Valton began, immediately on the defensive as a curious and visibly concerned Ruler arrived with his Crown Litigator.

"As did I, cousin," Tetrok replied, his eyes on Nebulaesa as Xeniok and Gulibol stood on either side of him. When Valton made no attempt to explain her presence, Tetrok explained his own choice. "It is my right to request the presence of the Ruler and his litigator at any audience in which policy matters are to be discussed, as I have reason to believe is the case here." This time he did not so much as glance at Nebulaesa. "You know the law as well as I, cousin."

♄

Across the city in Nebulaesa's villa, Saturna waited, trying to be patient. Tetrok's second precaution had been to summon her by personal invitation to visit him privately just prior to her ceremony. The holocom in her room showed the Hall of Audiences beginning to fill with spectators.

Traditionally, citizenship ceremonies were open to anyone who wished to attend, and while holocom made it possible for most Fazisians to watch from home or the workplace, many still preferred to attend in person. Saturna knew that her ceremony would be watched from the colonies, the outlyers, even from Titan, but it was the presence of so many in the hall itself that amazed her.

They've all come to see me! she thought. Where another so young might have had stage fright, Saturna could not wait to make her entrance. The only thing that disturbed her was Tetrok's invitation, or more accurately, her aunt's reaction to it.

Nebulaesa had told her niece that morning that she and Valton had some urgent business with Tetrok prior to the ceremony.

"Excellent! Then we can go to the Citadel together," Saturna suggested. "I will wait in the anteroom until you and Valton have finished and—"

"No!" Nebulaesa had said too sharply, clamping down on her thoughts barely an instant before Saturna could read them. Oh, what use Valton would make of the child if she accompanied them! "Wait here for me. I will return in ample time for you to take the skimmer back to the Citadel."

Saturna shook her head, puzzled. "It seems so wasteful when we could . . ." Something in her aunt's demeanor warned her not to press it. She shrugged. "No matter. I will wait here. I'm still undecided how I want to wear my hair."

The innocence of her remark reassured Nebulaesa; she was still so young, after all! But as Saturna watched the hall filling with citizens, she felt a prickling on her skin, like a kind of static. Idly she fingered the exquisite crystal Krecis had given her, which she wore always about her neck, even in sleep. Someone was talking about her, someone important! She did not know how she knew it, but she knew.

❧

Saturna's holo image, summoned by Valton, stood between him and Tetrok as if in full accusation.

"... concrete proof that this child, the first child born of Fazis on Titan, is in fact not Phaestus's child but Tetrok's!" Valton concluded triumphantly, his voice vibrating with excitement. "A child conceived in adultery, no doubt as the result of duplicity if not seduction, by one who would be Ruler. Thus will we inform the Fazrul, unless of course Tetrok agrees to step away from the royal succession!"

To an Earthian, what followed might have sounded like stunned silence. What it was, in fact, was an orchestrated cacophony of Fazisian mental transmissions ricocheting wall to wall across the salon.

*Such an accusation ... Adultery ... my son?*
*Ruler, I caution you, guard your thoughts ...*
*Father, this is some trick! Zeenyl and I never ...*
*Oh, Tetrok, you fool!*

Valton stood emanating smugness: I've got him ... at last!

⦿

Saturna's restlessness was communicating itself to the animals. Catlyke's fur was all on end and no amount of grooming seemed to settle it, and Mushii was beside himself.

*Come with you!* he insisted, scrambling about under Saturna's feet, all but tripping her up as she paced, her long skirts swirling about her ankles. With a last look in the mirror, she touched her hair, settled the crystal pendant in the cleft between her breasts, and decided it was time.

"Absolutely not!" Saturna said crossly, nudging him out of her way with the toe of her shoe. "How do you think that would look, me sauntering into the future Ruler's presence with you ill-mannered furballs in tow? You've embarrassed me quite enough in front of Valton, thank you!"

*Told you!* Catlyke thought to Mushii grandly; she of course had done no such thing. *All your fault!*

*Was not!* Mushii retorted; *Was so!* Catlyke replied. Saturna's head was humming. Bad enough her skin continued to tingle with the knowledge that she was being talked about somewhere, somehow, but these two were driving her to distraction.

"That's enough, both of you!" she cried, her temper sharper than they'd ever seen it before; they froze in midfuss and slunk off into a corner, curling around each other for comfort. Saturna glanced at the chrono. Her audience with Tetrok was in twenty-four minutes; if Nebulaesa didn't return with the skimmer in six she would be late. Quickly she made a decision.

"That does it!" she announced, and sailed out of the room.

‿

*This is some trick!* Tetrok's mind screamed, as he closed off his thoughts. Still, the irrefutable proof stood before him. Beside Saturna's holo was her DNA reading, beside that, his. The pattern was unmistakable; even an amateur could see the similarities. In this roomful of learned Fazisians, there was no denying the truth.

Valton felt exalted. For so many *years* he had been relegated to second position. For so many *years* he had had to live with the certainty that Tetrok would always be one step ahead and would one day be *his* Ruler. Now the tide had turned . . . Nay, the tidal wave of history had changed. Now it was he, *Valton,* who would inherit complete victory! The only serious impediment in his path was about to be removed. He could see the total dismay on Xeniok's face, the utter defeat. Tetrok was a traitor to all Xeniok and the Fazrul held sacred. Tetrok was done; Tetrok was history!

Nebulaesa, reading Valton's thoughts, was torn. In spite of herself, in spite of Tetrok's rejection of her, it tore at her very soul to realize her first and one true love was about to be destroyed. And she had played a major role in this pending catastrophe. Perhaps to ensure her own sanity, perhaps to maintain some semblance of mental self-preservation, she turned her thoughts to Zeenyl: Look what he, Tetrok, has done! Preferring my baby sister to me! Valton is right; he deserves whatever he has wrought.

A single thought flashed across Tetrok's mind: Krecis!

The experiment had been a success after all; it was the only possible answer. Yet if he tried to prove that he and Zeenyl had never been intimate, challenged Valton to examine the other parent's genome, it would endanger Nyota and Krecis, and would not save him or Saturna.

*Nyota!* he thought in the deepest recesses of his mind. *Oh, my love, we have a child!*

Tetrok might have lost control, but he was a Ruler born and bred. Collecting his thoughts, he addressed them to Valton, as if they were alone.

"Cousin, I caution you. If you bring this to the Fazrul, they will laugh you out of the Citadel."

"The proof is there!" Valton answered calmly, his confidence unwavering in the face of Tetrok's self-assurance.

Tetrok looked deeply into Nebulaesa's eyes, though his words were directed at Valton. "I do not know, Valton, how you came by this genetic evidence. I only know that you dishonor Zeenyl's memory by even suggesting that she would commit adultery."

Nebulaesa looked away.

"The evidence is unmistakable. You are Saturna's father!" Valton challenged. "You cannot deny it."

"And I shall not," Tetrok replied. "In truth, I am."

"My son . . ." Xeniok gasped, and his color drained.

With a gesture, Tetrok asked his father for silence.

Gulibol's logical mind had leapt into overdrive. This changed everything. As Phaestus's child, Saturna belonged to the ruling line only through Zeenyl, but as Tetrok's . . . ! Gulibol's eyes flashed as he moved toward Valton.

"Valton, you border on treason with your threat to the ruling lineage," he warned. "Ruler, I suggest—"

"Uncle," Valton interrupted, "I mean no harm to the ruling lineage, but you have made it clear that you will soon stand down, opening the seat of rule to your qualified heir . . ."

Valton let the word hang in the air, then turned to Tetrok.

"Cousin," he continued oilily, "you have, regretfully, disqualified yourself through your actions on Titan. It would greatly pain me to see our family disgraced and the lineage threatened, as our learned litigator has so wisely pointed out. But as a devoted servant of the people and a trusted member of the Fazrul, I have no choice but to expose your treachery. Unless, of course . . ."

Every mind in the great salon was silent in the face of the inevitable.

"... you step down in favor of your faithful servant and cousin. I, Valton, stand humbly before you."

An eternity elapsed as all eyes turned toward Tetrok. But during Valton's smug, condescending diatribe, Tetrok's mind had soared through time and space to Krecis on Titan.

*Krecis!* Tetrok thought: *You old slythik!*

"My son!" Xeniok's pained utterance startled Tetrok back to the here and now. Closing his mind to all others, Tetrok sent a message to the Ruler alone: *Father, trust me!*

"Never, Valton!" Tetrok stated evenly. "Never!"

Stunned silence hung in the air like the thickness of methane smog on Titan. Valton saw the resolution in Tetrok's eyes. He would not make it easy for him; he never had.

"You know, then, what I must do?" Valton snarled in sour disappointment.

"Do what you will," Tetrok responded coldly. "But leave us, you and Nebulaesa both!"

At that moment the great ornate portal swung open and all heads turned as a page appeared to announce the newcomer grandly:

"Saturna of Titan!"

Through the stunned silence, Saturna entered. She stood as a vision before them in flowing green-and-gold gossamer robes that emphasized the jeweled color of her extraordinary eyes.

Tetrok's heart clutched as he gasped in sheer awe and admiration of her beauty.

*Nyota ... Nyota ...* He fought to control his rampant pulse as for the first time he beheld the child-woman who was their daughter.

All the prescribed etiquette and protocol Saturna had rehearsed for weeks failed her as she looked at Tetrok. Her mind and her eyes were for him only. She scarcely noticed as the furious Valton swept past her, her defeated Aunt Nebulaesa trailing helplessly behind him. And though Xeniok the Fazisian Ruler himself and Gulibol the Crown Litigator stood on either side of Tetrok, it was as if they were not in the room.

Saturna was drawn to Tetrok as she had never been to anyone else. The attraction was something she could not fathom; she had no precedent for it. Beyond a feeling of recognition, of belonging, she knew this man in the very marrow of her bones.

Gently Tetrok opened his mind to her, to reveal to her only as much as he could allow her to know. Saturna stood transfixed as their minds melded. A single word—impossible but true—escaped her lips:

"Father?"

# CHAPTER 20

On Titan, Krecis watched the holocom broadcast with some concern as the Hall of Audiences filled first with spectators, later with members of the Fazrul, all waiting to see the new candidate for citizenship and hear her declare her intention. Commander Choy arrived just as the last guests were trailing into the hall. Their excitement added to Krecis' anxiety.

"We've got a problem," Luke said, inadvertently treading on the hem of a councillor's robe as he strode through the holocom to get Krecis' attention.

Krecis gave Luke his attention as he turned down the volume on the holocom. He knew Luke well enough to distinguish from his tone whether the "problem" was a true crisis or just a minor annoyance; this, he could tell, was a minor annoyance.

"Harley Block," he said automatically.

"I didn't know you were psychic as well as telepathic, OldOne," Luke half joked. "Yes, Harley Block. The freighter captain refuses to let us put him aboard. Some nonsense to do with insurance and quarantines, but if you want my opinion it's because they know him, and to know Harley is to love him. So we're stuck with him until I can wangle alternate transport."

Krecis wanted to ask why Luke didn't simply contact Commander Listrom and demand she send a ship to retrieve her provocateur, but there were subtle distinctions between Earthian military and civilian jurisdictions that he never would understand.

"The problem may not be insurmountable," he suggested. "There will be a courier to Mars shortly."

"You've gotten clearance to send Nyota another shipment

of algae,'' Luke said. Krecis nodded. ''Good. We can send all
the slime in the same ship. A joke,'' he explained, when Krecis looked at him oddly.

''A poor one,'' Krecis suggested, turning up the volume
again as Choy went on his way. The holocom showed the
packed Hall of Audiences.

As Valton and his followers entered the hall, he was in a
state of high agitation. He dared to defy me—that self-
righteous, egomaniacal—

''. . . but I shall gain the victory this day, my friends,'' he
assured those with him, fairly spitting venom. ''Trust me!''

''What will you do, Valton?'' they inquired. ''Tetrok is not
known to be a rash or foolish man.''

Valton smiled wickedly. He'd been livid when he stalked
out of his audience with Tetrok, but anger would not benefit
him now. He'd had to gather his wits and think. He had started
to storm into the Fazrul and condemn Tetrok for the traitor he
was, but Tetrok would have been granted a litigator and a
hearing and time to wriggle out of the accusation.

Not likely! Valton thought now. My dear cousin Tetrok who
would be Ruler—not very likely!

Then Valton had had his brainstorm. As head of the Offworld Services, he was also a member of the Fazrul. As kin
to Tetrok and Zeenyl, he was also related to Saturna. Thus
he was doubly welcome to attend her ceremony on the dais
if he chose to. Under the circumstances, he most assuredly
chose to.

''It will be a ceremony to be remembered,'' he told his
followers cryptically, leaving them to take his place on the
dais.

The hall was filled with Fazisians resplendent in their finest
clothing, crowding into the balconies for the best view of the
candidate as she strode the length of the central aisle to where
Xeniok, Tetrok, Gulibol, and the councillors sat on the dais
awaiting her.

And stride she did. With a regal carriage that belied
her youth, Saturna followed the prescribed route walked
by thousands upon thousands of candidates before her, following the protocols precisely, at the same time that she
transformed them into a kind of choreography, investing her

ceremony with the full grandeur it traditionally deserved but
also making it uniquely her own.

The buzz of anticipation became a hum of approval as she
made her way alone through the midst of the crowd and stood
waiting for Xeniok to address her. On the colonies and the outlyers, on Titan and even among a few knowledgeable Earthians,
Saturna had the attention, and the approval, of millions.

"Oh, Krecis, she's lovely!" Nyota Domonique whispered.
"Such poise, and she's barely a child! You've done yourself
proud, OldOne."

It was pure coincidence that she and Krecis should be
watching the ceremony together, he from Titan, she from
Mars. Her work had been at fever pitch for months and she'd
been out of touch with everyone beyond the microcosm of the
labs. She and her team were literally about to cure cancer.
Experiments using rhodium to modify cancer cells at the molecular level, begun in the previous century, had been refined
to the point where individual cancer-causing genes could be
identified and eliminated. All that was necessary now was to
run a polymerase series to modify each suspect gene. Between
the excitement of discovery and the joy of celebration lay a
lot of tedious and time-consuming work.

"It will need your complete attention," Nyota had told
her team in her weekly pep talk. "It can't be rushed, and I
don't want anyone asleep at the switch. Ten seconds' care-
lessness—"

" 'Can mean ten years' wasted effort,' " they'd finished for
her, having heard the speech before.

Nyota laughed with them. "I want everyone to get a good
night's sleep. We'll start the series tomorrow and work them
through in shifts until we're finished. I've got a case of Mangala Crystale reserved for the party afterward."

That caused quite a stir. Mars' own vineyards had just
yielded their first crop, and a bottle of first-vintage Martian
champagne was worth a year's salary. Unless you happened
to be Governor of Mars.

Back in her quarters, Nyota had found a message from Krecis about the algae shipment. Always eager to talk to him,
she'd hailed him back immediately. He took her call just as

Saturna's ceremony was about to begin, and invited her to watch with him.

"It's so sad that Zeenyl and Phaestus didn't live to see this!" Nyota mused, literally watching over Krecis' shoulder. "She seems like a remarkable young woman. I'm ashamed of myself for not keeping in closer touch with you all these years to watch her growing up. I'd love to meet her someday," she added, just as Xeniok began to speak.

"Would you?" Krecis asked, an idea forming in his mind.

". . . and welcome our sister Saturna to the homeworld of her ancestors . . ." Xeniok intoned the prescribed words. He seemed older than he had in decades as he continued the performance of the ritual. ". . . in the hope that she will not find us wanting and wish to make it her own!"

Nebulaesa had not dared take her place on the dais, but watched from the balcony, fighting to control her colors and her racing heart and block her rampant thoughts lest she disgrace herself before all of Fazis.

Tetrok stood at Xeniok's right hand, striving to maintain the dignity of his office on this most serious and auspicious of Fazisian occasions. Xeniok himself wrestled with his emotions. Saturna's—his granddaughter's—special day was simultaneously the most devastating day of his life since the death of his beloved wife. But his destiny was to be Ruler of a great people, and he turned once more to fulfill it, for as long as it might last.

&

*Isidros? Your mind is farther away than usual today . . .*

He looked at Niklosa with something like chagrin. A man might rule a world, but he could not fool Niklosa.

*Yes,* he thought to her, consciously pulling himself back, though he kept one tendril of his mind wrapped protectively about Saturna.

&

On Titan, Krecis nearly gasped in alarm at the sight of his old friend Xeniok. The Ruler seemed drawn and weak now, whereas during their last holocom not three orbits past Krecis had marveled at his strong, healthy appearance.

This was not illness, then. The Ruler was visibly distraught. Although he was covering well, he could not hide his pain from Krecis. What could have caused such a change? Krecis wondered as he adjusted the holocom to scan the dais, examining each of the dignitaries in turn as if to seek an answer among them.

Each member of the Fazrul seemed calm, but Litigator Gulibol's bearing was stiff, his face showing what appeared to be concern, while Tetrok sat almost rigid in his regal robes. Did Krecis only imagine that all three—Gulibol, Tetrok, and Xeniok—stiffened as Valton joined them, bowing ostentatiously before taking his seat beside Tetrok?

"It's amazing," Nyota said, catching her breath at the sight of Tetrok, "how two men can look so much alike and be so different."

Her voice jolted Krecis back from his thoughts. For a moment he'd forgotten Nyota's "presence."

"Just so," he mused.

☙

Valton's late arrival caused a small stir. Fazisians were polite by nature; no one, not even a kinsman, would be so rude as to make an entrance while the Ruler was speaking. Xeniok faltered upon seeing Valton.

". . . and welcome our daughter . . ." he repeated himself, ". . . our sister . . ."

He hesitated, visibly shaken. A murmur of concern coursed through the audience.

Valton's eyes fairly glowed. Now is my moment! he gloated, and rose.

"Uncle," he began in mock concern, but Tetrok was too quick for him, and reached his father first, motioning for Gulibol, who was already moving toward the Ruler's side.

"Cousin," Tetrok said in a loud, strong voice, "thank you for your gracious concern, but if you will all be seated the ceremony will continue, as is my father's wish."

His bearing brooked no argument, and his strength restored a semblance of calm in Xeniok.

"I am well, my son," he assured Tetrok for all to hear.

"Father, with your permission . . ."

Xeniok gave a wan smile and a nod of approval and took the Ruler's seat.

*

"OldOne, what's happening?" Nyota asked with great concern. "Is Xeniok ill? What does it mean?"

Krecis felt a chill permeate his being.

"I do not know, Nyota," he whispered. "We shall see momentarily."

*

"Members of the Fazrul, Litigator Gulibol, my esteemed friends: Fear not. Our beloved Ruler is not ill, he is but overcome with emotion. Extraordinary news has come to his attention which alters the ruling lineage and lends even greater weight to this Ceremony of Citizenship for Saturna of Titan."

A drone not unlike a swarm of bees rose throughout the great hall and as suddenly died down. No one wanted to miss a word.

Nebulaesa shivered as her coloring blanched. *Oh, my love, what have I done?*

Saturna stood silently before the dais, showing nothing of the roiling of her nerves. Casually she caressed the crystal pendant, wishing Xeniok peace of mind and Tetrok strength of purpose.

Xeniok sighed then, as Tetrok's voice rose strong and self-assured.

". . . for Phaestus, nephew of the WiseOne Krecis, and Zeenyl, my dear friend and kinswoman, the gift of a child was a blessing they feared they would never receive . . ."

Valton sat breathing in victory with smug satisfaction, knowing however elaborate his words, Tetrok was destroying himself. Was there any point in delaying the inevitable with this retelling of Krecis' infertility experiment? Phaestus, poor dupe, may have been cured after all, but not until after you fathered his child!

". . . and thus I fathered his child," Tetrok said, almost in tandem with Valton's thought, "at Phaestus's request, and in keeping with the ancient and honored tradition."

The concerted gasp of the audience, both mental and vocal,

slammed against Valton's mind like a wave. He had not been paying attention. *What?*

"At first I hesitated," Tetrok continued, "knowing that Krecis was on the verge of a breakthrough. But Phaestus's concern was not so much for himself as for his beloved Zeenyl, who had mated with him aware of his condition and in spite of her longing to have a child."

Nyota's lips trembled. "Krecis?" she whispered, her voice very small.

"The infertility experiment was not successful until after Phaestus was dead," he stated evenly, though he could not meet her eyes.

"By Fazisian law a man may give the gift of life when the request is made by both would-be parents," Tetrok was saying. "Phaestus made such a request on Zeenyl's behalf, and as her distant kinsman and Phaestus's friend, I was honored to comply.

"The WiseOne Krecis performed the insemination, and, in the ancient tradition, I gave my word to Phaestus and Zeenyl that out of respect for their privacy I would not reveal it. It was also their wish that in the event of their deaths, the child be reared by Krecis on Titan. It was never my choice to divulge their secret, until now. An accusation has been made, and I must answer it."

Gulibol inhaled so deeply he all but fainted; his relief that he had not formally sided with Valton was all that saved him. As a body, the Fazrul's coloring rose to such intensity that the dais fairly glowed. Only Valton sat in stunned disbelief.

"It is not possible!" he muttered, as his coloring blanched.

Nebulaesa's body was racked with a pain she could not stop. Tears flowed freely down her handsome face.

Light-years away, Nyota controlled her disarrayed emotions with great difficulty. All the pain of losing her child came back to her, as sharp-edged as it had been when it happened. How envious she had been of Zeenyl, how filled with guilt at that envy, how filled with remorse when Zeenyl died! Nyota relived it all, as if it had been yesterday.

But Tetrok was still speaking.

"Had this matter not been brought to the attention of the Ruler just this night by one who meant to discredit me, I

would never have been able, for I was honor-bound, to declare
to you, Saturna of Titan, that I, Tetrok, am your father.
Proudly your father."

For what seemed an eternity the Hall of Audiences was as
silent as the vastness of space. Slowly a deep, guttural moan
began. It rose in volume and intensity like a swarm of millions
of locusts. It stopped abruptly and began again a half-octave
higher and rose once more in volume.

Several times this happened—now low, now high, now both
together, until the hall fairly shook. The sheer awesome beauty
of the sound filled Xeniok's heart with joy. He stood with
dignity and took his granddaughter's hand, leading her to the
center of the stage beside her father. Saturna's eyes shone
golden green as she looked up into Tetrok's eyes of deep emerald.

The Fazrul stood as Gulibol moved toward his Ruler. Xeniok then announced in a voice strong and clear: "Fazisians,
I give you Saturna of Titan, now of Fazis!"

Only Valton stood apart, alone in impotent defeat as the
sound of the audience grew even greater, bathing the Ruler
and his family in a people's love.

☍

*Isidros?*

Niklosa waited. Her pupil's face was bathed in a glow of
near ecstasy. The old woman sighed in her mind. Whatever it
was, he would tell her when he was ready; he always did.

☍

Krecis sat motionless, his back still to Nyota. He dared not
face her lest she read the truth in his eyes. Nyota was too
caught up in Tetrok's revelation to notice. The chanting from
the Hall of Audiences enveloped them both even from so far
away. On the holocom, Xeniok was calling for order.

Strange! Nyota thought. What could possibly top this? But
top it Xeniok did.

"Loyal Fazisians," he pleaded, "hear me, I beg you!"

Krecis closed his eyes and sighed peacefully. He knew exactly what his wise old friend was about to do.

"I have lived a long and blessed life," Xeniok began. "My

greatest blessing was to have served you for most of that life . . ." A roar from the hall did not deter him. "I have always known I would step down when the time was right, when I believed my son, Tetrok, was suitably prepared and ready to succeed me. He must first, of course, be approved by the Fazrul and confirmed by the citizens of Fazis . . ."

Xeniok paused to let the reality of what he was saying sink in before he continued.

"As the Fazrul and all of Fazis are here in one place, I choose this moment to officially call the Fazrul to order, and do hereby present to you my loyal and beloved son, Tetrok, in hope that you will find him worthy to rule Fazis the moment I step down. If this be agreeable to you, by the power invested in me, I hereby charge Litigator Gulibol to transfer the rulership at once."

Gulibol stepped forward.

"As the Fazrul is officially in session and all are present, and as our esteemed and beloved Ruler has stated his wishes clearly, with unclouded mind and good and wise intent, how say you?"

For seven years the Fazrul had been aware of Xeniok's intent; nevertheless, they were momentarily stunned. Still, they were also of good and wise intent and, of the twenty present, all stepped forward except Valton. All eyes shifted toward him; he did not move, but stared blankly.

"Are you ill, friend Valton?" Gulibol asked. "How say you?"

Slowly Valton blinked as reality sank in. It had all been his, but now it was all gone. How could that be? As if in a trance, he finally stepped forward.

"So say you all!" Gulibol announced. "The Fazrul has acceded to and unanimously approved the wishes of Xeniok, Ruler of Fazis, and transferred that rule to his son, Tetrok. Citizens of Fazis, how say you?"

En masse in the great hall and on holocom, the Fazisians roared their approval. This would mean no less than a month of official celebration.

Once again Xeniok took Tetrok's and Saturna's hands and, striding to the edge of the great platform, raised them high.

"Fazisians," Gulibol intoned above the roar, "after one

hundred and fifty years of Xeniok's good and wise rule,
blessed by the Almighty One, I, Gulibol, Crown Litigator and
servant to the people of Fazis, contingent only upon the confirming vote of the people of Fazis, present to you . . . Tetrok,
Ruler of Fazis.''

❧

They stood bathed in triumph—Xeniok, Tetrok, and Saturna,
surrounded by Gulibol and all the Fazrul save one—as the
Hall of Audiences echoed with the Fazisians' ecstatic roar.

It was a day no Fazisian would ever forget, especially Saturna, for now she was one of them.

# Chapter 21

Standing forward now in the well of the foredeck, Saturna gazed out into the vastness of the universe as if she could bring Titan into view all the sooner. She had stood there for hours, the ship's crew leaving her undisturbed in her lonely vigil.

More had happened to her since the night barely a month past when she'd met Tetrok than in all the twenty years before.

❧

They had talked for days after that incredible night when he had so proudly proclaimed himself to be her father, not always using words. When at the end of each day they withdrew their minds from each other, Saturna was amazed to find the late-afternoon sun slanting across the floor, pooling redly on the flagstones at their feet.

She knew this man so well now. It was as if she had grown up beneath his protection; seen his face hovering over her, watching over her always from her earliest years; heard his voice instructing her, singing to her, telling her nonsense rhymes; sensed him listening to her every pronouncement with the greatest attention and seriousness. Was this what it was like to have a father? She had not felt such an acute degree of kinship even with Krecis.

Even as she had the thought, Saturna banished it, horrified at her own disloyalty. Yet Krecis had lied to her. There was so much about herself she desperately needed to know. Her next thought startled her all the more.

"F-father?" She tested the word, loving the very sound of it. "Did you love my mother, Zeenyl?"

She'd spoken the words, having sensed through the telesper portion of their dialogue that Tetrok often felt uncomfortable

with the intensity of her skills. There were questions he had
been reluctant to answer, still others that he had deflected,
barely, shutting her out of those places in his mind where he
did not wish her to go. Out of respect for this man who was
now Ruler, Saturna tried to restrain her talents, if not her curiosity, so she'd asked the question aloud.

It might have been better for her to ask it in his mind.

"Your parents, Phaestus and Zeenyl, loved each other very
much. They were my dear friends," Tetrok answered levelly.
"Why do you ask that?"

The mildness of his tone assuaged her fear that he might
consider it an untoward, possibly foolish question.

Saturna hesitated. She honestly did not know.

"Oh, it was a noble thing you did for them, and I'm grateful
for my life, only—only I feel so comfortable with you. As if
I've known you all my life. But when I try to visualize Zeenyl
... I used to think there was something wrong with me. I
could never *feel* Phaestus as my father. Now of course, I know
why. But you see, I never felt Zeenyl ... Do you think me
terrible, Father?"

Tetrok felt his soul wrench. He found the next moments the
hardest of his life since he had left Nyota on Titan over twenty
years ago. Although he wanted desperately to take this exquisite child in his arms and shout to the heavens, "Your mother
is Nyota, the only woman I've ever loved or ever will!" he
knew he could not.

"I find you close to perfection, Saturna," he said at last.
"Did you never discuss your lack of feeling with the psychologist on Titan?"

"Langler? Dr. Langler and I discussed a number of things;
he was the first Earthian I came to know quite well," Saturna
said; now it was she who was not entirely answering questions.
"You knew him too, didn't you?"

"I knew all the Earthians from the first expedition."

"Including Nyota Domonique?" Saturna watched Tetrok's
colors carefully as she asked this. But Tetrok had been preparing for this question since before Saturna arrived on Fazis.

"Yes, I knew Nyota quite well. She was an extraordinary
woman. She and Zeenyl grew very close ..."

Half of her listened as Tetrok told her—admiringly, even
lovingly—about the Fazisians' first encounter with Earthians

and his own interaction with Nyota. He spoke with the highest praise of her intelligence, her professional skills, even her beauty, without ever really saying how he felt about her as a person. Saturna had really been listening to the silences, the subtext beneath what was being said. The strangest thought had taken hold of her mind and would not let go.

"I have seen Nyota on the holocubes that cover the Earthians' first arrival on Titan. I used to laugh at their bulky space suits and how funny they looked hopping about!"

Saturna laughed. She was rewarded with the most magnificent sight and sound: her father's laughter.

"Don't let those suits fool you. Nyota was a most formidable woman!" Tetrok said, letting his guard down momentarily.

"Did you love her?" Saturna asked suddenly.

Tetrok's smile turned slightly wistful. "Is it necessary for you to know?" he asked.

Her mind demanded answers. It was almost beyond her control. She blurted out, "Is Nyota my—" Tetrok looked deeply into her eyes. She thought she detected pain.

"My questions are rude, Father; I'm sorry," Saturna said, realizing she was in mental territory which severely perturbed Tetrok.

They both seemed relieved that the conversation had stopped at this point. She knew then that she must have a serious conversation with Krecis immediately upon her return to Titan.

❧

Tetrok saw her off privately, and with very little ceremony. Almost as an afterthought, he presented her with a holocube addressed to Krecis.

"A message for an old and dear friend," he told her. "One whom I have in my preoccupation with business on Fazis neglected for far too long. It is not encoded; you may read it if you wish. However, guard it well. Let no one place it in the OldOne's hands but you."

Saturna shook her head, as Tetrok had known she would. "It's private, between you and Krecis, and it will remain so. And I will guard it with my life."

They embraced, warmly, and bade farewell. As he watched

her ship depart the system, Tetrok wondered if sending even such a simple message had been wise.

"OldOne," the message ran. "It is said that some truths take many years to grow to their full realization. It is also said that even a Ruler can learn wisdom from a child. Saturna has taught me her truth, and I have tried to teach her mine. All the rest I leave to your discretion, even as I commend your nurturing and teaching this extraordinary young woman over the years. I implore you, WiseOne, impart your wisdom to my daughter."

He had thought at first of encoding it, but that would immediately draw suspicion if it was intercepted. The very fact that he was giving Saturna a holocube to deliver in person rather than sending a holocom broadcast might seem odd. The message barely skimmed the surface of what Tetrok truly wanted to say, but how could he say it all? *Tell her the truth, OldOne, the truth which endangers all our lives! She has borne a burden of misplaced guilt all her life, wondering why she felt nothing for Phaestus or Zeenyl, wondering if this meant she was incapable of love. Tell her, Krecis, tell her everything!*

One of the first things a Ruler must learn, Tetrok thought with bitter irony, was to rule himself. Of course he did not have the indulgence to endanger Nyota or Krecis any further. This simple message, were it to fall into the wrong hands, would merely be interpreted as a new Ruler's somewhat poetic greeting to an old friend; even Valton in his paranoia could not prove otherwise. Only to Krecis would the message be clear: *Saturna now knows who her father is. I leave it to you, Krecis, whether or not to tell her of her mother!*

❧

*Krecis and I never had secrets!* Saturna's agitated mind nagged at her. Why had Krecis kept the truth of her origins from her? She would have understood, would never have demanded Tetrok's acknowledgment. Was there something wrong with her? Was that why she had never felt anything for her supposed parents?

*Why, Krecis-mine?*

She pondered these thoughts as she absently fondled her

lovely crystal pendant, wishing she could calm her rampant anxiety. Almost immediately she felt a sense of peace waft over her.

*I'm being foolish. The important thing is who I am now and what I know now. I know that by blood I am of the ruling lineage of Fazis. Great Xeniok is my very own grandfather. My Aunt Nebulaesa, though she is most cordial, is not my friend. Valton—my uncle—is not a good man. He is Tetrok's enemy and therefore mine. But Tetrok is not fully candid with me either, for all his charm. Yet his love for me I do not doubt.*

Saturna considered the others she knew who might help her find answers. *Gulibol is crafty but wise, yet not in the way Krecis-mine is wise. Langler is the only one on Titan who has never held back from me, but he knows nothing; I can sense it. How I wish I had someone to advise me!*

She caressed her pendant, feeling its warmth in her hand. Suddenly, she visualized Zeenyl.

*None do I feel free to talk to about my mother. Who was she, truly? Zeenyl was so very beautiful. Why do I not feel my beauty through her? With whom can I confide and find an honest answer?*

It had to be Krecis, in spite of the fact that he was far more devious than he pretended. *Father is right about you, Krecis. You are brilliant, you are great, and you are an old* slythik!

Suddenly Tetrok's words replayed in her mind: "Yes, I knew Nyota quite well. She was an extraordinary woman. She and Zeenyl grew very close . . . She and Zeenyl grew very close . . ."

"Titan coming on viewscreen, Captain," the flight commander announced.

The frigid luminescence of Titan, with the glory of Saturn beyond, loomed suddenly before Saturna's eyes, bringing her quickly out of her reverie.

"Communication with Titan, sir," the flight commander continued. "Commander Choy is hailing us."

Saturna turned to the comm officer. "Please connect me with my Uncle Krecis when you can, Lieutenant Kor."

Luke Choy's face appeared immediately. Behind him was Langler, actually smiling like a Cheshire cat, he was so happy to see her again.

"Welcome, Saturna of Titan and Fazis," Luke Choy announced with as much gravity as his boyish face could manage. "Krecis is very eager to speak with you. Stand by and I'll transfer you."

Saturna was more excited than she had expected to be as Krecis' familiar face came into view. His quarters were dimmed and he seemed inordinately subdued, but Saturna did not attribute much significance to this.

"Titan has not felt warmth since you departed, Saturna. Welcome back to Titan . . ." Krecis' voice seemed weak and thin. "There has been much preparation for this occasion of your return."

"It has been quite an adventure, Krecis-mine!" Saturna offered coolly. "But I hope no one's gone to too much bother. I will not be staying . . ."

"Not staying?" Krecis asked with some distress.

". . . for long," Saturna finished.

Krecis struggled to control the uncharacteristic rapid rise of his coloring. "Might I inquire . . ."

"I do not mean to be impertinent, my dearest Krecis," Saturna stated, more regally than he had ever heard her speak. "We have much to talk about. Oh, I nearly forgot. Here is a gift from Tetrok."

✍

Krecis sat in his study, knowing that he was soon to be interrogated by his brilliant student who had now become an informed adult. He hadn't succumbed to nervousness since he was a young lad in school, but now the full feeling was upon him.

All of Titan had assembled for Saturna's return. When she disembarked, still wearing her space suit, Krecis could not observe her coloring; but he couldn't miss the iciness of her tone. She had handed him Tetrok's holocube, as instructed, and requested a formal meeting at his quarters that evening before the banquet being held in her honor. After greeting Choy, Langler, and all her friends warmly, she quickly whisked off to her quarters.

The time had come for truth. Deceit, or whatever one wished to call his actions over the years, was now relegated to the rear; and it made Krecis very uncomfortable.

❧

He answered the gentle knock on his door and was somewhat startled by the magnificently beautiful creature who stood in the doorway. There seemed to be only a trace of the young woman he had sent to Fazis. His visitor on this night was a goddess, in dress, demeanor, and aura. Krecis' transfixion was interrupted by a voice which could have been that of the planet Saturn itself.

"May I come in?"

"Of course, my dear," Krecis said with a calm he did not feel. "Come in."

"You lied to me," Saturna began.

Much to the uneasiness of Krecis, Saturna meticulously laid out the deceit about her parentage she had been subjected to over the years. She was legalistic in her approach, logical, and extremely clear, just as Krecis had taught her. Pain was obvious in his eyes, but she finished her brief nonetheless. Her conclusion was both a question and a demand:

"Krecis, I now know who my father is. Who is my mother?"

"My dearest Saturna," he began. "First, let me apologize for the untruths I have put upon you. You must realize I only did this because I believed it to be necessary, considering the gravity of the subject."

"I accept your apology," she replied with little emotion. "Now please answer my question."

"As you may have suspected by now," he replied with less hesitation than he would have guessed, "your mother is Nyota Domonique."

Krecis caught Saturna as her body began to sink. He placed her in a large comfortable chair and brushed her forehead with his hand. She looked up at him. Tears welled up in both their eyes; they embraced with love.

For the next hour, Krecis told the entire Titan story to Saturna—the experiment, forbidden by both governments yet pursued anyway; the conspiracy with Zeenyl and Phaestus; his own decision to deceive Tetrok and Nyota for fear the experiment would ruin their lives; the accidental deaths of Zeenyl and Phaestus. Upon finishing, he was totally exhausted, yet more relieved than he had been for twenty years. At last! The terrible secret was shared. As the burden was lifted, Krecis leaned back in his chair and closed his eyes.

Saturna was transfixed. Her brain flashed images past her so rapidly she could barely keep up. Nyota! . . . Tetrok! . . . Phaestus and Zeenyl! Then the terrible truth! *Her very existence was a threat to the lives of her own parents!* Gathering herself, she looked at Krecis.

"I understand now. I . . . condemned you . . . for lying to me, before I understood the danger. Can you possibly forgive me?"

"Only if you can forgive me," Krecis said fondly.

Once again they embraced. The crystal pendant, which Saturna wore always as Krecis had instructed her (furious with him on the journey back to Titan, she had almost—almost—snatched it off her neck and tossed it into a box with the rest of her more ordinary jewelry), glowed between them.

"There is one thing more," Krecis added, as they each remembered their Fazisian dignity and restored their natural calm. "The crystal. It is more than just a jewel—"

"Oh, I know, Krecis-mine!" Saturna laughed. She had to tell him about the dinner party at Nebulaesa's where Mushii had embarrassed Valton. Krecis laughed as well, though his amusement was brief.

"Never underestimate Valton. He may be temporarily vanquished, but he is still dangerous."

"Valton had better not underestimate me!" Saturna said with sudden fire. Krecis marveled at her. She had left Titan a child; this was no child who faced him now. She held the crystal pendant in both hands, frowning at it thoughtfully. "You said it's more than just a jewel. Tell me."

Briefly Krecis told her that it contained her entire history and Tetrok's, and Nyota's, encoded to match Saturna's DNA.

". . . so that only you can access it. In the event anything happened to me before I could tell you . . ."

He did not finish; Saturna did not want him to. An hour ago she had thought she would never trust him again. Now she could not bear to think of a universe without Krecis.

"It's like a computer chip, then. A memory bank," Saturna said slowly. "What else? That's not what makes it calm me when I'm agitated and I rub it."

Krecis shook his head. "The crystal has properties even I do not fully understand. You will find that it radiates a nearly invisible beam which projects your thoughts and feelings onto others." He then explained the calming effect she could impose on others who might be angry, and the "Spock" effect. "Never treat it lightly, my dear. I really don't know its full power."

Saturna's eyes widened with solemnity. She had begun this journey of discovery plagued with doubt; now the OldOne of Titan and the new Ruler of Fazis, her father, had entrusted her with their very lives.

"All our futures are in your hands, Saturna," Krecis said, giving voice to her own thoughts. "What will you do now?"

The words when she spoke them came slowly, but decisively.

"Krecis-mine, I must go to Mars!"

☙

Saturna was beside herself with excitement as the small courier vessel, designed and constructed on Titan expressly for optimum speed to Mars, was made ready for transport.

She spent every waking hour locked into a flight simulator which duplicated the courier's design. While, like everyone on Titan, she was pilot-rated on surface vessels and high-orbit flyers, and she'd made it a point on Fazis to learn manual overrides on every vehicle available, Krecis felt it was too large a leap to navigate an interplanetary, however small and maneuverable, however high-tech the autopilot. Krecis half wished Saturna felt more nervousness than she showed.

"Should not we wait for a more experienced pilot from Mars?" he asked with concern, as Saturna helped him pack the cryo-hold with Nyota's precious algae samples.

"That would take weeks, maybe months," Saturna complained. "And it isn't necessary. I'll be all right, Krecis, honest. There's very little for me to run into between here and Mars; I'd be more of a menace at midday in the capital. Besides, you've given me the best starcharts, the course is laid in practically to the millimeter, and once I achieve insertion orbit over Mars their entire system's on tractors; they'll pull me in automatically and I won't have to do a thing. The only real liability is computer breakdown in transit, and you've even provided me with the best Hack in the system.''

They both grimaced at the pun. Harley Block was being shipped to Mars with a lot less ceremony than the algae. Saturna would be escorting him home.

''Are you sure that's wise?'' Governor Choy had fretted. ''Once they're out of range he's capable of doing anything with those computers.''

''As I understand Harley Block, he wants one thing and one thing only—to return to the safety of his home on Mars,'' Krecis said. ''He will do anything toward that end. The last thing he desires is to die in space.''

For his part, Harley confronted Saturna and her menagerie with a scowl.

''The last thing I need is pet hair in my systems!'' he announced.

''Catlyke and Mushii will stay with me,'' she countered. ''They won't go anywhere near your systems. The vacs will take care of shed hair. Even yours.''

''Fine!'' he said, resisting the urge to run his palm over his receding hairline, a trait Saturna had noticed the first time she met him. She dared not look at Krecis, lest they both laugh.

Harley stepped over Mushii—who growled and bristled at him—and ensconced himself without another word in the aft compartment with his precious computer array. Saturna shrugged; the arrangement was fine with her.

''While you are en route, I will contact Dr. Domonique and let her know it is you who will be bringing her the algae,'' Krecis said formally, when he came to see her off.

''What else will you tell her?'' Saturna wanted to know, glancing into the interior of the ship, making certain Harley was too far away to hear.

''I will prepare her to accept some wonderful news,'' Krecis promised, as he handed her a holocube. ''Give this to her when you arrive. Then, I am sure, you two will have a glorious conversation.''

Saturna smiled knowingly. She embraced Krecis one final time, sealed the hatch, draped Catlyke over the back of the pilot's seat, settled Mushii into a niche between two consoles, set the controls, and with at least a show of self-confidence, fixed her gaze on the airlock and, beyond it, the stars.

# Epilogue

"Hack"?

"Yes, Dolores?" Harley said, half paying attention. They were ten days out, and to keep his mind off the fact that there was nothing but a metal hull between him and the void of space, he had a wicked game of Asteroid Assault going on one holo monitor and didn't want to be interrupted.

"Remember that weird short wavelength you've had me monitoring for almost a year now?"

Harley's concentration flagged and an asteroid got past his perimeter, badly damaging one of his ships. He tried to boost its retrothrusters, overcompensated, and watched it self-destruct, leaving debris all over the screen. He'd have to call in a sweeper ship to clear that up before the rest of his squadron sucked it into their plasma converters.

"Hack . . ." Dolores repeated with a computer's patient persistence.

Harley watched two more of his ships get caught in the debris trail before he froze the game in midscreen.

"What is it?" he demanded testily.

It was his own fault for endowing the artificial-intelligence program with a personality. Worse, he'd given her a name and, lately, a sexy contralto voice and a lush physical manifestation to go with it. Fortunately Dolores hadn't figured out how to activate the holo by herself yet; when she did, he'd be in serious trouble. For now, it was bad enough that she'd taught herself to nag him; he'd have to see if he could delete that trait, pronto.

"I just thought you'd want to know that I've detected one strand of it being directed right at this vessel," Dolores explained, unoffended by his crankiness.

"What!" This made Harley sit up and pay attention. He dumped the video game and tied into Dolores's mainframe.

Sure enough, there was an incoming aimed right at them; by
now he could recognize the signature in his sleep.

Harley peered over the top of the array to NavCon; Saturna
wasn't there. Checking the chrono, he realized she had the
ship on auto and was taking a sleep cycle. Good! he thought,
and scanned all the systems to see if the w-wave (he'd taken
to calling it that, short for "weird wave") was having any
measurable effect.

*Nada!* he thought with a scowl. So what was this thing
anyway?

"What do you make of it, Dolores?"

"Insufficient data. However, I don't think scanning the inorganics is going to help."

"You have a better suggestion?"

"You're not esper-rated, are you?"

"You know damn well I'm not!" Harley snapped. He'd
gotten enough abuse for that on Titan; he wasn't going to
tolerate it from a computer. "Wait a minute—what are you
saying? Esper ratings, 'inorganics'? You're telling me that w-
wave isn't targeting the hardware? What then, our brains?"

"Not yours," Dolores pointed out. "And certainly not
mine . . ."

Harley peered over the top of the array again. Saturna had
not returned to the controls. She was probably asleep in her
hammock in the off-duty room, just outside the cryo-hold below. REM cycles? he wondered. Was someone or something
beaming messages to her in her dreams?

Harley scratched his head; he was way out of his league
here—something he was hardly going to admit aloud, especially in front of Dolores.

"Dolores, forget about it, huh? For all we know, it could
just be some uncategorized solar radiation. It's not worth losing sleep over."

"Do you want me to stop monitoring it?"

"No. Just don't bother me with it unless I ask, okay?"

"Okay."

Harley went back to his Asteroid Assault.

❧

Krecis thought very carefully about the holocom he was about
to communicate to Nyota. There was little doubt in his mind

that it could and most likely would be intercepted by Beth Listrom and Valton, among others. He had presented the Titan story with all the sensitivity he could in the holocube that Saturna would deliver. Hopefully, Nyota, with Earthian emotions quite different from Fazisian, would forgive his deceit as had Saturna and Tetrok.

He would couch his message to her regarding Saturna's visit to Mars as if it were part of her education, which would be consistent with the traditional Fazisian rite to expose those of royal lineage to extensive travel off Fazis Prime when they came of age. This should not arouse any significant suspicion from anyone, although he knew full well that Valton was naturally suspicious of everything he didn't initiate and control himself. The message in the holocube would have to suffice for the time being, since he dared not allude to the actual reason for her trip in this potentially intercepted holocom. He felt the final lifting of his secret burden as he prepared to contact Nyota.

♄

"You're sending Saturna in the courier ship?" Nyota repeated when Krecis told her. "Krecis, that's wonderful! It will be a joy to finally meet Zeenyl's daughter in person. I can't tell you how many times I've wished I could return to Titan just to watch her grow up; in some ways I feel as if I could love her like my own. But you might have given me a little more notice, OldOne, so I could prepare her a proper welcome!"

Krecis didn't bother reminding her that it would take weeks for the trip. Nyota was too excited and wouldn't have accepted his logic anyhow.

"I'll have the best quarters set aside for her, naturally, and make sure the climate control is adjusted, but if there's any special Fazisian delicacy she prefers, we'll have to come up with an appropriate substitute. Does she even like Earthian food? Why don't men ever think of things like that?"

Krecis watched her fairly bubbling over with plans and ideas.

". . . and take her on a tour of the volcanoes and our newest facility in the Mangala Valley. Is she interested in things like that at all? Now that she's been to Fazis, I suppose Mars will look like an outpost . . . but Olympus Mons is nothing to sneeze at."

"Not to worry," Krecis soothed Nyota. "I'm sure you two will do very well with each other. Keep me informed. I'm sure we will speak again after Saturna arrives."

When Nyota finally stopped talking, Krecis added softly, "There is one other matter. Saturna will be bringing you a gift . . . from Fazis."

"Oh, Krecis, just having her here will be gift enough," Nyota continued, her eyes welling up with tears. "The first time I met Zeenyl, *she* gave me a gift. I still have that necklace; I wear it often . . ." She collected herself and looked Krecis in the eye. "I will be honored, OldOne, to receive Zeenyl's daughter, and her gift."

They said their farewells and Nyota sat thinking for a long moment after Krecis' image faded from the room. Was it just sentimentality that had always made her feel as if Saturna were in some way her child as much as Zeenyl's? Had it been some premonition that Tetrok was her father, and not Phaestus?

Don't be ridiculous! Nyota chided herself. You're a scientist; you know better than that! Stop reading hidden meanings into Krecis' words and go talk to the commissary about preparing Fazisian-style meals.

As she walked the long-familiar corridors of her science station on Mars, Nyota remembered the unscientific feeling she'd had just before the *Dragon's Egg* made landfall on Titan so long ago. Something's going to happen! she thought now, as she had then. Something that's going to change my life! Anything more would have to wait until Saturna arrived.

♄

Saturna dreamed. Somehow she was a child again, walking between two adults, holding their hands. From time to time they would swing her off her feet in the light g of Titan, swooping her up in the air until she shrieked with glee. Other times they walked more sedately and she would try to emulate their long, measured strides with her child-short legs, trying ever so hard to be grown-up and Fazisian.

In the dream her perspective was what it would have been in reality, a child's-eye view, very close to ground level. Her father was tall, like all Fazisian males; she barely reached his waist. His warm brown hand held securely to hers, both the same happy-changing color. Saturna glanced at her other hand, the one her mother held. Her mother's hand, holding hers, did not change color. Her mother was smaller than the average Fazisian female, much smaller than her father. Saturna was certain that if she looked up at them, she would see that her mother barely came up to her father's shoulder. She turned back toward her father and looked up, knowing before she did so whose face she would see.

Tetrok. My father! In the dream, Saturna turned toward her mother and saw the face she had seen in countless holo images . . . *Nyota's.*

She awakened in the still-unfamiliar confines of the hammock in the off-duty room, her constant companions curled protectively on either side of her. *It's only strange because I'm in strange surroundings, facing a new situation. And because I've never dreamed about my parents before . . .*

The dream stayed with her throughout the weeks of the journey, waking and sleeping, inexplicable, until the Red Planet loomed on her monitors and the forward screen.

*Mars,* Saturna thought, waiting for clearance, waiting for the in-system tractors to lock on and lead her tiny ship in. *Named for an ancient Earthian god of war. A multiplicity of gods is in itself a peculiarly Earthian concept, and what does it say about a species which needs a god of war?*

She had approached on a leisurely flyby, making note of the scattered dots of environment bubbles, placed mostly cheek by jowl along the equator but occasionally dug in at the foot of a volcano or the edge of the polar ice; of the slow creep of terraforming, of green growing things inching their way out into the $CO_2$, setting down tentative roots in the cool red dust.

*What would Nyota, her mother, think of her? Would she be welcome . . . or would the terrible secret stand between them?*

The incoming beeped; she had clearance to land. The system tractors locked onto her ship with a lurch, and began to reel her in. Saturna sat with her hands in her lap; it was all automatic from here. It gave her time to watch the stars.

*Unknown!* she thought, as much about the world below her as about the stars which shone above. With all of this, she was excited beyond belief. After all, she was over twenty years old and about to meet her mother for the first time!